OTHER PLANS

MCGARRY STATESIDE - BOOK 4

CAIMH MCDONNELL

Caimh McDonnell

Visit my website at www.WhiteHairedirishman.com

First edition: October 2023

ISBN: 978-1-912897-51-3

AUTHOR'S NOTE

Hello, dear reader,

Don't worry, unlike my previous author's notes, I'm not going to get into the highly contentious area of how things are spelled in different parts of the world. That thing took on a life of its own and I won't be making that mistake again. Anyway, on to the racism.

Fair warning – this book contains racists and, brace yourself, I am of the opinion that racism is bad. It feels weird that these days that can be construed as a political statement, as opposed to what I'd always previously considered it, which is a statement of the blindingly obvious. If you are a racist I can only apologise, not for making your ilk into baddies, but for the fact that you've presumably read some of my previous work and missed, up until now, my strongly held opinion that you're an idiot.

. . .

Also, as it happens, the racists in this book are American. The reason for this is, well, it's part of a series where Bunny is in America – them being Swedish would've been weird. To be clear, this is not a general statement about all Americans in any way, shape or form. Racism is sadly a problem that crosses all borders, which is deeply ironic as racists hate it when things do that.

In summary, I don't regret any of the terrible things that are going to happen to the racists, but, sincerely, I do feel bad about Billy's nuts.

Happy reading,

Caimh

"Life is what happens to you while you're busy making other plans"

John Lennon

EXCEPTIONAL WILL

Sebastian Felix entered the room and looked carefully around him. It was his nature. He had got where he was in life by being a man who takes great interest in details. He raised an eyebrow at the clock on the wall. "Your clock is wrong."

"Is it?" asked the woman sitting behind the desk.

"Yes. It is two-thirty in the morning and certainly not five minutes to midnight."

"Thank you for the clarification."

They regarded each other for a long moment.

The woman's accent was West African, and she was dressed in the simple garb of a nun, complete with habit. Over the past month, Felix had undertaken extensive research into the Sisters of the Saint, since they had become of great interest to the Ratenda Cartel, and from what he could determine, they were not affiliated with any religious organisation. The most plausible theory he'd heard was that they were the modern incarnation of a rebellious order of nuns expelled from the Catholic Church, although nobody could say for certain in what century that had happened. What was clear was that they were definitely not your ordinary nuns, as the dossier he'd assembled of their rumoured past exploits emphatically demonstrated.

5

Impressively, despite the frankly mammoth resources they had thrown into finding them, the Sisters had eluded the cartel's attention for just over a month. At the outset, Sebastian had privately predicted that it would take, at most, three days. They were full of surprises – quite literally, in fact. Gaining entry to the building in which he was now standing had been an eventful exercise. It was a supposedly derelict school in an area of Brooklyn that had steadfastly resisted all waves of gentrification crashing around it. And then, the cherry on the cake was this woman; when armed men stormed her office, she had calmly demanded parley with whomever was in charge, while pressing the barrel of a Glock pistol under her own chin. Not your ordinary nuns indeed.

Felix indicated the chair on the other side of the desk. "May I sit down?"

"Yes."

He hesitated. "Before I do" – he pointed at the two men in full assault gear, including balaclavas, who were standing in each corner of the room behind him, their guns trained on the nun – "need I point out that if you attempt to turn that gun on me, these men will shoot you without hesitation."

She looked at each of the men in turn with a look that was pure nun. "Duly noted."

"And if by some – aha – miracle they don't, rest assured, my associate Lola will."

Lola stood behind him. He could hear her chewing gum. He hated the sound, but the rules didn't apply equally to everyone, and certainly not to a woman who killed with as much flair and enthusiasm as Lola did.

This time the nun gave an almost imperceptible nod. Felix pulled the chair out and sat down. "So, you wanted to speak to me?"

"Seeing as you offered a reward of – what was it – two million dollars for information regarding our location, should we not say it is you who wanted to speak to us?"

"Actually," said Felix, "it recently rose to three million."

The woman raised an eyebrow. "I should have congratulated the gentlemen from Los Diablos Rojos earlier, but sadly that was difficult, given the circumstances."

Judging by her smile, Felix could tell that he had failed to keep the look of irritation from his face. The Ratenda Cartel had indeed offered a reward for information on the whereabouts of the Sisters of the Saint, meaning that most of the estimated twenty thousand street gangs in America, not to mention sundry bounty hunters, criminals of all hues and certain "ambitious" members of law enforcement, had been keeping their eyes peeled for this particular golden ticket. Inevitably, casting such a wide net had resulted in a great number of false reports, including a naturist commune in New Mexico and a touring production of the musical *Sister Act* in Kansas City.

That it had been the Los Diablos Rojos who managed to locate them was a matter of pure chance – this wasn't even their area of New York. However, rather than enjoy their good fortune, the gang in question under orders from their former leader, one Señor Santana, had decided to prove they were "useful" to the Ratenda Cartel by ignoring their explicit instructions and attempting to capture the Sisters themselves. From the brief report Felix had received from one of his lieutenants, their assault on the school had been thwarted by unconventional defences that included an improvised water cannon, non-lethal electrocutions, a collapsing fire escape, magnetic doors and, as cartoonishly hard as it was to believe, an actual boxing glove on a spring. Felix had asked for, and received, clarification that the boxing glove wasn't someone's misplaced idea of a joke. He was not a man known for his appreciation of levity, and he was certainly not in the mood for it now. The fools had lost them the all-important element of surprise, which was why the entire building had been found empty, except for this one woman. Mr Santana was currently sitting in the back of a van outside and didn't yet realise he was the former leader of Los Diablos Rojos, mainly because he didn't realise he was soon-to-be-former in the most fundamental and permanent of ways. Lola could deal with him later. It made sense to keep her proclivities well tended-to.

"You know how it is," said Felix, trying to brush it off. "It is hard to get good help these days."

"I wouldn't know," said the woman. "We don't rely on hired muscle."

"Really? Was the Irishman who assisted you in stealing Carlos Breida from us a nun?"

It was her turn to look annoyed now. "That was a rare exception."

"And, in your defence, I believe you had to raise the man in question from the dead first."

The nun behind the desk held her tongue.

"Yes," he continued, "one Bernard 'Bunny' McGarry. We know about him. You would be amazed how much we know."

"What you do not know is where he, or any of my sisters, are located."

"I'm assuming that, until Los Diablos Rojos tipped our hand, they were here, so rest assured we shall comb the length and breadth of New York."

"The very best of luck with that."

"Luck will not be required ... What should I call you, by the way?"

"You may call me Sister Dorothy."

"Sister? You like to keep the nun pretence up, do you?"

"It is not a pretence."

"Your ... let us call it an 'organisation' is not affiliated with any church."

"It is interesting that you believe who is and is not a nun is defined only by men."

Felix stifled a yawn. "Yes, the patriarchy, et cetera, et cetera. We both know you do not behave like nuns."

"As defined by you."

"As defined by anyone."

"We believe that the world is full of vulnerable people who need more than kind words and prayers. In particular, it is full of women who men want to make into victims. We are nobody's victims. We can, and do, defend ourselves, and we will defend those who cannot defend themselves with every fibre of our being. Some fights are worth fighting."

Felix was aware that Sister Dorothy was no longer addressing him, but was instead staring at Lola standing behind him. He resisted the urge to turn around. "I'm sorry to interrupt your recruitment drive, but" – he waved a hand at the nun and the gun she still held firmly beneath her own chin – "is there a point to all the amateur dramatics?"

"Yes," she said, focusing her eyes back to him. "I wish to give you the opportunity to bring all this to an end."

"You wish to give us the opportunity? Did I hear that correctly? Was it not you who stole Carlos Breida from us?"

"You keep saying that word – stole. You cannot steal a human being. They are not possessions."

"Fine. Kidnapped."

"He went willingly."

"He has the mind of a child," snapped Felix.

"And yet his mind is exceptional," she countered. "He has perfect recall and the ability to remember long, complex series of numbers. Yes, we figured that out. If the reward is three million, I can only assume that whatever those numbers represent must be worth a hundred times that."

"It doesn't matter what they are. They are entirely useless on their own. It seems your *employers* don't understand that."

Sister Dorothy held her tongue once more.

Felix smiled. "Yes, we figured that out, too. It made no sense, given your organisation's previous profile, for you to come after us in this manner. Then we found out that some time ago you were searching for two members of your order who had gone missing. We put two and two together."

"Did you?"

"We did. Which leads me to ask, how many lives are you willing to sacrifice to get them back?"

"We do not sacrifice lives. If you attempt to take them, that sin lies on your soul."

"Oh, please. If you are going to claim the moral high ground, you might want to consider who you are working for."

"This from a lackey of a drug cartel."

"Actually, senior management. I have a degree from Princeton."

"Your family must be very proud."

"Throw all the mud you like, Sister, but recognise that you also have to be down in the gutter to reach it."

"We were dragged here. It is where you live."

He made a gesture with his hand to dismiss her point. "Regardless, deliver us Carlos Breida and we will stop hunting you. I am even willing to say that we will do what we can to get your sisters back from whoever is holding them."

Dorothy nodded. "Whoever is holding them," she repeated. "So, you don't even know who is attacking you?"

This woman was really getting on his nerves now.

"If you are expecting us to blink first, then you do not know the Ratenda Cartel. My boss, Alfredo Montoya, is someone you do not cross. He is a man of exceptional will. The kind that shapes the world around him. You do not attempt to stare down such a man."

"Oh, please, he pushes drugs to the weak and vulnerable. There is no true strength in that."

"It strikes me that for such a moral organisation, your so-called sisters seem happy enough to have left you behind. Did they think your wheelchair would slow them down?"

"It was my choice to stay. I am the captain, and this is my ship."

"How noble," he scoffed.

She ignored him and glanced around at the filing cabinets instead. "This room alone contains too much valuable information. Information that some people – mainly men such as yourself – would pay a great deal of money for, in order to find vulnerable people we have helped start new lives over the years."

"We have just met, and you claim to know me."

"I know your type."

"And what type is that?"

"The kind of man who needs men with guns standing behind him."

"And it seems you need a shredder. At least I brought what I need with me."

She shrugged. "Maybe."

"Honestly," said Felix, leaning forward, "how do you see all of this ending?"

"How do you mean?"

"The odds are stacked massively against you."

Sister Dorothy shrugged. "They normally are. By the way, I know the members of Los Diablos Rojos who failed to gain entry to this building earlier have long since pulled back, but have any members of your" – she glanced again at the men in balaclavas – "I don't know what you would call them, been injured during their assault?"

What they were called was the Jackals. Alfredo Montoya took a great deal of pride in them. They were his favourite toy, and an expensive one at that. The group comprised former members of special forces units from around the world, which the cartel paid a small fortune to keep on retainer, for circumstances just as these. Although there had never been circumstances quite like these.

Felix tilted his head. "I believe one of them broke his ankle on the stairs."

"The stairs?" echoed Dorothy, momentarily confused before the realisation dawned on her. "The waterfall of grease?"

"And the machine that fired tennis balls, yes. Whoever engineered your defences is wasted as what you call a nun."

"Oh, it would surprise you the uses we can find for her. Nevertheless, you should remove that man from the building immediately."

"And why is that?"

"Along with the contents of these filing cabinets, there is a lab upstairs with a great deal of sensitive research in it that belonged to the aforementioned individual."

"Research?"

Dorothy nodded. "You have to ask yourself, what can a mind that can take down one of your highly paid mercenaries with some old cooking grease and a tennis ball do with access to innovative technology?"

"I will have to go upstairs and find out."

"I would not recommend it."

"There is something I am curious about," said Felix.

"And what is that?"

"If you are a nun, whatever religion you consider yourself attached to, what is its stance on suicide?"

"Suicide?" She seemed confused by the question.

"Yes, or have you forgotten that you are holding a gun to your own head?"

"Oh, this?" she said, tapping her index finger on the gun. "This was just to get you in here, so we could offer you the chance to stop this nonsense, and so we could find out what you know."

Felix laughed. "You do realise that you will eventually tell us all you know, too?" he asked. "Lola here is very good at asking questions."

"Is she?" said sister Dorothy, looking at Lola again. "I wonder who it was that made her like that?"

"It is getting late, Sister."

"What time is it?"

He glanced at his watch. "Two thirty-seven."

"And on my clock? I'd look myself, only I don't want to make any sudden movements."

"Two minutes to midnight. So, if you're not going to kill yourself, which you have more or less admitted, should I instruct one of my men with guns to shoot you in the shoulder, forcing you to drop your weapon so we can get on with this, or would you just like to put it down?"

"How familiar are you with close-up magic?"

"I grow tired of these pointless conversations."

"Indulge me."

"I don't care about silly parlour tricks."

"I never did either until one of our sisters took it up as a hobby while recovering from a gunshot wound. She got remarkably good at it. She once told me the trick is in the misdirection. It is the hand that looks like it is doing nothing that is doing everything. Take our situation – you think you control all the cards, but you have to ask yourself, would we let these records, or the contents of that lab, fall into anyone's hands?"

Felix was getting an uncomfortable feeling in the pit of his stomach.

"Or," continued Dorothy, "when we removed the asbestos from these walls, did we replace it with explosives at a few key points, in order to execute a controlled demolition of this facility should the need arise?"

Felix forced another laugh. "Very funny. You're bluffing."

"Am I? You can wait until that clock reaches midnight to find out. Or you could shoot me now" – Dorothy slowly raised her left hand off the desk for the first time since Felix had entered the room – "and see if this dead man's switch is working?"

Behind him, Felix felt the Jackals and Lola tense.

"Just so we understand each other," she said, studying the small device in her left hand, "I take my thumb off this for any reason, and it will take the authorities months to identify the bodies."

Dorothy lowered the gun but kept her left hand raised. "You see, our whole order is full of women of – what was it you called it? Yes, exceptional will. I will do anything to protect them and the work we do. I also have stage four cancer so, well, this is more of a slight bringing forward of my schedule than some great self-sacrifice."

Felix stood up. "This isn't over."

"No." She turned to look at the clock. "But I make it about ninety seconds until it will be. Watch out for the grease on your way out."

———

They ran. Ninety-four seconds later, Felix had just enough time to start feeling ridiculous for falling for the ploy, when the four-storey building on the far side of the street imploded, as promised, neatly collapsing in on itself. A massive cloud of choking dust engulfed the street and a symphony of wailing car alarms burst into life.

Sixty seconds later, his chauffeured town car sped away from the scene, covered in a thick layer of dust. Felix shook his head. "Who the hell are these people?"

He caught something in the corner of his eye and turned to look at Lola. "Did I just see you smirk?"

A MAN'S GOTTA DO

"How much further?" asked Diller, from the front passenger seat.

Smithy's hands tightened around the steering wheel of the Winnebago. "I have no new information since the last time you asked, Dill."

"Okay, but just so you know, the urgency level is steadily rising from my end. No pun intended."

"I appreciate that," said Smithy, "and I'm going as fast as I can on this winding road without sending us off a cliff to be consumed in an inconvenient fireball."

The road in question was halfway up a mountain in Oregon, with forests of Douglas-fir trees stretching in all directions as far as the eye could see and, more importantly, no public conveniences anywhere in sight, as had been the case for quite some time now. The landscape was undeniably beautiful, although at that moment, Diller would have greeted any form of toilet with the kind of reverence normally reserved for dudes who walk across water or the person who invents a home printer that works continuously for more than three weeks.

"I don't understand why you just can't take a dump behind a tree like a normal person," opined Bunny from the sofa in the back.

"Because," snapped Diller, waving a hand towards the

windscreen, "out there is nature and you don't mess with nature. Bear attacks. All manner of bugs and insects. Poison ivy."

"What are the chances of getting attacked by a bear?"

"It happens. Every year. Since 1970, there have been seventy fatal attacks by brown bears, fifty-four by black bears and fifty-seven fatalities from snake attacks, which is the exact same figure for sharks."

"Are we worrying about shark attacks now, too? Halfway up a mountain?"

"And," continued Diller, "in the last year alone, Oregon has seen attacks by bears, cougars and wolves. There are wolves out there! One hundred and seventy-eight wolves at the last count."

Bunny puffed out his cheeks. "I'm glad to see someone made good use out of the single hour of Wi-Fi we got in the last four days. Did you check how many people were killed by trees falling over, or did no one hear those?"

"Leave Diller alone," huffed Smithy. "We all have our phobias. Oh, look" – he jabbed a finger at the passing treeline – "a clown!"

"Ha, ha," growled Bunny. "I told you that in confidence."

"You told that to everyone in this Winnebago in confidence, and you're the one taking shots at Diller."

"I'm not taking shots. I was just saying—"

"And," continued Smithy, "let's not forget, it was you who broke the john in the first damn place."

"No, I didn't."

"Yes, you did!" interjected Diller.

"No," repeated Bunny, "I was using it when it broke. That's not the same thing."

"Yes, it is," said Smithy.

"I was using it for its intended purpose," said Bunny. "It's not like I was using it to mix cement."

"I wish you had been. The smell would have been a lot more pleasant." They'd been driving around with the windows open for two days now.

"And," said Bunny, "if we're tossing blame around, how's that whole the-road-less-travelled thing working out for you, Robert Frost?"

Smithy said nothing to this, but Diller noticed his shoulders tense. It had been early this morning when, with nowhere in particular to be, they'd come to the crossroads. In one direction lay a newly constructed and busy road between the towns of New Bridge and Willow Creek. In the other direction lay a road that the woman at the gas station had explained was just a route up the mountains that took twice as long to get to the same place and which nobody went up any more. Something in it had appealed to Smithy's poet's soul, so much so that he'd recited the whole Robert Frost poem before turning, much to the annoyance of the car behind.

"And," continued Bunny, gathering up a head of steam, "it was your idea to stop for those chilli-dog things."

"I didn't tell you to eat six of them," objected Smithy.

"I was hungry!"

"Evidently."

"And, Mr I-can-fix-anything, if you're so damn clever, how come you couldn't fix the toilet?"

"Some things there's no coming back from. Really, we should take the poor thing outside and shoot it."

"How about—"

"Enough!" yelled Diller, causing the other two to stop in surprise. He was not a shouter. "Let's all just sit in silence and hopefully we will find a toilet somewhere in this godforsaken state before I physically explode. Alright?"

His request received a chorus of grumbled assents.

Silence descended in the RV until about fifteen seconds later, when Carlos Breida chirped up from the back, "Diller needs to go poo-poo!" The man uttered the words with the same wide-open, innocent smile he did most things. You couldn't be mad at Carlos, which, given the tense mood in the Winnebago that long pre-dated Diller's current predicament, was really saying something. At that moment Carlos was rewinding a yo-yo they'd picked up about three weeks ago. He spent most of his free time playing with the thing, occasionally giggling happily to himself.

Diller took a deep breath and tried to relax as much as he could without things becoming very unpleasant, very fast. It had not been a good month for many reasons, starting with the fact that it was never supposed to have been a month at all. When they'd left Nevada, having successfully busted Carlos Breida out of Longhurst Prison, morale had been high. They'd won. The unlikely team of Smithy, him and the Sisters of the Saint had pulled off a prison break from one of the highest-security facilities in the country. They'd done the hard part. At least, that was the theory. From there, the plan had been to head to New York where they'd exchange Carlos for the two captured members of the Sisters of the Saint – Bernadette and Assumpta – and Bernadette would then presumably be able to tell Bunny how to find his long-lost lady friend, Simone. It was a big stretch to call it a simple plan, but it was relatively straightforward, at least it was compared to the hoops they'd had to jump through to break Carlos and Bunny free. It turned out that there had been a lot they didn't know.

First off, their assumption that Carlos was some Ratenda Cartel bigwig had been way off. As soon as they'd actually got to speak to the man, it had become clear he was no gangster but rather an innocent possessed of a childlike mentality. Carlos was sweet and, increasingly, the only member of the quartet in the Winnebago who wasn't getting on anyone's nerves or getting annoyed by anyone else. He was greatly enjoying driving around the entire country, like it was the holiday of a lifetime, which, given the limited amount of information Diller had gleaned from him about his life up until this point, might well have been the case. Last week, when they had been doing a jigsaw – the same one they'd already completed four times – Carlos had said, out of nowhere, that his favourite thing about prison had been that nobody hit him. Diller was no expert, but the fact that he had a favourite thing about prison at all indicated quite how bleak his life had been.

The reason they were driving around the country was that the

Ratenda Cartel's response to Carlos disappearing had been way more emphatic than anyone had anticipated. The four men in that Winnebago and the Sisters had swiftly become the most wanted people in America. Carlos was, technically, an escaped convict, of course, as was Bunny (albeit one who hadn't been in prison under his own name), but law enforcement wasn't that interested in them. At least, not as interested as the Cartel.

From what information the Sisters had given them, every criminal or criminal-adjacent person on the continent was supposedly keen on finding them. Their week-long drive to New York in a specially constructed eighteen-wheeler had been halted and the Sisters had instructed them to swap vehicles to a Winnebago that was left for them at a truck stop. That had been two Winnebagos ago. They'd kept swapping vehicles and, as had been pointed out, the standard of transport had grown steadily worse. This RV had just two bunks, meaning that two of their number had to sleep on the remarkably uncomfortable chairs. In fact, on more than one occasion, Smithy had gone and slept outside – something Diller was very definitely not going to do. He was pretty sure Smithy did it just for the peace and quiet. He was not a man used to having company twenty-four-seven and it was wearing him down.

They'd been taking a circuitous route around the country, trying to stay off-grid rather than heading anywhere in particular, their theory being that a moving target was harder to find. They paid with cash from envelopes of money that had been left in the vehicles, and attempted to do nothing that drew attention to themselves. Most of the time, Carlos stayed in the Winnebago, given that a six-foot-six Latino who clapped his hands excitedly whenever he saw dogs was something people would remember. Their sole communication with the Sisters was a phone call they made every three days at 8pm EST from a payphone to a number they'd received in the last phone call, in which they were given an update. The updates had been scant on details, but it was evident that the Sisters were playing defence while trying to find a way to organise the swap safely. Diller and Smithy were now five weeks into the week they'd given up to help Bunny and the Sisters, and Diller had been able to email his mom only once and give her no information about where he was and why. Smithy had elected not to contact Cheryl, his estranged girlfriend, at all, and he hadn't been up for talking about his reasoning. So, yes, things were becoming a little tense.

And now, it turned out the straw that might break the camel's back was a busted toilet.

After about a minute, Bunny broke the silence. "Have any of you lads heard of the candiru fish?"

"Let's assume we haven't," replied Smithy.

"Right. Well, it's a fish they find in the Amazon, and if you go for a wee near a river, it can swim upstream, if you get my meaning, right into your doodah where it can, like, eat through your flesh and lay eggs. Only way to get rid of it is to lop the old lad off."

The Winnebago veered dangerously as Smithy turned to glare at Bunny.

"Why the hell would you tell him that?"

"What?"

"Dill is already irrationally terrified of the outdoors."

"It's not irrational," corrected Diller.

"'Tis in the Amazon," said Bunny. "Did you not hear that bit? The Amazon!"

"Sure, and the human brain is real good at rationally considering facts like that when taking a pee in the dark out in the middle of nowhere."

"What is a doodah?" asked Carlos.

"Never you mind, Carlos," said Smithy, before lowering his voice. "Great, now you're going to give him nightmares, too."

"I was just making conversation," said Bunny.

"That is your idea of conversation?" hissed Smithy. "No wonder you aren't getting invited to many dinner parties."

"I've had just about enough of your—"

As the Winnebago negotiated a bend, Diller pointed out the windscreen with such excitement that he nearly put his fist through the glass. In the distance was a flickering neon sign. "Look! A bar!"

Sixty seconds later, the Winnebago pulled into the parking lot of the Huntsman's Lodge. It didn't look in danger of garnering any Michelin stars any time soon. There were about half a dozen trucks dotted around with twice as many motorcycles lined up outside the front door and an eighteen-wheeler tucked away in the corner. On the far side of the parking lot sat a squat breeze-block building of about sixty feet in length with noticeably massive chains on the door.

"Alright," said Smithy, "you two stay here. I'll go in with Diller."

"I need to go too," said Bunny.

"But I thought you were all for doing it in nature?" countered Smithy.

"We're here now, and do you not think a grown man pooping in the car park might be a tad more conspicuous than just going inside?"

"Carlos wants to go poo-poo too!" came Breida's voice from the back.

"Fine," said Smithy with a sigh. "I guess we're all going. Fingers crossed this place ain't on the Cartel's grapevine. Let's just try to keep a low profile."

"Yeah," agreed Diller, "and let's just hope they aren't piping their water in from the Amazon."

HOW TO MAKE FRIENDS AND INFLUENCE PEOPLE

As Bunny stepped through the door of the Huntsman's Lodge, it took his eyes a few seconds to adjust to the gloom after the bright, late-summer sunshine outside. As he regained his vision, he could make out a wood-panelled bar with all manner of paraphernalia on the walls, stools at the bar, booths along one wall and, at the far end behind the pool table, a fenced-off area that featured a mechanical bull which looked as if it'd been around since before MC Hammer had been in his pomp. The vibe of the place was also that it was unlikely the jukebox contained any of MC Hammer's singles, not even 'U Can't Touch This'. At that particular moment, it was playing some swampy rock number Bunny didn't recognise. At least it was until it stopped suddenly mid guitar solo.

"Wow," came Smithy's voice from behind him, "an actual record-scratch moment. Thought that only happened in the movies."

"We should go," said Diller.

"Relax, Dill," said Smithy.

Bunny looked around at the faces of the two dozen or so patrons dotted around the bar that were staring back at them. To say there wasn't a great deal of warmth there would be a massive understatement – a polar bear would regret not having brought his cardigan. A plethora of leather, denim and sleeveless jackets were in evidence. Not enough to be considered uniform, but enough to be more than coincidence. Not that Bunny was in any position to criticise the sartorial choices of others. A combination of meagre prison rations and then the sheer boredom of life on the road had led Bunny to spend far too much time snarfing junk food and attacking diner menus with an ill-advised gusto. The result was that his waistline had expanded beyond the capabilities of his old clothes. His latest outfit, drawn from the haute-couture section of a discount store's closing-down sale, was a Hawaiian shirt featuring a non-IP cartoon duck, some loose-fitting basketball shorts and a pair of Crocs – because if you're going low effort, you might as well go all in.

Behind Bunny, the light streaming through the door was blocked out as Carlos entered and the pairs of eyes staring at them all shifted upwards to take in this new piece of information.

A peroxide-blonde woman of about a hard-roads fifty appeared behind the bar. "Goddamn it, Clint, you told me that jukebox was fix —" She broke off at the sight of the quartet of newcomers. "Oh … and what can we do for you gentlemen?"

"How do," said Bunny. "We were just dropping in to use the facilities and—"

"Customers only," she interjected.

"Course. We were going to grab ourselves some tasty beverages after," he said, having just clocked the Confederate flag on the far wall.

"This is a private members' club," growled a bald, thick-set man sitting on a stool at the bar and wearing a leather jacket like Travolta wore in *Grease*. Travolta wore it better. His facial expression resembled the one Travolta probably wore when he read the reviews for his legendary career-killing turkey *Battlefield Earth*. Travolta undoubtedly wore that better too.

"Private members' club," echoed Smithy. "Is that right?"

"Let's just go," repeated Diller.

"And exactly what are the membership requirements?" Smithy pointed around at the walls. "I don't see any notices up, and there's a sign outside that says 'all welcome'."

"Let's just ..." started Diller.

"Relax, Diller," said Bunny, smiling at the room. "We're just having a friendly chat."

"Nobody here is feeling particularly friendly," said the man.

"Jake," warned the barmaid, earning her a glare from the wannabe Travolta.

"What, *Gail*?" he replied, laying heavy sarcastic emphasis on her name.

They locked eyes. Gail broke away first, shaking her head as she moved down the bar, looking for something to do.

Jake turned and gesticulated towards the quartet with his bottle of beer. "You can all turn right around and head off back to where you came from."

"Where we came from?" repeated Smithy, and Bunny could feel the tension in the room rise another notch. People were shifting in their seats. Now that Bunny looked again, the people in question, with the exception of Gail behind the bar, appeared to be exclusively men. If it turned out this was a gay bar, that'd be an unexpected twist.

A man stepped forward from the back of the room, his long straw-coloured hair tied back in a ponytail. He was wearing blue jeans and a black T-shirt bearing an insignia Bunny didn't recognise. The man's wide smile was dripping with insincerity. "Gentlemen, apologies," he said, patting the man at the bar on the shoulder. "Jake here is a terrible greeter. No offence meant."

Jake grumbled something in response but left it at that.

"None taken," said Bunny mildly. "We're just passing through. We appreciate this is the HQ for your motorbike club."

"No, my friend," said the man. "We're the Paradise Sportsman's League."

"Fair enough," said Bunny.

"Paradise?" asked Smithy.

"That's right," he replied. "It's a little town a couple of miles up the road there. Been run down for a while now since the mill closed, thanks to all that cheap lumber coming in from overseas. Place is expecting a bounce-back, though, due to some recent good fortune."

This elicited some smirks from the watching audience, and they were all now undoubtedly watching.

"Glad to hear it," said Bunny. "I look forward to seeing it as we drive through. Once we've had a convivial drink, used the restroom and been on our way."

The man shook his head. "I'm afraid that's not possible. You see, this is a private members' establishment, and we have certain traditions."

"Traditions?" echoed Bunny.

"Yeah," said the man. "You've got to be initiated into the Sportsman's League. My name is Ronnie, by the way, and I'm the president."

"I see," said Bunny. "Well, 'tis nice to meet you, Mr President. To be honest, I'm not looking to take up a hobby, we're just passing through, and it has been a long old drive through this fine state of yours. We need a brief pit stop and then we'll be on our way."

"Diller need to go poo-poo," chipped in Carlos, which resulted in some sniggering from one of the booths.

"My sympathies," continued Ronnie, "but rules are rules. Anyone who wants to join has to ride Billy the bull."

"Really?" Bunny nodded at one of the men sitting in the corner who he had noticed was in a wheelchair. "Is that not a bit – what's the word ... ableist?"

"How do you think he ended up in the wheelchair?" asked Jake at the bar. This raised a laugh from almost all the patrons, with the notable exception of the wheelchair user.

"Fair enough," said Bunny. "I'm a great respecter of local tradition. I'll ride the bull."

"You can't," said Diller. "You're wounded."

The left side of Bunny's abdomen was still healing from the stab wound inflicted in prison in what could not be called a misunderstanding. The guy with the knife had meant to stab him and achieved that aim admirably. Luckily, the blade had avoided all organs, and the Sisters had provided the best on-the-go medical facilities anyone could hope for. Plus, it turned out Diller was a dab hand at changing bandages.

"I'll be fine," said Bunny. "'Tis only a bull." He nodded to the fenced-off area in the corner of the bar. "Would you mind if I used the restroom first, though? Things might get a tad unhygienic otherwise."

"Oh," said Ronnie, pointing to the mechanical bull, "that ain't Billy." On cue, someone pulled a rope and the double doors at the back of the bar flew open, allowing sunlight to flood in. A large black bull huffed his way into the enclosure as several of the men sitting nearby grabbed their beers and shifted away quickly. Billy appeared to be as tall as a man, as heavy as a truck, and as angry as if someone had just explained to him where steaks come from.

He gave the room a withering look, snorted a few more times then mounted the mechanical bull, maintaining defiant eye contact with anyone who dared look his way as he thrusted vigorously.

"Oh Lord," sighed Gail behind the bar, "I just cleaned that damn thing."

"They've an actual live, fecking bull who comes into the bar," said Bunny, shaking his head in disbelief. "Jesus, you really do see everything in this country." Even he had to admit that discretion might be the better part of valour here, stab wound or not.

"So," said Ronnie, "happy trails to you fellas. Don't let the door hit you in the ass on the way out."

"I'll ride it."

Bunny looked down at Smithy. "You will?"

"Sure," said Smithy. "I'll ride the bull."

"Please, can we just go?" pleaded Diller.

"I'm sorry," said Ronnie, "I don't know if we're insured to allow him to be ridden by children."

"Hilarious," said Smithy, stepping forward. "Never heard that one before. So, are we doing this, or is the Paradise Sportsman's League too chicken?"

Ronnie and Smithy locked eyes for a long moment before Ronnie raised his voice and, without turning around, said, "Pete, get Billy set up. Looks like we got ourselves a cowboy."

IN AND OUT

Bunny stood in the restroom of the Huntsman's Lodge. It was nothing to write home about, not unless you were writing a book entitled *Below-Average Bathrooms of the Pacific Northwest*. There was one small window with bars on it. It was unclear if they were meant to stop people from getting in or out. The good news was, at least they'd been allowed to use the place.

Bunny looked at Smithy. "What the hell are we doing here?" he asked in a quiet voice.

Before Smithy could answer, Diller came charging out of one of the cubicles. "I'll tell you what you're doing here. You're being idiots. Am I the only one who's remembered that we're supposed to be keeping a low profile? Now we've got an entire bar of knuckle-dragging Neanderthals waiting excitedly for us to leave this restroom so that Smithy can ride an actual live bull. Pretty sure that's going to be memorable."

Smithy and Bunny said nothing but looked at each other like a pair of schoolboys who had just received the mother of all reprimands.

The silence hung heavy, until Carlos farted loudly in the other cubicle before giggling happily to himself.

"In our defence—" started Smithy.

"What?" interrupted Diller, in a slightly calmer voice. "You're going to point out that this is clearly the clubhouse for a bunch of racist idiots. Yeah, I noticed. Pretty sure I noticed before you did. There's a framed portrait of David Duke, former Grand Wizard of the Ku Klux Klan, on the wall near the door."

"But we can't just—" attempted Bunny.

"Let them get away with being racist? Here come the actual white knights in shining armour. Do you really think the two of you making a stand is going to encourage them to judge people not by the colour of their skin but by the content of their character? We've got half the criminals on the continent out looking for us. We've been on the run for a month and you two have decided that now's the time to solve racism through the medium of bull-riding?"

"Well," said Smithy sheepishly, "when you put it like that ..."

Diller, clearly not done, wagged a finger between his friends. "This is a lot less about racism and a lot more about you two. You're a bad combo."

"Excuse me?" said Bunny.

"You two always have to prove you're the big man, and whether you realise it or not, you're egging each other on. Neither of you ever wants to take a step back in front of the other, which is how we've ended up trapped in a bathroom with a nice little mob building up outside."

Smithy nodded. "Everything you've said is both fair and correct, Diller. Clearly, Bunny and I have some things to work on."

Diller folded his arms and gave a terse nod.

"Having said that, can I ask, by any chance—"

"No, I have still not managed to go."

"But," began Bunny, "you were desperate?"

"I know. And then the tension of all this, I dunno – fight or flight, the body probably thinks taking a dump while in danger is not advisable. It's basic biology."

From the sounds emanating from the second cubicle, it was clear that Carlos was experiencing no such issue.

Smithy found the segue the conversation so badly needed. "Not to change the subject," he said, clearly doing so, "but have you noticed the accents?"

"What about them?" asked Bunny.

"They're from all over," said Diller. "Even from the few we've heard, those guys out there are drawn from far and wide."

"What does that mean?" asked Bunny.

Smithy shrugged. "I'm not sure, but probably nothing good," he said, as he moved to take his turn in the free cubicle.

Bunny and Diller stood there awkwardly for a few seconds. Eventually, Bunny broke the silence. "Can I ask – and you're right, we've messed up here, but, I'm curious – they've got one of them Confederate flags up on the wall outside ..."

"No," said Diller, anticipating Bunny's question. "Oregon was never part of the Confederacy. It was, however, formed as a supposed Whites-only state. They had actual Black exclusion laws."

"You're kidding."

"Nope. It was back in the 1840s, I think, but they only took the redundant language out of the state's constitution this century."

"Jaysus."

Diller nodded. "People have this idea that racism is a Southern problem, but it's not. I like to believe most people don't feel that way, here or there, but it doesn't mean there aren't big old pockets of it. Like this bar."

"Right," said Bunny. "How'd you know so much about this? I mean, the history and all that."

Diller shrugged. "You know I like to read, and I just retain stuff. Besides, I always dreamed of one day heading off on my own epic adventure to see our great nation, but as a young Black man, it pays to know what you might be heading into."

"Right. Makes sense. 'Tis a nice idea. The seeing-the-country bit, I mean."

"Yeah," said Diller with a slight grimace. "Although I might need to revise my plans to include some restroom provisions."

Smithy and Carlos exited their respective cubicles at the same time. Ignoring the out-of-order sign above the wash basin, Carlos turned on the faucet and looked annoyed at it when no water came out.

"It's busted, big guy," said Smithy. "You can wash your hands when we get back to the Winnebago."

"Before that," interjected Bunny, "I should probably ask – how are you planning on getting out of riding Billy the insane bull?"

"Oh, I'm not."

Just a hint of a smile was playing across Smithy's lips. In spite of himself, Diller pointed at him excitedly. "Wait, you've done this before, haven't you? Back in your mysterious past that you don't like to talk about?"

Smithy shrugged. "Maybe."

"Is it like riding a bike, d'ye reckon?" asked Bunny.

"Dunno. I've never ridden a bike."

"Christ on a Lilo, the man's ridden more bulls than bicycles. I can see why Diller is so obsessed with getting your backstory. There's a lot to unpack there."

"You can ask all the questions you like," said Smithy. "Just don't expect me to answer them."

"Okay, gents," said Bunny, addressing the group. "Like Diller so eloquently and rightly pointed out, we have got ourselves into a bit of a daft situation. So, Smithy will do his thing and then we'll get the hell out of here as calmly and discreetly as possible."

"And wash our hands?" asked Carlos.

"And wash our hands," confirmed Bunny. The fella had an admirable commitment to personal hygiene. "Right, then. Now, if you'll excuse me, I'm going to go into that cubicle and log my very own protest at this establishment's unacceptable ethos."

"Do your worst," said Smithy. "This place actually deserves what you can do to a toilet."

CUT 'EM OUT, RIDE 'EM IN

When they re-emerged from the restroom, Diller couldn't tell if the bar had got busier in their absence, or if it was the fact that all the patrons were now on their feet, standing around in an eager throng, that made it look that way. It was notable that a significant number of them were positioned between them and the door out, in case the four musketeers decided to make a break for it. If Diller was honest, he had been considering the possibility of doing just that.

The layout of the bar was rather odd. The fenced area at the back, containing the mechanical bull, could be expanded by the opening of a set of large double doors, which allowed Billy – the live bull in his enclosure outside – to wander in. Diller didn't drink so he couldn't begin to guess why the experience of sipping on your tasty beverage would be enhanced by having a pissed-off bull staring at you from the other side of the fence while you did so. Personally, he'd have just set up a dartboard, but live and let live – not that it was a popular sentiment in this establishment.

When Smithy had confessed that this was literally not his first rodeo, Diller had experienced a sudden surge of confidence in how things were going to go. As they approached the pen containing Billy the bull, that confidence dissipated fast. Billy looked truly massive and very, very angry, his nostrils already huffing like a steam train pulling out of the station. Diller personally didn't like the idea of a sport based entirely around enraging a beast, but now didn't seem like the time to bring up his moral objections. There probably were White supremacists out there who were big into animal rights, but it still felt like he'd be attempting to appeal to a niche demographic. Diller's fear of the outdoors was entirely separate from his feelings about animals, and he didn't see the two things as contradictory. He liked animals enough that he didn't want to go into their home uninvited and take a dump. It was just good manners and his momma had raised him right.

In contrast, Billy the bull was clearly very angry about how he was being treated and was letting everybody know about it. Somebody had thrown a rope around his neck and three men were trying to pull him into what Diller knew was called the chute – the enclosed area where the rider gets on, prior to holding on for dear life.

Bunny stood at the front of their little group as they pushed their way through, with Carlos bringing up the rear. Not for the first time, Diller wondered how much the big guy really understood what was going on around him. He was a gentle soul, albeit one who was keeping a running total of their mileage in his head and could tell you how many miles they were from Paris, Texas or Paris, France, at any given time. It was an odd trick.

The crowd closed in behind them, a giddy sense of excitement in the air. Diller could feel eyes on him. He had a bad feeling in his stomach, and not just because he'd probably caused himself internal damage by so badly needing the bathroom and then not being able to avail himself of it. He'd run up against racism before, of course he had, but in more subtle ways. It happened in New York, but it generally didn't have its own clubhouse and collection of flags.

As they walked, he scanned the room. There was a fire exit over on their right, the only other way out apart from the front door they'd come in, but that suddenly felt a long way away. The three remaining sides of Billy's enclosure were constructed of eight-foot-tall wire fencing topped with barbed wire. Along with the Confederate flag and framed David Duke portrait, the walls were adorned with pictures of people Diller didn't recognise, some faded framed newspaper articles, and a swordfish whose nose had somehow become bent out of shape.

He came to a halt so abruptly that Carlos walked into the back of him. Oh no. No, no, no. Hell, no! They had Momma June's. This would not stand.

Growing up, even when they hadn't had much, his mom had always made her signature dish for special occasions – fiery chicken wings. They were so hot that most people couldn't handle them, but Diller and his mom loved 'em. The most important ingredient was Momma June's Fire-Breathing Hot Sauce. It contained Carolina Reaper peppers, and it was so hot it'd burn your skin. The thing was, for a good few years now, you couldn't get hold of it. Anywhere. The rumour was that the company had gotten into financial trouble after being sued when their sauce killed a man. So how, then, did this bunch of knuckle-draggers have it sitting there on the tables? Bottles of the stuff, just lying around, waiting to be used.

On the label, Momma June was a grey-haired Black lady with her hair tied up neatly in a bun, smiling benignly upon the world. When he was younger, having never had a grandma of his own, Diller may have imagined her filling the role. These people could not have her, sitting there on their tables, ready and waiting to improve any meal. They did not deserve her. You can't be racist and enjoy Momma June's secret family recipe. This was a step too damn far. Just the thought of it was getting Diller all fired up.

Speaking of being all fired up, Billy was finally being corralled into the chute as they reached it. Everyone was giving him a wide berth and the three men on the end of the rope were all straining to pull him in. Jake, the particularly unfriendly bald guy who'd been sitting at the bar when they'd arrived, came up behind Billy with a long cattle prod and shocked him in the rump to get him the rest of the way there. The bull yowled in pain and slammed into the chute, causing the rope trio to stumble backwards, before another man rushed in to slam the gate shut and complete the process. Jake waved the cattle prod around, inordinately proud of himself.

"For Christ's sake," said Smithy, "take it easy. That ain't the way you're supposed to do that."

Ronnie, the president of the Paradise Sportsman's League, chuckled. "Would you look at that? The little fella's been a bull rider for all of a couple of minutes and now he's an expert."

"You don't need to be an expert to see when an animal's in pain." Smithy moved beside the metal bars on the chute. "When did he last see a vet? His hooves are overgrown." He pointed at the bull's side. "And look – bald patches, crusty lesions, this poor guy has ringworm. Treating it is simple. Why haven't you even done that?"

The smile dropped from Ronnie's lips. "I don't know where you come from, but round here, it's rude to come into someone's home and start throwing insults around. Texas Pete here is our expert cowboy."

Pete, a stick-thin, lanky guy with a crew cut and a squint, shrugged. "I'm not, though. Just because I'm from Texas doesn't mean I know shit about livestock. I was a day trader."

"None of that matters," snapped Ronnie, glaring down at Smithy. "Now, are you riding the bull or not, you little smartass?"

"I said I'd do it. I'm doing it. Doesn't mean I can't point out some basic animal welfare issues. How long do I need to stay on for?"

"Well," said Ronnie, "I know in official competition it's eight seconds, but seeing as you're coming up a little short, let's call it six."

Smithy's eyes narrowed. "And what's the record?"

"The record?" said Ronnie, laughing. He repeated it more loudly for the crowd. "Little guy here wants to know the record!"

Hearty laughter rang out around the room.

Ronnie turned back to Smithy. "It's twelve seconds. My guy Jake set it." The assembled crowd let out a couple of whoops in recognition of the achievement and Jake gave a self-satisfied nod.

Ronnie gestured to a set of shelves behind the bar. "If you beat it, you get that trophy."

"Yeah," said Jake. "I'll even polish it up all nice for you."

Diller glanced up at the trophy. He hadn't noticed it before, but then again, he'd been consciously avoiding looking at what was on the walls. It was a gold-plated bust of a bull and looked like it was the only thing in the place that was cleaned regularly.

The group stood there in awkward silence as Texas Pete, the non-cowboy, carefully lowered a rope around Billy as he snuffled and snorted. Once that was done, he turned to Smithy. "You're good to go."

"Where'd you learn to do that?" Smithy asked.

"YouTube."

"Great. Look up ringworm next," he said, taking the proffered leather glove and pulling it onto his right hand as he climbed up on the metal bars surrounding the chute. The audience were fanning out along the wooden fenced side of the enclosure, keen to get the best view possible.

Bunny stepped forward. "Shouldn't there be, like, a clown or something to distract the bull when he comes off?"

Ronnie gave Bunny a look that was more sneer than smile. "Feel free to step up, my friend. You and your associates are welcome to do all the clowning you like."

"Don't worry about it," said Smithy. "Just come put your arm in front of me when I'm getting on. Stop me being pitched forward if Billy here kicks."

Bunny did as instructed as Smithy carefully lowered himself onto the bull. Carlos moved closer to Diller and whispered, "Is Smithy going to be okay?"

Diller tried to look a lot more confident than he felt. "Sure, Carlos. Easy-peasy, lemon squeezy."

Carlos looked only slightly mollified by the assurance. Smithy put his gloved hand under the rope then leaned forward and murmured something in the bull's ear.

"Can we get on with this?" shouted Jake, which earned him a glare from Bunny.

"I'd say keep your hair on, but that bull has already bolted."

The crowd sniggered and Jake's face reddened noticeably. "Aren't you the clever one?"

"That isn't saying much around here."

Diller tried to shoot Bunny a warning look, but Bunny intentionally avoided making eye contact.

Smithy took a few deep breaths then looked at the man in charge of the gate rope and nodded.

After a moment of near-perfect stillness as the world held its breath, the gate was pulled open and a mass of bovine fury was unleashed.

THE RIDE

As soon as the gate was released, Carlos started counting without being asked.

"One Mississippi ..."

Billy wasted no time bolting out of the chute like he had been fired out of a cannon, planting his front legs before throwing his massively powerful hind quarters up in the air. Up close, it was his sheer power that struck Bunny. Billy was no longer an animal; he was now fifteen hundred pounds of anger and Smithy was the focus of it.

"Two Mississippi ..."

Smithy jerked violently and looked for all the world as if he was going to go flying over the horns.

"Three Mississippi ..."

He held on, his free arm flailing in the air. The crowd's roar was an unintelligible mix of cheers and jeers, depending on how they felt about watching other people's misfortune.

"Four Mississippi ..."

Billy's hind quarters spasmed, sending them upwards for a second time. Smithy's legs lost their grip on the bull's back and he tilted to the left, tumbling towards the dirt. Bunny and Diller leaped onto the fence, both unsure of what they were going to do if the business end of Billy got Smithy on the ground.

"Five Mississippi ..."

Smithy was almost off. His right leg was now on top of the bull and his face looked as if it was about to meet the dirt, which would only be the beginning of his problems. Bunny threw a leg over the fence. He'd been annoying people his whole life – fingers crossed, he could annoy a bull long enough for Smithy to make his escape without any permanent damage.

"Six Mississippi ..."

Bunny paused as, and he had no idea how, Smithy halted the tumble. His only lifeline was his right hand, which grasped the rope. Somehow, at least temporarily, that was enough.

Six! *He's made six*, thought Bunny, *that's all he needed*. That, and getting out alive.

"Seven Mississippi ..."

As Billy's front legs hit the ground again, Smithy pushed off from the beast's side with both feet and swung himself upwards. *It's like he's paragliding up a bull in reverse.*

"Eight Mississippi ..."

Smithy landed his manoeuvre and, unbelievably, he was now back on top of the bull, his legs once again either side of its spine.

Forgetting themselves, some members of the crowd cheered.

"Nine Mississippi ..."

Billy stopped bucking and instead started spinning around in a circle. Smithy, who was back on proper bull-riding form, left arm aloft, rode the momentum.

"Ten Mississippi ..."

Round and round they went. A whirling dervish of ferocity and defiance. Billy was kicking up a massive cloud of dust but Smithy seemed to have found his rhythm. Oddly, an image of two ballroom dancers popped into Bunny's head. They were a couple now. From a certain angle there was an odd harmony to it.

"Eleven Mississippi ..."

Bunny reckoned some of Billy's ferocity was starting to wane. Lost in the moment, he punched the air. "G'wan, ye good thing!"

"Twelve Mississippi ..."

The kicks weren't quite as high now.

"Thirteen Mississippi ..."

"Fourteen Mississippi ..."

Some members of the crowd started to applaud but quickly stopped when Jake glowered at them.

"Fifteen Mississippi ..."

"Sixteen Mississippi ..."

"Seventeen Mississippi ..."

Billy was running out of anger and breathing hard, but in a different way. Like Bunny did after he'd run up a hill. Come to that, like Bunny did after he'd run down a hill following a month of sitting in a Winnebago eating Cheetos.

"Eighteen Mississippi ..."

"Nineteen Mississippi ..."

Carlos got all the way to twenty-five before Diller managed to stop him from counting. By that point, Billy was completely out of puff and no longer bucking at all. Smithy sat astride him calmly as the bull stomped around the enclosure, glowering accusingly at his audience, as if this was somehow all their fault.

After about a minute, Billy came to a near stop just in front of the chute. Smithy gave the bull a firm pat then leaned forward and whispered something else near his ear. Then, with a final flourish, he leaped off the animal and landed with his feet on the middle rung of the fence, arms raised, the perfect Olympic dismount.

Forgetting himself, Bunny hugged him.

"Hey, easy," protested Smithy.

"Jesus," said Bunny, releasing him, "that was fecking incredible. Are you alright?"

"No," Smithy whispered through gritted teeth as he continued to receive the ovation the audience was not giving him. "My shoulders are killing me, my nuts are never coming back down, and my ass must look like a Pollock painting." He took another bow. "Get me the hell out of here. I don't want the racists to see me cry."

PRIZE-GIVING CEREMONY

Bunny had never experienced anything quite like the mood in the Huntsman's Lodge following Smithy's ride. The closest thing he could imagine was something like being surrounded by sports fans whose team had just suffered a totally unexpected and massively embarrassing loss. Having said that, Bunny generally only attended GAA matches, and while the fans' exchanges got heated, it rarely, if ever, went further than a bit of banter. Any eejit attempting to start something with a supporter from a rival county quickly got a clip round the earhole from one of his own. The same could not be said for here. The members of the Paradise Sportsman's League were not responding in a terribly sporting manner. There were darkly muttered grumblings and a conspicuous lack of congratulations. The quartet moved towards the door, keeping close together as they did so.

"Right so," said Bunny. "Well, we'll be off."

"Hang on," said Gail from behind the bar. "I got to get the ladder for the trophy."

Smithy and Bunny shared a look. Even they knew when not to push it.

"That's okay," said Smithy. "We don't—"

"He ain't getting the trophy," snarled Jake.

Gail paused and looked at him. "But ... Ronnie said so. Said if he—"

"Doesn't matter," snapped Jake. "The little fucker cheated."

"Hey," said Bunny, "calm down. He didn't cheat."

"Sure, he did. He's not ..." You could almost see Jake's brain working away, trying to come up with something. "He ... he's not the right size. It's an unfair advantage."

"Advantage?" echoed Smithy, the disbelief in his voice clear. "When I walked in here, you were all making jokes about my size, and now, somehow, it's an advantage?"

"Okay," said Diller, "we should probably head—"

Gail turned to Ronnie. "Ronnie – you said he'd get the trophy. Do I give him the trophy or not?"

"No," said Jake.

"I didn't ask you," said Gail. "Ronnie?"

The crowd of about twenty or so people all turned to look at their president. The words came out of his mouth as if they were laced with razor blades, cutting his throat to shreds on the way out. "Give him the trophy."

"I don't want the trophy," Smithy protested.

"Aha!" shouted Jake, raising his hands. "See, he doesn't want it because he knows he cheated."

"I did not cheat," said Smithy, emphasising each word.

"And," continued Jake, "I don't think that bull was right. Like, like ..." His eyes lit up as a couple of brain cells banged into each other and formed something approaching an idea. "I reckon they interfered with him."

"Are you out of your tiny mind?" snapped Bunny. "We came in here looking to use the toilet. It wasn't our idea to ride the fecking bull in the first place."

Ronnie stepped forward, holding out his hands. "Hang on, hang on. Everybody calm down."

"Great idea," said Diller.

Ronnie turned to look at the crowd. "Pete, do you think that bull might have been interfered with?"

"I mean ..." Texas Pete scratched the back of his neck and looked down at the floor as he spoke. "I suppose. Yeah, it's possible."

"So, Pete's an expert now, is he?" asked Smithy. The man himself at least had the decency to look embarrassed.

"I knew it," said Jake, almost leaping up in the air. "The midget even pointed out all that stuff about Billy being sick. See, he knew what he was doing."

"First off," said Smithy, "the word is dwarf. And second, anyone who knows anything can see you haven't been taking proper care of that animal."

"Because you snuck in last night and were messing around with him."

"Can you even hear yourself?" asked Bunny. "We didn't know this dump even existed before we pulled up outside."

Jake turned to address the room. "You mark my words, this is all some woke propaganda bullshit. This'll all be up on the internet with some hidden-camera nonsense, you see if it isn't."

"Are you high? We came in here to use the restroom," said Smithy. "Now you've got us drugging your bull."

"Hang on a minute," said Ronnie. "Nobody mentioned drugging. Why would you bring that up?"

Smithy threw out his hand in exasperation. "That's what *you* were saying. We beat you fair and square and you can't take it, so you're acting like a bunch of babies."

"Alright," said Ronnie, "nobody is leaving until we get Billy tested for drugs."

"Ara, would you grow up," growled Bunny. "Believe what you like, but I've got better things to do than wait around for your bull to pee in a cup. You can" – he stopped himself from saying what he was going to say next, which involved a firm suggestion on where they could relocate the trophy – "keep the trophy. We're off. Good luck."

"We need to check them for cameras!" hollered someone from the back.

"NO!"

Bunny turned, shocked to discover that the final shout had come from Diller. He took a step forward to address the room. "C'mon, be sensible. You were all here. We came in to use the restroom and get a drink. We didn't want any trouble. You said we had to ride the bull, so my friend rode the bull. That's all. We're only passing through. Just forget about it. We're leaving. This is over."

A moment of silence followed his farewell.

"Okay, then," said Diller. He nodded pointedly towards the door and, after the slightest of pauses, Smithy and Bunny turned towards it.

Bunny took a couple of steps.

Some of the things you learn from walking a beat as a member of the blessed Garda Síochána or any other police force stay with you. For example, you get a sense for when someone is screaming and shouting and it's all just pantomime, empty thunder, meaning nothing. You also get a sense for those other sounds. Quiet sounds. Sounds that aren't loud enough to be actual words. It can be the noise a man makes when he abandons all sense of reason and gives in to his angry ego, when he can't take the fact that the world isn't spinning in his direction.

Already ducking without even consciously knowing why, Bunny glanced back over his shoulder. He did so just in time to see Jake, only a few feet behind them, drawing his hand back in order to launch his beer bottle at the back of Smithy's head.

He never got the chance to release his missile, though, as, to Bunny's surprise, Carlos Breida's big, ham-hock-sized fist smashed into the side of Jake's face.

And then all hell broke loose.

WHY STEVEN SEAGAL IS OVERRATED

As an aspiring actor, Diller considered himself a student of film. You had to be. If your aim was to be in movies, it made perfect sense to him that he should endeavour to understand all facets of the medium. That was why, a couple of months ago, he'd spent the best part of a week doing a deep dive into the action-movie staple that was the bar-room brawl scene.

In any discussion of which was the greatest offering, there first had to be a defining of parameters. For example, was gunplay allowed? If you're talking shootouts in a bar, Clint Eastwood as a one-armed man in an ass-kicking contest in *For a Few Dollars More* took some beating, or rather handed it out. That also gave you the under-appreciated Robert Rodriguez classic *Desperado* as a strong contender. Yes, Antonio Banderas's character's balletic firearm technique was unconventional, and his survival was largely thanks to his opponents' almost pathological inability to shoot straight, but it had style. Diller would forgive a lot for style. Plus, it featured Quentin Tarantino getting shot in the head, and anything that put a stop to one of the world's great directors from acting could only be a good thing. Come to that, if the eligibility requirements were relaxed further to allow vampires, then *From Dusk Till Dawn* was a strong contender too.

However, if you're talking pure hand-to-hand combat, there was one clear winner. With apologies to the hammy, film-long bar-room brawl with the occasional bout of self-reflection and feat of sexual prowess that was Patrick Swayze's *Road House*, *Terminator 2: Judgment Day*'s "I need your clothes, your boots and your motorcycle" scene was the daddy of them all. Arnie's greatest work was achieved by asking him to play to his strengths and not to act. To just stare. A cigar was stubbed out on his chest, he threw a guy onto a hot stove, effortlessly took out a bunch more and did so while stark naked. Ladies and gentlemen, we have our victor.

Diller was aware that his independent study of this matter did not correlate with opinions expressed on the internet. He'd checked afterwards and there was a remarkable amount of support for the idea that the best bar-room brawl was in *Out for Justice*, featuring Steven Seagal. Leaving aside the horrendous "hey, forgeddaboutit" New York accent that offended Diller's hometown pride, he still couldn't get behind it for one simple reason: the considerate nature of Seagal's attackers. He'd analysed the scene carefully. Seagal was attacked by ten ne'er-do-wells in total – one of them came for him twice, on the second occasion minus the front teeth he'd lost on his first attempt. What's nice about the scene, though, is that they all, oh so politely, ran at him one at a time. Diller didn't know much about "real violence", but even he knew that attackers did not take it in turn to rush at someone. He'd made the mistake of saying as much in one particular comments section and then had the internet screaming and shouting at him for weeks. He wished the internet was here now, because reality was rather making his point for him.

Carlos's intervention to prevent the sneak attack on Smithy had resulted in a full-out bar-room brawl. It wasn't in the classic cinematic saloon-fight tradition where someone hits someone else and then, inexplicably, everyone else stands up and starts randomly punching the person nearest to them. No, in this particular instance, the clientele of the Huntsman's Lodge either moved out of the way or attempted to fight Carlos, Smithy and Bunny. Crucially – and pay attention here, Steven and the internet – they were not doing so one at a time.

Diller was watching events unfold from under a table. He'd dived there just as things kicked off. He was not a fighter and never had been. It wasn't that he was a coward – at least that's what he chose to believe. He'd done plenty of brave things in the last couple of years, particularly since he'd known Bunny. Trouble had a tendency to follow the Irishman around, leaving aside the trouble he'd come to America seeking. So, Diller had been brave when required. He just hadn't thrown a punch while doing it.

He scanned the room desperately, trying to find some way to assist his friends. *Fire alarm? Hmmm. Setting that off was unlikely to persuade the angry mob to evacuate in a calm and orderly manner. Even if this place had sprinklers, which he seriously doubted it did, it'd just get everyone wet. Maybe he could start an actual fire? Extreme, but that Jake a-hole had now found his cattle prod and was steadily trying to work his way behind Smithy to attempt another cheap shot. So fire it was. How would—*

Diller didn't get a chance to continue exploring his options in the field of pyromania, as the table he was sheltering under disappeared. While most of the patrons of the Huntsman's Lodge had been keen to meet the other three members of Smithy's team, some of them had hung back. Clearly the two gentlemen now standing over Diller hadn't done so because of a squeamishness about violence, they simply preferred to assault someone who wasn't going to fight back. One of them sported a neck beard to draw attention from a receding hairline, and the other was so overweight that from Diller's perspective on the floor, his head was nothing more than a threatening fringe over an expanse of plaid shirt.

"And what do we have here?" asked the neck beard, kicking Diller's feet.

The large man bent down, his face now looming into view, like the blond cherry atop an approaching avalanche. "Looks like we caught ourselves a nig—"

Diller didn't get to hear the rest of his sentence as the large gentleman's hands flew to his face, but he could guess where it had been heading.

Diller had no regrets when it came to his aversion to violence, but he did feel bad about his larcenous tendencies. There had been a dark time in his life a few years ago, when his mom's situation had put them under severe financial pressures, and in the absence of other options, Diller had resorted to stealing. He'd hated it, to the point that it had made him feel physically ill, but at the time, rightly or wrongly, he hadn't seen another way. As fate would have it, the last person he'd robbed had been Bunny. That had been his turning point.

It was therefore surprising to Diller that he had somehow ended up with a bottle of Momma June's hot sauce in his hand. He didn't know when he had even picked it up. Possibly while diving for cover, but he had zero recollection of doing so. Could it even be considered theft? Given the situation and the establishment, it could be argued that he was liberating it rather than stealing it. Besides, it had been left sitting on the table in the implicit understanding that patrons could help themselves. Only if he left the premises with the bottle could it be considered actual theft. Right now, he was just using it. Not, admittedly, in a way the manufacturers would recommend or accept liability for, as he'd just splashed it in an overweight man's face, but he liked to think that Momma June herself would approve.

The fat man yelled in pain and grabbed at his eyes. This momentarily distracted his friend enough that Diller was up on his feet and off before anyone else could react. He might not be a fighter, but he could certainly run. Amid the furore of the ongoing battle behind him, Diller couldn't tell who was shouting at him and who was just shouting, but something whistled past his right ear as he darted around the tables. He caught sight of the fire exit in the right-hand corner of the room, but it wasn't until he was about to slam into it that he spotted the chain around the handle. He tried it anyway to confirm his worst fears. Damn it, that was a fire-code violation right there. He turned around to see Neck Beard and two new associates bearing down on him. Ten feet away and fanning out. The guy to the left was sporting a Fu Manchu moustache and looked as if he'd been hit in the face repeatedly with a shovel. The one to the right's facial hair of choice was a goatee and he looked like he'd been the shovel.

All Diller had in his defence was half a bottle of Momma June's hot sauce and an apologetic grin. A glance over Neck Beard's shoulder was enough to confirm that the cavalry wasn't coming as it was too busy taking a kicking. He might, if he got very, very lucky, get the hot-sauce-to-the-eyes trick to work one more time, but that would still leave two highly motivated individuals keen to put an end to his seasoning spree.

The only person showing any interest in this confrontation wasn't actually a person at all. It was a bull. Billy was standing in his enclosure about ten feet away, watching events unfold with fascination.

Diller's options were limited.

Very limited.

Three angry asshats or one angry bovine.

Diller feinted left with the bottle, which bought him just enough time to dart right. He was up and over the fence before anyone had a chance to stop him, even if they had felt so inclined. Judging by the laughter that followed him, he was pretty sure they wouldn't have bothered.

Diller stumbled to the ground in the middle of the pen. He looked back to see his three would-be attackers spread out along the fence, determined to make sure that getting out would be considerably harder than getting in. Each wore a look on his face collectively best described as "racist Christmas morning". Diller scanned his surroundings feverishly. He could attempt to scale the eight-foot barbed-wired-topped fencing that encased the enclosure on the three sides that didn't face the bar, but that would invariably leave him trapped at perfect goring height.

With no other options, he turned to face the problem. The massive problem. The immense, enraged problem. Billy trotted around him once and stopped in one corner, scuffing the dirt with his hoof, huffing his nostrils. This close, the sheer enormity of the beast was overwhelming.

Billy's eyes fixed him with a bloodshot stare. Head down. Horns pointing directly at his target. Diller was dimly aware of the hairy bunch laughing gleefully somewhere in the background, but that seemed insignificant. He was not a religious man as such, although he did believe that Smithy could hear the voice of God in his head. Logically, that meant God was probably watching them. After all, if he was chiming in, he needed to be up to speed with what was going on and all that. Besides, God was supposed to be everywhere, wasn't he? Still, as Diller kneeled there on the hard ground, he decided to appeal to a lower, more immediate power. He clamped his eyes shut.

"Please, Billy – I know you're having a bad day, but believe me, so am I. I just wanted to go to the friggin' bathroom, that's all. You know how that is. When you've gotta go, you've gotta go. And for the record, I think it's horrible that they keep you cooped up in this enclosure. I really do. If I get out of here alive, I'm dropping a dime to animal welfare or whoever else about it. Swear up and down. Right after I call whoever I need to talk to about that chained fire exit. I mean, what the hell? I just want you to know that ..."

Diller lost his train of thought. The feeling of heavy bull breath blowing into your face will do that. It was hot and wet. He didn't dare open his eyes, but he was ninety-nine percent certain that the head of a massive bull was inches from his face, and that if he did look, all he would see were two furious nostrils.

"Please, Billy, honestly, I'm a good guy. And these people, they're terrible, terrible people. Let me be and ... I'll go vegetarian!" He felt the bottle in his hands and, oddly, some part of his brain, one of the teeny-tiny parts not now frozen in abject fear, issued a correction. "I mean, I'll give up beef. Beef. Yeah, beef. Can't do better than that, can I?"

Diller clenched his eyes tighter still as a wet nose now brushed against his forehead.

GUN SHOTS IN CHINA SHOPS

Chaos.

Pure chaos.

This was less of a fight and more like an attempt to stand your ground while someone blasted you in the face with a hose, only the hose was filled with violent bikers. Sorry, sportsmen. The only advantage Bunny, Smithy and Carlos had – if you could even call it that – was that their opponents outnumbered them to such a degree that they were literally falling over one another to get a shot in. The trio had ended up standing with their backs to an empty booth, corralled there more by the sheer weight of numbers coming at them rather than the result of any deliberate plan. Bunny had no idea how many people they were fighting; it was just a wall of angry arseholery.

Someone had already hit Bunny over the back with a chair. A damn chair! As if having a massive numeric advantage wasn't enough, they'd chosen to weaponise furniture. Bunny had caught sight of a flash of long brown hair and a gold tooth at the other end of the chair. He was going to remember the fella. The force of the blow meant he'd nearly gone down there and then, but he'd managed to turn his stumble into an uppercut that gave some weaselly gobshite with ridiculous-looking mutton chops and an overbite some blood to soak up. While he'd been doing that, a fist with LOVE tattooed across the fingers had landed a haymaker, and Bunny's right eye was now swelling up. It was all one step forward, two steps back – only each step involved getting repeatedly punched in the head, literally and metaphorically. So far he'd protected his abdomen from the blow that would undo all Diller's hard work repairing his stab wound, but the longer this went on, the more likely it was someone would land a shot that would take him down hard.

To his right, Carlos was swinging his arms around wildly, clearly distressed. Bunny had seen the big fella take a right hook that would have floored a normal man. He had the body for confrontation but not the soul. Bunny would have liked nothing more than to get him out of there right now, but that was a pipe dream. The door was on the far side of the room and he had most of a biker gang – sorry, sportsman's league – between them and it.

Smithy was faring marginally better, at least. This was clearly the first time any of these boys had fought a dwarf, but Smithy had been in plenty of fights before where he'd been a dwarf. It was a simple matter of angles. Smithy was an expert at making taller people shorter through the medium of the expertly delivered lower body shot, and once you were down, you were in his world. Despite all that, it was only a matter of time. Unless the trio could find a way out, they were going down. One of them would fall and the other two would follow in quick succession. And once they were down, they wouldn't be getting back up.

Bunny caught a blur of motion out of the corner of his eye and Carlos yowled, having just been shocked by the cattle prod. Darting towards the weapon, Bunny snatched the end of it and predictably found the bullet-headed, sour-faced Jake at the other end. Bunny made to yank it away and Jake pulled back, buying the feint. Bunny then shoved it hard and, between the two of them, the handle made wonderful contact with Jake's face, smashing him backwards.

One of the "sportsmen" attempted to use Bunny's state of distraction to tackle him, but before he could, he crumpled to the floor, Smithy having literally chopped the knees from under him.

Bunny spun the cattle prod around, shocked the would-be tackler and kicked him over.

The sizzling crackle from the cattle prod as Bunny waved it around gave the baying mob some pause.

"Alright," shouted Bunny, "we're leaving."

"Carlos, let's go!" screamed Smithy.

Smithy grabbed hold of Bunny's shirt and they attempted to shuffle awkwardly along the wall towards the door. As they moved, Bunny jabbed the cattle prod in as many directions as he could, to maintain the uneasy peace, while being careful to stop anyone grabbing the end from him as he had done.

"Diller!" shouted Smithy. "Diller?"

No response.

"Keep moving," Bunny urged through gritted teeth. "We can't help him if they pin us down."

"Dill," called Smithy. "Time to leave, buddy."

Carlos, shuffling on Bunny's other side, pointed towards the rear of the bar. "Dill is playing with the bull."

Bunny, focusing on the barely restrained mob in front of him, couldn't tear his attention away. "He's doing what?"

Before he could get an answer, the air was rent asunder by the sound of gunfire. Everyone on all sides dived for cover.

When Bunny looked up, Jake was standing in the middle of the room on a chair, some kind of assault rifle in his hands and a gleeful look on his blood-smeared face.

"Yeah," he roared. "You got no idea who you're dealing with, you sons of bitches."

Ronnie got to his feet beside the bar. "Are you insane?" he yelled.

"What? You want to let these assholes come into our Lodge and make fools of us?"

"Now we got holes in the goddamn ceiling," shouted Gail from behind the bar, pointing up angrily. "And you probably killed the AC unit. We only got that fixed a month ago."

"Screw you, Gail."

"You are such a dumbass, Jake."

He pointed the gun in her direction. "What did you say to me?"

"She called you a dumbass," said Ronnie. "Because you are. Who said you could take one of those guns out?"

"Screw you too," said Jake. "I'm handling the situation. Someone has to."

"What the fuck is that supposed to mean?"

Before they could delve into their power dynamic further, everyone looked towards the back of the bar where a noise unlike anything any of them had ever heard before had just erupted.

———

One Minute Earlier

Diller, on his knees, eyes clenched shut, tried not to tremble as the hot, wet breath played across his face.

His entire body was an electrified ball of anxiety, waiting for the inevitable.

The inevitable was interrupted by the inexplicable. Diller flinched as the sound of gunfire ripped through the bar. His eyes flew open. On the upside, this interruption clearly attracted Billy's attention too, as Diller found himself now looking up at the massive rear end of a whole lot of bovine. He peered around it to see Jake standing in the middle of the room on a chair, an assault rifle in his hands, seemingly pointed at Diller's friends.

This was bad.

Really bad.

Diller looked down at the bottle of Momma June's hot sauce that he was still holding.

As ideas went, it was an awful one for a whole host of reasons. The only thing working in its favour was that it was the only one he had.

BULLY FOR YOU

For the second time in just over a minute, everyone in the Huntsman's Lodge dived for cover. The first time had been because a lunatic had opened fire with an assault rifle. This time an exceedingly angry animal had broken free from its confinement and was now picking up speed. Billy had crashed through the wooden fencing of his enclosure and, even for a bull, seemed positively irate.

Bunny had never really understood the whole bull-in-a-china-shop thing. He got what it meant, of course, but he didn't understand why that particular frame of reference was chosen. Bulls were agricultural animals, and hence belonged in the country. China shops clearly belonged in urban areas. People might drive through the countryside and decide to stop to pick some strawberries, or possibly get some fresh eggs, but nobody was looking for that sign that read "china shop, next left". And while during his days as a member of the Irish police force, Bunny had met some lads from the country who had come up to the big city and lost the run of themselves, not even the most lonely of young farmers had brought with him a bull to act as a wing man when approaching the terror that was big-city women. So how would the china-shop situation ever have come up?

There were other animal-related clichés that Bunny did not understand. Supposedly, goldfish had legendarily short memories while elephants were in possession of the exact opposite, but he had no idea how anybody could be certain of those two facts. More to the point, the most important question at this moment in time was how good was a bull's memory? Bunny had dropped the cattle prod when the shooting had started, something he was now rather glad about. It almost certainly would not pay to be the idiot holding that in Billy's line of sight. However good the bull's memory was, it was clearly good enough. Undoubtedly, it helped that Jake, who had been the last person to use the cattle prod on Billy, was not only right in front of him, but also standing above everybody else on a chair.

Billy careened through the furniture as if it weren't there. Some of the sharper thinkers amongst the sportsmen dived over the bar, realising that it was the sole available cover that was worth a damn. It quickly became apparent that the only thing in the bar that had even a slim chance of stopping Billy was the gun. Unfortunately for Jake, he was far too gripped by terror to think of using it. Instead, he froze. It was the chair that saved him. Standing on it meant that instead of finding himself impaled on the horns of the problem, Billy took the legs from under him and, after being taken for a brief ride, Jake came crashing down to earth. He hit the floor awkwardly and screamed, but given how things could have gone, this was still a good result.

For his part, Billy kept going, not even slowing down as he reached the large, tinted, plate-glass window at the front of the bar. When God closes a door, he opens a window, or at the very least provides an instant solution to the bar's sudden lack of a functioning air-conditioning system. Billy hurtled through the glass and out into the midday sun, shattered fragments spraying in all directions in his wake.

As sunlight flooded through the former window, it took Bunny's eyes a second to adjust. They did so just in time to witness a bull standing up in the middle of the row of motorcycles he'd just landed in, stomping his hooves on them while he turned a half-circle as if deliberately attempting to cause as much damage as possible. He was bringing a real bad break-up vibe to proceedings. Then he scanned the bar with a withering, bloodshot glare of pure hatred. The room held its breath, awaiting the animal's next move. After several tense seconds, Billy glanced to his right, then to his left. With a final huff of his nostrils, he turned and bolted towards the road, his yearning for the great outdoors narrowly outweighing his desire for vengeance.

The collective easing of tension lasted only a matter of moments, but long enough for the sportsmen to realise there had been a fundamental shift in the power dynamic of the room. Almost everyone had understandably placed their entire focus on the rampaging bull, but one man had not. The type of man with the mentality to ride a bull for a record-smashing amount of time. Smithy held the assault rifle aloft and fired a couple of quick rounds into the ceiling.

"Oh, come on," pleaded Gail.

"At the risk of being a cliché," began Smithy, "hands in the air." He played the gun across the patrons, many of whom were pointedly refusing to raise their hands. "Personally, I'm having a pretty crappy day, so honestly, if one of you wants to get shot as a message to these other fools, I'm fine with that."

There was a noted uptick in compliance.

"Okay," Smithy continued. "Now, if you'd all like to avoid doing anything monumentally stupid for the next couple of minutes, my friends and I are getting the hell out of here."

Bunny pulled Carlos to his feet, and they were joined by Diller, who dashed from the back of the room along the path Billy had cleared, being careful to stay well away from any of the patrons as he did so. Huddled together, the quartet slowly backed out towards the door they had entered through all of thirty eventful minutes ago. When they reached it, Smithy handed Bunny the gun. "Cover them. I'll get the Winnebago."

Diller and Carlos followed him out, leaving Bunny standing in the doorway, holding the gun. He surveyed the room.

President Ronnie popped his head briefly above the bar but ducked back down when Bunny pointed the gun in his direction.

"I would say don't do anything stupid, Mr President, but it feels like that bull has already bolted."

"You'll regret this, you Scottish bastard."

Bunny's grip on the gun tightened. "Do you know what? You would appear not to have a single redeeming feature, ye cloth-eared gobshite." At the sound of a horn being honked, he glanced over his shoulder to see the Winnebago idling outside with the back door open. He turned back to the room. "If I were you, boys, I would strongly suggest you do not follow us, and maybe use this as an opportunity to reflect on some of your life choices. I'd probably start with reviewing your policy on weary travellers being allowed to use the facilities. Fair warning, my Tripadvisor review is going to be less than flattering."

The Winnebago was already moving when Bunny jumped in through the back door and Diller slammed it shut behind him. Some canned goods went flying off the shelf in the kitchenette area as Smithy pulled a sharp left turn to get them back out onto the road.

"What the hell was that?" yelled Smithy.

"Could you be more specific?" asked Bunny. "A lot of stuff just happened." He moved to look out the rear window. "I've had some tricky shites in my time, but that one does rather take the biscuit."

"I meant the bull," said Smithy. "Why did he go on the rampage?"

"Oh," said Diller, looking sheepish, "that was me." He held up the remains of the bottle of Momma June's hot sauce. "I sorta hot-sauced his nether regions."

"You did what?" said Bunny. "Great balls of fire, Diller. I mean, I know you saved us and all, but still."

"I feel really terrible about it," said Diller, with aching sincerity.

"At least we're alive to feel terrible about it," said Smithy. He paused as he guided the Winnebago around a bend before continuing. "Is everyone okay?"

"A few bumps and bruises," said Bunny, "but I'll live."

"Me too," said Diller. "Carlos, are you alright?"

The big man had squeezed himself back in beside the small Formica table and was studying the jigsaw puzzle intently. He looked at Diller as if he didn't really understand the question before nodding happily.

"Okay, then," said Diller. "I guess we can just chalk this up to experience."

Bunny examined the gun in his hands. He was no expert, but he'd never seen anything like it. It felt as if it was made of some kind of metal he didn't recognise, and the barrel, instead of being smooth and solid, had an array of holes in it. The stock appeared to be made of a type of moulded polymer. The whole thing looked slick and cutting edge.

"I wouldn't be so sure about that, Dill. Hey, Smithy, you know we're heading back the way we came?"

"I do. I figured it's time we cut our losses and get the hell back on the road more travelled."

"But they're not going to come after us," said Diller. "Are they?"

Bunny considered the gun in his hands again, a sense of dread growing in his stomach. "That'd be the sensible course, but those boys aren't the most sensible of—"

He looked up and out the rear window. On cue, the first three motorcycles came into view around the corner behind them. "Ara shite, just once I'd like to be wrong."

NOW THAT'S HOW YOU GET RID OF A BAD SMELL

Bunny and Diller hunched down as they peered out the Winnebago's rear window. A trio of motorcycles was speeding towards them along the blacktop; two with passengers, one of whom was in a sidecar, the other riding pillion on the back of another. Bunny recognised the sidecar guy. He was the sod who'd hit him with the chair.

"Can this thing go any faster?" shouted Bunny.

"It's a Winnebago," answered Smithy. "It can't go as fast as it's currently going."

"Well, we aren't outrunning them."

"No shit, Sherlock," replied Smithy. "Alright, look – they're probably just trying to intimidate us. It's not like they're––"

Bunny dived on top of Diller, pulling him down milliseconds before the bullet smashed through the rear window before exiting through the Winnebago's metal roof.

"Seriously!" yelled Smithy, to nobody in particular. "These shit-stains need a course on conflict de-escalation in the worst way possible."

Bunny couldn't help but agree. He'd noticed the guy in the sidecar pulling the gun just in the nick of time.

"That chair-chucking, gold-toothed, gun-loving, goat-humping gobshite."

A pause followed, during which Diller grabbed Carlos and cajoled him onto the floor, before Smithy asked, "What?"

"Doesn't matter," said Bunny. "Me and the gun fella got some history."

"Also, he is shooting at us."

"Yeah," agreed Bunny. "And there's that."

"If you'd like to resume your personal battle, they're coming up on us fast," said Smithy.

Bunny picked up the assault rifle he'd dropped while diving for cover. "As a preference, I'd rather not shoot anybody."

"I hear that," replied Smithy. "Thing is, if someone is going to get shot …"

"Yeah," said Bunny, looking down at the gun, "we'd much rather it was them than us." *And if it has to be anyone, it might as well be Chair Guy*, he added to himself.

There was now a spiderweb of cracks in the laminated glass of the rear window surrounding the hole where the bullet had entered. Bunny reckoned it had been a decent shot if you were aiming to kill, but a terrible one if you were just trying to scare somebody. As if to emphasise the point, a second shot penetrated the glass, a foot to the left of the first one.

"Y'know," said Bunny, "I could really get to dislike these people."

The Winnebago tilted alarmingly as it turned a corner.

"We seriously need to get them to back off," shouted Smithy.

"No kidding." Bunny leaped to his feet and took a quick look at the three bikes behind him. The one with the sidecar sat in the middle, flanked by the single-rider bike on the left and the bike with the passenger on the right. He jammed the tip of the gun through one of the bullet holes in the glass and pulled the trigger, sending a trio of shots into the road surface a couple of feet ahead of the bikes.

All three riders hit the brakes. The bike on the left, which had been in front of the other two, veered into the path of the sidecar, its rear wheel making contact and sending the lone rider flying. As

Bunny ducked back down, he could see Chair Guy looking back towards his fallen comrade even as he raised the gun again.

"One down ..." shouted Bunny as he hit the floor in time to hear a third bullet smashing through the glass above his head. The sidecar passenger registered his ironic displeasure at being shot at.

"Six to go," finished Smithy.

"Wait, what? Six?"

"Four more bikes just came around the corner behind them."

"Great," said Bunny with zero enthusiasm.

"Do I want to know how many bullets we got left?"

Bunny studied the gun in his hands. "We had three, three shots ago."

"Terrific," said Smithy. "I think it's time to get creative before they figure that out."

"Great advice."

Bunny looked around the back of the Winnebago. The only thing that sprang out as having the potential to do fatal harm was the smell.

———

Two minutes later, Bunny was moving Carlos into position and instructing him on how to stay low while using his powerful legs to kick out the rear window. Diller, meanwhile, was crawling around on the floor, attempting to figure out if any bits of the Winnebago were detachable enough to be hurled out the back.

"And nobody will mind?" asked Carlos.

"Nobody you care about, I promise."

"You need to speed this up," shouted Smithy. "I think they've figured out you're out of bullets and they aren't holding back any more."

As something of a confirmation, another two bullets smashed through the window, while a couple more could be heard striking the body of the Winnebago.

"Not to worry you," hollered Smithy, "but the fuel tank isn't a million miles from where they're shooting at."

"That's only occurring to you now?" snapped Bunny. "Okay, Carlos, time to make like a mule." This earned him a blank look and he remembered who he was talking to. "I mean, kick the window."

Carlos did as he was told and, on the second attempt, the remaining glass flew out of the frame and onto the road below.

"Hang on," shouted Smithy. "Bend coming up."

Bunny glanced across at Diller as the RV took the turn to the right. "Anything?" asked Bunny.

Diller shook his head. "It's almost like they don't want bits of this place flying around when you crash. I'm going to try and pull the fridge out."

"Don't worry about it. Best give me a hand with this," he said, opening a cupboard.

Diller nodded.

"Okay," shouted Bunny towards the front. "Tell me when they're close."

"They're close," hollered Smithy.

"Really close."

"They're really ... BILLY!"

The Winnebago veered violently to the left, in a way that would have sent anything still on a shelf tumbling.

"What the—" started Bunny, as he bobbed his head up to see the bull that Smithy had swerved to overtake, running along the right side of the road in the same direction they were travelling. In an odd moment, Billy looked up and, in that fraction of a second, Bunny could have sworn that the animal winked at him – right before one of the motorcycles changed direction to avoid him, causing the bike behind it to course-correct the other way and collide with the bull's left rear buttock. While Billy didn't enjoy the contact, he came off best from the impact, as the rider wiped out and the bike crashed to the ground, leaving him in their collective dust.

"Alright," shouted Bunny, keen to capitalise on the confusion. "Go!"

After a month of living off canned food, there was something therapeutic about hurling every last tin they had out the rear window in a frenzied rush. Most of the aluminium missiles bounced off their pursuers, but one came into tremendously satisfying contact with the face of the guy riding the bike with the sidecar.

"Ha!" roared Bunny. "Got the prick! Thank God none of these idiots wears a helmet!" Chair Guy desperately tried to grab control of the handlebars as the bike skidded off into the treeline, his colleague already hanging half off his bike, hands raised to his bloodied face.

"Take that, ye furniture-flinging fucknugget!" roared Bunny.

"We're out of cans," shouted Diller.

He and Bunny ducked back down as one of the pillion passengers pulled out a handgun and attempted to open fire on them. Thankfully, that was a lot harder to do than shooting from a sidecar was and the bullet flew wide.

"Looks like they're coming up both sides of us," reported Smithy, as the Winnebago swayed back and forth across the road. "This thing moves too slow to keep 'em boxed out for long."

"Give them the left," shouted Bunny, "and tell me when they're nearly beside us."

"They're already there."

Without another word, Bunny scrambled to his feet, fighting against the erratic swaying motion of the RV. One of Smithy's issues with life on the road, was his reliance on gas station coffee, which, he said, tasted as if it had passed through several other people before it had reached you. Eventually, he had gotten around this problem by buying himself a nifty little travel coffee press. You threw in the ground beans, some hot water, steeped it, pressed a button and voila! Thanks to its double-walled, vacuum-sealed design you had a flask full of hot coffee that'd stay warm for hours. Bunny grabbed it, pulled off the lid, opened the side door and threw its contents outside. Smithy had brewed up a couple of hours ago now, but even tepid coffee hitting you in the face while travelling upwards of eighty miles an hour is reasonably distracting. Certainly, the rider on that side felt so as he screamed, smacked against the side of the Winnebago then spun out into the trees. Bunny didn't see his landing, but it sure sounded messy.

"Another one down!" he shouted in triumph.

"Nice," said Smithy. "The guy on the other side got by us, though."

"What's he doing?"

"Accelerating away around the corner up ahead," replied Smithy. "And his two remaining colleagues are hanging back."

Bunny, who was hunched down again, popped his head up to look back and confirm that was indeed the case.

"That's ..."

"Yeah," said Smithy. "This guy and his passenger might be round the corner ready to riddle us with bullets head on. Everyone stay low. I'm going to ..."

"What?" asked Diller.

"Not figured that part out yet," admitted Smithy. "Really hoping something will come to me."

They had reached the turn now, and the Winnebago shifted down in speed slightly to take the left.

"Anything?" asked Diller.

"Still working on it," said Smithy. "We—"

As they came round the bend, Bunny didn't get a chance to look out the front window before Smithy slammed on the brakes so hard that he ended up in a heap on the floor, Carlos and Diller on top of him.

"What in the shitting hell?" screamed Bunny.

Smithy yelled something over the sound of screeching brakes that Bunny couldn't make out.

"What?" shouted Diller.

Taken by surprise, one of the bikes following them smacked into the rear of the Winnebago, sending the passenger flying up and half through the window. Bunny hauled himself to his feet and dealt with that particular problem by landing a kick on the interloper's unprotected head, which sent him tumbling back out the window even while the juggernaut of an RV was still braking.

When the Winnebago finally came to a juddering halt, Bunny glanced out the front windshield. A figure was kneeling in the middle of the roadway in front of them. "Holy ..."

Smithy was already out of the driver's seat and grabbing Diller. Bunny reached for Carlos and, with all his might, shoved him towards the side door that was still dangling open. "GO, GO, GO!"

All four of them stumbled out onto the blacktop. Bunny had managed to push Carlos about half a dozen steps towards the trees when he heard a booming noise from up the road ahead of them. The guy's aim must have been good – not that it was the hardest of shots. A fraction of a second later, the Winnebago exploded, the force of the blast lifting Bunny off his feet and throwing him several yards across the road before colliding with the trunk of a tree.

As he lay there, temporarily deafened, his ears ringing and the air filled with smoke and falling debris from their former transportation-cum-living-quarters which had just been eviscerated, his last thought before he passed out was how the hell did a bunch of dumbass bikers get their hands on an anti-tank missile?

LIFESTYLES OF THE RICH AND THE MOST WANTED

"I feel absolutely ridiculous," declared Dionne.

She could see Tatiana, sitting opposite her, doing everything in her power to suppress a sigh.

"And don't think I can't see you rolling your eyes behind those big sunglasses."

"You can't," said Tatiana.

"No, but I can sense it, and I'm right, am I not?"

"Is it really the car that is bothering you?"

"It's not a car, it's a stretch limousine. And it is ridiculous."

"Of course it's ridiculous," said Tatiana, sounding annoyingly calm. "That's the whole point. It is ludicrous, but not as ludicrous as pulling up to the private terminal at JFK in a Hyundai."

"Hyundais are perfectly good cars," said Dionne.

"I didn't say they weren't. In the same way that a Subway sandwich is an excellent meal, but you don't serve it at a presidential banquet. A limo pulling up to the private terminal is something people see every day at the airport. A Hyundai, on the other hand ... You put me in charge of the escape plan, Sister, and this is it."

Despite having been a member of the Sisters of the Saint for quite some time now, Tatiana only ever referred to the others as sisters when she was annoyed with them. Dionne had clocked this a while ago. The woman had remarkably few tells, and she wasn't even sure this qualified as one, seeing as she was probably doing it deliberately.

Dionne folded her arms and stared out the tinted window. "I did, but I didn't say do this."

"Exactly the point. You left that responsibility to me, and ask yourself, Sister, can you think of any mode of transport less likely for three members of the Sisters of the Saint to use to get out of New York than a limo leading to a private jet?"

"It's ... it's extravagant."

"Again, precisely the point. I came up with fifteen escape plans and, given the time constraints, the threat level and our need to be on the other side of the country as soon as possible, I judged this to be our best option."

Since they'd left Brooklyn, they'd swapped vehicles twice and outfits once, taking every counter-measure possible to leave no trail. In other circumstances it might be seen as paranoia, but if the day had proven anything, it was that everyone really was out to get them. Still, all of that took time, which was why it was now almost two in the morning and they were still in New York.

"Do I want to know how much this private plane is costing us?" asked Dionne.

"Nothing," said Tatiana.

"I ... Really?"

"I called in a favour."

"But?"

"The person doing the favour has no idea who we are." Tatiana lifted her large sunglasses from her face. "Have you met me? You gave me this task because this is kind of my thing. Disguise. Misdirection. You said, get us out of New York, and I am getting us out of New York. What's more, I'm doing it in such a way that none of the people looking for us will think of in a million years. They're expecting us to be running in a state of panic, so calmly strutting, however fake and ridiculous it might feel, is the play. If the style bothers you, feel free to flagellate yourself for the duration of the six-hour flight if it'll make you feel better, but let's be honest" – she waved the sunglasses between the two of them – "this isn't about the stupid car or the ludicrous airplane."

Dionne turned and looked out the window before glancing at Zoya sitting beside Tatiana. With her headphones on, blaring out something with a thumping backbeat while her fingers flew across the keys of the laptop perched on her knees, Zoya seemed oblivious, no doubt focusing on distracting herself from the fact that she was outside. Her agoraphobia was bad at the best of times, and this was certainly not one of those times.

When Dionne spoke again, her voice was quieter, stripped of all the irritation. "No, it isn't. Sorry."

"No problem," said Tatiana. "If it helps, I feel like screaming too."

Dionne pursed her lips and nodded.

"We could ..." started Tatiana, but Dionne waved away the suggestion before it was even made.

"No, we couldn't. Sister Dorothy" – Dionne felt a pang pass through her as she uttered the name – "was extremely clear in her instructions. We were to go, not tell her where or how, and we were to do nothing to assist her or contact her. She would get herself out and—"

"I'm just saying—"

"I know!" snapped Dionne, more harshly than she intended. "I know," she repeated in a softer tone, "what you're saying, and believe me, I've thought about nothing else, but she is the head of the order and her orders are her orders."

"There are cancer specialists in LA."

"Yes, I know that too, and trust me, I made that point. Her response was that she didn't want to slow us down and she didn't want us having to find her specialist medical assistance to be either a distraction or a possible vulnerability." Dionne turned to face the window again, not to look at anything in particular but to avert her gaze as her eyes were beginning to tear up. "You know how stubborn the woman can be. She wanted to ensure the HQ wasn't compromised, to find out as much as she could from them, and to then make her own escape."

Tatiana said nothing for several seconds then, in a soft voice, murmured, "Yes."

Dionne knew better than anyone that underestimating Dorothy was the quickest way to make a fool of yourself, but still. She was weaker than she showed, and a wheelchair-bound woman of her age getting herself out of a building before … Well, it was a big ask. She and Tatiana were leaving a lot unsaid in the conversation, and they both knew it. A reasoned reading of the situation they had left Dorothy in led to only one conclusion. That being said, they had to cling to hope; first for themselves, and second, because there were others to consider.

As if on cue, Zoya spoke up. "We could still check if she got out?"

"How are you able to hear us over the music?" asked Tatiana.

"I got a strange range of skills," the young woman responded.

"Clearly."

"I could also do some checks to see if Dorothy is—"

"No," said Dionne firmly, causing Zoya to draw her neck back in surprise. "Dorothy has the emergency number she can ring, and the other avenues. It's up to her to contact us. Sorry, Z but she was really, really clear on this and she is in charge."

"Actually," said Zoya, "she isn't. Not any more." She nodded at Tatiana. "We were both there when she said, super clearly, that you're in charge now. So, technically, you could countermand her instructions."

Dionne rubbed the palms of her hands over her eyes. She couldn't remember the last time she'd had anything approaching a good night's sleep. She ran her fingers through her hair before she finally spoke again. "Yeah, I thought of that, too. So did Dorothy. Her last words" – she hesitated as the phrase jarred – "I mean, the last thing … The thing before …"

"We know what you mean," said Tatiana.

"Right. She said that the priority was getting you all out, then doing whatever we have to do to get Assumpta and Bernadette back, and then to protect the order. She made me swear on an actual Bible."

"But you're not—" started Zoya.

"You don't have to be religious to take it seriously when a friend who *is* religious makes you put your hand on their Bible and promise to fulfil their wishes. And ... Well, she said, imagine I was in her position and how would I feel, if after all those years in charge, the people you love won't go along with your final wishes." Dionne hesitated. "As leader. I meant as leader."

None of them said anything for a while. Dorothy was as stubborn as she was resourceful, but each of them was still coming to terms with the fact that she might also be dead.

Eventually, Zoya broke the silence. "So, a couple of things ..."

"What are the odds this is good news?" asked Dionne.

"Not super high," confirmed Zoya. "Before we get to the main thing, can I ask" – she turned to Tatiana – "to use a turn of phrase from the Irishman, how in the shitting hell do you know Kim Kardashian?"

"What?" said Dionne.

"We're about to get on Kim Kardashian's private plane."

"You're kidding me?"

"Relax," said Tatiana. "Okay, first off, how did you figure that out?"

Zoya pointed at the laptop. "Hi, have *you* met *me*?"

Tatiana nodded. "Point taken, and yes, it is true. It's a long story. I'll tell you some parts of it if you absolutely insist."

"I do," said Zoya firmly. "You can tell me on the plane, then, because we deffo need to discuss the other thing first." She pointed at the laptop again. "The dot just disappeared."

"Excuse me?" said Dionne.

"The dot. The tracker on the Winnebago so we know where the four musketeers are. It disappeared about twenty minutes ago."

"Right," said Dionne slowly. "How worried should we be?"

Zoya sucked her teeth. "Well, that depends ..."

"On what?" asked Tatiana.

"I don't know, because I have no idea how it can disappear."

"Wait," said Dionne. "Aren't they up in the mountains of Oregon? I mean, cell phone reception up there probably isn't great."

"I'm offended you think that's what my tracker is running through."

"So, what is it running through?"

"A US military satellite. Don't worry, the US military totes don't know that."

"How?" asked Tatiana.

Zoya gave a tight smile. "It's a long story. I'll tell you some parts of it, if you absolutely insist."

"Touché," said Tatiana. "So how would this thing have lost them, then?"

"No idea. Assuming someone hasn't shot down a satellite and, y'know, started World War Three, we should be able to find these guys anywhere on the planet."

"Except Oregon, apparently."

"Wait a second," interjected Dionne. "Maybe they're going through a tunnel or something?"

"Theoretically possible," conceded Zoya, "but if they are, they've been going through it for a long time, and it's deep."

"Broken down?" suggested Tatiana.

"The tracker's got its own power source."

"Could it have run out of batteries?"

Zoya gave Tatiana a withering look.

"Sorry," she murmured. "Withdrawn, Your Honour."

"You bet your sweet patootie."

"So what, then?" asked Dionne.

"I mean," said Zoya with a shrug, "could just be some sort of technical failure, but ..."

"But what?"

"Well, not to be all braggadocious about it, but my stuff doesn't break down."

"Crap," said Dionne. "It really doesn't, does it?"

"Not so much, no."

"So what are we saying?"

"I'm saying I don't know what the hell I'm saying, as it's either broken down, which is possible if a smidgen unlikely, or ... I dunno. Someone found it and smashed it to pieces, which would take a real good hammer, by the way, or ..."

"Or?" pressed Dionne.

"Satellites crashing from the sky. A meteor has hit them. They've fallen down a real big hole. The great state of Oregon has crumbled into the sea."

Dionne scratched at her forehead. "Great. Could really have done without this today."

"True dat," said Zoya.

"I don't suppose ..." Dionne looked at Zoya, who narrowed her eyes in response. "I know we said that for security they weren't going to have any cellular devices, and that the only direct contact between them and us would be the phone calls."

"Yes," said Zoya suspiciously.

"I don't suppose you – and I'm not mad if this is the case, I'm just—"

"I haven't spoken to Diller in weeks."

"Really?" said Dionne. "Is everything—"

"Because," said Zoya, cutting her off, "we have protocols in place to protect them and us, and I've been sticking to them."

"Right," said Dionne, nodding and feeling incredibly awkward. "Good. Excellent. Well done."

"So," said Tatiana, helping Dionne out of the hole she had dug for herself, "we've got no way of contacting them?"

"Not until they call on schedule tomorrow evening."

"We could wait until then," said Tatiana. "I mean, there could be a perfectly reasonable explanation."

"Yeah," said Dionne, "but that isn't how our luck has been heading recently, is it?" She tapped her fingers on the arm rest. "Okay, invoke Archangel."

"Joy's currently doing that thing in Sacramento," said Tatiana.

"That's today?" said Dionne.

"Yeah," said Zoya. "Last thing I did before we bailed was confirm my end." She looked at the watch on her wrist. "She should be doing the grand finale right about now."

"Okay, then," said Dionne. "Send her their last location and tell her it's urgent."

"She's not going to be happy," said Tatiana.

"When is she ever?"

"True."

They looked out the windows as the limo started to slow down.

"Right," said Tatiana, "we're here. Remember, when you get out, act like you think you're all that. No chatting to the security. Don't try to grab your bags, and whatever you do, don't look impressed by anything."

"Alright," said Zoya, snapping her laptop shut. "But if there are snacks on this plane, I'm going to town on them. Pretty sure the Kardashians don't eat, anyway."

IT COULD BE WORSE

It could have been worse. It was definitely bad – terrible, in fact – but Bunny was consoling himself with the consideration that it could have been even worse. He'd come round while being thrown roughly into the back of a jeep, but at least he was still alive to enjoy being manhandled. Given that he'd been in an RV a few seconds before it had been blown up and dispersed over a wide area of Oregon state, it was important to remember that. He didn't know how long he'd been out for, but a couple of jeeps and a truck had turned up during that time, to join the several motorcycles that were already there. It was fair to say the opposition was enjoying quite the "mission accomplished" moment. There were plenty of high fives and "hell yeahs" going around. It wasn't every day you hunted down a Winnebago with just a considerable numeric advantage and an apparent arsenal at your disposal. Plucky group.

While it hadn't been possible to talk, Bunny had managed to look around and confirm that the other three were at least alive. He'd watched them being loaded into the other vehicles. None of them were looking too clever, but they didn't appear to have been seriously hurt either. Smithy was now wearing a poorly applied bloodied bandage on his forehead, but other than that he seemed to be fine. At some point during proceedings Bunny had twisted his left ankle, but that wouldn't make even the top five problems he was currently dealing with. It hurt like hell, though, not least because once the sportsmen had got him in the jeep, they'd duct-taped his feet together at the ankle and his hands behind his back at the wrists. They'd also been considerate enough to tape his Crocs onto his feet. Seeing as the only other footwear he owned had just been blown to smithereens, it meant he wasn't going to die barefoot. He was sure he'd read somewhere that in some cultures, dying barefoot was considered very bad luck. The shoeless part. The dying part was considered universally unlucky. Not that he intended to die, but the way the day was going, he couldn't rule out the possibility entirely.

They were being transported back to the Huntsman's Lodge and suddenly everyone seemed to be armed. At least, everyone not on their side. That wasn't surprising – this was America, after all – but the weapons looked rather shiny and hi-tech. Then there was the fact that the Winnebago had been blown to smithereens in front of their very eyes with what had looked a hell of a lot like a bazooka. It might have been called something else, but given that Bunny's experience with heavy ordnance was drawn mostly from watching Second World War movies, he was going with bazooka. And surely, even here, you couldn't buy that kind of thing down the road in Wacky Wally's World of Guns?

Bunny said nothing for the duration of the ride and just kept his head down. Making a run for it was not an option. There are times to rile up your opponent in the hopes of them making a mistake, and there are times to keep your trap shut and your powder dry. This situation definitely called for the latter. So Bunny sat in the back seat, enjoying the evening breeze on his skin as he watched the dappled sunlight playing through the trees. Metaphorically speaking, it made sense to smell the flowers while you could, especially when you were heading towards all kinds of shit. At that particular moment, he had two guns trained on him and they were being held by individuals who weren't overly concerned whether he lived or died. The best he could hope for was not to give them a reason to come down in favour of the second of those two options.

He also took advantage of the opportunity to do a little self-assessment: he was feeling groggy, and the late-evening sun hurt his eyes when it hit them directly. His left ear was still ringing, too. All signs pointed towards a concussion. Given how close they'd been to a large vehicle going up in a fireball, he'd still got off pretty lightly. If the explosion hadn't caused the concussion, what happened after certainly did. As he'd been pushed into the jeep, a can of beans thrown from a couple of feet away had smashed into the back of his head. He'd turned to see the chair-wielding cheap-shot gobshite grinning at him. Bunny had taken a sliver of grim satisfaction from the fact that the man's T-shirt was bloodstained and his smile was missing its gold-toothed glint. Overall, it didn't come as a massive shock that the Paradise Sportsman's League weren't following the rules of the Geneva Convention, despite being somehow as well armed as any army on the planet.

As the convoy pulled up in front of the Huntsman's Lodge, it was met by yet more whoops and hollers from the members who'd stayed behind. This place needed a darts team in the worst way. Things got a little fraught as they were being led inside when one of the assembled pillars of the community threw a cheap shot into Diller's right jaw, sending him crashing to the ground. There wasn't much Bunny or the other two could do about it, but they'd given it a go, anyway. This had resulted in much slamming of gun barrels into unprotected areas and a general display of why the Stanford prison experiment had needed to be stopped. The fun and games ceased when President Ronnie came outside and instructed his men to bring the prisoners into the storeroom.

And then there they were, roughed up, taped up and thoroughly fed up, sitting on the concrete floor of a cage in the storeroom at the back of the Huntsman's Lodge. Bunny assumed the cage was probably meant for storing high-value booze, but these gobshites had also been keeping a bull, so who knew? Like every such room Bunny had ever been in, the place smelled of disinfectant, a fact that seemed a tad ironic given how it obviously hadn't been cleaned in quite some time. He noticed rat traps under a couple of the shelves and a shiver passed down his spine. Logically, he knew that rats weren't exactly his biggest concern right now, but the part of his mind that worried about them wasn't the same part that did logic.

One of the more youthful members of the Sportsman's League was sitting on a chair across from them, on guard duty. Bunny noticed he kept picking up the assault rifle hanging from a strap on his shoulder and looking at it like a child with a new toy at Christmas. The dude looked young. Old enough to shave, but that was only evident by how bad he was at it. Bunny probably didn't look too hot himself, but then again, the last time he'd decided to trim his beard was in the back of a moving Winnebago over a rough bit of road in South Dakota. Or Wyoming, possibly. The entire trip was bleeding together now. Not this bit, though. This bit was certainly standing out.

"Is everybody okay?" asked Smithy.

"No talking," snapped the guard.

"Why?" asked Bunny. "What harm is it doing?"

The guard furrowed his brow then repeated, "No talking."

This scintillating intellectual discourse was interrupted by the arrival of President Ronnie as he strode through the swing doors from the bar. "Leave us, Chip."

The kid got up and Ronnie watched him skulk off. The League's glorious leader was now wearing a handgun in a holster on his belt. It didn't make the ponytail look any less ridiculous.

Once they were alone, Ronnie turned back to them, leaned against the wire mesh and favoured them with a haughty smile. "So, I hope you're enjoying your stay. Can I get you anything, gentlemen?"

"I need to wash my hands," stated Carlos.

"Is he a retard?"

"Cleanliness is next to godliness," said Bunny quickly, as he reckoned Smithy's response was going to be considerably less polite.

Ronnie cracked his knuckles. "I'm going to ask this only once: who do you work for?"

"We don't work for anyone," replied Smithy, not even attempting to keep the exasperation from his voice.

"Bullshit."

"If you remember," said Bunny, "we came in here, like, two hours ago, asking to use the bathroom."

"Yes, and look at all the trouble you caused. You just happen to wander in this week of all weeks? I'm not buying it."

"Look," said Bunny, trying for reasonable, "clearly, things got out of hand, but we just wanted to get out of here and be on our way. Hell, we were trying to leg it when you blew our Winnebago to smithereens."

"Yes," said Ronnie, his eyes flashing, "you were trying to get out of here with one of our XM7s. All the proof you'd need."

"Proof of what?"

Ronnie drew his handgun from its holster. The room fell silent. He licked his lips then sat down in the chair vacated by the truculent Chip. "I am not naïve. I always knew that someone would inevitably try and interfere with Project Paradise."

"I don't—" started Bunny.

"Silence!" snapped Ronnie, jabbing the gun in his direction. "I don't want to hear any more of your nonsense. Soon we will have the resources to own this town once and for all. A haven of American purity in a sea of filth. Nobody is going to replace us. Paradise will become a beacon of hope for the oppressed." He shifted the gun around and Bunny guessed he'd spent a fair bit of time posing with it in front of the mirror. "You will not interfere with our plans. The Colonel is coming tomorrow, and then, after consulting with him, I'll decide what to do with you." Ronnie laughed. "Believe me, he'll know how to get answers. In the meantime, I strongly suggest you keep quiet. Otherwise, there'll be no decision to make. My men are highly trained and they will not hesitate to deal with you."

He turned and marched out of the room, the swinging doors to the bar flapping back into place in his wake.

There was a moment of pause.

"No guard," whispered Smithy.

Bunny tugged at the tape firmly binding his hands behind him. "How do we ..."

"On it," said Smithy, raising his shoulders and working his arms behind his back while keeping a close eye on the doors.

"Did anyone understand any of that?" asked Diller.

"Not a lot," admitted Bunny.

"Is everyone okay?" checked Smithy.

"More or less," said Diller, a slight waver in his voice betraying him. "I lost a tooth, but it was hurting anyway, so the guy did me a favour. How's your head?"

Smithy grunted. "I'll live."

Bunny attempted to shift himself around. "My left ankle is buggered. Not helped by those pricks taping it to the other one. Are you okay, Carlos?"

The big man looked at all three of them before speaking. Bunny had to strain to hear him. "My tummy hurts where the man poked me."

"Oh," said Diller. "Sorry to hear that. I'm sure it'll be alright. We'll be out of here soon."

"They took my yo-yo."

"Don't worry, we'll get it back," said Bunny, before adding, "as soon as I've used it to throttle a certain chair-wielding, baked-bean-throwing, cheap-shot merchant."

He caught Diller's pointed look then, glancing at Carlos's innocent face with its worried expression, felt instantly guilty. "I mean, everything will be fine, and us and your yo-yo will be out of here in no time."

"I'm very sorry," said Carlos.

"What?" said Bunny, noting that the big man looked as if he might cry. "You've nothing to be sorry about."

"I am sorry I hit the man. It started all the trouble."

"No," said Bunny. "You stopped the man hurting Smithy. You did nothing wrong."

"Yeah," agreed Diller. "None of this is your fault. If anyone should be sorry, it's me. We wouldn't have stopped here if I hadn't insisted."

"That's a load of crap, Dill," said Smithy, still working his hands behind his back industriously, and not taking his eyes off the doors. "I'm the one who should be sorry. Taking the road less travelled got us into this mess. And then the whole bull-riding thing was a little much."

"Ara stop," said Bunny. "I broke the loo. I helped wind these pricks up. Still, none of us owes anybody an apology. Remember, we just came in here trying to use the toilet. That's a basic human right. It's not our fault these dipshits are several hotdogs short of a barbecue."

This particularly accurate assessment was received with a few seconds of silence.

"Although I have to admit," Bunny continued, "I have no fecking idea how the hell we ended up here."

"Things did rather escalate," agreed Smithy.

"I might not owe you guys an apology," said Diller, "but I owe poor Billy the bull one. I put hot sauce on his ... well, a place that no male needs hot sauce. I feel awful, doing that to an innocent animal."

"Hmmmm," said Smithy. "Even then, those a-holes were mistreating him long before we got here. Think of it like you provided the impetus for him to move on and remove himself from a terrible relationship."

"Did anyone else see Billy?" asked Bunny.

"Last time I saw him," said Smithy, "I was taking evasive manoeuvres to avoid rear-ending him with a Winnebago."

"Did you see him take out one of the bikers?" asked Bunny. "'Twas a moment of sheer beauty. I don't know art, but I know what I like."

"Personally," said Smithy, "him charging through the bar and flipping that Jake doofus off his little chair like a rag doll – that was a moment of ecstatically realised karma."

"He certainly—" Bunny broke off at a noise outside in the bar.

They all looked up and Smithy instantly relaxed his shoulders as young Chip came hurrying back through the doors, looking shocked to find that nobody was in there, save for the four prisoners.

"Here he is," said Bunny. "We were wondering where you got to."

"Shut up," said Chip, returning to his seat.

A wave of silence passed across the room before Diller cleared his throat. "Sorry to bother you, but I don't suppose there's any chance I could use the restroom?"

"No!" growled Chip.

Diller nodded. "Yeah, figured as much."

SACRAMENTO SLUMLORD SOUFFLÉ

Andre Eskola awoke with a start. There was a woman in bed with him, but it wasn't the one who'd been there when he'd fallen asleep. That one had been a high-priced escort, originally from Colombia by the name of Melissa, on whom he spent a pretty penny every couple of weeks. She made the trip up to Sacramento from LA because Andre appreciated the finer things in life. He also liked those finer things to be incredibly flexible when it came to how he chose to enjoy them. The bed was designed in such a way as to conceal the manacles discreetly underneath it when they were not in use. He couldn't help but notice that he was wearing them now. This gave him great displeasure. He was supposed to be the one holding the key.

This other woman also looked remarkably different from her predecessor. For a start, she was casually holding a gun in one hand and a plastic bottle of some liquid in the other. Melissa was tall, with a figure to die for, dark eyes, sun-kissed skin and silky, curly, black hair cascading around her shoulders. Her smile had a certain effect on any hot-blooded male. In contrast, the woman now standing over Andre Eskola was short, plump and Asian, with fuzzy stubble for hair and an eye patch over her left eye. She was wearing a pair of leather bike pants and some kind of combat vest over a

Tom Petty T-shirt. Her smile also had an effect, albeit a very different one. The one eye Andre could see twinkled with malevolence and the grin below it filled him with terror. He kicked against the restraints that were holding all four of his limbs to the bed.

"Oh, good," she said in a husky voice, "you're awake. I was worried I was gonna have to shoot you to get your attention."

"Who the fuck?"

"You can call me Sister Joy. Charmed, I'm sure."

"Where's Melissa?"

"Oh, she left. Fun fact: as she did, she threw up in one of your big fancy flowerbeds outside before getting in her car. Gotta wonder what it says about you as a lover that a woman you're paying, no doubt handsomely, is so disgusted by you that it makes her physically sick."

Andre strained against the manacles again. "Fuck you, bitch," he spat, then raised his voice. "Marco!"

"Polo." Joy shifted casually and, with a minimal amount of movement, stood on Andre's testicles. She waited for his howls of agony to die down before she spoke again. "I ain't a big fan of the B-word, and I'd suggest you remember your manners, Mr Eskola. You're already not going to enjoy this, but it's up to you to decide just how bad it's going to get."

Andre said nothing in response, having temporarily lost the power of speech.

As Joy waited for him to come back from his trip to a very personal world of pain to the world of the conversant, she scratched her armpit with the muzzle of the gun and looked around his bedroom. "One of the many things I'll never understand is why the hell rich people got such a boner for marble. Marble floors – I mean, they ain't comfy to walk on. Slippery when wet. You drop something, it smashes. Okay, they wipe clean pretty easily, I'll grant you that, but still. It's one of those things people get just because it's expensive. I mean" – she waved the gun around loosely – "this bedroom is, what, a couple of hundred square feet? Whole thing got a marble floor, and I bet it's some fancy-pants Italian marble because, of course, nothing but the best for ol' big shot Andre Eskola, property tycoon."

Having regained the use of his faculties, Andre drew as deep a breath as he could and roared, "MARCO!"

"Polo," Joy responded again. "Or is Marco the name of that big bodyguard dude you got?" She moved around a little until she was in his eyeline. "About six-seven, six-eight. Bodybuilder type. Looks like somebody put an Easter Island statue in an Armani suit. Walks with a pronounced limp. That him?"

"He doesn't have a limp," snapped Andre.

"Yeah," she said mildly, rolling her head around her neck as if working out a kink, "he does now."

"MARCO!"

She sighed. "I mean, maybe I'm full of crap and he's about to come stomping through that door." She hopped off the bed and sat on the edge, seemingly confident that the restraints would prevent Andre from taking advantage of her having her back turned to him. "How long do you want to give it before we assume that isn't happening?"

Andre licked his lips. He needed to focus. Whatever this was, it was a negotiation. Everything was. He just needed to figure out what the deal to be made was. "Okay," he said. "Let's just calm down."

She glanced over her shoulder at him. "What gives you the impression I'm not calm? You're the one screaming your lungs out."

"How much do you want?"

"'Scuse me?"

"How much do you want?" he repeated.

Joy barked a humourless laugh and shook her head. "I don't want your money."

"Bullshit. Everyone wants money."

She got to her feet and turned around to look at him directly. At this angle he could see her face clearly; the vivid scar that ran down the left side, broken up by the eye patch. "No, they don't. Really, people want what it represents. For most folks, that's security. A home. Somewhere to raise a family. Not having to go to bed at the end of the day worrying. Being able to get a good night's sleep." She nodded at the restraints. "Speaking of which, I was able to put those on you without you waking up, Andre. I'm guessing you must've taken something pretty strong. Tell me, do you have trouble sleeping?"

"None of your business."

"I'd like to think you do. That somewhere in there, beneath all the excess and narcissistic arrogance, there's some little voice whispering your wrongs to you in the wee small hours."

Despite himself, Andre felt his anger rise again. "Did you go to all this trouble to come hear my confession? You aren't a priest."

"No. I am a nun, though."

"Bullshit."

She tilted her head. "I mean, not a normal one, I grant you. Found out a couple of years ago that I had six months to live—"

"I don't—" Andre gave a girlish screech as the woman shot a hole in the mattress a few inches below his right armpit.

"Don't interrupt people, Andre. It's rude, and it makes them think you're not interested in what they have to say. Oh, and side note – marble, bad for ricochets, too. Luckily, this bed has got a thick base. Now, where was I? Oh yeah, had me one of those epiphanies. Not a burning bush, now." She laughed. "Have had that in the past too, had to drink a lot of cranberry juice and ride side saddle for a while. But no. This time I got my own version of the Ten Commandments. No drink, no drugs, no cigarettes, no gambling, no sex, no chocolate, no meat, no killing and no dairy. I also found myself a little sisterhood. I ain't never really belonged anywhere my whole life until now. Between you and me, I kind of like it. The only things I've ever been good at ain't the kind of skills that lend themselves to being good, if you catch my meaning. Breaking into a high-security mansion. Taking out a bodyguard monster. Knowing how to do some other stuff we'll get to, that ain't the skill set of an upstanding citizen. Nowadays, though, I found a way. Because I found somewhere I belong. Because of my Ten Commandments. Andre – you're a former accountant, aren't you? Notice anything about them?"

He had. "There are only nine."

She favoured him with a smile and an appreciative nod. "Ding, ding, ding! That's right. Very impressive, Andre. Being able to count like that under pressure. The tenth one took me a while, but I got there. With apologies for the double negative, I ended up with 'no more not giving a shit'. I guess I mean pretending to. Deep down I think I always did, and I was just drowning it out with the booze and the drugs and the everything else, but maybe that's just hindsight. See, back in my bad old days, I reached a point where I was convinced I only cared about myself. Other people's problems were just that – other people's. Now, we can talk all night about the various reasons I ended up there, but ultimately, doesn't matter. We're all supposed to care, y'see. About the world and the people in it, which brings us back to you."

"I'm sorry," he said.

"Great. What for?"

"I ... Whatever brought you here."

This time, the bullet, fired from a more acute angle, hit just below his left armpit. "Wrong answer, Andre. Don't just say what you think I want to hear. I'm trying to give you a chance at redemption here. But you've got to work for it. So, tell me ... who is Savannah Jackson?"

"I don't—"

The bullet exploded into the pillow a couple of inches from his left ear.

"Jesus! Be careful."

Joy actually laughed as she shook her head. "C'mon, Andre. If you think I'm overly worried about hurting you, then you have not been paying attention." She pinned the gun under her armpit and used her freshly liberated hand to slap the various pockets of her vest. "Hang on a second, I got it here somewhere." She drew out something small and black that Andre couldn't see properly. "Ha! Told you."

She turned to the TV at the end of the bed and pointed at it with the thing in her hand. After a second, the TV sprang into life and a picture Andre had seen many times before appeared on it.

"Would you look at that?" Joy said. "I ain't too technically minded, I don't mind telling you. But a friend of mine, Zoya – the girl can do stuff with technology. I mean, this is nothing compared to most of it, but still. It's like knowing an honest-to-goodness magician." She glanced back at him. "Can you see that okay, Andre? Or do you need me to put another pillow under your head?"

He said nothing.

"Okay," she continued, "I'll take your silence as an affirmative. So, like I was saying ..." She pointed at the picture of a teenaged girl – white, mousy-brown hair, green eyes and rosy cheeks – holding a puppy as she beamed the widest smile at the world. "That there, as you well know, is Savannah Jackson. Fifteen when the photo was taken, never reached sixteen. I know everyone always speaks highly of the departed, but even allowing for that, bright as a button, good student, loyal friend, loving daughter and animal lover. Volunteered weekends at an animal shelter. Was going to study veterinary sciences or something like that."

"I don't know what you've heard," said Andre, "but that was a tragic accident."

Joy nodded, pocketing the pointer and taking the gun back from under her armpit. "Sure. Just so we're clear, you mean the fire that burned down the building you owned, the one the residents were trying to fight you evicting them from?"

"I'm on record as saying that building wasn't safe."

"And why was that? Because not only did you not service it, but you also had your goons go around breaking pipes, damaging walls, ripping out wiring. All to get those people to leave their homes so you could redevelop the site."

"That was never proven in a court of law."

"No, it wasn't. The whistleblowing witness who was there when one of your boys set the fire, he disappeared. Dead? Paid off? Running scared? Which is it?"

"I don't—"

This time, the bullet whistled by his right ear.

"You are not a good student, Andre. How have you still not learned the rules of the game?"

Andre pulled at the restraints again. "If this is being recorded, I want it on record, everything I am saying is under duress."

Joy paused for a long moment then squinted. "Recorded?" she repeated, incredulous. "What do you think this is? You think I'm here taking a deposition? You already got off, Andre. Relax. Same as you did in all those other cases. Your lawyers are crazy good. And then there are the other people you employ. They're ... Well, the word good hardly seems appropriate. Let's go with effective. Last I heard, you were suing a paper for referring to you as 'the slumlord of Sacramento', which, let's be honest, is way nicer than what most people call you. And you're worried I'm doing all this to record you saying something? Just how strong was the thing you took to block out the voices, Andre?"

"Fuck you!" he growled.

"Well, at least you're back to being yourself. I see this process as very much like peeling an onion. We gotta work through some layers. Let's see if we can't speed things up a little."

Using her thumb, she popped the lid off the plastic bottle she was holding and poured its contents all over Andre's supine form. He tensed as the cold liquid splashed across his naked skin. Some fell into his open mouth and the taste of it confirmed what his sense of smell was picking up. Gasoline.

He spluttered and spat before he found his voice again. "What are you doing?"

"Think of it like role play, Andre. Give you some idea of the terror poor Savannah must have felt when the smoke filled her room. They reckon she went back to get the family dog." Joy's voice became quieter and harder. "The kid really loved animals."

"You can't do this."

"Why's that?"

"You ..." Inspiration hit him. "You can't kill me. Your commandments thing. No killing!"

She nodded in approval. "See? See what happens when you

listen, Andre? I hope that's one of the lessons you're going to take from our time together."

A pinging noise signalled the arrival of a text. "Damn it. Apologies, I thought I'd turned it off." She tossed the now-empty plastic bottle away and reached into her pocket to fish out a cell phone. She tutted as she read the message. "Well, would you look at that. A dot has disappeared. I know that means nothing to you, Andre, but it isn't good news. To be honest, I had my heart set on seeing this all the way through, and then there's a monster truck rally in Sacramento tomorrow night I got a ticket for. You ever been?"

Andre simply looked back at her, unable to think of any response to that question.

"You should check 'em out. They're a lot of fun. Big trucks crushing stuff, jumping over stuff, breathing fire. Motorcycle acrobatic things, too. I mean, it ain't Shakespeare, but damn, if it ain't a fun night out." She tucked her phone back into her pocket. "Now looks like I got to go elsewhere. I hate having my plans interrupted." She seemed to remember she was talking to a man who had woken up chained to his bed and now found himself covered in gasoline. "Sorry, look who I'm telling. Speaking of which, I guess I need to expedite things here a little."

She took the small black device back out of her pocket and pointed it at the TV again. The picture changed to the twenty-four storey New Dawn Tower. Andre knew it well. He'd built it.

"Yeah, you know what that big, shiny, penis-substitute is. I know that. Your pride and joy. Literally built on the spot where poor old Savannah Jackson died. Do you want the good news or the bad news?"

Andre had no words.

"Cool." Joy pointed at the screen. "Well, that's a live feed and" – she checked her watch – "you're going to want to stay glued to it because at seven minutes past midnight, which is about ten minutes from now, a few fires are going to break out."

"No!"

"Oh, don't worry," she continued, "the alarms work fine, and I've got a friend watching, so the three security guards will get out okay. They're the only ones in the building. I've also set things up in such a way that firefighters aren't going to be able to go up beyond the second floor, and because there's no threat to life, they've got different protocols. They'll be perfectly safe." Her voice lowered, and she looked him directly in the eye. "I mean, I'm not a monster. And hey, don't worry about it. You're insured."

"Yes," he said, "I am. So this is just a pointless act of terrorism."

"Terrorism? It feels like we call everything that now. Probably fair." She ran a hand over her scalp. "The bad news is, owing to a really quite spectacular oversight on behalf of your company, your insurance runs out at midnight tonight."

"Impossible."

"Impossible?" she repeated. "No. Unlucky? Maybe. A lot of people might go with karma. I mean, especially when they check and it turns out you received all kinds of emails, letters and calls about it, and yet, amazingly, you and your executives just ignored them." She turned back to look at the building on the screen again. "Like I said, it's like watching an actual magician work."

"Please," he begged. "You'll ruin me!"

Joy nodded. "That's very much the plan, yes. Your empire is carved out of other people's pain and tonight you get to watch it burn. It's the very least you deserve."

"You're insane!"

She shrugged. "I've been called worse." Her phone pinged again. "Right, I'd better leave. Do you want the lights on or off?"

"I'll get you for this, you bitch!"

"And there's that word again. I feel you haven't learned all I hoped for from this conversation." She nodded back at the screen. "Still, the night is young."

And with that, Sister Joy walked out of the room, turning the lights off as she went, leaving the TV screen as the only source of illumination.

After a minute, she walked back in again.

"I almost forgot."

As Andre screamed and hollered all manner of abuse at her, she lit a candle and left it on the bed between his legs.

"Don't want you being all alone in the dark."

"But ... but ... no killing!"

She pointed at the candle. "Oh, what, this? I mean, it's kinda like your situation, isn't it? You gave an order to someone who said something to someone else and so on, and poor Savannah died, but I bet you tell yourself that isn't your fault, don't you? All I'm doing is lighting a candle. That's all. Maybe it'll react badly with the gasoline, maybe it won't. Who can say?"

In the time it took for her to walk out again, Andre Eskola vacillated between pleading and abuse three times.

———

Six hours later, when nobody could reach Andre on the phone, the COO of his company came to his home. He found him on his bed, in quite the state, having screamed himself hoarse. The candle had fallen over and miraculously not caused a fire. Later analysis would confirm he was in fact covered in domestic cleaning fluid, which smelled rather like gasoline, but had a special formula that does not burn.

The same could not be said for New Dawn Tower.

WE GOTTA GET OUT OF THIS PLACE

Bunny had always enjoyed his trips to Dublin Zoo, but this experience was changing his perspective on that. He didn't know for how long they'd been sitting in the cage, but he could see from the three-by-two-foot window, which was high on the back wall, that it was now dark outside. He'd dipped in and out of consciousness a couple of times but not managed anything you could truly classify as sleep. Their regular visitors made sure of that.

The Huntsman's Lodge was really jumping tonight. Music pumping from the bar could be heard above a hubbub of raucous voices. Gail the bartender was regularly in and out of the storeroom, restocking, changing barrels in the corner. She neither looked at them nor said anything to their guard. Chip was back on his second stint, having been relieved for a couple of hours by a very large fat guy with red eyes who spent a lot of time shooting daggers at Diller.

In the absence of any other stimulus, Bunny was enjoying hate-listening to the songs that were being played on the jukebox. If one he liked came on, it stoked the fire of his righteous ire. Hearing these fuckwits singing along to the Neil Young classic 'Rockin' in the Free World' had been a particular low point. This bar was where irony came to die, possibly after being tied up in the back storeroom first and given a severe kicking.

For the majority of time, they sat in silence, Chip and his rotund buddy not being big fans of the art of conversation. Bunny got the impression they were lowest on the Sportsman's League's totem pole, seeing as everyone else seemed to be out in the bar living it up, while their job was staring resentfully at the caged beasts in the back. Not that they weren't on the receiving end of regular visits. For the most part it had just been some unimaginative taunting, although there had been the throwing of quite a lot of bar snacks and the spraying of beer. One particularly inebriated visitor had wanted to spray something other than beer, but thankfully Gail had passed through at that point and made it very clear that nobody was taking a piss in her storeroom. A certain formerly gold-toothed individual had come in, said nothing and hung a noose on the cage's wire mesh. Bunny clocked Smithy taking some deep breaths and trying very hard not to give the asshole the reaction he was looking for. With a grim satisfaction, Bunny noted that at least when he gave them that shit-eating grin of his, it was minus a gold tooth. He hoped he'd swallowed the thing and it was lodged somewhere diabolical.

Every now and then, Bunny yawned or belched loudly, or pleaded with the guard for a meal or the chance to use the facilities. On each occasion he got told to shut up. Diller likewise made the odd impassioned request relating to his urgent need to use the bathroom. He was similarly rebuffed. Insults were hurled, guns pointed, sneers sneered. Bunny didn't mind too much. Whenever they were doing that, they weren't watching Smithy, who was using the distraction to work his hands behind his back, which was the whole point. Bunny hoped Smithy was doing a whole lot more than scratching his arse, because right now, he represented their only slim hope of getting the hell out of there.

He also didn't know how much time they had. The parade of visitors was getting steadily more drunk and belligerent in tone, and Bunny was worried that, despite what El Presidente had said earlier, it wouldn't be long before all that free-flowing booze mixed with the festering hostility in the air to coalesce into an ugly idea. He kept trying not to look at the noose.

Bunny glanced at Smithy and was considering launching into another impassioned speech about what he'd give for a ham sandwich, when he heard the doors swing open. Jake was standing there, bottle of beer in one hand, bull-riding trophy in the other, and a drunken sneer writ large across his face. The bull-riding-trophy hand was in a cast. Clearly, his latest rather brief bull ride had inflicted a little damage.

It was saying something about the antagonistic air of the man that, out of the vast assortment of visitors they'd received throughout the evening, none of them had caused the temperature to drop quite so much. This, thought Bunny, was what happened when you took away the only thing a small man had been considered good at in his largely crappy life. If you added that resentment to his permanent anger at a world he believed owed him something, you got the look that was in those bleary eyes at that moment. This was where impotent rage turned truly ugly.

"Hey, Jake," said Chip.

Jake didn't even turn to look at the kid. "Go take a break, Chip."

"Ronnie said—"

"And I'm saying something different," snarled Jake. "I'm second in command around here and don't you forget it. Or do I need to carve a little org chart onto your ass?"

"No, Jake. Sorry, Jake."

Chip got to his feet, clearly hovering between feeling he should say something and the heartfelt desire to be elsewhere. "When should I—"

"When I want you to come back in and sit here doing nothing, I'll come and tell you. Until then, piss off."

Chip was already out the door before he'd finished the sentence.

A look passed between Smithy and Bunny.

"Jesus, Jakey boy," said Bunny, "I didn't realise what a big man you were until I saw you ordering a dumb kid about. Impressive."

"Is it my imagination," offered Smithy, "or is there a real big drop-off in respect around here between the guy in command and the next one down?"

Jake spat on the floor. "Look at you two, with all your clever words. Look where you ended up, bitches – sitting in a cage."

"True enough," said Bunny, "but at least I'm in here with three friends. You, Jakey boy, seem to be wandering about on your own."

"Fuck you."

"Yeah, Bunny," agreed Smithy, "mind your mouth. Jake here is pretty impressive. Despite our differences, he's come here to give me my trophy. That's real class."

"Screw you, midget. You cheated."

"Ha. Right," said Smithy. "Or did a *midget* waltz in here and make you look like an idiot?"

Bunny turned to the others. "How long was the previous record?"

"Eight seconds," supplied Diller.

"Shut the fuck up," said Jake, smashing his empty beer bottle on the ground. "It was twelve."

"Twelve?" echoed Smithy with a snigger. "I could probably do that right now. You wouldn't even have to untie me."

Bunny laughed and Diller joined in.

"Shut up. You interfered with that bull, you goddamn pervert," snarled Jake.

"Did I?" said Smithy, a mocking lilt to his voice. "You got proof of that?"

"He was drugged. Everybody said so."

"Riiiight," said Smithy, deliberately drawing the word out. "Would this be the same bull that rampaged through your shitty little bar and ran several miles down the road a few minutes after I'd rode him to a standstill? That bull?"

"That's him, alright," said Bunny. "Didn't he flip you like a little pancake on his way out the door, Jakey boy?"

Jake lifted his T-shirt, drew a gun from his waistband and pointed it at Bunny.

"Stop calling me that, asshole."

"Would you look at that," said Smithy, pulling it back slightly. "Jake here has got himself a golden gun."

He really did. When Jake turned it, so it was no longer pointing directly at him, Bunny got a better look at it. It seemed like a fairly ordinary handgun, only it was gold-plated.

Bunny whistled. "Ye can't buy class."

The irony in the statement seemed to pass Jake by entirely. He gazed at the gun with an expression of pure love that was rare to see in this day and age. "This was a present from my cousin. He's coming tomorrow. He's going to fuck you retards up."

"He sounds delightful," said Bunny.

"Show some respect," slurred Jake. "Goddamn war hero. Me and him sorted this whole thing out. Gonna put Paradise on the map. Me and him got it done."

"Is that right?" said Smithy. "He sounds awesome. I can't wait to show him that trophy I won."

"The fuck you did."

"Yeah," continued Bunny, "marching around outside in the bar, with your golden gun and that trophy you don't deserve, I'm sure nobody is laughing at you, Jakey boy."

Jake kicked at the wire. "I said, don't call me that!"

"Careful, Bunny," said Smithy. "Big brave Jake here might shoot an unarmed man sitting in a cage. That's how he likes to fight his battles."

"I think he's just annoyed," said Bunny, "after I cattle-prodded him earlier on. Looked like he might have wet his panties."

Jake shoved the gun back into his jeans. "Screw you. With a word, I could have all four of you taken out back and shot."

"Yeah," said Smithy, "and that word is 'Ronnie'. As in" – Smithy pitched his voice to a grating whine – "please Ronnie, can you hurt the big bad men? They were mean to me. Boo hoo."

"Wasn't Robin second in command to Batman?" asked Bunny.

"Chewbacca was technically second in command of the *Millennium Falcon*," said Diller.

"Yeah. It's really just another word for sidekick," said Smithy. "For the guy who can't hack it."

"Fuck you," hissed Jake. "You fucking little midget."

Smithy sighed theatrically. "Yeah, you already said that. Not the most original of thinkers, are you?"

"I'll fuck you up."

"Not without the okay from Daddy Ronnie you won't."

Something in that sentence was the straw that broke the camel's back. Bunny would bet good money it was the word daddy that did it.

"I'll show you," he hollered, moving across to enter the combination into the lock on the cage door while still holding on to the trophy awkwardly.

Bunny glanced at Smithy, who was now working his hands furiously behind his back. He gave the briefest of nods.

"I wouldn't worry about it," said Bunny. "They've probably not given Jakey boy the right code."

They watched him fumble awkwardly with the lock as his cast got in the way.

"Yeah," agreed Smithy. "He's way too much of a fuck-up. Besides, he—"

Jake roared as the combination lock clicked open. He tossed it aside and surged through the cage's gate.

Bunny was already rolling himself across the ground for all he was worth. There was no set plan. The best they could have hoped for was chaos, and chaos was what they now had.

After three purposeful strides, Jake was above Smithy, his right boot raised, all set to smash Smithy's unprotected face. With a strained grunt, something snapped and Smithy brought his arms around just in time to catch Jake's boot and absorb most of the downward force. This was enough to throw Jake off balance, and enough for Bunny's flailing legs to take Jake's left leg from under him. It was all Bunny could do not to scream as his weakened left ankle made contact with Jake's standing leg, but it was a small price to pay to see him come crashing down to earth beside him.

Because even God sometimes enjoys a well-timed pratfall, Jake dropped the bull-riding trophy before he landed and, for the second time that day, he got to feel the business end of a bull's horns, this time as they jabbed painfully into his descending left arse cheek. Before Jake could scream, the still-bound Carlos threw himself on top of him, knocking the wind out of him. Then, in a flash, Smithy had Jake locked in a sleeper hold. Bunny had marvelled a couple of weeks ago, when they'd had an arm-wrestling competition, at how freakishly strong Smithy's arms were. It was as if God had taken the strength of an ordinary man and distilled it into a smaller, considerably more intense package.

Bunny watched the light fade from Jake's eyes as he lost consciousness.

"Smithy," said Diller, "he's out."

Smithy kept straining.

"Smithy!"

A look came over Smithy's face, as if he was coming back from somewhere far away, and he let go.

"Good man," said Bunny. "Now, untie the rest of us."

With difficulty, Smithy released the tape from around his own feet then stood up and staggered out of the cage. Over on a nearby shelf he found a wire cutter beside the remains of the roll of duct tape. Smithy grabbed it and set about freeing the rest of them, starting with Bunny.

"How long do you reckon we have?" asked Diller.

"Hopefully long enough for Carlos here to help me over to that window," said Bunny, "because I'm not sure how well I can walk right now." *And then we'd better hope Carlos can fit through the thing*, he added to himself, *as it wasn't like going out the front door was an option.*

Now freed, Bunny pulled the gun from the unconscious Jake's waistband. "We need to tape this gobshite up. Diller, grab that roll and start with his big mouth."

Diller did as instructed as Smithy hacked away at the tape around Carlos's hands.

"Where are we going now, Bunny?" asked Carlos.

"Out the window, fella."

"What's out there?"

Bunny shrugged. "Doesn't matter. Whatever it is, it's got to be better than what's in here."

INTO THE WOODS

As escapes went, theirs was not the most dignified. Diller had slipped through the window to check that the coast was clear. Then, thanks to his sprained ankle, Bunny had to suffer the ignominy of Diller pulling him through while Carlos shoved his fat arse from behind. A button pinged off his shirt into the darkness, never to be seen again. Once that was done, Diller and Bunny had struggled to heave Carlos's colossal frame through the small window. For a while there, it had looked as if that was where the whole plan was going to come unstuck, but eventually they'd managed to get the big fella through, even if it had required Diller to climb back in to assist with the pushing from the other end. It was like being stuck in some weird version of that old riddle of the farmer trying to transport a chicken, a bag of grain and a fox across a river in a rowboat. There were some noticeable differences, though; for example, Bunny had never heard a version where the farmer's diminutive friend was also covering a door waiting for someone to stumble through and turn the whole thing into a messy shootout.

Eventually, all four of them got through the window and found themselves huddled behind the Huntsman's Lodge beside the dumpsters. The garbage smelled so stomach-churningly bad that, hungry as he was, Bunny was glad he hadn't been given anything to eat. The hot day had given way to a muggy night with a hint of a breeze to take the edge off, which pushed sporadic patches of clouds across the sky, playing hide-and-seek with the moon. To their right sat Billy's now-empty enclosure, once again shut off from the main bar. To their left, a path around a corner led along the side of the building towards the front of the Lodge. Slivers of light passed through the slats in the big, barn-like doors that separated the enclosure from the bar, mixing with the moonlight to give the self-liberated quartet as much illumination as they were likely to get.

"We could try to go around to the parking lot," said Smithy. "See if we can steal a car?"

Bunny shook his head. They could hear raised voices outside. "Somebody is going to see us, then we've got one gun against a fecking arsenal and I amn't any great shakes on the moving front."

"How's your ankle?"

Bunny had taken his first proper look at it when he'd fallen gracelessly out the window. It had only been a few hours since the injury, but it was already swollen, with patches of dark bruising amidst the red swelling. "I'll live, but don't expect a foxtrot any time soon."

"Whatever we're doing," said Diller, "we need to do it fast, before someone notices we're gone."

Bunny scanned their surroundings again. The Lodge backed onto woods that stretched down the hillside for literally miles. Douglas-firs towered over them, and beneath, the inky darkness of the unknown did not look inviting.

He nodded towards the trees. "I guess we head that way. Let's get as far away as possible and figure out our next move from there."

"Okay." Smithy touched Diller's arm. "You alright with that?"

Diller gave a sharp nod. "If it's a choice between that and a heavily armed lynch mob, I'll take my chances with the wolves."

And so they moved off.

It was slow-going, mainly because ten yards into the trees and the light offered by the Huntsman's Lodge was all but gone. That, plus the thick canopy overhead, meant they were left attempting to walk through near-total darkness, save for the occasional patches of moonlight that came and went. Every twig that snapped seemed impossibly loud, like a siren ringing out in the night.

They quickly fell into formation with Smithy leading the way, Bunny leaning on Carlos for support and Diller bringing up the rear. It would have been a pleasant enough walk in daylight, but at night the ground became a malevolent traitor, one footfall away from taking them down. They walked in silence, save for Smithy hissing the odd warning about protruding roots or branches. Large patches of brambles grew beneath the trees, which they tried to work their way around when possible. The air was sweet with the scent from the fir trees and still muggy as it hung on to the heat from the day. Bunny was soon sweating from the effort. Carlos, propping him up on his left side, made no noise apart from his heavy, steady breaths as he marched on.

After what was probably only a couple of minutes but felt like an eternity, they were far enough away from the bar for the music to have faded to a suggestion on the faint breeze.

"We need to up the pace," urged Bunny.

"Easier said than done," Smithy replied.

"I know, but we have to. Don't go slow on my account."

They left the rest unsaid as the sword of Damocles hung over them. Every nerve in Bunny's body was on edge, constantly expecting the next second to be the one when the alarm was raised and the night became filled with angry shouting voices and impending doom.

Smithy moved forward with more purpose and the others matched his pace.

"Is it always this loud?" asked Diller, clearly trying his best to sound relaxed.

Bunny knew what he meant. Any time he heard someone banging on about the wonderful peace and quiet of the great outdoors, he wondered if they were going to a whole different great outdoors than he was. The one he knew was noisy at the best of times, filled with birds cackling and calling to each other, God knows what rustling through the undergrowth. Even trees could be surprisingly noisy with a bit of wind rushing through them, and don't get him started on the dawn chorus – he was fully convinced birds were morning people reincarnated with the sole purpose of ruining everybody else's lie-in. Shower of chirpy pricks, the lot of them.

At night, though, being surrounded by it like this, nature took a darker turn. The noises became sinister. Every inky-black outline looked like some malicious entity come to wreak unspecified vengeance. This was where the natural world had humanity at a disadvantage and didn't it know it. Those long-forgotten instincts in the back of the human mind, that had all but faded away to nothing as you sat on your sofa watching David Attenborough banging on about puffins, suddenly woke from hibernation, staggering into the dim light to remind you that nature didn't want you here and it never had.

Overhead, an owl hooted loudly, and Diller made an involuntary noise from the rear of their pack.

Bunny cleared his throat. "Don't worry about it, Dill. 'Tis nothing. They use recordings of sounds like this to lull people to sleep."

Diller grunted. "Man, what I'd give for a car alarm."

"Shush," said Smithy, stopping and holding up a hand.

"Wolves?" asked Diller.

"Worse." Smithy left a pause then started striding forward. "C'mon."

"What?" insisted Bunny.

"The music stopped."

"Ara crap."

They were moving faster now, because safety had suddenly become a relative term. Bunny nearly fell as Carlos, hanging on to his left arm, collided with the trunk of a tree in his rush to keep up with Smithy. He heard Diller lose his footing behind them and stumble to the ground. "You alright?"

"Fine, fine," said Diller. "Keep moving."

The pain from Bunny's ankle was growing more pronounced, but that was the least of their troubles.

"Crap," hissed Diller.

Bunny glanced back over his shoulder and saw what he was referring to. Flashlight beams could be seen dancing around behind them, fanning out through the trees in several directions.

"Keep moving," said Smithy, picking up the pace even further.

It wasn't as if there was any other option.

The pace was now such that they were all in a constant state of stumbling, battling to stay upright as they strove to put some distance between them and the pursuit. Carlos gave a yelp as a low-hanging branch poked him in the eye.

Bunny looked behind them again. The torch beams were growing closer. He could hear distant voices too, indistinct shouts. They weren't heading directly towards them yet, but it was surely only a matter of time.

Up ahead, Smithy said something that Bunny couldn't quite make out. Diller fell into the back of him then grabbed hold of Bunny to stop him from pitching forward. Bunny couldn't see Smithy now, but he could hear him kicking and shoving his way through the vegetation to their left, going sideways when they needed to be going forward. Was he disorientated? What had he said? Sunny in the night? That didn't—

The ground disappeared from under Bunny's feet and he tumbled to his right. It was all he could do not to cry out as he slammed into the damp earth and began rolling downwards. A sharp rock dug into his side as the world spun before he came to a halt, the trunk of a fallen tree pausing his descent. Then the immense form of Carlos slammed into him, sending the tree and them both tumbling further down the slope. Bunny wrapped his arms around his head as rocks and branches threw jabs from all sides.

Finally, the spin cycle stopped and they were at the bottom, Carlos mercifully landing just beside Bunny as opposed to on top of him this time. The big man cried out softly in pain and Bunny reached out to pull him upright. "Are you okay?"

"We fell," said Carlos.

"Yeah, but are you alright?"

The cloud cover shifted, allowing the moon to throw more light down upon them, and revealing that they were at the bottom of a hollow about twenty feet deep. It had felt a lot deeper on the way down.

"My finger hurts." Carlos held his right hand up and Bunny could see well enough to appreciate that the digit in question, the index finger of his right hand, was bent at an angle it really shouldn't be. He could just make out the baleful look in the big man's eyes too.

"We'll fix that later, but for now, we need to be really quiet."

They both looked up at the sound of Diller and Smithy scrabbling down the slope after them.

"Gully to the right," said Bunny, as much to himself as anyone else. "Shite."

As the other two reached the bottom of the hollow, Carlos was trying to get to his feet.

"Stay down," hissed Smithy, pointing upwards. "They're coming."

Bunny could make out beams of flashlight picking out the trees above, and for the first time, he heard a distinct voice from the pursuit. "C'mon, this way!"

"Over here," whispered Diller, pointing behind Bunny and then pulling him up to his feet.

Ignoring the complaints from the various parts of his body, his left ankle being head of the queue, Bunny got up into a hunched position and half stumbled, was half dragged towards the side of the gully nearest to their pursuers. Once there, they pressed their backs up against a ridge of rock about four feet in height. Directly above them, a large tree stood at the top of the gully looming over it.

"I'm telling you, this way," shouted the voice again, sounding much closer this time.

Diller tapped Bunny on his knee then pointed at his feet. With effort, he pulled his legs into him, to make himself that bit smaller. It still felt horribly exposed. All four of them sitting there, the rock at their backs, mulch on the ground beneath their arses, staring up as the light from a torch danced across the trees above.

"For Christ's sake, Todd," shouted another voice, "slow the fuck down. You've got the only flashlight."

"I heard something, Razor."

"Alright, but stop running or I'll break my goddamn neck. Which way?"

There was a pause. "I don't know. What's down there?"

Bunny held his breath as light played over the slopes of the gully.

"Ooowee, look at this."

"That's why I'm saying to be careful. I'm not killing myself running around these woods at night."

"I'm telling you I heard something."

All four escapees watched in silence as the flashlight swung to the left, picking out different parts of the gully.

Bunny bit his lip as he watched it move along, steadily moving closer and closer to them. At the sound of a noise beside him he looked over to see Smithy had pulled out the ridiculous golden gun. This was no angle from which to engage in a shootout. They were fish in a barrel, albeit ones with at least a slim chance at fighting back.

"Can we—"

"No," snapped the voice with the torch. "I heard something. I heard something!"

The light was moving with a dreadful methodical rhythm now as it passed over the slopes, checking every inch. It swept left, then right again, and then it would be on them as ...

The beam jerked upwards towards the sound of distant gunfire far off to the right.

"Shit," said the flashlight bearer.

"Someone must have got 'em," said his compatriot. "C'mon. We're gonna miss it!"

The quartet listened in silence for a few seconds to confirm that their pursuers were indeed moving away.

Another rapid burst of gunfire in the distance was followed up by two single shots and then a third. Silence. Or rather, there was a return to the dull nocturnal roar of nature, which had changed in tone because some idiot was shooting.

"Fecking hell," exclaimed Bunny, exhaling loudly.

"That was close," confirmed Diller.

"I don't know about anyone else," said Smithy, "but I'm starting to come around to Diller's point of view on this whole great outdoors thing."

"Yeah," agreed Bunny.

"I know this is probably an odd thing to say," said Diller, "but didn't this feel exactly like that scene in *The Lord of the Rings* when the hobbits were running from the demon dudes on horseback?"

"Weirdly," admitted Smithy, "I was thinking the exact same thing." He laughed, releasing a little tension. "We really need to get out more."

"Seeing as we're talking random nonsense," said Bunny, "this might be the concussion talking, but you know that riddle with the farmer in the boat trying to get his chicken, a bag of grain and a fox across a river?"

"I do," said Diller, sounding extremely confused by the question.

"'Tis bothering me. Can anyone remember why the feck a farmer is trying to get the fox across?"

They all sat there and considered it for a few moments as, in the distance, they could hear the glorious sound of heavily armed imbeciles shooting at something that wasn't them.

WEST COAST PROBLEMS

From her position hunched down in the back seat of the RAV4, Zoya glanced surreptitiously out of the window to check that Dionne was still sitting outside at the picnic tables. They'd pulled over at a truck stop that looked as if it made up for what it lacked in spit and polish by providing the very real opportunity to contract salmonella or purchase meth.

At least Zoya thought she was sitting in the back of a RAV4. She wasn't that big into cars, and she'd been in and out of so many over the course of the last day that it was hard to keep track. After being picked up at San Diego International Airport by a limo, they'd been dropped off at a hotel, where they'd flagged a cab which took them to an all-night diner. There, they had picked up a car and changed clothes, or, in the case of Tatiana, changed into another person entirely. The woman's way with disguises was freaky. She could go into a restroom and come out twenty years older and forty pounds heavier. Anyone could put on a wig – hell, she and Dionne had, but Tatiana did so much more than that. She said it was all about changing posture, subtle padding, blah, blah, blah. Zoya preferred her own personal explanation – the woman was a straight-up witch. The good kind, obviously, but a witch nevertheless. At a certain point, that became easier to believe than her being able to change into different people at will with stuff you could buy from a dollar store.

Remaining in the car had been easy for Zoya. She'd pretended to be asleep, and Dionne had left her, knowing that she wouldn't want to get out anyway. Sweet, sweet agoraphobia. The gift that keeps on giving. It meant she could finally log on and get to work.

The being-asleep thing was plausible, not least because she hadn't got any sleep the entire flight. None of them had. Bizarrely, the Wi-Fi on the private plane had been out. Honestly, how could the filthy rich live like that? The food options had also been alarmingly healthy. They'd received an apology that the full à la carte menu wasn't available owing to the skeleton crew. To maintain their cover, they'd just had to make do with the insane level of opulence while feigning mild dissatisfaction. In different circumstances, Zoya would have got a real kick out of the whole thing.

Despite what Dionne said, there was no harm in Zoya taking a looksee. She knew what she was doing and, more importantly, she knew how to make sure other people wouldn't find out about it. The truck stop's free Wi-Fi was weak, but there was a private network that had some juice. It was password protected, but, like most things, Zoya had a tool for that. Once in, a quick scan confirmed that there had been no contact from Dorothy on any of the channels. It hadn't been twenty-four hours yet, so that wasn't unexpected. She'd only break with protocol in an emergency. Zoya then kicked off some checks on hospital admissions, scanning databases for anyone roughly matching Dorothy's description, and nothing came back. She wasn't sure if she should be happy about that or sad.

She knew she shouldn't have done the next bit, but she did it anyway. Birdy – Zoya's drone – was docked on top of a disused water tower a mile away from the order's HQ. Even with her cutting-edge cloaking technology, Zoya didn't enjoy taking Birdy out for a spin in a highly populated area during the day, but this was an exception. She could lie to herself about why she was checking, but the simple fact of the matter was that the school had been the closest thing Zoya had ever known to a proper home, and now it was gone. Some part of her needed to look.

Even knowing what to expect, she'd gasped when the image being beamed across the country from Birdy had come into focus on the screen. There it was. A pile of rubble where their home base had once been. A tape cordon surrounded the whole thing and, judging by the barriers, it looked like the authorities had closed off the block. Her home, her life's work, Dorothy – all those things had been where that still-smoking pile of rubble now lay. Fingers crossed that one of them, the most important, had made it out.

Zoya bit her lip. Dorothy was a bad ass. If anyone could ...

She scanned the rubble again. She knew Dionne hadn't wanted her to look. Now she felt like she had a better idea why.

———

Dionne didn't glance up from the legal pad she was busy scribbling on when she heard the voice.

"Hey, how you doing, darling?"

"Not interested," she said firmly. In the corner of her eye she'd clocked the man approaching the table at which she was sitting. It was bad enough she'd had to suffer lukewarm fries, a stodgy burger and an inexplicably hot coffee that had burned the roof of her mouth, now she was going to get hit on by some dumbass trucker who thought a woman sitting on her own was an automatic invitation.

She rolled her eyes as the man sat down opposite her.

"I'm just being friendly."

Dionne finally looked up in order to favour the man with her full, pissed-off, laser-beam glare. "And if you're still sitting here in three seconds, I'm gonna ..."

Dionne actually gasped.

The man wore his hair long, over his well-groomed beard, which was a dense thicket of brown hair that touched his chest and covered most of his face, save for sparkling hazel eyes and a crooked-toothed smile. The man coughed, as if to dislodge the down-home accent, then spoke again, everything staying the same except for the voice.

"Were you expecting someone else?" asked Tatiana in a low register.

"No," said Dionne, "but I sure as hell wasn't expecting this."

"I said I was going to do what I could to further muddy our tracks once I dumped the car."

"Yeah, but ..." Dionne looked her up and down again. "If you're looking for notes, the double denim is a little on the nose for a truck driver."

"Clichés are clichés for a reason."

"Wait," said Dionne, pointing towards the truck stop's parking lot. "I was keeping an eye out. Did you pull up in a truck with, for want of a better word, another man?"

"Sure did. Benji. Nice guy. Gave me a lift here to pick up a rig from a buddy. He's going through a bad divorce right now, but they're trying to stay civil for the kids."

Dionne shook her head. "There really is something freakish about you."

"I'm going to take that as the compliment I'm sure you meant it to be, sugarplum."

Sugarplum. The unusual sobriquet made Dionne pause then widen her eyes. "Holy crap! You, or whoever this is ..."

"Norm," Tatiana supplied, slipping back into the down-home accent again.

"Norm," repeated Dionne, "tried to pick me up a few months ago in that coffee shop over in Queens, didn't he I mean, you?"

He/she smiled at Dionne and spoke once again in Tatiana's voice. "I needed to test him out, and you're the most observant person I know."

"Be honest – do you just see the entire planet as being full of people you can bamboozle?"

Norm shrugged and returned to his voice. "I'm just trying to get by, little lady."

"Freaky," said Dionne. "Completely freaky."

"So," said Tatiana once again, "did everything go okay your end?"

"Yeah. No problems. Our whizz kid is asleep in the back of the car."

Tatiana nodded. "I mean, you know she isn't, right?"

"Oh, yeah. She was faking being asleep when I pulled in. She's no doubt running checks and probably even has Birdy in the air by now."

"Isn't that a direct contravention of your orders?"

"Yes," admitted Dionne, "but she had the courtesy to wait until now to do it, and this way, if there is anything, she'll tell me. If there isn't, we need never discuss it."

"You're already sounding like a natural leader."

"Oh, stop."

"I still can't believe she didn't realise that we'd told the pilot to turn off the Wi-Fi on the plane."

"That's the thing with really smart people – they don't always think of incredibly simple things like something just being unplugged. She still didn't get any sleep, though."

Tatiana scratched at Norm's beard. "Worth a shot anyway. And hey, the kid is more resilient than you think."

"She's going to have to be," said Dionne, puffing out her cheeks and glancing over at the car. "You and I both know that the odds of Dorothy having managed to get out are not good."

"Yes. And if she did, the odds they wouldn't find her ..." Tatiana didn't articulate the rest of the thought. There were worse things than not escaping, and they both knew it.

After a few moments, Tatiana pointed at Dionne's tray. "Not enjoying the fine dining?"

"No," confirmed Dionne. "I don't think the cook on the early shift is their finest."

"Nah, the food here is always terrible."

"And yet you recommended it as a rendezvous?"

"Because it's on the way to LA and there's very little in the way of cameras. I didn't choose it for the gastronomical fare on offer."

Dionne looked around. "In which case, I get why *we're* here, but I feel sorry for everyone else."

Norm nodded at the pad Dionne had been scribbling on. "Whatcha doing?"

"I'm trying to come up with a list of everyone we know in LA, or elsewhere within reach, who might owe us a favour."

"How are we looking?"

Dionne shrugged and pushed the pad across the table. "A few but, got to be honest, I'm struggling to figure out a plan here. If yesterday proves anything, it's that we can't wait around any longer. We have to arrange the exchange to get Bernadette and Assumpta back fast, and then, well, after that, I guess whatever comes after that."

Tatiana reached across and took the pen out of Dionne's hand. "Well, there's a big one you forgot. Bunny. I take it he's in?"

"He's *so* in I feel guilty. He came here to find that Simone woman because she's in some unspecified, but deep, trouble, and he's spent most of his time trying to help us get Bernadette and Assumpta back."

"Y'know," said Tatiana, "I've never asked this, and I guess now is a terrible time to do so, but are we sure that Bernadette will know where to find Simone?"

"No," said Dionne. "But to be fair to us, we made that clear to him."

"Man, the guy is certainly determined. What about Smithy and Diller?"

"That I don't know. They didn't sign up for the shitshow that was the last month. I'm guessing they might want to get back to New York and their lives."

Norm pursed his lips. "Maybe, maybe not. I only met them briefly, but they struck me as the sort that might not be able to turn their backs on a tough fight."

"And we certainly have one of those coming," said Dionne with a sigh. She looked down at the pockmarked wooden table that had so many things carved into it that nothing was legible. Her voice came out barely above a whisper. "I don't know what we're going to do, T. I really don't."

"What we're going to do," began Tatiana, "is get to LA, and then, when that's done, we're going to do the next thing. C'mon, we should get back to the car before the child protégée does something even she can't fix."

They got up to leave and Dionne discarded her unfinished food in one of the nearby trash cans. "And look on the upside," she said, dusting off her palms, "unless Joy locates our missing Winnebago, we might not even need a plan."

"She'll sort out whatever it is," said Tatiana as Tatiana, before switching back to Norm's gruff rumble, "I can feel it in my loins."

"Ugh. Gross."

"Speaking of which," said Tatiana, "you should probably walk ahead of me. We've worked damn hard to be incognito. Don't want Z screaming the place down when a big hairy dude tries to climb into the passenger seat."

THE MORNING AFTER

Bunny sat with his back to the trunk of a massive tree and tried to gather his thoughts. It said something about how well their night under the stars had gone that he felt genuinely nostalgic for the accursed Winnebago, smell and all. Still, in what was becoming something of a theme, Bunny had to acknowledge, even if only to himself, that things could have been considerably worse. First and foremost, they'd escaped. Admittedly, this didn't feel much like freedom, but it was still a big step up from that bloody cage. They were lucky that it was summer and that the overnight temperature had been mild. Come to that, it had been dry too, which was also fortunate as he seriously doubted any of them had the know-how or enthusiasm to build a shelter. That being said, there was every chance Diller had read a book on it at some point and might remember some of it, if only he would stop looking at every tree and bush as if it were a knife-wielding serial killer.

After their pursuers had headed off on a wild-goose chase, the quartet had picked themselves up and slowly made their way further into the forest. They'd walked, or in Bunny's case limped, for another half-hour or so before exhaustion determined that this clearing was where they were staying for the night. Thankfully, their pursuers seemed to have given up too, as there were no further sightings. Bunny had no idea what they had been shooting at, and he didn't really care as long as it wasn't them. Having said that, the idea that they had mistakenly engaged in a gun battle with themselves warmed his old bones in the darkness. Carlos, bless him, had sat in silence as Bunny reset his broken finger, getting it right on the second attempt. With the help of a bit of duct tape from Bunny's Crocs and a twig, Diller had fashioned a makeshift splint for him.

The problem was that surviving in the wild was one thing, but doing so with essentially what you had on your back when you got off a Winnebago to go for a dump, was really something else. They weren't dressed for it in the slightest. Bunny was wearing shorts, a Hawaiian shirt that was now missing several buttons, and Crocs, for God's sake. What he'd give for a decent pair of trainers. They didn't have any means of starting a fire, which, to be fair, they wouldn't have done anyway, any more than they would have sent up a flare that would have made it easier for their pursuers to find them.

After the adrenalin had worn off and they finally stopped for the night, Bunny figured all of them had been contemplating the same two questions in the exhausted silence – how the hell had this happened? And how the hell were they going to get out of there?

Poor bewildered Carlos was the most wanted man in America, and the one thing they needed to do was keep a low profile. This situation, as embarrassing as it was, was now evidently life threatening. It brought new meaning to the phrase wrong place, wrong time. He kept imagining explaining it all to Dionne or Dorothy and then finding himself wanting to curl up into a ball.

The other fun side effect of the adrenalin wearing off was that Bunny's body was keen to offer him a comprehensive update on his various aches and pains, and the reports were not good. Their escape, subsequent blind stumbling through the darkness, and then the fall down the gully had done nothing for the state of his ankle. On top of that, he had picked up numerous other bumps and bruises, whether from cheap shots, explosions, or the aforementioned tumble. The temptation to give in to the feeling of utter bloody misery was strong, but he didn't have that luxury. It wasn't like they had some sort of hierarchical structure, but still, he needed to step up, or at least limp up, and lead. He might not be the smartest, but he was the oldest. More importantly, Smithy and Diller had only been in that Winnebago in the first place because of him. It was his job to get everybody out of this in one piece.

So it was that, after whatever meagre sleep they had snatched, at the first light of dawn Bunny had got everyone up and moving again. At least he'd tried to. Smithy had disappeared, so Bunny was now sitting there waiting for him to come back. He entertained the idea that somehow, inexplicably, Smithy would return with a full fried breakfast and news that he had a brand-new Winnebago with a working toilet parked just down the hill. It would certainly be a remarkable upturn in their current run of rotten luck.

"Did he say where he was going?" asked Bunny.

"I didn't even see him leave," said Diller, who was sitting on the ground in the middle of the clearing while seemingly trying to look in every direction at once. Bunny had often heard people banging on about how to successfully conquer your fears by immersing yourself in them. Initial results from Diller were putting a rather big dent in that theory. He looked as nervous as a cat at a rocking-chair convention. It said something for the irrational fear responses of the human mind that he'd looked considerably calmer when he was the only Black guy in a building filled with racists.

Smithy finally returned a few minutes later with a five-foot-long branch that he had stripped. "Sorry," he apologised, "that took longer than anticipated." He presented the branch to Bunny. "Thought you might need a crutch."

It must have been the tiredness, but the simple act of kindness caught Bunny off-guard. Embarrassingly, he found himself welling up, but thankfully for all concerned, he was able to hide it behind a coughing fit before getting to his feet. He took a few tentative steps across the clearing, the crutch wedged under his left armpit. "That's tremendous. Thanks a million, Smithy."

"*De nada*," returned Smithy, sitting down on top of a rock.

"No," said Bunny, "'twas a cracking idea. Seriously, I appreciate it."

"Speaking of ideas, have we got any?"

"To be honest, I'm still confused as to who the hell this shower of goat-bothering bin-sniffers are. I mean, clearly they're a bollock-load of bigots but how have they got all those fancy weapons?"

"And why," added Diller, "are they so obsessed with stopping us leaving?"

Bunny clicked his fingers. "He mentioned something, that arsehat President Ronnie, about this being a big week for them, didn't he?"

"And somehow," concluded Smithy, "these idiots have got it into their heads that we're here to disrupt their operation."

"They might also be looking for their thing back," said Diller.

"What thing?" asked Bunny.

Smithy pulled the golden gun out from the back of his jeans. "I'm assuming Dill means this."

"And what kind of a gobshite wants a golden fecking gun?"

"Dunno," said Smithy. "Big Bond fans, maybe? Either way, seeing as it's also our only weapon, it's not like we can turn around exactly and give it back to them."

"How many bullets has it got?"

"Well, gun fans, it says on the side here that it is a Wilson Combat Tactical Supergrade EDC X9, and as far as I can see, it has an eight-round capacity, so if we're going to shoot our way out, some of those douchebags are going to have to stand in a very convenient line."

"Is it like *gold* gold?" asked Bunny.

Smithy spun it around and examined it in the morning light. "I dunno. I mean, it doesn't cost that much to gold-plate something, does it? And it's a modern handgun, so it's not like it's some kind of antique."

"Besides," said Diller, "these a-holes owe us a Winnebago."

Bunny raised an eyebrow at him. Diller was not quite himself.

"What? They do."

Bunny considered enquiring if Diller had managed to make peace with nature to a point that had allowed him to relieve himself, but he decided against it. Some things it was best to leave a man to work his way through alone.

"Technically," said Smithy, "they owe the Sisters of the Saint a Winnebago. Speaking of which, it's today we're supposed to call in, right?"

"That's right," confirmed Bunny.

"So, when we don't, at least they'll know something is wrong."

"I was really hoping we could get out of this without it coming to that. I don't know about you, but having to be rescued because I got into trouble trying to take a dump is going to do some shocking damage to my fragile ego."

"At this point, I think if the worst thing we get out of this situation is a bruised ego, I'll take it."

"Fair point," conceded Bunny. "Let's see if we can't save ourselves first anyway. As I see it, we can keep heading downhill and hope we eventually hit a road."

"That could take days," said Smithy. "You can barely walk. We've got no food. All that and …" He glanced at Diller. "Well, what are our other options?"

"The only other possibility is that we head back up towards the road but away from the Huntsman's Lodge and try to find some way of getting out of here."

"We have to assume they're looking for us."

"Agreed," said Bunny. "But if we head out into the wild blue yonder, they could do that too." An image popped into his head of dogs being used to hunt them, but he decided not to mention it. "How far away was that town?"

"Paradise?" said Smithy. "No idea. Maybe a couple of miles, if we're lucky."

Bunny nodded. "Does anyone know how to steal a car?"

Smithy looked sheepish. "I may know how to do that," he confessed, before adding, "although it's been a while."

"Stealing is wrong," said Carlos, looking up from poking the ground with a stick he had found.

The other three shared a look between them.

"It is," confirmed Bunny, "but not if we do it off these fellas who blew up the Winnebago on us."

Carlos looked up and squinted. "They took my yo-yo."

"I know. And we're going to make them pay for that. You mark my words."

"Alright, then," said Smithy, standing up and stretching. "Paradise here we come."

THANK YOU FOR YOUR SERVICE

Cynthia Gardner looked out the tinted window of the black SUV and watched the monotonous treeline zip by. That was neither her real first nor second name, but it had been so long since she'd used them, she doubted she'd even react if somebody were to shout them at her in the street. Hers was not a life of class reunions and get-togethers with old friends.

Occasionally, she caught sight of her own reflection and found it to be an oddly disconcerting experience. She'd allowed her hair to grow longer and dyed it chestnut brown instead of its normal black. She'd also had extensive plastic surgery, but not for reasons that had anything to do with vanity. Facial-recognition software was becoming more sophisticated by the day, and it worked on data points. The only way to evade it successfully was to alter enough of those points. So, she had a new chin, a lowered brow, a nose that she had picked from a catalogue, and so on. Now, nobody would recognise her because even she didn't recognise herself. In the past week, she'd realised that she couldn't remember her birthday. She'd had so many different ones during the course of her career, and, as odd as it sounded, she couldn't be one hundred percent certain which one was right. June, she was sure. She gave one of those involuntary giggles at the thought.

People had been surprised when she had suddenly dropped out of college after a year and enlisted. Her classmates were bemused; her family scandalised. Her reasoning then, as now, was nobody else's business, and she had never explained herself to anyone. After coming through basic training with flying colours and taking a series of interesting tests, she had been identified as someone with "a unique set of skills". That was a carefully chosen phrase designed to flatter her ego. She had, of course, known that already, her instinct for such things being one of the many reasons she'd so suited a career in PSYOP, or psychological operations to give it its full title, one that nobody ever used. They were the dark shadow of the war machine, whose existence was only begrudgingly acknowledged and whose methods were never discussed.

Inevitably, PSYOP had led her into other areas. Once you're in the shadows, the org chart becomes considerably more fluid. She had done everything her country had asked of her, even if her country was unwilling to acknowledge that it had ever made any such requests. Her career had been filled with briefs that were so deliberately vague as to make everything that she subsequently did plausibly deniable to those above her in the already murky chain of command. Directives were phrased like wishes, goals parsed in terms such as, "It would be very helpful if ..." And they had loved the results until they hadn't.

She had been a highly valued resource and then, when she was no longer convenient, they had tossed her aside. Worse, they had attempted to explain her. Apologise for her. "The subject was, in hindsight, severely traumatised by the incident in Kandahar and should have been withdrawn from active duty then and there to receive extensive counselling." Patronising bullshit. Kandahar had freed her, released her from the caged thinking of what was, and wasn't, acceptable. War was war, and the concept of rules was an idiotic fallacy superimposed by those who had never been face-to-face with the beast. It came down to sheer will. The victor was the one who would be willing to do what the other would not. She had been willing to do what it took to get the job done, and she had been a rockstar until she wasn't. A little collateral damage, the threat of a congressional hearing, and suddenly the high command was running for cover like scared little piggies.

They didn't even have the decency to try to kill her. That she found irksome. They would have if she were a man. In its way, it would have been a sign of respect. But no, because of her gender, they needed doctors to explain away her actions, assure themselves that something had gone wrong somewhere, as opposed to her having fulfilled their requests to the very best of her considerable abilities. She was not broken. It was they who were broken. Even now she wondered if, while clinging to their tedious plausible deniability like a life preserver in a stormy sea, they'd been so busy convincing others they were ignorant of all she had done, and how she had done it, that they had actually forgotten what she was capable of. It was like leaving a fire unattended on the presumption it would burn itself out. They wanted her to disappear, to place her quietly in a nice secure facility with padded walls and happy pills where they could forget she ever existed.

They got what they wanted, in a way. She did indeed disappear. One day she was there, the next she was gone, leaving in her wake two orderlies who would live to regret high command's decisions regarding how to deal with their little problem. One of them would never walk again, while the other, the one who had believed himself to be on a promise of a sexual liaison, would certainly never be doing anything like that again. He'd probably cry if the thought ever popped into his weak little mind.

So, she had walked out of the front gates of a facility with a previously blemish-free security record and became a ghost. Now she was entirely free of all restraints and going into business for herself. They would rue the day. First things first, she needed some seed capital, hence this little adventure. She had made sure to have things in place – that plan for a rainy day.

As the SUV pulled into the parking lot of the Huntsman's Lodge, the first thing Gardner noticed was the husk of what appeared to be a burnt-out Winnebago in one corner. The second thing she noticed was that many of the men milling about were carrying weapons. Her weapons.

"What the fuck?" said Draper in the passenger seat, summing up her sentiments precisely.

He and Newton, who was driving, had stayed with her because they had become personae non gratae at precisely the same moment as she had. Newton had been with her for the majority of the last six years, Draper for an eventful four. They had both remained admirably tight-lipped when questioned. She didn't kid herself that it was out of loyalty to her, more that it was a finely honed survival instinct. The reason they both knew where so many of the bodies were buried was because they had wielded the shovels, often interring their own handiwork. Gardner preferred to have about her people with a razor-sharp sense for self-preservation. Such individuals made logical decisions and you could rely on that. Loyalty was just sentimentality dressed up in fancy words, and such things led to emotional decision-making. She had considered herself loyal to her country and look how that had turned out. Loyalty was a flag waved by fools. She didn't trust Newton and Draper, but she trusted that she understood their motivations, and that was far more valuable.

They were early. The reason for this was simple: Gardner had not worked with these people before and if you wanted to know who you were getting into bed with, the easiest way to find out was to catch them with their pants down. Still, she had not expected this. It was 6:30am and the parking lot was full of motorcycles and pickups while the steady stream of men in hunting gear were passing in and out of the front door of the Huntsman's Lodge. She also noticed that the large window beside the door had been covered with a sheet of hastily applied plywood.

They exited the vehicle, and with Newton and Draper automatically falling into step behind her, Gardner strode towards the front door. A group of three men, decked out in full camo gear, was standing to the left of the entrance, smoking and chatting. The man nearest to the door sported a head of bushy brown hair and worked a thick cigar around his mouth as he watched them approaching, one hand resting on his pot belly and the other on a state-of-the-art weapon that the US government would be extremely interested to discover he had in his possession.

Gardner spoke in a calm, flat tone. "I wish to speak to Ronnie."

With tedious predictability, Pot Belly looked at his two colleagues, smiled and made a bad decision. "Do I look like his secretary, sweetheart?"

Gardner, doing what she had done for a living, was well used to being the only female in an otherwise all-male environment. Still, having to handle the same old chauvinism and lack of respect was, more than anything, boring. Over the years, she had dealt with it in more subtle ways, but this morning, she really wasn't in the mood.

Her right hand caught Pot Belly's half-finished cigar mid-air as he spat it out when the heel of her left hand chopped into his throat. Meanwhile, her right leg swept his feet from under him, and he landed on his back on the wooden porch decking with a satisfying thud. Before he had even hit the ground, Draper had his sidearm out and was covering his two friends, while Newton covered the rest of the parking lot.

Gardner crouched down beside the man who wasn't anybody's secretary. He clutched at his throat with both hands and gasped for air. As she bent down, a giddy little giggle escaped her lips. She had developed the tic after the incident in Kandahar, but she didn't even notice it any more. Other people did, though.

The quality of her voice didn't change from the same calm, flat tone with which she had begun the conversation.

"In case you're wondering, I hit you in the trachea, more commonly known as your windpipe. Right now, you can't breathe. You're panicking, thinking you might not breathe again. The good news is you will. Probably. I would say in about a minute or so. Rest assured, if I wanted you dead, you already would be. So, while you have this time, I would like you to use it to reflect on what just happened and what action points you can take from this interaction." She studied the thick, half-finished cigar that she held in her hand then casually moved it until the lit end was a couple of inches from the man's eyes, which widened in appreciation of the potential that the situation could get a whole lot worse for him. "I want you to remember that I asked you a polite question and that, really, everything that happened after that moment was your choice."

Her attention was diverted as two men stepped out the front door.

"What the hell?" said the first one.

"Logan?" said the second, looking at Draper.

"Jake," said Draper in acknowledgement, not lowering his weapon.

"I take it this is your cousin?" Gardner asked Draper, who confirmed it with a nod.

"And I'm Ronnie, president of the Paradise Sportsman's League," said the first man.

Gardner straightened up. She could see Ronnie regarding her and then mentally redrawing some maps in his mind. The only contact between them up until this point had been through Draper. She had needed bodies to carry out her plan and a location to hide what they acquired. Draper had assured her he knew someone who could provide both. Throughout their discussions, he had referred to "the Colonel" and Ronnie and Jake would have filled in the gender for themselves.

"You must be—"

"Yes," she said, "I am."

"We weren't expecting you until tonight."

Gardner looked around pointedly and nodded. "I can see that."

At least he had the sense to sound sheepish. "We should probably have a discussion in private."

"Yes. I think that would be best."

———

Fifteen minutes later, Gardner was sitting on one side of a gloomy booth inside the Huntsman's Lodge. The air smelled as if it had been trapped in there since the Nixon administration. Newton stood leaning against the bar. The room was otherwise empty except for the two men sitting opposite her, Ronnie and Jake, who were just finishing giving their version of the events which had taken place the day before. It was riddled with inconsistencies and outright lies, as evidenced by the large pile of broken furniture in the corner of the bar, directly in her eyeline, and which their story did not account for.

Ronnie had done most of the talking as he was, for want of a better phrase, the closest thing in evidence that could be referred to, even jokingly, as "the brains of the outfit". Still, he clearly hadn't had enough time to get his story straight, and his tells – as he worked on the fly to fill in the gaps and rework the most embarrassing elements – were painfully evident. As was the unease between him and his associate every time Jake spoke. With each word Ronnie tensed further, anticipating having to fix yet more damage. Jake was Draper's cousin, but he clearly came from the shallow end of that gene pool. Draper had looked embarrassed before Gardner had sent him off to the warehouse across the parking lot from the Huntsman's Lodge to do a much-needed stock take. Normally, she would have sent Newton, but she had observed the tension in him rise as he'd walked into the bar and noticed what was on the walls. Draper had conveniently left that part out when he'd explained the nature of his cousin's little group. Newton, a Black man from one of the more godforsaken corners of Alabama, would be no doubt keen to discuss that in considerable detail with his compatriot. It could wait. Right now, they had bigger fish to fry.

Gardner examined the fingernails on her right hand as she spoke. "Can you describe this group of men to me again, please?"

"There was a big Mexican guy," began Ronnie, "a Scottish guy, a dwarf and a ..." There was a slight pause and a subconscious flicker of his eyes in Newton's direction before he finished with, "African American gentleman." Classic overcompensation indicated the phrase that had been replaced.

"I see. Was one of them riding a unicycle at any point?"

Gardner was not known for her sense of humour, but there was an undeniable element of grim farce to all of this.

"You think this is funny?" snarled Jake.

"No," she confirmed, without making eye contact with him. "Believe me when I say, I do not."

"We think they were agents of the deep state," Jake continued, to a barely suppressed eye roll from his compatriot.

"The problem with that assessment," she began, "is that, frankly, if such a thing existed, then until recently it would have been me. If I had been sent here to interfere in this arrangement, it would not have been in a Winnebago, and you would not have been left with bumps and bruises."

"I don't appreciate your tone."

"Jake," said Ronnie, a note of reprimand in his voice.

"Fuck you, Ronnie. She comes in here, acting all high and mighty." Jake straightened himself up. "I think you've forgotten who did what here. It was me and the boys who robbed the two eighteen-wheelers. Us who swapped the cargo into the new trucks. Us who transported it across two state lines. I ain't even seen you until this morning, lady."

Gardner chose this moment to look at him. "I am very well aware of your contribution to this endeavour, Mr Draper. At any point did it occur to you that the US military rarely transports shipments of state-of-the-art weaponry in unguarded trucks? You managed to successfully hold up two unarmed truck drivers. From there, you went to the location as instructed and did the simple tasks assigned to you, before driving a couple of hundred miles, a feat everyone from frat boys to octogenarians will manage today and every day without incident. You essentially proved capable of taking candy from a baby, and now you'd like to be patted on the head and told you're a clever boy."

Jake was about to respond, but Gardner sensed Newton behind her, moving a few steps, placing himself firmly in Jake's eyeline. Putting enough doubt into this idiot's tiny mind to still his tongue.

She continued. "The clever part, if you will, of this endeavour was making it so that a high-value shipment disappeared into the ether and got rerouted as a shipment of MRE rations, which nobody who has ever eaten them is going to spend any time trying to get back. That was the part I did. Along with finding us a buyer. Someone willing to put up the money upfront, to grease the wheels to make this happen. The kind of buyer you do not want to disappoint, believe me. Rest assured, Jake, I am the most dangerous person you have ever met in your sad, insignificant life, and these people – our backers – terrify me. They are going to be here tomorrow night. I have neither the time nor the crayons to explain to you how bad it will go for us if they go away disappointed."

"Okay," said Ronnie, trying to sound placatory, "I get it. *We* get it. Some mistakes have been made, but we're going to fix that. I've got men stationed on the road five miles either side of here, stopping any vehicles leaving, so they aren't getting out that way. There's nothing but forests for miles, save for the town of Paradise and" – a flicker of pride passed across his face – "I've already taken down the phone lines and the cell tower, so these guys aren't calling anybody. It's just us and them, and we're heading out right now to hunt them down. One of them has got a bum ankle – there isn't any way they'll have gone far."

"I hope you're right."

Behind her, she heard the door to the bar open and Draper's distinctive footfall as he marched across the room. "We have a problem."

"Tell me something I don't know," muttered Gardner.

"It's gone."

She looked up at him as he reached the booth, her eyes widening. "You are kidding?"

The expression on his face made it clear he wasn't. She didn't ask if he was sure. She did not surround herself with people who were not thorough.

"What's gone?" asked Ronnie.

Gardner turned back to him. "There was a gun. To be exact, a custom Wilson Combat Tactical Supergrade EDC X9 that was gold plated. It's a gift for the individual this shipment was originally intended for before we rerouted it. Where is it?"

"I don't know what you're talking about," said Ronnie.

"No," said Gardner, looking him directly in the eye, "you don't." She'd had special training in reading people, which only added to her innate, finely honed instincts. None of that was needed here. The body language of these two fools screamed so loudly it could be read from space. She turned her attention to Jake. "But he does."

"I got no clue what you mean," insisted Jake.

Before anyone else could move, Draper drew his Glock and trained it squarely on his cousin.

"What the fuck, Loggie. You pulling a gun on me?"

"I am, and the next words out of your mouth better be the truth or, so help me God, I'm going to put a bullet straight into your brainpan."

"Fuck—"

A bullet hit the wall three inches from Jake's head.

"That's your only warning. Don't test me, Jake."

Behind him, Newton also pulled his sidearm and watched the doors.

Ronnie glowered at him. "Have you got this gun?"

"No," insisted Jake, staring at the muzzle of the gun trained on him. "They have it."

"What?" hissed Ronnie.

"They took it when they ... when they escaped." He turned to Gardner. "Look, you can take it out of our end."

She paused. The urge to kill everyone within a hundred yards who wasn't Draper, Newton or herself was vying with the very real need to ensure her own survival. Their buyers were not the kind of people who took disappointment well. Even worse, in order to emphasise the necessity of getting the gun back, she was going to have to reveal sensitive information to these mouth-breathing clowns.

"The problem with that," began Gardner, "is that the gun in

question is not a gun. Not *just* a gun. It has a concealed data port in the grip that contains some highly sensitive information. *That* is what our buyers are paying for. Taking it out of your end would not be covered by the deaths of you and everyone you've ever met," she concluded before adding to herself, *delightful though that would no doubt be.*

Gardner slid out of the booth and addressed Draper and Newton. "Suit up. This is something else now." They both nodded as she turned back to the other two. "I want every man you have, in this room, in ten minutes. Is that understood?"

"Now, hang on," protested Ronnie.

"No," said Gardner. "Through your gross incompetence this is now a whole other situation. We have no time for niceties. Is that understood?"

He nodded.

"Excellent. And, to clarify, when I said we needed every man" – she pointed at Jake – "not that one. If he's still here in ten minutes, you're digging a hole."

"Who the—"

Before Jake could say another word, he was interrupted by the man he considered his best friend punching him hard in the face.

RALLY THE TROOPS

Ronnie looked around at the assembled members of the Sportsman's League, who were currently sitting around the Huntsman's Lodge's tables, talking amongst themselves. A few of them had breakfast beers on the go. He'd have preferred it if they hadn't done that, but it didn't seem like the right time to be a hard ass about it, seeing as he'd pulled them all in on short notice. He'd put the call out late last night and, by and large, they'd responded.

Including himself, twenty-eight active members had shown up to deal with the situation. A couple of them lived in Paradise, but the others had come from further afield. First thing, he'd sent out two men in each direction to check any, and all, vehicles attempting to leave the area. He then sent another four to watch Paradise in case the fugitives turned up there, and instructed two bikers to patrol the road, looking for anything suspicious. That left them with eighteen men to go on the hunt. Derek Friend had recovered from his run-in with the Colonel earlier, and while he wasn't feeling too happy, he'd reluctantly agreed to stay.

The woman herself was now standing by the bar, flanked by Draper and Newton, watching in silence. Out of necessity, he'd given her a version of events from yesterday that omitted quite a few details. He was fully aware that all the stuff with Billy the bull would not have gone over well. Similarly, while telling her about the escape had been unavoidable, he'd neglected to mention the subsequent "shootout" when Jonny Lebronsky swore that he'd seen them. At first light Ronnie had gone out into the forest to check and he was pretty sure the drunken idiot had opened up on an old, abandoned hunting blind.

Ronnie had also told Jake to get the hell out of there. The guy might be his oldest friend, but there was no denying that this was all his fault. If he hadn't gone and got one of the guns and escalated the situation, then things wouldn't have gotten out of hand in the first place. If he hadn't then got drunk and been jumped by four men locked in a cage, they would not now have a problem. And, most importantly of all, if he hadn't taken that stupid golden gun … Ronnie blamed himself for leaving him in charge of the warehouse, but then, he'd handled the robbery and the transportation end of things. This should have been relatively straightforward. Now, all that was left to do was clean up this mess and complete this deal with no further complications. They were so close, if they could just get their shit together for a couple of days.

"Alright," said Ronnie, clapping his hands to get everyone's attention. "Settle down, fellas. Settle down."

After a few of seconds, the hubbub of conversation subsided.

"Okay. Thank you for coming. As I'm sure you're all now aware, we got ourselves a little problem. Some bunch of assholes think they can come in here and steal from the Paradise Sportsman's League. We're going to show them just how wrong they are about that."

A murmur of agreement passed around the room along with some "fuck yeahs" from a few of the younger members.

"That's right," said Ronnie, "it's time to go hunting."

Todd Munken stood up at the back. "And whoever bags them drinks free for a month!"

Munken's words received an enthusiastic response that was almost, but crucially not entirely, universal.

"No," said Gardner, stepping forward, "they won't. Seeing as the cell network is unavoidably down and we don't have enough walkie-talkies, each two-man team will be issued with a flare. At the first sign of the quarry, you will shoot your flare into the sky, remain in place, then Newton and Draper here will come and deal with the situation."

"Who the hell—" started Todd, but Ronnie stepped forward quickly and waved him down.

"I was coming to that. Fellas, this here is Colonel Gardner, and she is our partner in the endeavour you all know about."

Gardner turned to glare at him. "They all know about it?"

He hesitated. "Not the ... finer details."

She shook her head in disbelief.

Ronnie continued quickly and pointed at Draper. "This is Jake's cousin and" – he glanced at Newton – "these folks are all patriots, here to help us out."

"No," said Gardner, "we're not. Here to help you out, I mean. I am now in command of this situation, and you will do exactly as I say."

A considerable amount of grumbling went up in response to this.

"Well, now ..." started Ronnie, looking back at her. "Hang on a second."

"No, I will not." Gardner took a step forward. "The situation is very simple. Owing to inexcusable errors on your part, this deal has now been put in jeopardy. Capturing these men has now become priority number one. In fifteen minutes, my two associates will create rockslides five miles either side of here to shut the road and close off this area entirely."

"How're we supposed to get home?" shouted someone from the back.

"You're not," answered Gardner. "Not until tomorrow evening, when all of this has been resolved."

Ronnie winced as a further round of grumbling passed through the room.

"I didn't come here to get ordered around by some woman," shouted Todd. "I got an ex-wife for that."

"We are on a war footing," said Gardner. "If anyone doesn't like it, the door is there." She pointed firmly at the front door.

After a few seconds, Ronnie grimaced as Texas Pete stood up and gave an apologetic wave. "I'm out. This is all getting a little heavy for me."

"Pete," said Ronnie, a tone of warning to his voice.

"Nah, man. I'll see you around."

He turned to go.

What happened next happened so fast that Ronnie found himself too stunned to react for a couple of seconds. In one fluid motion, Gardner drew her sidearm and fired two shots into Pete's back, sending him tumbling to the floor.

The first to react were Draper and Newton who, as quick as a flash, moved to flank their boss with their guns out, covering the room.

Several people spoke at once, their voices raised in a mix of shock and anger, and all of whom were silenced when Gardner calmly fired two more shots into the ceiling.

"I repeat, we are at war," she said loudly, "and the penalty for desertion has not changed for centuries. Does anyone else require a clarification of their responsibilities going forward?"

The room fell silent. Ronnie glanced over at the unmoving form of Pete. He'd put good money on the man being dead.

"Excellent," said Gardner, returning her gun to its holster. "I'm glad we could clear that up."

Ronnie turned as the door to the storeroom swung open and Gail came through, carrying a tray of glasses. "Who the fuck is shooting in —" She stopped as her eyes fell upon Pete, lying face down on the floor in a pool of his own blood.

"Pete? PETE!"

The glasses came crashing down to the floor.

Ronnie intercepted Gail as she attempted to run towards the body. She pushed at him before collapsing in his arms in tears.

"Split into two-man teams," barked Gardner, seemingly oblivious to the woman who was now in hysterics not four feet from her. "Corporals Draper and Newton will issue you with your flares and your assignments." She smiled at the room. "Happy hunting."

THE ROAD LESS TRAVELLED

Not for the first time, Bunny, Smithy, Diller and Carlos hunched down and held their breath as they listened to the roar of a motorcycle engine passing by. The holding-of-breath part was, of course, entirely unnecessary, not to mention ridiculous. Bunny only realised he was doing it the third time they'd all huddled down to avoid being seen by traffic on the road, but at this point it felt as if it'd be bad luck to stop doing it, seeing as they hadn't been spotted yet. Stupidity like that was how traditions got started.

As the sound of the engine faded into the distance, Diller was the first to pop his head up. "Coast is clear."

With a groan, Bunny got to his feet and leaned on his crutch. All this subterfuge was playing havoc with his gammy ankle.

"That's the second time that guy has gone by," said Diller.

"Yeah," agreed Smithy, "driving slowly and taking in the scenery. These guys haven't lost interest in us, have they?"

"Well," said Bunny, "'tis nice to feel wanted."

For a road that was no longer anyone's first choice to get anywhere, there had been a fair amount of traffic along it, mostly bikes and mostly heading toward the Huntsman's Lodge. Maybe they were just having themselves a big old racist barbecue, but Bunny doubted it. Luck hadn't been on their side so far and nothing indicated that was about to change.

And with that, they started trudging on. Tired and hungry as they were, the morning had been slow-going. After a couple of hours, they'd found the road again and since then, they'd been following it from a distance, careful to remain out of sight.

A while back, Smithy and Bunny had a discreet conversation during which they'd agreed that unless they got really desperate, the carjacking route wasn't one they were going to take. In theory, waving down a passing car and then pulling a gun on the owner should be fairly straightforward, but the reality would never prove to be that simple. Leaving that aside, a lot of the sporadic traffic on the road appeared to be probable members of the Paradise Sportsman's League, which meant the odds of them pulling over to help were not favourable. Would anyone stop for a bunch of strange men coming out of the woods, waving their arms about? They could, of course, wave the gun about, but any passing motorists might prefer to put their foot down and take their chances in that scenario too, and Bunny couldn't blame them. They'd have made the right choice as well, because Bunny and company were definitely not going to shoot at a vehicle full of innocent people. And then, of course, there was the sheer ickiness of it all. Ma and Pa Johnson out for a drive with the two kids and the cocker spaniel – were they really going to force them out of their car at gunpoint and leave them by the side of the road? They might be desperate men but there were still lines you didn't cross.

So the plan, in so far as they had one, was to find a car to steal and get the hell out of there. Yes, it was still theft of a motor vehicle but, ideally, they wouldn't be doing it at gunpoint in front of two traumatised kids and a beloved family pet. They'd take a car, or indeed a vehicle of any kind, and once they'd got to safety, they'd make sure it was left in a safe place with a note of apology and details of where the owner could be found. If he had the time, Bunny would even stick in a nice "we're sorry" cake and a bone for the hypothetical spaniel.

If they couldn't find transportation, there was also the option to call the number they had for the Sisters of the Saint. That idea was currently about as popular as the carjacking one. First, in practical terms, it would take time for the Sisters to send help, so it'd still leave Bunny and the boys playing hide-and-seek with lads who weren't smart enough to cut holes in sheets. Second, more than anything, Bunny did not want to have to explain their predicament. Broken, hungry and hobbled as he was, he still had a little bit of pride left. One option that was not under consideration was phoning the authorities. Two of their number were still wanted men, after all. Maybe when they got out of here, dropping an anonymous dime was on the cards but that did nothing for them in their current situation.

After another fifteen minutes they reached the latest in a series of bends in the road. When they followed this one round, miracle of miracles, they were not greeted with the sight of more forestry. There were still plenty of trees, but tucked in amongst them on the far side of the road was a definite sign of civilisation. At first, all they could make out was some wire fencing and an entrance, but as they moved along more came into view. Nestled against the sheer rock wall of the mountain that curved around the back of the compound stood what a battered sign indicated was McPherson's Yard. The broken carcasses of wrecked cars stood piled three and four high, stretching all the way back towards the rock wall. Above it all towered a mobile crane.

Smithy let out a whistle. "Would you look at this. Haven't seen somewhere like this in a while. Check out those cars. Peeling them away layer by layer would be like taking a trip through American history."

"Apologies for interrupting your reverie," said Bunny, "but it also looks like the kind of place that might have a few working cars knocking about."

Smithy nodded. "I reckon you might be right. What say Dill and I go take a looksee, and you and Carlos hang back here?"

"Shouldn't we stick together?" asked Diller.

"Nah," said Bunny. "What Smithy is being too polite to say is that I'd slow you down. Best you two nip in and out. Me and the big fella will wait here."

Smithy pulled the gun from his belt and held it out to Bunny.

"Are you sure?" asked Bunny.

He nodded. "I feel shitty enough about doing this. I'm not doing it at gunpoint. If we can't sneak it, we'll be back."

Bunny took the gun, and he and Carlos watched in silence as the other two sneaked to the edge of the road, glanced around, then hurried across.

"What are we going to do now?" asked Carlos.

"I'll tell you what we're going to do," said Bunny, lowering himself carefully to the ground. "I spy with my little eye …"

WITH FRIENDS LIKE THESE

Newton stood behind the black SUV as Draper, map spread out on the hood, gave instructions to the last of the two-man hunting parties to set out.

"So, I need you two to head south-south-west," said Draper.

"Yeah, I know, I know," replied the blond man, who must have weighed a good three hundred and fifty pounds, as he pointed east. "Thataway."

"No, goddamn it," growled Draper, doing nothing to hide his exasperation, before pointing in the right direction. "That way."

"We know," said the fat guy's friend quickly. "Danny is only jerking your chain."

"Well, his career in stand-up comedy is off to a rocky start. Head that way and use the top of that peak there to navigate by if you get turned around. And if you catch sight of the fugitives ..."

"Send up the signal," said the skinny one, patting the signal flare that they had all been issued with.

"And wait for us."

"Y'know," said the big guy, "me and Walter have seen some action in our time too."

"Is that right? How many foreign countries have you HALO-jumped into? Newton back there and I took out an entire Taliban encampment, just the two of us – you boys ever done that? And he killed a Ugandan general with a sniper shot from two thousand metres. You want to tell me what your high score on *Call of Duty* is, fat boy, or do you want to shut the fuck up and do what you're told?"

The little guy put out his hand. "Alright there, soldier. Danny meant nothing by it. Let's all take it easy."

Slightly mollified, Draper started to fold his map away. The little guy, clearly not finished, moved slightly closer and lowered his voice. "Hey, man. Can I ask – the Colonel ... Is she, like, full-on crazy? I mean she shot Texas Pete like it was nothing."

"To be clear," said Draper, pausing the map-folding so he could give the man his full attention, "are you inviting me to engage in the active undermining of a superior officer?"

"Erm ..."

Draper grabbed him by the collar of his jacket. "Would you like me to tattoo Article 92 of the Uniform Code of Military Justice on your ass, or would like to get the hell out of here and do your damn job?"

Holding the guy an inch from his face, Draper waited for an answer.

"The ... the second one."

"That's what I thought." Draper pushed him away. "Now, I want to see you two running to get out there and start hunting the enemy."

The duo started walking quickly towards the treeline.

"I said run," shouted Draper, prompting them to do exactly that. Then he turned to Newton and laughed. "Fuck, Newt, these dudes are something else. Look at the fatty waddling."

Newton folded his arms. "Not exactly wrong on that final point, though, were they?"

Draper finished folding his map away and gave Newton a look. "C'mon. You know Gardner has always been a little ..."

"Whatever she used to be, she's now stone-cold insane," finished Newton. "Let's not pretend we didn't know that going into this, but we wanted the final big pay day. Still, she didn't need to gun that poor fucker down. And by the way, we aren't covered by any articles of the Uniform Code of Military Justice any more, seeing as we deserted to avoid prison."

Draper widened his eyes. "What's got into you?"

"What's got into me?" Newton turned to him. "Seriously? I mean, beyond the fact that Gardner has gone completely off the deep end?" Newton jabbed a finger towards the Huntsman's Lodge. "Do you think that maybe there were a few details about your cousin's little bike club you forgot to mention?"

"That?" asked Draper. "You're worried about that? None of these idiots are going to fuck with you."

Newton threw up his hands. "No shit, Logan. I could take out this whole jamboree in about fifteen minutes with just a spoon. These guys don't want to mess with me. But I got nieces and nephews, goddamn it, and I don't want to be working with White-supremacist, Nazi assholes to further their aims in the country that I gave seventeen years of my life to defending."

"They're harmless," said Draper, with a dismissive wave of his hand.

"No, they're not. Thanks to us, they're now heavily armed and about to get a serious cash injection."

"They're—"

Newton reached into his back pocket, took something out and tossed it at Draper. "They're what?"

Draper held it out. It was a noose.

"I found this hanging on that cage in the storeroom. Of the Scottish guy, the dwarf, the Mexican guy and the guy who looks a lot like me, who do you think that was meant for?"

"I didn't—"

"Yeah," said Newton. "You sure didn't. Forget what we talked about. Once this is done and I get my money, I don't want to see you or Gardner ever again." He pulled a pack out of the back of the jeep and tossed it at Draper. "Your C4 is in there. I'm going to go blow the road to the west, you do the east."

He hopped into the driver's seat.

"How am I supposed to—"

Newton started the engine. "Get one of your new buddies to give you a lift."

Draper stepped back as, with a squeal of tyres, Newton hauled ass out of there.

NINE LEGS OF JUSTICE

This was the second time Smithy had been in a junkyard in recent years, and just once, he thought, it'd be nice if he could simply wander around, drinking it all in, and not be there in a high-pressure life-or-death situation. He didn't know a great deal about cars, but he liked the idea of a junkyard. There was a certain romance to them. Old wrecks from bygone eras, little slices of Americana. Cars with tailfins. Big chrome bumpers. Gas-guzzling behemoths that were far bigger than they needed to be. Like the song said – Automatic. Systematic. Hydromatic. Whatever the hell hydromatic was supposed to mean. No cars in the world looked like those old American cars, and no country in the world loved their cars like America did. All of which meant time strolling among the wrecks would be a morning well spent. Unfortunately, he and Diller were here to sneak in and steal a car to get themselves out of the insane situation in which they currently found themselves. Cheryl always said that Smithy was not destined for the quiet life, but he was starting to think maybe a little bit more of that wouldn't be such a terrible thing.

They passed through the open gates into an area of shade provided by a thick metal sheet which hung between the two columns flanking the entrance. Smithy paused for a moment to look more closely at it and the chains hanging on either side of it. In a certain light, the term portcullis wouldn't be entirely inappropriate. If that came down, you weren't getting through it. Beyond it, just inside the fence, a line of crushed cubes that had once been cars formed a three-foot high wall.

He stared down the main track. Initially, the old cars looked as if they were piled up willy-nilly, but as he moved a little further into the yard, Smithy could see that there seemed to be more of a system to it. The piles of cars formed several rows radiating out from the sole entrance they'd come through – five or six, from what Smithy could see. That meant there was the main track down the centre of the yard and then other, smaller tracks, branching off it. The main track led into an open circular area that formed the heart of the yard. At the far right of it sat a large wooden cabin with the crane beside it, and four vehicles to the left. A Mustang had its hood open with an array of tools lying next to it. Filling out the line was a battered station wagon to the left, along with a Volkswagen Beetle and one of those old-school vans that Scooby-Doo and the gang used to head off solving crimes in. Smithy wasn't fussy – anything that would get them the hell out of here was fine by him.

He nodded to their left, towards the narrow path that ran between the rows of wrecks and the outer fence of the compound. "C'mon, Dill, this way." Better to take the less-obvious route that offered the most cover. Crouching down, they moved as quickly and quietly as they could along the side of the yard. The eight-foot-tall fence bore a sign on it warning that it was electrified, which Smithy highly doubted. Nobody needed that kind of security in a place like this, did they? Mind you, there were also the sturdy concrete columns where, normally, fence posts would be, and the smaller wall of crushed cars continued in this direction too. As they moved along, Smithy found himself noticing the smell of the place. It was the aroma of the surrounding woods, mixed with rust and oil and the scent of soft decay. It wasn't unpleasant.

They were soon able to see more of the yard. Over to the right of the cabin was another building, seemingly propped against the cliff.

It looked as if it had once been some kind of sawmill, but had long since fallen into disuse. There was also what Smithy reckoned was a crushing machine to the right of that, and behind the cabin, yet more piled wrecks formed another wall. Towering over it all as it curved around the entire back half of the yard was the massive sheer face of the cliff, immense and imposing, as if proclaiming to anyone whose gaze fell upon it that it had been there long before you and would be there long after you were dust.

"Wait," hissed Diller.

Smithy froze and looked back at his friend, who was pointing to the stack of cars beside them. "I saw something. Like, a small, red light flashing."

They both stared at the pile of rusting old cars. Smithy couldn't see anything.

"Where?"

"I don't know," said Diller. "I just saw ... something."

Smithy considered it. Diller was an observant guy, and if he said he'd seen something, he undoubtedly had. Still, as far as he knew, junkyards didn't have alarm systems. Traditionally, they had big slobbering dogs who could rip a man limb from limb. That thought did not provide him with much comfort. Smithy liked dogs, and the last thing he wanted to do was have to fight one off.

Eventually he said, "Don't worry about it," because what else could he say? And they continued on.

Smithy kept his eyes peeled, but he couldn't see any signs of life. It was around 10am, so it was safe to assume the proprietor was awake. Maybe they'd got lucky and happened upon the place after they'd headed out. He glanced over his shoulder at the way they'd come. There was also the chance that they'd be trying to get out in a stolen car to find their way blocked by the aforementioned proprietor returning, possibly bringing back his pack of rabid Dobermanns from a trip to the vets that had put them in a real bad mood. Given how their luck was running, that felt like a real possibility.

The duo continued around the side of the yard, the sheer wall of rock looming ever more imposingly the closer they got to it. Smithy tried to blank it out. Something about it he found oddly oppressive.

Finally, they drew level with the cars in the clearing. He leaned in close to Diller's ear. "I reckon we try the Beetle first. Both get in, and if it works, we floor it."

Diller nodded.

Smithy stared across at the cabin door on the far side of the clearing. Still no sign of movement. From this new vantage point, he could see that another path led off through the wall of wrecks behind it but he couldn't hear any movement back there either. He nodded at Diller and they both scurried across the twenty or so feet of open ground towards the Beetle.

Smithy's fingers were on the door handle of the car when he heard the growl. Some deep-seated caveman instinct made the hairs on the back of his neck stand up. Without being asked, he raised his hands and slowly turned around.

The second most noticeable thing behind them were the three dogs – not a Dobermann in sight. In fact, between them, they had a combined total of nine legs.

The growl had come from what looked like the result of an unhappy union between a chihuahua and a pit bull. It was only about a foot high and had more teeth than should really be possible to fit into a head that size, all of which it was baring in a display of barely restrained homicidal rage.

Beside it stood a dog that looked like every canine in America had contributed to its gene pool. Its fur was a shaggy mane of brown and its eyes were unreadable, mainly because they were barely visible under a long and particularly curly fringe. Its tongue lolled out the side of its mouth. It was missing its front right leg.

The third dog was missing both back legs but made up for it with a rather nifty set of wheels in their place. He looked vaguely like a sheepdog, but wouldn't be receiving an invitation to any family reunions any time soon. His disposition was particularly cheery, which wasn't something you could say about everyone present.

The woman standing directly behind him, for example, who was glaring at them down the most noticeable thing – the barrel of a rifle. Dressed in a green vest and combat trousers, with her blonde hair cut puckishly short, her arms featured multiple tattoos and a silver stud pierced her right eyebrow. When she spoke, it was in a soft accent that Smithy couldn't place.

"I'm afraid I have two pieces of bad news for you, gentlemen. The first is that Beetle doesn't have anything in it – engine-wise, I mean. The second bit of bad news" – she clicked back the hammer on the rifle – "is that this definitely does."

"Okay," said Smithy. "I acknowledge this looks bad."

"Well, it's very nice of you to say that." The small dog yapped a couple of times and the woman spoke to it without looking down. "Easy, Princess. The nice man has already acknowledged that this looks bad. I'm sure he's about to explain how it isn't what it looks like." She turned the rifle towards Diller a fraction. "While he's doing that, I'd really appreciate it if your hands were considerably higher in the air, sir."

Diller duly obliged.

"Thank you. Now, where were we?" she asked. "Oh yeah, I remember." She turned the gun back towards Smithy. "We were acknowledging it looks bad."

"Okay," conceded Smithy. "It *is* bad. We were attempting to steal this car."

"And stealing is wrong."

"It is," agreed Smithy. "For what it's worth, we were only doing it because we're desperate."

"I see. You two able-bodied men can't find yourselves honest work in this tricky economy. What a state this once-great land of ours is in."

"No, I ..." Smithy studied the woman, trying to decide where to go next. He reckoned she was probably in her late twenties. Her hands were covered in grease from whatever she'd been working on, and from where he was standing, he couldn't read any of her tattoos. In his experience, tattoos told you a lot about a person. In the absence of any better idea, he decided to go with the truth.

"Okay. The Huntsman's Lodge is just a few miles up the road

there. It's the clubhouse for a group that calls itself the Paradise Sportsman's League."

"I'm aware." There was noticeable tension in the woman's voice.

"Right. Well, long story short, we tried to drop in there yesterday to use the bathroom, it didn't go well, they're now hunting us."

"Let me guess," she said. "Did you forget to raise the toilet seat?"

"Honestly," said Smithy, "I could tell you the full story, but it wouldn't sound a whole lot less ridiculous than that. They're a bunch of knuckle-dragging, racist a-holes and we're trying to get the hell away from them any way we can."

"Does this explain the explosion I heard yesterday?"

"Yes," said Diller. "That was our Winnebago."

"Sorry for your loss. And the shooting last night?"

"Yes again," confirmed Smithy. "That was the knuckle-draggers shooting at something they thought was us that thankfully wasn't."

She nodded. "Lucky you. And out of curiosity, what makes you think I'm not another knuckle-dragging, racist a-hole?"

Smithy shrugged. "You've got three dogs."

"Excuse me?"

"Dogs are excellent judges of character."

"Really? You think jerks don't have dogs?"

"Yeah," conceded Smithy, "I guess they do. Never said it was a perfect theory. These three dogs seem nice, though."

On cue, the dog that had previously been referred to as Princess yapped a couple of defiant barks, outraged at this assessment of her character.

"And ..." The woman started to say something but trailed off. "Okay, I can believe part of it – in so much as I don't think your friend's complexion would go down well with that establishment's clientele."

Diller nodded. "You can certainly say that again."

"That's as may be. I'm not naïve enough to believe my enemy's enemy is automatically my friend. You could just be a different type of ass-wipe. It's a big, bad world, and there are many colours in the glorious rainbow of shitty people."

"Amen," agreed Smithy. "In the circumstances, I think a show of good faith would be appropriate. Put down the gun."

The woman barked a laugh. "Yeah, I'm sure as shit not doing that."

"Sorry," apologised Smithy, "I wasn't talking to you."

And with that, out limped Bunny from behind the row of wrecked cars on the far side of the clearing, with Carlos trailing nervously in his wake.

"What the—" started the woman, oscillating her gun between the two pairs of men.

"Relax," said Bunny, turning his gun so that it was pointing up in the air. "I mean you no harm." Slowly and deliberately, he dropped the weapon on the ground and took a step back.

The woman looked down at her dogs. "All three of you should be entirely ashamed of yourselves."

Princess did look suitably appalled with herself, but the other two just kept smiling away. The one on wheels trundled forward and licked Smithy's hand.

"Jesus, Lollipop!" the woman cried, exasperated. "This is an armed standoff. There is no licking."

"Well," said Smithy, "we're not armed any more, so you win."

The woman was thinking about that when a large explosion in the distance caused them all instinctively to duck down. It came from their left.

"What the hell was that?" she asked.

"No idea," said Smithy. "But I bet it wasn't a good thing."

"It came from the far side of town. It might be—"

Before she could finish her thought, another explosion went off in the other direction. This one sounded closer, but to the right.

"Seriously? What is going on?"

"Oh," said Smithy, looking over at Bunny, "I've got a bad feeling about this."

"I have a theory," shouted Bunny from the far side of the clearing.

"And what might that be?" asked the woman.

"Fair warning, you're not going to like it."

"I guess I'm just going to have to cope with the disappointment."

"Right," said Bunny. "If you were hunting four guys and you didn't want them to leave the area, what would you do?"

"Cut off communications?" offered Diller.

"The phones and internet have been down since last night," said the woman.

"Really?" asked Smithy.

She shrugged. "It's a common occurrence around here, thanks to the aforementioned sons of bitches."

"And then ..." said Bunny.

"Damn it," said the woman, lowering the gun. "You'd block the roads?"

"You'd block the roads," confirmed Bunny.

"Holy shit," said the woman. "They must really want you guys bad. You must've made one hell of a first impression." She sighed. "C'mon, my enemy's enemy, I'll put a pot of coffee on. I'm Beth, by the way."

She turned and walked towards the cabin, with the dogs following immediately behind her.

Smithy looked across at Bunny and Carlos and then all four of them followed her.

"I don't suppose you've got a helicopter?" asked Bunny.

"Funnily enough," replied Beth, "no."

"Right," said Diller. "What about a toilet?"

THE ART OF PUBLIC SPEAKING

If he was honest with himself, Rory Davenport would admit that his career in law enforcement was not turning out the way he'd hoped. When he'd done his sixteen-week police academy training in Salem, there had been classes in firearms, defensive driving, and scenario training on their specially constructed city-streets lot. He'd excelled, even winning himself a marksmanship trophy. He'd then come back to Paradise to "take over the family business", as everyone kept saying.

Rory's father had been the sheriff in Paradise for over twenty years, but he'd been having heart troubles and early retirement was in the offing. In hindsight, Rory didn't even really remember them discussing it. It was more presented to him. You could do your training, do some courses and then, after your probation, you could take over. You couldn't call it railroading. Nobody had ever demanded anything, he'd just sort of gone along with it. Maybe his dad had assumed that was what Rory wanted, and he'd never said otherwise.

His mom had died when Rory was in high school. Out of nowhere, a perfectly healthy woman had just keeled over while pruning her rosebushes. A sweet, wonderful woman had died that day, and inevitably, her passing had carried a lot away with it. Rory realised a while ago that he couldn't remember the last time he'd heard his father laugh. Not that there'd been much to laugh about around here recently. Almost twelve months into his eighteen-month probation period, Rory felt as if he spent most of his time dealing with angry people he couldn't make less angry. There'd been a lot of it and, frankly, what was really getting him down was that they were right to be angry.

What Rory was facing at this present moment in time was considerably more fury than he had previously had to assuage, both in intensity and in number. He was currently standing on the porch of Paradise's small sheriff's office with a crowd of over twenty residents gathered around him, all talking at once.

Kimberley Reese – whom he had taken to junior prom down in New Bridge only for her to spend most of the night dancing with that Chad Penning douchebag who played wide receiver on the football team, even though they never passed the ball – was standing there in her waitressing uniform. "Jesus Christ, Rory – those crazies have blocked the road both ways. How am I supposed to get to work?"

Janice Dockery, who had been a district nurse before she retired a couple of years ago, wore a face like thunder. "They've gone too far this time, Rory. Something has to be done. Blowing up roads is still illegal in this country."

Old Man Randall, who'd been old longer than Rory had been alive, was also standing in front of him, his bushy eyebrows bobbing up and down so that he went from big eyes to no eyes to back again all in the space of a sentence. "I can't do my Wordle because the internet is down again. Tell 'em to put it back on. I need my Wordle."

Chuck Clarke, who ran the town's only store, was hovering to one side, holding a box of Pringles under his arm for no apparent reason. "There either is law or there isn't law, and you and your dad are supposed to be that law."

Lots of other townspeople were gathered behind them, all shouting things along similar lines, possibly with fewer references to word puzzles.

Rory stretched out his hands. "Folks. Please, folks – I understand you're upset but let me speak, please."

"Normally, I'd drive down to Willow Creek to use the Wi-Fi in the library there," complained Old Man Randall, "but I can't even do that. I got a four-hundred-and-sixty-seven-day streak to keep going."

Rory glanced at him then scanned the last of the crowd. "Look, we don't know what the hell they're doing blocking the roads, but my ... the sheriff went up there right away to find out." Much to Rory's annoyance, he'd been told to stay behind. Not in the dad voice either. In the commanding-officer one he almost never used.

"What about the phones, Rory?" asked Janice Dockery. "The phones?"

"As you know, there's been an ongoing problem with the exchange box being vandalised but, at this time, we do not have any proof of—"

A collective mass groan drowned him out. He couldn't blame them. Everybody knew it was Ronnie Pierce and his damned Sportsman's League. They'd made everyone in the town a low offer on their properties and were now doing everything in their power to make getting out look like the best option. Landlines and the cell tower went down every other week, and the phone companies weren't interested in doing anything about it. The cell tower had been out since last Tuesday. They called and called to complain, but the companies were becoming slower and slower about coming out to fix it. They saw Paradise as a money pit that should be someone else's problem.

Then there'd been four power cuts and counting in the last six months, plus that scare with what turned out to be harmless food dye turning the drinking water green. Everybody knew who was doing it, but they were all but powerless to stop it. Despite appealing to the state police, all that happened was they sent some officers up for a few weeks, the trouble stopped and then started up again as soon as they left. Rory's dad had even written to the FBI, but they didn't want to help either. Everyone agreed what was happening to Paradise was terrible, but eventually, they wore out their goodwill and found themselves back to a two-man sheriff's department, powerless to do anything except stand there and get shouted at.

Currently, the town didn't have a mayor, after Bert Unger had suddenly upped and left a couple of weeks ago. Nobody had done anything about that yet either, mainly because they were collectively beaten down by the whole thing. When Leo Watts had disappeared, Rory and others had thought that surely now something must be done. They'd gotten state police and other agencies to come and assist with the search, had even sent up a helicopter for three days, but someone going missing in the Oregon mountains wasn't exactly unprecedented. Suspicions abounded, but there was no proof of any foul play, even if Beth McPherson swore that the last time she'd seen him he'd been leaving to go up and fix the phone exchange himself. Leo could fix anything. Rory had liked him for a lot more than that reason.

Quite a few people had already left, and many more were teetering on the brink of doing the same. To Rory, there was nothing more frustrating than sitting around, watching the town you loved being torn to pieces and being powerless to stop it, in spite of the badge pinned to your chest. He'd grown up thinking his dad, the sheriff, was an all-powerful, benign god, watching over everybody. Now he watched on as, day after day, this slow, invisible siege under which those assholes from the Sportsman's League had laid the town wore him down further and further. His mother's death had taken so much of the man, and this was taking the rest.

At the back of the crowd, Darrell MacQueen pointed an angry finger in the direction of the Huntsman's Lodge. "You and your dad need to stop pussyfooting around. March in there and arrest every last one of those bastards."

His outburst prompted Janice Dockery to turn and fix him with a steely glare. "Oh, you're the real big man now, Darrell. I ain't seen you standing up to them."

He looked taken aback by the rebuke. "I'm not the law!"

"And Rory here and his dad are only two men. They ain't the army you want to pretend they are."

"I pay my taxes," added Darrell weakly.

"Congratulations. Why don't you go up to that dumbass lodge and tell them—"

Janice broke off as she and the rest of the crowd noticed Rory's father's patrol car coming back down Main Street, a black SUV following in its wake.

The crowd fell silent. Well, most of them did.

"I even got *parer*," said Old Man Randall. "And that was a real hard one. Hardest Wordle there's been. Almost half of everybody missed that. I got it in four. *Parer*, I thought – that's a small knife for doing fruit, vegetables and what not." He stood slightly taller and puffed out his chest. "Got it in four."

Rory nodded absent-mindedly as he and the assembled townsfolk watched the two vehicles pull up. Sheriff Alan Davenport, Rory's father and boss, stepped out of his cruiser and put on his hat. Behind him, all four doors of the SUV opened. Ronnie Pierce got out of the passenger side. Rory didn't recognise the other three people. A muscular Black guy eased himself out of the driver's seat and leaned against the hood, with a similarly tall, stocky White guy emerging from the back. He was joined by a considerably shorter brown-haired woman in a pant suit. Rory noted that all three of the unfamiliar faces were carrying sidearms. Rory would have bet his meagre probationary salary on the two men being either current or ex-military. The woman was harder to read, but she strode forward with an assured air.

"Alan, please tell me you've finally arrested that son of a bitch," said Janice Dockery, pointing a finger at Ronnie.

Rory noted the tight grimace of irritation pass across his father's face. He held out a hand. "Nobody has been arrested, Janice."

A collective groan went up from the crowd. A lot of them were being noticeably less demonstrative now that Ronnie was there, smiling that shit-eating smile of his at them.

Ronnie had been a couple of years ahead of Rory in high school, and he'd been a scumbag back then too. Him and his buddy Jake. They'd been inseparable. The two of them had specialised in finding anyone who was smaller than them to pick on. Rory could still remember receiving a nuclear wedgie as punishment for walking down the hall.

Kimberley Reese held up her hands in despair. "The road is blocked and I can't even call into work. I'm going to get fired, Sheriff. What the hell is going on?"

Before Rory's dad could say anything else, the woman in the dark pant suit stepped up onto the porch beside him and raised her voice to address the crowd. "Ladies and gentlemen, my name is Colonel Gardner and I work with the Department of Homeland Security. I am sure you have many questions about this morning's events, and I will answer them as best I can. There are currently four persons of interest at large in the area that we believe present an imminent and credible threat to national security."

A couple of townsfolk let out an audible gasp. Rory looked at his father, who subtly shifted his left hand in only the way a parent can to tell their child to stay quiet.

"Under no circumstances," continued Colonel Gardner, "should you approach these individuals. They are four males – a large Hispanic man, mid-thirties; a slightly built African American, early twenties; a Caucasian dwarf, late thirties, as in an individual under four feet ten inches in height; and finally, a man who is described as early fifties, with a strong Scottish or Irish accent." Rory noticed her glance at Ronnie. "Reports vary."

"And why has the road been blocked?" asked Janice Dockery.

"It's been determined that for security reasons these men have to be prevented from leaving the area. We apologise for the inconvenience."

"Couldn't you just set up a roadblock?" asked Chuck Clarke.

"No. I decided my men, who are munitions experts amongst many other things, would best serve the operation by creating rockslides, as vehicles can, and will, ram roadblocks, even when armed guards are present. Also, at this time, we have deemed it necessary to disable all avenues of communication. We would ask you to return to your homes immediately and shelter in place."

"I said it," said Darrell MacQueen to nobody in particular. "That explosion yesterday and all the shooting. I said it."

"Hang on," piped up Janice Dockery, a woman who was always going to have follow-up questions. "If these people are terrorists or whatever, shouldn't there be lots of agents and the army or whatever here?"

"I will not discuss operational concerns," countered the Colonel. "All you need to know is that every step is being taken to ensure your safety."

"And hold up," Janice continued. "What the hell would terrorists be doing here? We haven't got anything worth blowing up."

"Again," said the Colonel, a noticeable steel rising in her voice, "I will not be discussing operational concerns."

"What should we do if we see these terrorists?" asked Darrell MacQueen.

"You should immediately inform my men, or a member of the Paradise Sportsman's League, who are assisting us with this matter."

There was a considerable amount of angry muttering from the assembled crowd of Paradise residents before Janice Dockery gave it a voice. "You're using him and his gang of goddamn criminals?"

Rory watched closely as the Colonel's eyes narrowed. "I am in command here, madam, and I have made the decisions I have deemed necessary to handle this situation."

"But what about—"

The Colonel cut Janice's response short with a downward chop of her hand. "I have given you all the information I can. Please return to your homes and be vigilant."

"But—"

"The longer we spend answering questions, the less time we have to resolve this situation. Please return to your homes immediately. The Department of Homeland Security thanks you for your cooperation." The Colonel turned and pushed through the door into the sheriff's office, with the White guy immediately behind her. Ronnie Pierce and Rory's father followed behind. The other guy stayed leaning against the vehicle, casually surveying the road.

"Alan?" pleaded Janice, but he just shot her a what-can-I-do shrug and continued through the door as the crowd rapidly dispersed, chattering amongst themselves as they hurried away.

"This is bullshit," muttered Janice, shaking her head and turning to go.

That left just Old Man Randall standing there, looking thoroughly crestfallen. "But ... I got a streak. I got a streak."

THERE BE DRAGONS

Given that this meet-and-greet had started with "Sorry, yes, I am trying to steal your car," what followed had gone surprisingly well. They'd taken seats outside the cabin on some battered deckchairs and a couch that looked like it had seen the Vietnam War but didn't want to talk about it, while Beth had served them coffee and iced tea. The trio of dogs hung around, regarding their visitors with great interest. The small one, Princess, sat there glowering at Smithy, waiting for the first sign of trouble. The three-legged one, called Cerberus for reasons that were never explained, instantly laid his head on Carlos's lap, much to the big man's delight, and who soon became entirely engrossed in petting the pup. Lollipop neatly reversed his wheels to position himself beside Beth's chair and stared intently at the new arrivals – playing good cop to Princess's bad.

Diller, once directed, had made a less than dignified sprint for the toilet, which had naturally led into Bunny and Smithy explaining in detail how they had ended up here. What won Beth over was her knowledge of the parties in question, Jake and Ronnie in particular, as was made clear by her interjecting with the occasional "asshole" and "motherfucker" when their roles came up in the story. Bunny found it oddly reassuring. The last day had been so intense, it was rather comforting to have someone else confirm that they hadn't all collectively lost their minds, and that the situation they found themselves in was indeed insane.

Diller came back just as Smithy was talking Beth through their great escape into the woods, which Bunny guessed technically qualified as their second escape, the first featuring Billy's grand exit and the Winnebago's last act. His friend looked like a new man. It was as if the metaphorical weight of the world had been lifted from his shoulders, or eased from elsewhere.

When the story had finished, Beth shook her head in disbelief. "Where's Billy now?"

"The bull?" said Smithy. "No idea, but I can't help thinking he's better off anywhere than there. They weren't treating him right at all."

"Leo said that. He even tried to talk to them about it, but those assholes don't listen to anyone." A pained expression came over Beth's face and the conversation rather ground to a halt. None of them wanted to ask. It turned out they didn't have to.

"Leo is my fiancé," explained Beth in a quiet voice, rubbing the back of Lollipop's neck. "Or was ... He ... He's been missing for ..." She paused and looked up at the sky. "Forty-one days now. He went up to fix the phone exchange when it went down again and then he disappeared."

Bunny, Smithy and Diller swapped looks, none of them knowing what to say.

Lollipop lay his head in Beth's lap and she scratched behind his ears as she spoke. "I'm not a fool. I know he's dead. We did the whole search thing, but they never found a body. One of the state troopers tried to console me with the idea that maybe he'd just run off. Y'know, like, he got cold feet." She gave the saddest smile Bunny had ever seen as she looked up at the three of them briefly. "He didn't. We've been together for five years and I know the man. He was excited about getting married. He was determined to defend this place and" – she leaned down and kissed Lollipop on the top of his head – "he loved us. We went to get a dog three years ago, ended up getting three because he couldn't leave any of them behind. Took the ones nobody else wanted. Has the biggest heart you've ever seen, that man. Or at least he did. He's dead and they killed him. Those Sportsman's League bastards killed him because he was standing up against their little plan to take over this town, and he was the kind of man that people rallied around. They didn't need that."

"But," said Bunny, "can't the police do something?"

Beth ran the backs of her hands across her eyes. "Apparently not. What you've got to realise is that these sons of bitches effectively have us under siege. They're trying to run us all out of this town. We got here two years ago, Leo and I." She waved a hand around. "This was my grandpa's place. I used to come out here every summer. I loved it. He left it to me and we thought it was perfect. Leo was a man who could fix anything. I'm an artist. The light here is superb and the space and, well," – she looked down at the ground – "we got here not that long before that asshole Ronnie set the wheels in motion. Slow at first. I mean, the new road really cut the lifeblood out of the town. Janice Dockery – she's one of the locals – I can remember her describing it like we were suddenly amputated and left to wither away as progress moved on around us. Then Ronnie and his cronies, they came up with their messed-up idea of making this town into their own little White-supremacist Shangri-La. They didn't start off saying that, of course."

"Yeah," said Smithy. "They never start off with that."

"And now," said Bunny, "don't ask me how, but those cockwombles have got a whole shedload of sophisticated weapons and they've got something big going down."

Beth nodded. "The only thing they were missing was enough money to buy everybody out. I guess that'll give 'em it."

"Will everyone sell?" asked Diller.

"Enough will," conceded Beth, "and then the rest are going to find themselves living in some KKK fun park. I mean, wouldn't you move?"

"You're not going to, though," said Smithy. "Are you?"

It wasn't really a question. As they'd been sitting there, Bunny had started noticing things too. From this side, the positioning of the stacks of wrecked cars and other things looked even less random. "You've been putting defences in place."

Beth nodded. "I ... Well, we had been. Mainly Leo. He was the practical one. There'd been a couple of incidents, you see. Our back-up generator got damaged. A couple of the cars Leo was fixing got set on fire. Someone took a shot at us from the road."

"Holy crap," said Diller.

Beth waved away his concern. "Thankfully, whoever it was couldn't shoot for shit."

"And the cops?" asked Smithy.

"We've got Sheriff Davenport and his son, Rory. He's a good man and Rory's a sweetheart, but what are they supposed to do? It's not exactly hard to avoid a sheriff's office of just two men, and Ronnie and his gang are clever enough to simply lie low when the state police come around. It's like trying to punch fog." She patted Lollipop on the rump. "As for your situation, your best bet is to get out of here and go talk to the state troopers. Maybe all this talk of guns might finally spur them into doing something serious."

Beth caught a slight cooling in the air and she looked around at the quartet. "Why am I getting the feeling that talking to law enforcement might not be high on your to-do list?"

"It's complicated," said Bunny.

"I'll bet it is." And then, to his surprise, Beth got to her feet. "Your business is your business. C'mon. I'll give you the ten-cent tour."

"We don't want to impose," said Smithy.

"To be honest," continued Bunny, "we need to get out of here."

"Yeah," she concurred, "I figured that, but you aren't getting out by road today. Not if they've done what you suspect." She nodded at Bunny's crutch. "And it doesn't look like you're going to be able to hike out of here for a while, so I figured we'd better come up with some other sort of plan in the meantime."

"We don't want to bring trouble to your door," said Diller, giving voice to the thought that had been pecking away at Bunny.

Beth pointed a finger at the ground. "This is my home and those sons of bitches want to force me out of it by any means necessary. Thanks for the concern but, realistically, trouble was always coming. At best, you might've just moved the schedule forward a little." She stretched out her back. "To be honest with you, I was getting kind of bored waiting for it. C'mon, let's go see the sights. Please keep your hands inside the car at all times and no flash photography."

Beth walked them up the sloped path behind the cabin between yet more wrecks, her rifle slung over her shoulder as the trio of dogs walked in front of her. "Like I said, I'm an artist," she explained. "I was based in LA for seven years after art school, but that life started wearing me down. Leo and I leaped at the chance to come here. Peace and quiet. Space." She ran her hand around the back of her neck. "That was the idea, anyway."

As they walked towards the sheer rock face, she noticed them all looking up at it towering above them. "I'd tell you that you get used to it, but you never do. Eighty-six feet of rock. Used to give me nightmares when I stayed here as a kid. Grandpa McPherson used to tell me not to worry. That he was able to drink his special juice and become one hundred feet tall, so he could hold it up if it started falling."

"Don't suppose he left any of that juice behind?" quipped Bunny.

"Funny you should mention that ..."

"What is this place?" asked Smithy, looking around. "Or, I mean, what was it?"

"That's a surprisingly complicated question. It's been everything. Was a gold mine at one point, probably a prospecting camp before that. Afterwards, it was a lumber camp for quite some time. We're not sure exactly how long it's been in our family or how we got it. Grandpa told me a story about his grandfather winning it in a card game, but I think that might have been a myth. We found a few things that suggested it's had a few other uses over the years, but at some point it transitioned to being a junkyard and, well, that's what it was until Grandpa passed. My dad's a probate lawyer in Orlando these days, so it came to me."

She led them into a cave at the base of the cliff, the darkness quickly swallowing the morning sunlight. "This used to be the entrance to the mine. The shaft is down the back there, long since filled in."

Beth pulled a lever on the wall. Above them, fluorescent lights flickered into life, one after the other, to reveal an enormous cavern filled with metal sculptures.

It was like something out of a fairy tale – a cavern filled with wondrous creatures. All the pieces seemed to be made of repurposed scrap metal. Dominating the collection was a massive horse that stood at the back of the room, towering over everything. To their left, a large rhino was in full charge, something in its face conveying its snorts as it powered forward. Bunny found the twisted metal helped to conjure the sound of thundering hooves to mind.

To their right, the evolution of man was realised in metal, except this time, it included a further three stages beyond the original five, to show a hunched man staring at his phone, another sitting in an armchair drinking a beer, and the final one, down on his knees, throwing up neon. It was certainly arresting. In the far corner were three monkeys seeing, hearing and speaking no evil, while a fourth wore a gas mask and held an umbrella over its head. Numerous other sculptures populated the space. A giraffe with a toxic cloud around its neck. A gorilla holding a machine gun with a bandolier of bullets across its chest. And in the other corner, a large dragon, mouth wide, roaring at the world.

"These are amazing," said Smithy.

"They really are," agreed Diller. "You didn't mention you were brilliant."

"Oh," said Beth, waving the compliment away, "I bet you say that to all the girls who catch you committing grand theft auto. I was supposed to have a big show coming up before, well, y'know."

The centre of the cavern was dominated by another large piece, which looked different from the others, even to Bunny's untrained eye. Welding gear and tools lay dotted around it on the floor.

"Is this what you're working on now?" asked Diller.

"Kinda. Don't ... It's not finished."

The work in progress showed the figure of a woman, staggering forward, one knee already on the ground, neon spears that had rained down from the sky pinning her in place. One of them went straight through a rusted heart. The agony on the metal face as it howled in wordless pain wedged itself in Bunny's brain.

Bunny didn't, as a rule, frequent art galleries. He didn't have anything against art; it was just that it'd never been his thing. It felt a bit like wine. He liked nothing where people wearing cravats got to tell you what was good and what was bad. As far as Bunny was concerned, you should lose the ability to issue judgements on anything as soon as you've made the conscious decision to leave the house wearing a cravat. Not that he was a philistine, it was just that if pushed to pick the only piece of art he could take with him to a desert island, he'd plump for a large print of that *Far Side* cartoon with the fella playing the cymbals in the orchestra with the thought bubble "This time I won't screw up! I won't, I won't, I won't, I won't ..." And the caption "Roger screws up again." With that in mind, Bunny really didn't feel like he had the language to convey his opinion of Beth's work in a coherent manner, so he went for a sincere, "These are fecking class."

"Can I ask—" started Smithy, looking like a man who had a lot of questions, but he was cut off by a loud pinging noise.

Beth pulled a device out of her pocket. "Oh, crap. I'm guessing you guys don't know anyone who drives a black SUV?"

"No," said Bunny.

"In which case, let's assume this isn't a social call."

"Ara shite," exclaimed Bunny. "The fecking golden gun is still outside on your porch."

"Great," said Beth.

"What are we going to do?" asked Diller.

Beth looked around the room. "I think it's time you guys got to see one of the McPherson family secrets."

THROUGH THE KEYHOLE

By the time Beth reached the cabin, the black SUV was already parked up, with a brown-haired woman in a pant suit standing in front of it. Two large men, one Black and one White, flanked her on either side. As Beth approached, both of the men placed their hands on their gun holsters and the woman held up an ID.

"Ma'am, I'm Colonel Gardner from Homeland Security." She nodded at each of the two men in turn. "These are Agents Draper and Newton. I'm going to need you to drop the weapon."

Beth looked down at the rifle she had unslung from her back and now held loosely in her hands. She held on to it, careful not to make any sudden movements. "Homeland Security?" she asked, as the trio of dogs caught up, all stopping to stand protectively in front of her, Princess growling.

"Yes," said Gardner. "Gun, ma'am. I will not ask again."

"What the hell is Homeland Security doing in Paradise?"

Without anyone saying anything, the two men took a few steps forward and drew their weapons.

"Gun, now," barked the one she'd indicated was called Draper.

Beth looked between the agents. It wasn't as if she had a choice. If she so much as twitched, either of them could drop her in a heartbeat and nothing in their demeanours suggested they wouldn't.

"Alright," she said, "take it easy." She lowered the gun to the ground slowly then stood back up. "I'd still like to know what the hell you're doing on my property."

"Homeland Security," repeated the woman. "We have reason to believe there are four terrorist suspects in the area."

"Terrorists?" said Beth, her voice laced with disbelief. "In Paradise? We don't even get Jehovah's Witnesses or travelling salesmen. What the hell would terrorists want here? Are they planning on blowing up some trees?"

This question was studiously ignored by Gardner. Instead, she issued a description of four men who did sound rather familiar, although Beth was ninety-five percent certain that the one who had introduced himself as Bunny was not Scottish.

"Have you seen these men?" Gardner asked.

"No," said Beth, "I—"

She broke off as one of the back doors of the SUV opened and Ronnie Pierce stepped out.

"What the—" The red mist descended and Beth ran at him. She was intercepted by Agent Newton, who grabbed her before she could get more than a few feet, his powerful arms enveloping her. Struggling, she jabbed a finger at Ronnie. "You murdering bastard. Get the fuck off my property!"

Gardner stepped in front of Ronnie. "Ma'am, I'm going to need you to calm down."

"Screw you."

The guy restraining her grunted, having just been bitten on the ankle by Princess. He lashed out his foot, sending her flying with a yelp.

"Princess!"

Now that she'd spun around, Beth saw Cerberus and Lollipop moving forward too. She also caught sight of Draper, turning his gun towards the advancing dogs.

"Stay!" she screamed. "Stay, boys. They're fine, they're fine."

Both dogs stopped moving, anxiety obvious in their wide eyes that were darting around to take everything in. Beth caught a flash of movement to her right. "Princess. Down!"

Reluctantly, the little dog who had been hurtling back in for round two fell into the down position, still baring her teeth.

Beth turned to Draper, who was training his gun on the two boys. "They're okay. They're okay."

"Draper," ordered the woman in the pant suit.

After a brief pause, the agent holstered his weapon and Beth relaxed a little.

With that immediate threat over, she looked back at Colonel Gardner and jutted her chin in the direction of the SUV. "What the hell is he doing here?"

"My patriotic duty," Ronnie answered on her behalf, that smug grin on his face. "I'm helping Homeland Sec—"

He was interrupted by Colonel Gardner spinning around and delivering a vicious backhand slap to his face that took him clean off his feet.

He looked up at her from the ground, his eyes wide with outrage. "What the—"

"I told you to stay in the car," she snapped.

"I—"

"Get back in there now."

Without another word, Ronnie picked himself up and, holding a finger to his nose that had already started to bleed, he scampered back into the SUV, slamming the door behind him. Once he was gone, Colonel Gardner nodded at Newton, who released Beth from his grip.

She pulled herself away, straightened up her T-shirt then pointed accusingly at the car. "What the actual fuck?"

"He is assisting us with our enquiries."

"And since when does the mighty Department of Homeland Security need assistance from White-supremacist douchebags?"

"Circumstance acquaints a man with strange bedfellows," replied Colonel Gardner.

"It's actually misery," said Beth. "Misery acquaints a man with strange bedfellows, and I'm going to need a considerably better explanation than misquoted Shakespeare. I'd like to start with taking a closer look at your ID."

Oddly, for the first time in this exchange, Gardner now looked annoyed. "I don't have to explain myself to you. We will be searching your property."

"Search warrant," demanded Beth.

"I don't need one under the Patriot Act," said Gardner.

"Not true. I still have my fourth amendment rights."

"Probable cause," countered Gardner. "If you don't like it, feel free to take it up with the American Civil Liberties Union."

"I will. In the meantime, I'm refusing your request."

Gardner gave a tight smile. "Luckily it wasn't one. This can happen with you in cuffs or not, but it is happening. The choice is yours. Now, is there anyone else on the property?"

"No."

"You live alone out here?"

Beth folded her arms. "I've got my dogs, one of which your goon just assaulted."

"He bit me," said Newton, looking put out by the accusation.

"*She*. And look at the size of you. Pussy."

"Don't insult the agent, ma'am," said Gardner. "To repeat, you live alone?"

"Yes." She jabbed her chin towards the SUV. "Ever since your little friend in there and his buddies murdered my fiancé."

This drew no response. Instead, Gardner addressed the two men. "Draper, with me. Newton, stay here and if the jack-in-the-box pops out again, feel free." She didn't specify what Newton should feel free to do.

Beth marched over to the cabin, snatching up her hoodie on the porch as she did so.

Colonel Gardner stopped and considered the crate that was serving as a table. "There are several glasses here."

"Yeah," Beth shouted over her shoulder without looking around.

"I didn't bother cleaning up as I wasn't expecting company or the jack-booted thugs of the US government."

Gardner was forced to take a step back as the three dogs obediently filed into the house after their owner. When Gardner finally got inside, Beth was busy making a fuss over Lollipop.

"If we could make this quick," Beth said, "this little guy needs to have his diaper changed."

"Ugh," said Draper from the doorway. "Gross."

"Bite me, agent. I signed up to deal with his shit. Yours, on the other hand ..."

It was one of the more unpleasant experiences of her life, having to stand idly by while two complete strangers rifled through her things. She did her best to keep her temper, but it was difficult.

"Seriously," she snapped at Agent Draper as he opened the drawers under her bed, "you think four terrorists are going to be hiding in my underwear drawer?"

He gave a tremendously punchable smile-cum-sneer. "One of them is pretty small."

"It strikes me that I've not seen your ID, Agent Draper."

Draper shrugged as he continued to wander about her bedroom. "I left it in the car."

Eventually, after going through the cabin, the old mill that was now just a storage shed and the entire yard, they moved on to the cavern. Beth stood there as Draper and Gardner looked around the space. In a way, it felt even more invasive than the rest of the search, their hands all over her work, Draper pointlessly touching stuff while pulling faces.

She tried to distract herself with the dogs as best she could. Cerberus, the big, dopey, three-legged idiot had broken new ground. He liked everybody, absolutely everybody, to an almost pathological degree, and even he had shown no affection towards their most recent visitors. She bent down and made a fuss over all three of the animals. Previously, Lollipop had followed her around religiously, while Cerberus was Leo's shadow and Princess, of course, was the strong independent woman. Since Leo had been gone, though, all three of them remained by Beth's side from dawn till dusk. She checked Princess again and confirmed once more that her earlier run-in with the other agent hadn't left any lasting damage.

Beth held on to her anger because she figured in this situation it made her harder to read. It felt better than being scared too. That way, she was not only giving them nothing, but it also meant that she felt braver. Brave enough that she'd used the action of picking up her hoodie to also snatch up the golden gun before the searchers saw it. Some small part of her was also rather proud of the solution she'd come up with at short notice to hide it from prying eyes.

Draper was over by the rhino, pulling at the plates of metal that formed its body.

"Seriously," said Beth loudly, directing her complaint at Gardner, "what part of your search for terrorists requires this baboon to rip apart my life's work?"

Draper gave her a sour look.

Gardner, who was wandering around with her hands clasped behind her back, as if she was on a day out at the museum, rolled her eyes. "Play nice, Corporal."

"Corporal?" echoed Beth, "He was an agent a couple of minutes ago?"

If this slip-up phased Gardner, she showed no sign of it. She came to a stop in front of the dragon, considered it for a few moments, then started moving towards it.

"I'd be very careful over there," warned Beth.

"And why would—"

Gardner jumped back as a gout of flame sprouted from the dragon's mouth and the tiny metal cow that had been sitting on the plinth in front of it was replaced with a little metallic hamburger.

"It's still a work in progress. Flame can be a tad unpredictable."

Gardner raised an eyebrow. "Indeed. Is that not dangerous to have near your dogs?"

"No. They know not to go where they're not wanted."

If Gardner got the not-too-subtle insinuation, she made no

acknowledgement. Instead, she resumed her walkabout, as if perusing rather than invading.

Finally, she stopped under the nose of the horse and pointed up at it. "We will be leaving soon, but first, I'm going to need you to open this up."

"Excuse me?"

Gardner smiled. "I might just be a simple government employee, but I know a teeny-tiny little bit of history. Let's see who's inside the horse, shall we?"

"There's nobody in there."

Gardner was circling the piece now, looking for a door amidst the tightly welded sheets of metal. "Prove it."

"It doesn't open," said Beth.

"Have it your way," said Gardner. "Draper, go pick up that welding kit, would you? We're going to have to operate."

"Oh, for God's sake," exclaimed Beth.

Gardner moved towards the rear of the horse and stood on one of the hooves. "Actually, never mind. I can see a gap in the back here. Big enough that I can shoot through it and we'll see if there's anything inside worth hitting."

"Jesus," said Beth. "You're some kind of psycho."

Gardner's head spun around and suddenly her voice sounded very different, the faux sweetness gone. Every word came out wrapped in barbed wire. "I don't like that word."

Taken aback by the ferocity in the other woman's retort, Beth fell silent. As she walked across the cavern, Draper fell into step beside her, the dogs following behind.

"There's really no need to—"

"Open it, now," snapped Gardner.

Draper drew his weapon as Beth stood in front of the plinth. With a last glance at Gardner, she moved to the back of the horse and pulled its tail. The sculpture's undercarriage sprang open and what Beth knew were sixty-seven stuffed animals came raining down onto the bottom of the plinth, spilling onto the floor.

"There," said Beth. "Happy? It'll take the best part of an hour to put them back."

Draper and Gardner, guns drawn, kicked their way through the stuffed toys and looked up into the now-empty insides of the horse.

"What the fuck is this supposed to be?" asked Draper.

"Art, apparently," was Gardner's reply.

"Awesome," said Beth sarcastically. "Do you mind if I quote you on the flyers for the show?"

Gardner pointed to the back of the room. "What's over there?"

"The shaft of an old gold mine that has been blocked up for about a century."

"I want to see inside it."

"Did you not hear me?" asked Beth. "The shaft has been closed since before I was born."

"And a minute ago the horse didn't open."

"I can't make rock disappear."

Gardner stared at Beth for a few long seconds. "Have it your way," she said, turning to Draper. "I can. You got any C4 left?"

He nodded. "Hell, yeah."

"Go get it."

"But—"

Before Beth could lodge any further objections, they all looked up at a shout from outside.

A few seconds later, Newton ran into the cavern, stopping to look around in surprise when he entered.

"What?" snarled Gardner.

"Oh," he said, refocusing. "Flare. We got a flare. South-south-east. About two clicks."

"Yes!" said Draper. "One of the dipshits must've found them."

Gardner nodded. "Let's go." She started striding back towards the entrance of the cavern, not looking back as she said, "Ms McPherson, thank you for your time."

———

Beth sat down on the plinth and neither said nor did anything except scratch Lollipop behind the ears for a couple of minutes. She watched the closed-circuit feed on her phone as the three supposed employees of the Department of Homeland Security got into the black SUV which then tore out of the gate. Then, out of an abundance of caution, she walked outside and looked around to make sure that her eyes were not deceiving her and that nobody else was around. Finally, she went back into the cavern and stood facing the Trojan horse.

"Alright," she said loudly. "Mind your fingers."

With that, she pushed in two innocuous-looking panels on the plinth and then, using every ounce of her strength, she pushed the sculpture aside to reveal the eight-foot by ten-foot wood-lined cavity beneath it. Even on the discreetly concealed wheels, the horse was an awful lot of metal and wood for one person to move on their own. As it slid back, hands appeared from the space below and helped.

"Everybody alright?" she asked.

Bunny, Smithy, Carlos and Diller blinked up at her.

"Sitting in the dark in a tight enclosed space with three grown-assed hairy men," said Smithy. "Just what I needed to stop me getting nostalgic for the Winnebago."

"How much of that did you hear?" asked Beth.

"Voices," said Bunny. "Indistinct, remarkably scary voices."

"Yeah, wasn't much fun at my end either."

"We really appreciate it," said Smithy. "And how the hell do you have a secret almost-room under your cave?"

"Remember when I said my grandpa told me he had special juice that made him a hundred feet high?"

"Moonshine still?" asked Bunny.

She nodded. "We found that out back of the old mill. We reckon he stored some of the barrels here. It was hidden under a big old carpentry bench the old rogue had placed there, even though he never did much carpentry. Probably dates back to my great-grandpa. I don't know the details, but it's safe to assume the family made some money out of prohibition."

"Doing the Lord's work," said Bunny.

The four men started to climb out.

"Is it just me," said Diller, "or did that remind anyone else of the scene in *Inglourious Basterds*?"

"I was thinking exactly the same thing," agreed Smithy.

Bunny shook his head. "There's something really wrong with you two."

"Yeah," said Smithy mildly. "Speaking of which, as someone who was just trapped in a confined space with you and your ass, we may need to discuss your diet."

"Sorry to interrupt," said Beth, "but when exactly were you going to tell me you were wanted terrorists?"

"Excuse me?" said Bunny.

Beth proceeded to give them the brief highlights of her visit from Colonel Gardner and her friends.

"Homeland Security?" said Smithy, when she'd finished.

"I'd bet my ass that they aren't really," replied Beth. "They had that bastard Ronnie with them. I have no idea who they really are, but they're some very serious people."

Smithy sat on the edge of the plinth. "While we were down in the hole, trying real hard to be quiet, I was thinking about this." He looked at the others. "Diller and I, we're not wanted men."

"Should I be hearing this?" asked Beth.

Smithy shrugged. "Too late. If it's any consolation, none of us have done anything wrong, it's just … a really complicated situation."

"Whatever," said Beth. "I think I've gone too far to go back now, and besides, you seem to be pissing off all the right people around here."

"And we aren't even trying." Smithy turned back to look at the others. "Like I was saying, Bunny and Carlos, you can't go to the police for obvious reasons, but Diller and I can."

"I guess," said Bunny, sounding none too sure as they all looked around at each other.

"It isn't my preferred option either," conceded Smithy. "I just think it's our only one. Priority number one is us getting out of here, but whatever the hell these people are up to, we can't pretend it has nothing to do with us. Somebody needs to put a stop to it. We've got a heavily armed fascist militia and they're up to something really bad. I think we're way past the point where we can just walk away and pretend like none of this is happening."

Bunny scratched at his beard. "You make an annoyingly good point."

"Sheriff Davenport is a good man," said Beth before pointing at Bunny and Carlos. "You two could stay here, hidden, and I could drive these two into town."

"If I have to go back in the dark hole," said Carlos, "could the doggie please come with me?"

Beth gave him a smile. "I don't think you'll need to, but I'm sure Cerberus will take very good care of you."

On cue, the dog himself hopped over smartly and started licking Carlos's hand, eliciting a delighted giggle from the big fella.

"Alright," said Bunny, "so I guess we've got a plan. You should probably take the—" He hoisted himself up suddenly. "Shite. The gun. Where is the gun?"

"Relax," said Beth, bending down to pat Lollipop. Her hand came up a second later holding the golden gun. "Not even the Department of Whoever-the-hell-they-really-are wants to look in this boy's diaper."

THE WELCOMING COMMITTEE

Sister Joy hit the auto drive on her bike then reached into her sidecar to grab a can of Fresca. It wasn't that warm, especially not up here at altitude, but it paid to stay hydrated.

Recently, she'd rather unnervingly found herself developing an enjoyment of fresh air. It was undeniably refreshing. The one thing you could say for Oregon is that it had absolutely tons of the stuff too. As states went, it was one of the leading providers of the not-very-much-you-needed to produce all this fresh air. She was driving through forests, a lot of which had been here longer than the country had been a country. It really made you think. And around all those trees was air. Vast volumes of the stuff. The good kind too. Probably packed full of oxygen, or maybe it was just the whole nice-smell thing. Joy felt as if she hadn't smelled anything for years; maybe it was that she just hadn't been paying attention or, seeing as she'd been smoking two packs a day along with many other vices, maybe she just really couldn't smell a damn thing. It could be that, or the whole "living each day like it's your last" cliché that inevitably came as part of the package, being two years into a six-months-to-live death sentence that she was somehow still cheating.

Earlier in the ride she'd also been disgusted to find herself enjoying the view. Scenery, for Christ's sake. Between that and her new-found enjoyment of fresh air, she was beginning to worry she'd lost her edge. Admittedly, the night before, she'd committed arson to burn a scumbag slumlord's empire to the ground, but that had been yesterday. So far today, she'd been getting high on scenery and fresh air. The request to go find the Winnebago full of America's most wanted hadn't been ideal, but she'd long since resigned herself to answering the call whenever the Sisters asked. Still, that monster truck rally would have been pretty sweet.

As the bike guided itself around a corner, she flipped the visor down on her helmet. The morning sun sat squarely between the line of trees on either side of the road, hitting her right in the face. A couple of hundred yards ahead of her, at the end of this straight stretch of blacktop, she could see what looked like a landslide blocking the road. In Joy's limited knowledge of such things, rockslides typically happened in winter. It'd explain why the Winnebago would have stopped moving, but not why it would have gone dark. Unless, of course, it was buried under all those rocks.

Joy was a naturally observant person, so she had noted that all cell signals had dropped out about a mile back. That was kind of interesting. What was even more interesting, as the fancy display thing on her helmet confirmed, was that the rockslide up ahead was being guarded by two men bearing what looked a lot like assault rifles. This wasn't a few rocks tumbling down because of natural, time-related erosion either; someone had blown the rockface beside the road then spread the rocks out for good measure to make a mound of stone, nearly six-foot high in most places, that no four-wheel drive was getting over. Joy hit a button on her handlebars and there was a brief flutter of what sounded a lot like wings from behind her.

She gunned the engine a little, noting that the two armed men were now climbing over the rockslide as she approached. That was also interesting. They'd been guarding the *other* side of it. More focused on keeping people in than out. As she approached, she got a better look at them. Two White guys, wearing biker jackets, jeans and surly expressions. One had an honest-to-god handlebar moustache, and the other was under the mistaken impression that a bandana could hide male pattern baldness.

Joy pulled up to a stop and killed her engine.

"You can't be here, man," said Handlebar.

Joy pulled off her helmet.

"Holy shit!" exclaimed his buddy. "It's a chick. Sort of."

"You're the smart one," said Joy, running a handkerchief over her own bald pate. "I can tell."

"Did you not see the signs up the road?" said Handlebar, keen to reassert his authority. "The road is closed."

"Says who?"

This gave them pause and they looked at each other. "What the hell d'you mean, says who?" asked Bandana. "Says this massive rockslide."

Joy shrugged. "I can get round that, especially if you two kind gentlemen pick up my bike here and carry it across."

Bandana chortled. "And why the fuck would we do that?"

"Being neighbourly."

"You ain't my neighbour."

Handlebar shifted his gun. "Where you from, anyway?"

"A small town called none of your business, in the northern part of the great state of blessed ignorance."

"You got a smart mouth on you," said Handlebar.

"You think that's good? You should see me doing Sudoku. I got mad skills."

"Shut the fuck up and get the fuck gone," said Bandana. "Nobody wants whatever you're selling. My grandad fought against your kind in Vietnam."

"Really?" said Joy. "Was he Vietnamese? Because my grandad from Boise flew choppers for the US Navy over there."

"Bullshit."

Joy swung her leg over her bike and dismounted.

"And what the hell do you think you're doing?" said Handlebar.

Joy stretched out her back and groaned. "Damn, long ride to get here."

"Did you not hear me?"

"Oh, I heard you fine, I just missed the part where there was any authority compelling me to answer your questions or follow your orders. I mean" – she pointed at their dress – "unless Oregon state troopers or the local sheriff's department have had a radical overhaul of their uniform code."

Both men scrambled down the side of the pile of rocks to get closer to her. Bandana brandished his gun. "This here gives me all the authority I need, bitch. Or did you not notice the gun?"

"I did, actually," said Joy, leaning against the side of her bike, folding her arms casually. "It's a good deal more impressive than your vocabulary. That's an XM7, if I'm seeing it right. State-of-the-art. Thought they were military only."

This caused Handlebar to shoot a nervous glance at his compatriot. Enough to tell her plenty.

Bandana took another few steps forward until he was standing three feet from her. "This is your last warning, bitch. Turn around and get gone."

Joy tutted. "See, there was a time I'd have cussed you out and then done far worse just for calling me that word, twice, but I've given up swearing amongst many other things. These days, I'm all about practising that self-restraint."

Handlebar joined his compatriot and they both stood pointing their weapons at Joy's head. "Are you crazy or you just got a death wish?"

"Neither," she said. "I just want to get over that rockslide and be on my way. Now, are you two going to get out of my way?"

"Fuck no," said Bandana.

Joy nodded. Unseen, the little remote in her right hand finished guiding the thing the two bozos hadn't noticed behind them at about a height of ten feet. It was a nice little piece of design. Something she'd suggested to Zoya as a crude idea, but Z had made it far more than she'd imagined. The thing that looked like a little bird as it flew along with the bike and then stopped when it stopped. Damn, that girl was a straight-up genius. She called it the Woodpecker, for obvious reasons.

Joy pressed the button and both men spun around as a deafeningly loud rat-a-tat warble, the type synonymous with Woody Woodpecker, ripped through the air. The extendable baton up Joy's left sleeve was now out and making firm contact with the back of Handlebar's head, even as Woody set off the flashbang to temporarily blind and disorientate them. Joy remembered to shut her good eye this time, having learned that lesson in the testing stage. She then threw a well-placed kick into the back of Bandana's knees, causing him to tumble to the ground, along with his slightly less fortunate colleague. She dropped the Woody remote and drew her Taser from the concealed slot on her belt. Both men gyrated as the shocks passed through them, and then, while they were still trying to remember their own names, she quickly relieved them of their weapons. She tossed one into the sidecar and trained the other on them.

"Don't say I didn't ask nice," said Joy, "but you two had to be all unneighbourly about it."

"You fucking—" started Bandana, before being interrupted by Joy's combat boot making contact with the side of his head.

"Seriously, I know somebody somewhere thought highly enough of you two that they've got you out here guarding a pile of rocks, but how dumb are you, exactly?" She looked at the men who lay at her feet, both holding their heads. "I'd also like to point out that I was kind enough to not break any bones during this little tête-à-tête. Don't go thinking I won't, as you pair of princes are already getting on my last nerve." She shifted the gun. "Luckily for you two, I'm in need of a couple of big strapping men to carry Lauretta here – that's my bike – over this big old pile of rocks. And believe me when I say this, fellas, you definitely do not want to drop her. You really wouldn't like to meet me when I'm angry."

She stepped back as the two men, spirits broken, clambered to their feet. Maybe she hadn't lost her edge just yet.

"And remember, boys – lift with the knees."

THOSE WHO WAIT

Rory Davenport squeezed the Seattle Seahawks-branded stress ball in his left hand, while drumming the fingers of his right on the desk. He felt like screaming. Throwing something. Doing ... something. Anything. Instead, he was stuck here, sitting in the office, feeling worse than useless.

He tossed the ball onto his desk in disgust, knocking over the container of pens as he did so. "I just don't get it."

Sitting in the opposite corner, his father, Sheriff Alan Davenport, looked up from the paperwork he was filling in and gave an exasperated sigh.

"What?" said Rory defiantly. "I don't get it. I just don't get it."

"I appreciate that, son. You've said it more than a few times now."

"Yeah, and I'm going to keep saying it. We – you – are the sheriff of this town, where right now we've got agents supposedly from Homeland Security—"

"They *are* from Homeland Security," said his father, not looking up from shuffling through a stack of forms on his desk. "I checked their IDs. Not my first rodeo, Rory."

"Okay, but then what the hell are they doing teaming up with

Ronnie friggin' Pierce and his bunch of reprobates? Why the hell would a government agency be doing something like that?"

"Speaking as a proud veteran, our government has a rather spotty record on that kind of thing. You should google the words CIA and South America. It ain't going to make you overflow with pride."

"I would do," snapped Rory, "but those asshats have knocked out the internet, along with the phones." He waved across at the corner of the room, where there was a noticeable empty space on the table. "And, unbelievably, the Department of Homeland Security confiscated our ham radio, and you let them."

This final jab clearly got through the normally impenetrable Alan Davenport's armour as he slammed down his pen. "I didn't let them. They're Homeland Security. They don't give you a choice."

"You're the sheriff—"

"And they're the government, Rory. I've been doing this a lot longer than you, son, and sometimes you've just got to do as you're told."

"That's crap, Dad. Terrorists are supposedly running around this town and we're law enforcement officials who've been told to sit here and stay out of the way. All because Homeland Security and a bunch of biker-gang assholes who've been holding this town to ransom for six months are out dealing with it. And you think that's right?"

"No," said his father, leaning back in his chair and suddenly looking all kinds of tired. "I think it stinks. I'm mad as hell and, if it makes you feel better, this is my worst day ever wearing this uniform. I also cannot go out that door and defy Homeland Security without it costing me my job and, more importantly, messing up your career."

"What career?" asked Rory huffily. "You mean so I can go back to giving Darrell MacQueen a warning for driving with an open container and helping Janice Dockery get her dumb cat out of trees."

"Community policing—"

"What community?" said Rory, standing up because he had the strongest urge to kick something and he needed to redirect the energy. "Ronnie and his band of douchebags have been destroying this community, and now, somehow, they're suddenly in charge? I mean, what are we actually doing here, Dad? Are we police or just showroom dummies in uniforms? This town is dying and we're" – he kicked the side of his desk, which earned him nothing but a sore toe – "filling out stupid fucking paperwork."

He turned around and looked at the poster on the wall explaining to anyone who cared the values of a gun safe. He couldn't bring himself to look at his father right now, for fear he might say something he couldn't take back.

There was a long pause and then, when Rory's father spoke again, his voice was quieter. He undoubtedly didn't realise, but it was the same soft tone he'd used when he told Rory about his mother's sudden passing. Some conversations you do not forget. "Rory, I've ... I've been meaning to talk to you about everything. Look, I know that since you did your basic training, coming back here ... Let's be honest, it's not what you want from life."

Rory turned to speak, but his father held out a hand. "Please, just let me finish. I appreciate you came back here because, well, you're a good son, and I thank you for that. Sincerely. You always have been. There hasn't been a day in your life that you haven't made me proud. But, well, I think making you come back here—"

"You didn't—"

"Okay, I didn't make you come back, but I didn't stop you. Either way, that was a little selfish of me. Neither I nor your mother ever envisioned a life for you where you'd just stay put here. This town, whether we like it or not, is not what it was, and it's never going to be that way again. With your scores from the academy and – well, I know a few people – you could get a job with any police force in the state, or even go further afield. Somewhere much more fulfilling than here."

"But this is my home," protested Rory.

"Is it, though? I mean, I barely recognise it."

As tears of frustration stung Rory's eyes, he jabbed a finger toward the front door. "That's because it's being taken from us, and we're letting it happen."

His father stared down at a form in his hand, just to have

somewhere to look. "Son, you're a young man and, well, let's just say, things look different from my end of things. The sad truth is, there's some battles in this life you can't win and this, this is one of them. Keep it to yourself, but Chuck Clarke told me last week he and the family are taking what they can get and getting out. His sister has a paper business over in Kansas. He goes, lots more will follow and ..."

Rory turned around and walked over to their only cell, the one that nobody had been in during his time there, bar a couple of boys sleeping off a big one and that asshole Doug Kent that time he'd got physical with his wife. He rested his head between the cell bars. "So, we give up and just let these people, the worst of the worst, win?"

"We survive, son. I could move near Portland, see more of your aunt and your cousins. And you? Well, that's really up to you, but I'll support you whatever you want to do."

"Whatever?" said Rory.

"Whatever," repeated Alan.

"Okay, then," he said. "I choose to stay and fight."

A long, drawn-out pause filled the room. Rory couldn't see his father and he didn't want to. He didn't want to look at the face of the man who was now his whole family, because if he did, he'd have a hard time not breaking into tears, and that wasn't going to do anybody any good.

Luckily, nobody had to find the next words to say as they were interrupted by a knock at the door – the side door, which was actually only a fire exit.

Rory moved across the room and raised the blinds to peer out. "It's Beth McPherson."

Beth was a regular visitor. For the first couple of weeks after Leo's disappearance, she'd called by every day, and every day Rory had felt bad. Then she'd stopped coming and he'd felt worse, because it meant she'd given up on the idea that they could help.

Alan sighed. "We'd better see what she wants."

Rory opened the door. "Hi, Beth."

"Hey, Rory," she said, glancing around. Her battered old station wagon was parked behind her in the alleyway between the sheriff's office and the diner that'd been closed for four months now. "Are you alone?"

"It's just me and my dad in here."

Rory felt his father moving to stand behind him. "Beth."

"Alan."

"What can we do for you?"

"You know these supposed terrorists that the supposed Homeland Security and Ronnie and his scumbags are looking all over town for?"

"We're aware," said Alan.

"I got a couple of them hidden under a blanket in the back of my car. I think you're going to want to hear what they've got to say."

OUTLAWS AND LAWMEN

Beth sat watching nervously as Smithy finished laying out his version of events to the sheriff and Rory. Diller seemed willing to let him do the talking, only nodding along when he felt it was appropriate. She was aware it wasn't the whole truth and nothing but the truth, as she'd been in the car while Smithy and Diller had got their stories straight, but the really important truth was there, and that was all she'd cared about. In this altered version, they'd picked up two hitchhikers and become separated from them when they'd busted out of their illegal detention in the storeroom of the Huntsman's Lodge. She guessed Sheriff Davenport wasn't buying that, but he listened in silence as Smithy laid out the whole thing. Rory was much less of a closed book than his father, and his eyes widened in outrage as Smithy went on.

"These guys seem to have a massive supply of brand-new, state-of-the-art-looking assault rifles, and, like I said, they took out our Winnebago with actual heavy ordnance."

"We didn't hear the explosion," admitted Rory, "because we were out checking the fencing down the mountain where somebody had smashed into it, but we heard all about it when we came back. I ..."

He trailed off, having noticed the look that his father was shooting him.

"And," said Beth, "I had these supposed Homeland Security people out at my place earlier, searching it, and I'd bet you dollars to doughnuts they're not really who they say they are."

"Their ID checks out," said the sheriff.

"Okay, but *they* don't. At one point, that Colonel Gardner swapped from referring to one of her guys as an agent to calling him corporal instead."

Sheriff Davenport shrugged. "I mean, there's probably a fair bit of crossover between the military and them but I take your point."

"Besides that," continued Beth, "she bitch-slapped that son of a bitch Ronnie right in front of me. Much as I enjoyed it, you cannot tell me that's something bona fide government agents go around doing."

"She has a point, Dad," said Rory. "I mean, enlisting those Sportsman's League dicks, that ain't right."

"There were three of them sitting just out of town," said Beth. She'd been tense as she'd driven past the bikers on the way to the sheriff's office, wondering what she'd do if they tried to search the car. "Like they're suddenly in charge."

"And I knew those Homeland Security people didn't seem legit," continued Rory. "Coming in here, confiscating our radio."

"Seriously?" said Smithy.

"Yeah," continued Rory, pointedly avoiding looking in his dad's direction. "Gave us this bullshit about how they had to secure all communications to prevent the terrorists from escaping."

"And did they explain exactly what kind of terrorists we're supposed to be?"

"I asked that," said Rory. "They said you were radical incels."

"What?" said Smithy, genuinely outraged. "Those involuntarily celibate pricks who blame all the ills of the world on women? That's ... I'm a feminist," he declared, actually stamping his foot to emphasise his point. "There's a whole lot wrong with the world but I've never once blamed it on women."

"Thanks," said Beth.

Smithy folded his arms and shook his head. "I mean ... I mean ..."

"For the record," said Diller, unable to suppress the hint of a grin, "I don't blame stuff on women either."

"I got racists and fake Homeland Security going around telling people I'm an incel," fumed Smithy. "This is ... I mean. I ..." He threw out his hands. "I've seen the Indigo Girls live, three times." He held up three fingers to drive home his point. "Three!"

Beth, as the only woman in the room, felt obliged to comment. "Okay, well, thank you for that, Smithy. We should probably get back to the matter in hand."

"I got the complete works of Maya Angelou. And three Frida Kahlo prints."

"Smithy," said Diller. "I think they get it."

"I've done work for nuns," continued Smithy, before looking up. "Well, kind of. Sort of. Y'know what, never mind about that bit."

"Okay," said Sheriff Davenport. "Let's just all calm down for a minute and think." He walked across to his desk then turned around. "If you are who you say you are, or, at least, not who they say you are ..."

"I definitely am not," said Smithy emphatically.

"Then I presume you'd be happy to talk to the FBI?"

Smithy shrugged. "I mean, I guess. As long as they're legit, because like Beth said, there's no way these people are."

The sheriff nodded. "Right. Here's what we're going to do. Rory, you're going to escort Beth back to her place and stay with her."

"But—"

The sheriff cut him off firmly. "But nothing. We both know Ronnie and his crew are gunning for her. I need her safe. In the meantime" – he turned to Smithy and Diller – "I'm going to need you two to stay here."

"Where are you going?" asked Rory.

"I'm climbing up to Widow's Peak where that unmanned weather station is."

"Why?"

"Because there's an emergency radio hidden up there."

"I didn't know that," said Rory.

"Exactly," replied his father. "Nobody does. It's about a mile from here. I reckon I can make it in under an hour. Get word to Pat down in Willow Creek, and the boys in New Bridge. They can contact the Bureau and then come up here, fully loaded, to back us up."

"I could go with you," said Rory.

"No, you can't."

"But—"

"I'm not your father now, son. I'm your superior officer and I have given you an order."

Rory went to say something, caught himself, then nodded.

"Good boy. Everybody clear on the plan?"

They all bobbed their heads in assent.

"Right, then," said the sheriff. "Beth, Rory here will accompany you home. Everyone stay calm and this'll all be over in no time."

"Just ..." began Smithy. "Sorry, last one. *Thelma and Louise* is one of my top five films. Probably top three." He scanned the faces looking down at him.

Tense as she was, Beth couldn't stop herself laughing. "Do you want us to wait while you burn a bra or ..."

"Okay, I'm done."

CAR AND OTHER TROUBLES

Rory sat in silence as Beth punched the steering wheel of her car repeatedly and used some language that his mother would have referred to as unladylike. She'd been a bit old-fashioned in some regards. Mind you, Beth was using a couple of phrases that Rory hadn't heard before either.

They had travelled about eighty yards up Main Street before the station wagon died. In between the barrages of profanity, Rory, who was no car expert, was able to pick out that Beth appeared to believe the issue was with the car's battery.

When she had calmed down and stopped assaulting her vehicle, she turned to him. He tried to look like he wasn't a teeny bit terrified.

"So, the battery?" he asked.

"Yeah," said Beth. "Sorry. The battery. I've been meaning to get a new one."

"Not a problem. Have you got a jump-starter?"

"I've been meaning to get one of those too."

"Okay, well, don't worry about it. We've got a kit back at the office. Luckily, we didn't get too far, so I can run and go get it."

Once they were both out of the car, Beth popped the hood and Rory looked around. The street was deathly quiet. Paradise had never been a thriving place – certainly not recently – but at that moment it looked like a ghost town. Clarke's store was not only closed, but its shutters were down. Rory had only discovered it even had shutters a few months ago when someone, no prizes for guessing who, had thrown rocks through the window. The only sign of movement on the entire street was some curtains he noticed twitching – Janice Dockery monitoring comings and goings.

Rory looked down the street and saw his father exiting the office and climbing into his patrol car. "Or even better, my pops can just …"

To head up to the weather station at Widow's Peak, his dad should be driving right by them up Main Street, to then leave the car at the parking spot about a mile up the road before hiking the rest of the way. So why then was he turning the car around and heading in the other direction?

With a horrible sinking feeling in his stomach, Rory watched the town's patrol car drive off. "Oh, no."

"What?" said Beth.

Rory didn't answer. His mind was racing, trying desperately to come up with a different answer to the one that had popped into his head. "No, it …" He bit his lip. "He … can't be. He wouldn't."

Beth stepped around the car and put her hand on his arm gently. "Is everything okay, Rory?"

"My dad …" Rory licked his lips, unsure if he could say what he was about to. "He …" Rory nodded up the road. "He headed off in the patrol car – that way."

"Right," said Beth. "But … oh!"

Her reaction confirmed his worst fears. The thing he didn't want to believe. "Shit."

"Yeah."

She grabbed her shotgun out of the back seat and started running towards the sheriff's office. "C'mon, Rory," she shouted without looking back. "We don't have much time."

———

Smithy and Diller sat in the sheriff's office, in the dark save for the occasional sliver of light sneaking through the closed blinds.

They both jumped when they heard a noise outside.

"Maybe he forgot something?" whispered Diller.

"Get behind the desk."

Diller did as instructed. Smithy picked up a golf club that was sitting in one corner of the room and stood behind the door with it held above his head.

A second later, Smithy gasped as Rory all but stumbled through the door. "Jeez, kid, you almost got your head taken clean off."

Beth came in behind him and slammed the door shut. "We need to go."

"What?" said Diller. "But the sheriff ..."

"He's not going to do the radio thing. He's gone to tell them where you are."

Smithy looked over at Rory, who had rushed to one of the large filing cabinets and was pulling open drawers.

"But why would he do that?"

"I don't know," said Beth.

"Wait," said Diller. "How come you came back?"

"The darned car broke down. We need to" Beth broke off at the sound of a car engine outside. She pulled open the blinds to peer out. "Damn it! We're too late. He's back already and he's got company."

"What are we going to do?" asked Diller.

They turned as, in the office, a shotgun was racked. Rory was holding it. An unreadable look on his face. "Whatever we have to. I am still an officer of the law and I'm not handing you over to them. No matter what anyone says."

THE DRINKING MAN'S THINKING MAN

How dare they!

How fucking dare they.

That whole friggin' Sportsman's League would be nothing without him. Nothing! And that snake in the grass, Ronnie. It'd been their idea, the whole thing, and then he'd turned his back on him and betrayed him at the very first opportunity. Not just betrayed him, but actually punched him in the face so he could pretend to be the big man in front of that crazy Colonel bitch.

Jake ran his tongue around the inside of his left cheek, probing the swelling. Not that he could feel much. Ever since that pissant Jonny had driven him home under Ronnie's instructions, Jake had been hitting the booze real hard. He was sitting in his lounger in his front room, most of the way through a bottle of Jim Beam, with a six-pack on the go. At this point, he couldn't remember what was chasing what. He looked at his hand, still in its cast. He was as much of a victim here as anybody. Shit goes wrong. It had before, and he'd fixed it. Okay, he'd messed up, but if they'd just given him a chance, he'd have fixed this too. God damn it, this was his town. That should count for something.

Truth be told, Jake's house wasn't much. A two-bed shit heap whose decor was no more fetching than the memories it contained were happy. It was what his father had left him after he'd died. His mother had bolted long before, realising she couldn't stand another minute of the old man. Jake couldn't really blame her. There was a rumour she was now living only forty miles or so away in Daler. The fact that his father couldn't be bothered to drive even that short distance to get her back told you all you needed to know about their star-crossed love.

Jake was looking forward to a considerable upgrade in accommodation when they owned this town. He had his eyes set on Chuck Clarke's place. Even when they were kids, it'd been one of the fanciest houses in the town. Clarke and the Mrs had put in that hot tub a couple of years ago. Jake was never invited around to try it, mind. He'd have the last laugh when the place was his, and for pennies on the dollar too. His eyes wandered around his current abode. Drifts of beer cans and leftover TV-dinner trays filled every available surface. He needed a cleaning lady. Hell, he needed any kind of lady. It had been too damn long.

The one thing this house had going for it was location, location, location. It was only a block away from Main Street. Which is the reason he leaped to his feet when he heard what he reckoned was a gunshot.

He'd show 'em.

He'd show 'em all.

TURNCOATS AND GHOSTS

Sheriff Alan Davenport eased himself out of his patrol car and immediately turned to the three men pulling up behind him on motorcycles. "Remember what we agreed. I'll go in there and calmly bring them out."

"Yeah, yeah," said Tommy Drake, the only one of them he knew by name. "We'll wait here as instructed," he drawled as he shot him a sarcastic salute.

Davenport's knuckles itched. He hated these assholes almost as much as he hated himself right now. He and Tommy were only acquainted because he'd arrested the guy for driving while intoxicated when he'd ridden his bike into the back of Mrs Wilson's parked car. And now, here he was, sneering back at him like suddenly he was the one in charge. Hell, he was. Or at least his bosses were. Alan had made a deal with the devil, and he was wondering if he could live with himself for doing it. He'd started questioning himself as soon as he'd got into the patrol car. Maybe if he hadn't turned the corner to find Tommy and his compatriots right there, he might have landed on a different answer. Too late now.

He just needed to get this over with. Then he could get on with the rest of his life and, more importantly, Rory could get on with his.

"Stay here," he said.

He turned around and started walking up to the office. He was about twenty feet away when he noticed that the front window had been pulled up slightly.

"Stay back," came the shout from inside.

"What the— Rory?"

"I said stay back, Sheriff, and I meant it."

"What are you doing in there?"

"Of the two of us, I'm not the one who I think needs to be explaining his actions here."

"It's not what it looks like."

"Really?" Rory was trying to hide it, but Sheriff Davenport could hear an undercurrent of emotion in his son's voice. "Because it looks an awful lot like you sold these people out."

"I'm coming in."

He flinched as a bullet fired from a handgun hit the ground a few feet in front of him.

He took a couple of steps backwards, shocked. "Rory!"

"I probably wouldn't be able to shoot you, Dad, but, fair warning, I've given these fellas free rein of the gun cabinet and they just might manage it."

"You need to listen to me now, Rory – I'm your superior officer."

"Not any more. Not since you swapped sides."

Sheriff Davenport looked around, horrified, to see Tommy and the other two bikers fanning out around him, their rifles trained on the office. He threw out his hands. "Wait. Hang on, I'm handling this."

"Sure looks like it," said Tommy. "Nico, cover the side door."

The bald guy with the goatee nodded and positioned himself on the corner beside the old diner. The other guy positioned himself behind Davenport's patrol car, both of them with their automatic rifles trained on the sheriff's office.

"This is not what we agreed," protested Davenport.

"Plan has changed," replied Tommy curtly.

"I demand to speak to Ronnie and that Gardner woman."

"I'm sure they'll be here presently. We radioed it in. In the meantime" – Tommy raised his voice – "anyone in there shoots again and we're going to shoot back."

"You can't do—" Alan reached for his gun, only for Tommy to cover him with his rifle. "Don't, Sheriff. Do not."

"I'm the law," said Alan. "You can't—"

"Sure I can. Hands in the air."

———

Inside the sheriff's office, Smithy was looking out one window, with the sheriff's deputy, who, positioned at the other window, had just defied his superior officer and father.

"Damn it!" hissed Rory.

"What's happening now?" asked Beth.

"They've taken the sheriff's gun," said Smithy, "and they're handcuffing him to the truck parked on the far side of the street."

"Lay down with dogs," said Rory, bitterness lacing his voice, "get fleas."

Smithy glanced up and saw Beth looking at Rory, clearly thinking the same thing he was. The shotgun Rory had given him rested in his hands.

"We need to get out of here," said Diller.

"That we do," confirmed Smithy. "I think that one guy just said he called for help. Our chances aren't great, busting out against three of these guys. It'll be impossible against reinforcements."

Rory, still with his service weapon in his hand, turned to Diller. "We've got another rifle, if you'd—"

"No," interrupted Smithy, before Diller could reply. "Guns aren't Diller's thing."

"Have we got a plan?" asked Beth.

"I'm trying real hard to think of one. All suggestions welcome."

"Are there any other ways out of here?" asked Diller.

"Just the two doors," said Rory.

"You know what this reminds me of, Dill?" asked Smithy.

"Ending of *Butch Cassidy and the Sundance Kid*?"

"Yeah," he said, parting the blinds to take another look at the street outside. "I liked it a whole lot better as a movie."

———

Tommy Drake had positioned himself behind the truck parked opposite the front door of the sheriff's office. Razor was to his left, behind the patrol car, and Nico was to his right, over beside the old diner, covering the side door. Spread out like this, they had the whole place locked down. The only downside of his current location was that he was beside the whiny dumbass of a sheriff.

"You listen to me, Tommy," said the sheriff. "I'm an officer of the law and you will release me immediately."

"Can't do that, Sheriff. Your loyalties are questionable."

The sheriff strained at the cuffs that secured him to the back of the truck. "My son is in there. You or any of your idiots open fire, so help me, I'm going to hunt down and kill every last one of you."

Tommy smiled. "Well, now, that isn't very law abiding of you, is it? I mean, what about our constitutional rights?"

The sheriff almost screamed. "I will kill you, you bastard!"

"Yeah, well, we'll see about that when the boss gets here. Word of advice, though – I wouldn't piss off the Colonel. If you ask me, she has one of them impulse control problems."

"Tommy," shouted Razor, from behind the patrol car, "what's the play here?"

"Stay frosty, man. We're just waiting for the cavalry to show up. Let them sort this out."

"Don't we— Whoa, what in the hell?"

Razor didn't say another word because he was now distracted by the same thing as Tommy. Down the middle of the street, a motorcycle with a sidecar was trundling towards them at about fifteen miles per hour. Two things about that scene were unusual. First, nobody was riding it. And second, it was blasting a Tom Petty song. Unless he was very much mistaken, it sounded a lot like 'I Won't Back Down'.

———

"A motorcycle with no rider just rolled up outside," said Rory.

"Does it have a sidecar, by any chance?" asked Diller, moving forward.

"Yes," said Rory, looking back at him. "Someone you know?"

"If it's who I think it is, I've never met her. But if she's James Bond, I know her Q."

Rory shook his head. "You guys really have a weird way of talking."

"Fair point," said Smithy. "Be ready."

"For what?" asked Beth.

"No idea."

———

"What the hell is this?" shouted Nico from over by the old diner.

"I've got no clue," replied Tommy, as the thing came to a stop in front of him. "Whose bike is that?"

He looked over at Razor, who held up his hands. "Never seen it before."

Tommy glanced from left to right. There was nobody up the street in the direction it had come from. The whole place looked deserted.

The bike seemed to have once been a Harley Davidson with a sidecar, but it had been tricked out in ways Tommy had never seen before. He licked his lips. "I don't care whose it was, boys, it's mine now."

"No fair," complained Nico.

"Shut up. Finders keepers. I'm claiming it." He moved around the front of the truck, still crouching down to get a better look at the thing. Wow, it was something else. The keys were even in the ignition. He leaned forward to turn off the engine, which was purring like a kitten.

As soon as Tommy grabbed the key, several hundred volts of electricity passed through his body, causing it to convulse violently, which took up all his attention. That and collapsing to the ground immediately afterwards. If he had any capacity remaining to notice things, he would have heard a strange popping sound from the opposite direction to that from which the bike had travelled. It would oddly remind him of the noise made by that T-shirt cannon he'd stolen one time, from a kid at a high-school football game.

A second later, he would have seen something about the size of a cola can landing beside Nico before exploding into a cloud of dust, one that left his compatriot blinded, coughing and spluttering as he staggered around. Then he would have noticed that Razor, not so named for his lightning-quick mind, had realised that something was up and turned around just in time to take a beanbag fired into his chest from ten yards away.

The word beanbag really doesn't conjure up the right image, given that most people's experience of the things involves enjoying the idea of sitting on one right up until the point they try it, at which time they quickly acknowledge that chairs were invented for a good reason. The beanbag that hit Razor square in the chest was just over a couple of inches in diameter, but it was travelling at about ninety yards a second and filled with lead shot. It broke some ribs and knocked the wind out of him. A couple of seconds later, the Doc Marten boot he took to the side of the head knocked the sense clean out of him.

The boot belonged to a shaven-headed Asian woman who wore a pair of leather biker trousers and a combat vest over a Tom Petty T-shirt. She moved fast, racing across and firing a second beanbag into the still-spluttering form of Nico, already down on his knees, rubbing his eyes and presumably trying to figure out what was happening. The beanbag put him down and stopped him wondering about anything except when the pain would stop. The woman moved swiftly across, bent down and tossed Nico's gun well out of reach.

By this point, feeling like a bolt of lightning had struck him, Tommy had managed to pull himself to his feet. The last thing he noticed was the woman cocking the shotgun for a third time and sending a beanbag straight towards him. Experts will tell you that the maximum range at which a beanbag round is effective is twenty yards, and, luckily for Tommy, he was standing twenty-two yards from the woman as she fired. Unluckily for Tommy, this woman was a hell of a shot. He could only assume that the aforementioned experts had never taken one of those rounds right between the eyes. He'd definitely be writing to them about this, just as soon as he lay down unconscious on the ground for quite some time.

———

The front door of the sheriff's office opened and Diller popped his head out. "Sister Joy?"

"You must be Diller?"

"I am."

"Charmed to make your acquaintance. Our mutual friends sent me. What's going on here?"

Smithy appeared in the doorway. "You did all that to them and you don't even know?"

Joy shrugged as she looked around at the three men on the ground. "I took a guess. Care to bring me up to speed?"

"No time. We've got company coming. Let's go."

As Smithy spoke, Beth, Diller and Rory dashed out of the sheriff's office.

"Rory," shouted the sheriff, from his position handcuffed to the back of the truck. "Please, listen to me."

"No," said Rory, refusing even to look at his father as he moved around to the driver's side of the patrol car.

"He with us?" asked Joy.

"No," said Rory firmly. "He's with them."

Joy moved over to her bike. "Where are the other two?"

Smithy pointed his shotgun in the opposite direction to the one she'd come from. "Couple of miles that way. Junkyard."

Joy climbed on her bike and shoved the shotgun into its holster on the side. "Tell me—"

"Look out!" screamed the sheriff.

His warning gave Joy enough time to dive to her right, but it was not enough for her to avoid the bullet, which hit her in the back as she did so.

Beth spun around from where she was getting into the front seat of the patrol car just in time to see Sister Joy fall to the ground and the figure of Jake Draper standing behind her, turning his gun in her direction.

Instinct.

She raised her rifle and fired.

There was an odd moment of almost stillness as Jake looked down at the bloody wound blooming from his chest, and then he stumbled to the ground.

"I ..."

Smithy rushed past Beth, shotgun trained on Jake, but he wasn't getting up. He kicked Jake's gun away and leaned over his unmoving form. Diller, meanwhile, rushed over to Sister Joy, who, remarkably, sat up as he reached her.

"Fiddlesticks," she said. "Times like this I really miss being able to curse."

"You're okay?" asked Diller.

"No, I've just been shot."

Diller bent down to examine her back but she pushed him away.

"Kevlar. Our mutual friend made me this jacket and she's got some mad skills. Still hurts like a ... Man, the clean version of the English language is real limited." She clambered to her feet and worked her left arm around, wincing as she did so. "I'm gonna feel that in the morning."

"Is ..." Beth stood beside Smithy, looking down at Jake Draper lying face down in the street, blood pooling from his wound. "Is he ..." Her voice trembled.

"It was you or him," said Smithy.

"And it's a lot better it was him," finished Joy.

"But ..." Beth dropped her gun. She turned around, bent over and placed her hands on her knees.

"We need to go," said Smithy.

"No," said Beth. "I should …"

She turned at the sound of a voice she recognised.

"I got this," shouted Janice Dockery, waving her hands at them frantically as she ran out of her house towards them. "Go. Get out of here. Now."

"But …" started Beth.

"Go!" urged Janice.

Diller picked up Beth's gun and dragged her towards the patrol car as Rory hopped into the driver's seat, gunned the engine and performed a U-turn.. Smithy heard Joy's bike kick into life behind them as he dived into the front seat.

As Diller slammed the back door shut, Smithy spotted a black SUV and two motorcycles joining Main Street directly in front of them.

"What are we …"

The rest of his thought was lost as Rory slammed his foot down on the gas pedal and drove straight towards the SUV.

NEVER PLAY CHICKEN WITH CRAZY

Smithy was aware that in some quarters he was considered an aggressive driver, those quarters being pretty much anyone who had ever got into a car with him. He could blame this on having been a New York cab driver for a while, but really, it long predated that. He was a man with well-documented anger-management issues, and behind the wheel was often where such issues came to the fore.

Still, in his opinion, Deputy Sheriff Rory Davenport drove like an absolute lunatic. His response to seeing that black SUV a couple of hundred yards in front of them had been to slam his foot on the gas and drive straight at it. On either side of the two-lane thoroughfare were what appeared to be mostly houses, chocolate-box renditions of the American dream, with cars in the driveways and more than a few white picket fences. The kind of houses that should not line a road along which a sheriff's patrol car was being driven by a maniac straight at a large, black SUV, which may belong to a government agency, or to crazy people pretending to be from a government agency. Other branches of the emergency services were going to end up being involved pretty soon, because it seemed certain that Rory Davenport was going to kill everyone on the road.

Smithy knew that the young man's emotional state was probably very fragile, given the rather dramatic falling out with his father they had all just witnessed. On the other hand, he was also particularly aware that a high-speed collision was rarely recommended as a way of working through emotional issues. Not even in California, and they'd try almost anything there.

"What's the plan?" Smithy screamed, his nails digging into the arm rest.

"Them moving."

Smithy scrabbled for the seat belt he now realised he was very definitely going to need. "Oh no."

The "oh no" was a reasonable, arguably understated response to the current situation, so nobody queried it. In reality, for want of a much better word, the "oh no" in question was at least partially the consequence of a familiar tingling sensation in the back of Smithy's brain, which meant only one thing. After a rather dramatic accident a few years ago, Smithy now often heard the voice of God in his head when confronted with certain stressful situations. This would be traumatic for anyone, but doubly so for an atheist. He was fully aware it was just an odd residual side effect from head trauma. Unfortunately, there was no convincing the damned voice of that.

"ANY FINAL WORDS? CONFESSIONS? CONVERSIONS?"

"Seriously, God – bite me!"

"What?" yelled Rory.

Saying that out loud was embarrassing. Luckily, in a few seconds, nobody would be alive to bring it up and Smithy, if most of the world's major religions were correct, could take it up with God directly.

———

Meanwhile, in the SUV, Ronnie Pierce was no longer enjoying the fact that he'd been allowed to drive. He'd always wanted to get behind the wheel of one of these big old tanks. When things calmed down and Project Paradise was a success, he reckoned he might even get himself one. He was going to be mayor, after all. It was the kind of thing that would be expected of him.

He was rapidly going off the idea, though. He'd been behind the wheel for only a few minutes and now someone was driving a patrol car straight at him while, in the passenger seat beside him, Colonel Gardner was screaming, "Ram them. Ram them. Ram them!"

She was crazy. Whoever was behind the wheel of the patrol car was also crazy. That was altogether too much crazy.

———

Fifty yards.

Rory had his foot to the floor and he wasn't lifting it.

"Everybody hold on," he roared.

It was an entirely unnecessary piece of advice. The other passengers had, rather unsurprisingly, noticed that they were heading for a head-on collision and were bracing themselves for all they were worth. In the back seat, Diller and Beth were screaming. In the passenger seat, Smithy had his eyes shut and was talking to a higher power, mainly about how he didn't believe in him.

———

Ronnie angled the car a little to the left. Just a little. Unfortunately, Gardner noticed and reached across to pull the steering wheel back to the right.

"Are you insane?" he yelled.

"RAM THEM!"

———

Forty yards.

Gardner reached her leg across and slammed it on top of Ronnie's, forcing the gas pedal to the floor.

———

Thirty.

Screaming now, Ronnie noticed it was Rory Davenport driving the car. At least he thought it was. He looked different.

———

Twenty.

Everybody screamed.

———

Ten.

Ronnie, obeying every instinct in his being, tried to pull left but Gardner wrenched the wheel out of his hands. Unfortunately, or fortunately, depending how in love you were with the gift of life, she overcompensated and threw the car into a hard right turn. They would have flipped over had they not received a course correction. Luckily, the patrol car slammed into the rear left wing of the SUV and helped it to straighten back up again.

One of the two motorcycles following them wasn't so lucky. As it hit the front of the patrol car, the rider was sent hurtling into the windshield in front of Smithy, before rolling up onto the roof, where he collided with the flashers before tumbling down the rear window and onto the ground. The car's momentum forced the motorcycle under its wheels, whereupon, not unlike its owner, it sustained quite a lot of damage.

Rory managed to right the patrol car and keep it on the road. The windshield's safety glass was now a fractal of confusion where a biker had collided with it, and Smithy couldn't see very much through it. Still, from what he could see, the front of the car looked pretty messed up, which was not entirely surprising given that it had just endured two high-speed collisions.

"Everyone okay?" asked Smithy.

"I'm pretty sure Rory has lost his mind," answered Beth.

Rory laughed at this, which did nothing to dispel the theory.

Smithy turned to look through the rear window to where he could see that the black SUV had wiped out someone's picket fence and collided with a parked car, but was already reversing to give pursuit.

Joy had somehow negotiated her bike through the mayhem and was following behind them, while the other biker was checking on his buddy.

"Oh," said Rory.

Smithy turned back around to see that the "oh" was in response to a cloud of black smoke coming out of the front of the car.

"Yeah, kid," said Smithy, "pretty sure they're going to be taking that out of your pay cheque."

Smithy looked down. Rory still had his foot to the floor, but the car was going barely fifty miles an hour now. They were passing through the outskirts of town and houses were starting to be replaced by trees. Damn, this place had a whole lot of trees.

Joy pulled up beside the car on her motorcycle and signalled at Smithy to lower the window.

"Does this come down?" he asked Rory.

"No," came the reply. "It's bulletproof but they don't come down."

Smithy turned to Joy, pointed at the front of the car and pulled a face.

It was hard to tell at this speed, but Joy appeared to roll her eyes before she looked over her shoulder then accelerated away in front of them.

Smithy watched as she disappeared around the bend in the road ahead.

"Where's she going?" asked Beth.

"I have no more information than you do," said Smithy, craning his neck to look out the rear window again. The pursuing motorcycle was coming up behind them really fast now. Smithy picked up his shotgun. "Be ready, Diller."

"Ready for—" started Diller but stopped when Smithy unclipped his seat belt, hopped up on the seat and started to smash out the front windshield with the butt of the shotgun.

"What the hell are you doing?" shouted Rory.

"Not sure," responded Smithy as, on the fourth blow, the windshield finally gave up the ghost and fell out, tumbling off to the side.

"Are you crazy?" Rory yelled over the wind rushing in and the sound of a slowly dying engine that'd had more than enough of his crap.

"That's rich coming from you, kid," roared Smithy in response. "I saw this in a movie once."

In the back of the car, Diller yelped, not least because during a chat he and Smithy had had last week, while killing time as they passed through a particularly dull stretch of Kansas, that sentence had been Smithy's choice for his final words.

Securing the shotgun firmly in his hands, Smithy turned around and pushed himself out into the gap that had recently been occupied by the windshield. Belatedly realising what Smithy was doing, Diller dived forward from the back seat and grabbed hold of his legs. Fortunately, the Paradise patrol car was not a fully equipped police cruiser, hence its lack of features such as a Plexiglass screen dividing the front and back. Neither Smithy nor Diller would ever know, or care, about this but it had been a compromise the sheriff and the then-mayor had made a couple of years ago, in an effort to stretch the budget to cover the department taking on a probationary deputy. Their patrol car was what you got when you only took the most basic package.

The car's engine spluttered, causing Smithy to lose his balance.

He fixed his gaze on Rory in the driver's seat. "Hold her steady."

"I'm doing the best I can."

"Do more."

Smithy shifted his attention to the rapidly approaching biker. The thought struck him that, as far as the Sisters of the Saint were concerned, the safe delivery of Carlos, in order for them to get back the two missing members of their order, was priority number one. Still, Joy wouldn't just leave the rest of them. Would she?

Would she?

ENJOYING SOME FRESH AIR

If there was one defining characteristic of Smithy's life, it was that other people made a far bigger deal about his size than he did. In fact, he'd gone out of his way to do not only what everyone else did, but to also do it better. Still, even he would have to admit, begrudgingly, that there were certain situations where a foot or two of extra height would come in handy. It turned out that hanging out of the gap where a windshield used to be while attempting to use a shotgun to hold off pursuers in a high-speed car chase was one of those situations.

Diller was stretched awkwardly over the centre console, half in the front seat, half in the back, while hanging on to Smithy's legs for dear life, as Rory attempted to drive without elbowing Diller in the face. A little more height and Diller would have had more leg to hold on to. A little more height and it would have been a whole lot easier for Smithy to lean to his left while holding a shotgun. A little more height and he could have shot over the top of the car for that matter.

Still, beggars couldn't be choosers and Smithy had to work with what he had. The wind was whipping around his ears, and he was aware that it was carrying a lot of smoke and steam from their increasingly distressed-sounding engine. They were going barely forty miles an hour now and had become depressingly easy to catch up with. This was Smithy's second vehicular chase in as many days and, just once, it would be nice to be the one in the faster vehicle. Variety being the spice of life and all. The black SUV was gaining on them but that wasn't the most immediate problem.

Smithy caught sight of the biker coming up on their right-hand side, racked the shotgun and fired. It wasn't that he hadn't tried to hit the biker, it was just that, given the circumstances, he hadn't been overly optimistic about doing so. It was more important to send the message; that message being, stay back, I've got a shotgun. In any case, that was how he consoled himself when he clearly hit a tree that wasn't anywhere near his target. These were not optimal shooting conditions. Smithy racked the shotgun again. One shot gone, three to go.

Rory shouted something which Smithy couldn't make out.

"What?"

"I said—"

The rest of the statement was both lost and rendered redundant the SUV rammed into the back of them. Smithy lost his balance and, suddenly, his lean-out was now a full-on fall. He felt Diller's hands scrambling desperately for purchase and then, after the longest fraction of a second of his life, he found himself dangling precariously out of the car, upside down. Context was everything, particularly when it came to speed. That forty miles per hour, which had felt so desperately slow a few seconds ago, felt a whole lot faster now. The road rushing past, four inches from your head, will do that.

The motorcycle reappeared on the passenger side of the car, mainly because the SUV ramming into the back of them left little room for it to be elsewhere. Another juddering collision passed through the car as they were rear-ended again.

Smithy fired. In hindsight, he wasn't even certain he'd intended to, and it might have just been the jolt jockeying his trigger finger. Either way, the shot hit the ground harmlessly and the recoil sent the gun spinning out of his hands.

"Ah crap."

The car surged forward for a third time as the SUV rammed them once more. This time it kept in contact, pushing them forward. Flailing around with his now-empty hands to grab hold of something, anything, all Smithy could see was rapidly passing blacktop and the front wheel of the approaching motorcycle, its rider apparently feeling a lot braver now the shotgun was out of the picture. Smithy was about to get kicked off the side of the car he was travelling in like a barnacle being scraped off the hull of a ship. This was going to hurt. This was going to really …

The steel-capped boot was inches from his head when the rear passenger-side door to the patrol car flew open. It thumped into the bike, sending it careening off the road and into the trees. Some small part of Smithy's mind that wasn't entirely gripped with terror roared with delight. Beth was not only a fine artist, she had a gifted musician's sense of timing.

The hands holding him shifted and he fell a couple of inches more, the road now brushing against the tips of his hair. Finally, a hand grabbed the belt of his trousers. He looked up to see Diller leaning out of the car above him, hanging on for all he was worth.

"Who's holding you?" Smithy shouted.

"Not sure," responded Diller, his face a picture of strained determination. If Smithy had to pick anyone in whose hands he'd happily place his life, it would be Diller. Still, right there and then, it'd have been nice if his best friend had spent more hours mindlessly lifting weights rather than reading books.

They were coming up to another bend in the road and the pressure from the SUV increased as it continued to rear-end them. Their pursuers were clearly attempting to use the bend to shunt them off the road while Rory fought desperately to keep them on it. Helplessly, Smithy watched as the ground beneath him changed from blacktop to gravel as the car was edged off. A stone flew up and smacked him between the eyes. With every ounce of strength he could muster, he did whatever you would call a vertical sit-up and felt the air around him whoosh as a rock on the ground narrowly missed out on the chance to take his head clean off. Smithy grasped Diller's

T-shirt and held on with grim determination. Then, thankfully, the car lurched back to the left and once again had all four wheels on the road.

He could hear Rory shouting something but couldn't make out what it was. Then he noticed Diller looking in front of them instead of behind. He followed his gaze. Fifty yards ahead of them was a thick wall of billowing red smoke.

"What the—"

The SUV thumped into the back of them and Smithy noticed the hem on Diller's T-shirt was beginning to tear. Behind him, he could see Beth holding on to Diller's legs and Rory driving with one hand while using the other to grab on to Diller's belt.

"This is intense!" Diller screamed into Smithy's face. He had a point.

As they approached the cloud of smoke, Smithy glanced backwards to see that the SUV had backed off a little, clearly wary of whatever the hell this was. It was a solid instinct. You didn't drive into a cloud offering zero visibility if you had a choice. The SUV did. They didn't.

Just before they entered the smoke, Smithy winced as an explosion went off to their right. He saw the flash first then noticed the massive tree as it started to topple onto the road.

In one of life's rare moments of synchronicity, all four people, be they in the car or currently hanging out of it, screamed the word shit at the loudest volume available to them as they passed beneath the tree. They all watched helplessly as it tumbled towards them before narrowly missing the back of the car as it landed.

It was swiftly followed by the sweetest sound in the world. Forget a baby's laugh or one of Mozart's twenty-seven piano concertos, Smithy would take the SUV pursuing you crashing into a freshly fallen tree every time.

As the patrol car slowed, Diller, with help from Beth, finally dragged Smithy back inside.

They all slumped into their seats, panting heavily.

"That was ..." began Smithy.

"Yeah," said Diller. "Wasn't it, though."

"What ..." said Beth. "I ... What just happened?"

Smithy craned his neck to look through the rear window. The only thing now following them was a motorcycle with a sidecar.

As their car trundled on, making spluttering noises, Joy's bike pulled up beside them. She gave a brief salute before zooming off ahead once again.

"Who the hell is she?" asked Rory.

"Sister Joy."

"Sister?"

"She's a nun," confirmed Diller.

"A nun?" he echoed, sounding beyond outraged. "A nun? What kind of nun?"

"Ever seen *The Sound of Music*?" asked Smithy.

"Not that kind of nun," said Smithy and Diller in unison.

———

Two minutes later, they caught up with Joy, who had stopped outside McPherson's Yard. As the patrol car trundled through the gates, Bunny and Carlos came out of the cabin to meet them. The car spluttered and hissed before it issued its last gasp and ground to a halt. Then the front bumper fell off.

Bunny, leaning on his crutch, spent a long moment looking at the vehicle then considered the gaping hole where the windshield used to be.

"So," he said, in a casual tone, "how'd it go?"

MEET THE NEW BOSS

Tommy Drake was scared. Petrified, if he was being honest. So far today he'd been electrocuted and knocked unconscious with a beanbag that had smashed him right in the face, breaking his nose in the process. He'd happily go through either of those things again rather than do this. He swayed unsteadily on his feet, having only come around a couple of minutes ago, soaking up the blood still oozing from his shattered nose with a bandana, waiting for the tsunami of fury to land. He'd broken his nose before when he'd come off his bike and hit a tree. Jake Draper had reset it for him. Jake wouldn't be doing that this time around, that was for sure.

Nico, the lucky bastard, had been able to get on his bike and ride on to help keep an eye on the McPherson place. Apparently, after the fugitives had left town, that was where they'd holed up. Nico and a couple of the guys were tasked with monitoring the place from a distance, making sure they didn't try to make a break for it. Tommy and Razor were still in town outside the sheriff's office because Tommy was woozy, plus his face was messed up, and Razor couldn't ride thanks to what he reckoned were a couple of broken ribs.

They'd stood around while that old lady had worked on Jake, but as far as Tommy could tell, he'd been dead pretty much as soon as the shot had hit him. Ronnie had been over there, kneeling down beside the body, bawling his eyes out for several minutes. They'd been tight, him and Jake. Went way back. Jake was the hothead and Ronnie the calm and considered one, at least most of the time, but Tommy had seen Ronnie lose his temper once before and it had not been pretty. That Beth McPherson was going to pay for gunning down Jake, he had no doubt.

Speaking of a temper, Tommy would still much rather have dealt with Ronnie than with this Gardner woman. She wasn't much physically, but she had a look in her eyes that made him want to run for the hills and not stop. They'd all seen her shoot Texas Pete for just saying he was leaving, and she wasn't even mad then. This time, they'd really messed up. No doubt about it, Nico was the luckiest son of a bitch in town not to be here.

"So," said Gardner, "I think you're going to have to explain it to me again as I'm a little slow. Dim. Doddery in the mind. The three of you had the sheriff's office surrounded?"

"We did," confirmed Tommy. "Absolutely. And we were waiting, waiting just like you said, when we radioed in."

"Yes, well done. I guess, then, my next question would be, if you had them trapped inside the sheriff's office, why are they not still inside the sheriff's office?"

"There was this woman ..."

"And there were three of you."

"Yeah, but ... she ..."

"And," said Gardner, tossing the blood-covered beanbag in the air and catching it, "she was kind enough to take you down with non-lethal force. Am I right in assuming the three of you got your asses kicked by a small, female pacifist?"

"That's not ..."

"I mean," continued Gardner, "one of you getting caught by surprise – maybe. Two, given that you were on high alert, would be harder to believe. But three? Three? Beanbags, pepper bombs. Did she throw in any high-powered camomile tea at any point?"

"Her bike also electrocuted me." Tommy couldn't believe those words had just come out of his mouth. He wanted desperately to suck them back in as Gardner's eyebrows rose up her forehead.

Gardner paused. "I'm sorry, her what did what?"

"You see ... it drove up, only there was no one on it. And I—"

Tommy had no idea where that sentence was going and he was therefore incredibly relieved when Ronnie marched over. "I'm going to straight up murder that bitch!" he roared, his eyes red.

"That is certainly a possibility," said Gardner wearily.

"Fuck that. This is personal now."

Tommy stepped back as Gardner casually tossed the beanbag she was holding into Ronnie's face. "No," she said, "it's not personal. It's still business and nothing is more serious than business."

"He was my best friend."

"Yes, I noticed how close you were when you punched him in the head earlier on and threw him out of your little gang."

Tommy felt Ronnie's eyes on him, so he did his very best to hide his reaction to that bombshell.

"Brothers fight," said Ronnie, sounding rather less sure of himself. "But this ... I'm heading up to the McPherson place right now and—"

"No," Gardner said, with considerably more venom, "you're not. You and your merry band of halfwits running around half-cocked have resulted in this shambles. I make that three times these people have evaded you. Three! While they seem to exhibit basic competence and appear to have a non-lethal fairy godmother who's popped out of nowhere to save them, I can't help feeling that our side is really not bringing its A game."

"But—"

Gardner took a step forward, her hand resting casually on her holstered weapon. "Interrupt me again," she said. "Just once. Do it. Please. I beg you."

She left a long gap which, wisely, Ronnie made no attempt to fill.

Eventually, she took a step back. "Now. What we currently have at our disposal is the dregs. The three idiots from this part of the debacle, two of whom are wounded. Those other fools – one who went off his bike here and broke his collarbone, the other who is currently watching the McPherson place after ending up in the trees. Then there are the two dum-dums who were ... What was it? Oh, yes, found handcuffed around a tree after they got jumped while guarding a landslide. I mean, they literally failed in their attempt to guard rocks. Which explains how this tiny woman on a bike got through and" – she waved a hand dismissively – "some other dribs and drabs. Plus, of course, you, me and your friend's corpse, which, to be fair, I imagine would be more useful than he was when he was alive. I can always use a paperweight."

Tommy got the definite impression that the words "too soon" were not in this woman's vocabulary.

"So," she continued, "what we're going to do is wait for Draper and Newton to get back from what I can only assume was a false alarm, and for your hunting parties to return. The enemy is holed up in that yard and not going anywhere. We have twenty-four hours to bring this debacle to a resolution, so we will take our time and attack when it is advantageous to us. Do you have a problem with that?"

Ronnie paused then shook his head. Tommy reckoned that was a wise choice as there was a non-zero possibility she'd have put a bullet right between his eyes if he'd given any other answer.

"Excellent," said Gardner. "Now, where is the sheriff?"

Tommy and Ronnie exchanged glances.

Gardner turned to Tommy. "You told me that once he'd had second thoughts on our deal, you'd handcuffed him to a truck somewhere."

"I did," said Tommy. "That one over ..." He looked at the truck, which was conspicuous for its lack of sheriff attached to it, then dived his hand into his jacket pocket, to confirm that the key was gone. "Someone must have released him while I was unconscious."

Gardner scratched her fingernails on her forehead irritably and let out a heavy sigh. "Honestly, this little catch-and-release programme you clowns are running here is really quite something. Fine."

She strode into the middle of the street and raised her voice. "Good people of Paradise, your attention, please. It seems one of you has rescued your sheriff from his erstwhile captivity. That's fine, he is yours to keep. I'd be careful, though, as he is not terribly good at keeping his side of a deal. Ask him about the one he made with us. In the meantime, if you all just stay out of our way, we will be gone from here in twenty-four hours. But if you attempt to interfere, I will treat anyone who does so as an enemy combatant and proceed accordingly. In addition, I will burn this place to the ground. And, Sheriff, I'm reliably informed that your son is now with the fugitives. Stay out of our way and he'll live. Otherwise, well" – she pointed to where Jake Draper's body still lay on the road – "accidents happen."

————

Little did she know that right then, Sheriff Davenport was no more than twenty yards away, watching her from an upstairs window across the street. His palms itched. He needed to get hold of a gun. He needed to get to his son. He needed to make this right.

He looked away and stared down at the carpet. "With God as my witness, I'm going to fix this."

Old Man Randall didn't look up from his book of Sudoku puzzles. "Just fix the damned internet. Some of us got lives to lead."

LOCK IT DOWN

Bunny and the others watched as Beth McPherson ran around the junkyard like a whirling dervish. She closed the gates then pulled a lever to release the thick metal sheet that swung down into place, resting snugly against the gateposts. Nobody was getting through that without a whole lot of heavy ordnance. She pulled some more ropes, and metal barriers flipped up atop the front two rows of wrecks, making them look more like towers. Then she ran back to the cabin and Bunny heard the hum that signalled the electric fencing had come on. After a short while, she returned and tossed her rifle and a box of ammunition onto the hood of the Mustang.

"Okay, fence is on. Barriers down." She pointed at the top of the two piles of cars nearest the gate, where she had flipped up the barriers. "We got positions up there, with pretty thick sheet metal as cover. Leo said they'd be ... Leo said ..." She clenched her jaw, turned away, almost making it behind the car before she threw up.

"Is she—" started Bunny, but Smithy held up a hand to silence him then spoke just above a whisper.

"That asshole Jake tried to blindside us and Beth shot him."

Bunny raised his eyebrows in a question.

Smithy nodded in answer.

"Oh." Bunny looked back at where Beth was hunched down on her knees, while three alarmed dogs took turns trying to lick her face.

Rory, Diller and Joy came back from looking out the front. "We got a couple of bikers monitoring us from up the road," Joy said. "Seems like they're just watching, at least for the moment."

Rory looked around. "Do any of these cars work?"

Bunny shook his head. "Beth said the only one that would run was the station wagon."

"I'm afraid that died on us," explained Rory. "And that patrol car ain't going anywhere."

"It was a minor miracle it made it here," confirmed Diller.

"And while I like it cosy," said Joy, "I ain't getting more than one of you in that sidecar. It'd be a tight squeeze for the big fella on his own."

They turned as one towards Carlos, who was trudging back to the cabin for some reason.

"I can take a look at some of these," said Smithy, indicating the row of four vehicles. "See if there's any chance of getting them up and running. No guarantees."

"Alright," said Bunny, "give it a go."

"Oh." Diller pointed at Rory. "This is Deputy Rory. He's on our side."

Bunny shook the deputy sheriff's hand. "I'd certainly hope so. And while we're at it, you all should probably meet Sister Joy. This is Diller and Smithy."

"We've met," said the nun with a nod.

Bunny and Joy had met only the once, on what, he'd been told, was one of her very infrequent trips to New York.

"You're probably wondering what's happening?"

"Tell me later. I'm assuming it's a long story."

"That it is. By the way, not that we're not incredibly glad to see you, but how did you know there was a problem?"

"There was a tracker on your Winnebago."

"Nobody told us that," said Smithy, sounding outraged at the very notion.

Joy shrugged. "Would you rather there wasn't?"

"No, it's just ..." Smithy hesitated. "The principle of the thing."

"I'll tell you who has lots of principles. Corpses."

"It's just a bit Big Brother," said Smithy.

"Big Sister, surely?" quipped Diller.

"Anyway," said Bunny, "I don't suppose there's any chance of the cavalry showing up?"

"I am the cavalry," she said. "Mind you, weren't you supposed to make your regular phone call around now?"

Bunny checked his watch. "I guess."

"Well, they sent me on the suspicion something might be wrong. Seeing as they won't be able to raise me either now, what with there not being a phone signal round here, pretty sure they'll be certain something is wrong."

"Don't you have a satellite phone?" asked Diller.

"I did," she confessed. "Smashed it over a guy's head. Never really worked right since."

"Was it worth it?" asked Bunny.

"Felt so at the time," she said, looking around. "Am I regretting it now?" She considered this. "Actually, no. He had it coming."

"Okay," said Bunny. "Well, we can try to figure out our next move, but as of right now, Diller – and Rory, is it? Grand, would you two young fellas hop on those perches Beth pointed out and keep an eye on the opposition, please?" They both nodded. "Smithy, check the cars. Joy, if you can check the defences, I'm going to go talk to Beth."

Joy put her hand on Bunny's chest. "No, you're not. I know your heart is in the right place, but she doesn't need shock mansplained to her. Give her a few minutes to gather herself and then, when she's ready, she'll come talk to us. In the meantime, you and me can check the perimeter."

"Fair enough," said Bunny. "I ..."

He trailed off as he noticed Carlos walking over to Beth. He handed her a glass of water then walked over to the group. "Beth is sad."

"Yes," said Bunny, looking up into his big, guileless face, "she is."

"The dogs will cheer her up. Dogs are good at that."

SUPERMASSIVE BLACK HOLES

The three sisters sat there in silence, all wishing for the laptop to make any kind of noise.

"How late are they now?" asked Dionne.

"They should have checked in fourteen minutes ago," said Zoya.

The other two nodded.

"Have they ever been late before?" Tatiana asked.

"Three minutes is the record," said Zoya. "Well, was. Phone booth was in use."

"And can we reach Joy?" asked Tatiana.

"Nope."

"Right."

They both settled back into silence, with Zoya sucking the ends of her hair until she noticed Dionne giving her a look. She spat out the mouthful of strands and folded her arms.

"Hey, T, can I ask, is this what they call one of them sunken living rooms?"

"Yes," replied Tatiana, "although I believe they also call them conversation pits."

"Right."

They had arrived at their new accommodation a couple of hours ago. It was something of an upgrade from an abandoned school. It was a mansion, a full-on frickin' mansion. In Bel Air, no less. Zoya was only what Bunny had once called a "wee lass", but she'd seen *The Fresh Prince* – who hadn't? It was classic TV. She'd even seen the reboot. In other circumstances this would be cool AF. A little part of her wanted to tell Diller about it, then she remembered that Diller, along with now four other people, including Joy, was missing. Suddenly, being in a big, lit mansion seemed pretty irrelevant.

"Have you seen there's an enormous pool out back?" said Tatiana.

"Great," said Dionne. "I'll get my swimsuit."

"I'm just saying," said Tatiana, put out by the tone of rebuke in Dionne's voice.

"I'm sorry," said Dionne. "I ... You've done a great job. And thank Ms Kardashian."

"Oh, this isn't Kim's place – are you kidding? No. We really don't want to be somewhere with paparazzi stationed outside twenty-four-seven."

"Whose is it, then?" asked Zoya.

"Remember how we discussed how there were some questions you didn't want answers to?"

"That's one of those questions?" asked Zoya.

Tatiana nodded.

"Cool. Cool, cool, cool."

"How long have we got it for?" asked Dionne.

"As long as we need."

"Really?" said Zoya. "So it's, like, ours?"

"Well, I wouldn't go knocking down any walls or anything."

They went back to sitting in silence for a whole minute. Zoya almost started sucking on her hair again then remembered and stopped herself just in time.

Eventually, the hush was broken by Dionne starting to pummel a cushion repeatedly.

"Is that helping?" asked Tatiana.

Dionne stopped. "Not nearly as much as I'd hoped."

"So, how much longer are we going to give this?"

Dionne looked up at the ceiling. "No longer. It's decision time."

"Is there anyone we can send?" asked Zoya.

"There was. We already sent her. Everybody else is scattered, and seeing as we sent out 'the castle has fallen' alert about HQ, they're all going to be keeping radio silence for forty-eight hours because we put that protocol in place for some stupid reason. And even then, who do we send? I mean, has a massive black hole opened up in the Oregon mountains and are we just going to keep feeding people to it?"

"So, what do we do?"

Dionne got to her feet. "We keep feeding people to it. Zoya, you're going to be on your own for a while. I know that's not ideal but ..."

"I'll be fine."

"Tatiana, we need a vehicle. Something big enough to pick up some hitchhikers, because I'm hoping against hope this is all some spectacular series of mechanical failures that we'll all be laughing about when we reach Oregon."

"That doesn't seem like something I would laugh about."

"I was— Y'know what, never mind."

"I can get us a vehicle," said Tatiana. "But we haven't got any weapons."

"Well, let's just hope this is one of those non-violent black holes you always hear about. Now," – she stopped and looked around – "how many bathrooms does this place have?"

"Eight, I think."

"Great. Can you please tell me where any of them are?"

GAIL FORCE

Bunny scratched at his beard and studied the meagre spread of objects laid out on the trunk of the Mustang. "I think I've determined our biggest problem."

Smithy slammed the car's hood closed and wiped his hands on a rag he'd picked up. "Is it that we haven't got a serviceable vehicle to escape in? Because we haven't got a serviceable vehicle to escape in."

"Definitely nothing you can do?"

"Not unless you want to put your feet through the floor and Fred-Flintstone it out of here."

Bunny hummed an unhappy tune to himself. "We might need to consider it."

"I seriously hope you're joking."

"Which brings us back to my problem – we have that golden gun, Rory's sidearm, Beth's rifle." Bunny picked up the older shotgun and pulled the trigger. Nothing happened. "This thing, I'm guessing, has been sitting in a cupboard since before both of us were twinkles in our respective daddies' eyes, and its main use might be as a battering stick."

"I could look at it," said Smithy.

"Problem is, even if it worked, we've nothing to put in it."

"Oh."

"So that's all the weapons we have."

"Plus, your friend Sister Joy seems to have quite the bag of tricks."

"So I hear," agreed Bunny. "Although, in case you haven't noticed, it's a non-lethal one. Dionne mentioned it once. Some kind of code she lives by."

"Having seen her in action, take it from me, she's the most lethal non-lethal human being on the planet."

"She's going to need to be because, you see, the problem isn't guns, or at least *just* guns. The really big problem is ammunition. Beth has half a dozen shells for her rifle. Rory has one spare clip for his nine millimetre. Unfortunately, from there, we got the golden gun with whatever is left in that, leaving us with three armed people plus a badass nun against a whole lot of heavily armed cockwombles ..."

"And whoever this Gardner woman is, plus her two agents."

"That's right. And while it's extremely handy that Beth and Leo put some defences in place ..."

"We're still basically sitting ducks against a heavily armed enemy that vastly outnumbers us, and the only reason they're not trying to take us right now is that they don't know quite how overwhelming their advantage is?"

"Well," said Bunny, "I was hoping to put it in a more positive light than that, but yeah, essentially that."

"We've been in worse situations," said Smithy.

"Have we?"

Smithy stopped to think about it. He puffed out his cheeks. "Nothing springs to mind."

Bunny sighed. "I so enjoy our little chats."

They both looked up as Rory shouted from the far end of the yard. "Incoming!"

———

Smithy ran towards the gate, with Bunny limping behind him as fast as he could. Beth came tearing out of the cabin, and she and the dogs

232

overtook Bunny. As they all reached the gate, Joy was standing there, waving them down.

"Calm down, calm down," she said. "It ain't the full-scale invasion. It's just one woman."

"What?" asked Beth, coming to a halt.

"It's Gail," shouted Rory, from his place atop the pile of wrecks to their right.

"*Gail* Gail?" asked Beth. "The bartender from the Huntsman's Lodge? That Gail? What the hell does she want?"

"Damned if I know. Looks like she ran all the way from there to here, though."

They all stood there and watched as Gail sort of ran up the side of the road towards them. "Sort of" because she had the gait of someone who hadn't broken into a run in a very long time and was not enjoying the experience. She staggered the last few yards to the gate, her face red and puffy and her breathing sounding not unlike she was preparing for the last big push to pop out a baby.

"Hey, Gail," said Rory, "everything okay?"

Panting hard, she pointed a finger in the direction of town. "They got ... little guy ... Black guy ... sheriff's office ..." She scanned the faces of the people behind the fence and realised that Smithy was standing there looking at her. She jabbed a finger at him. "He's ..." She looked around at the rest of their number, eventually seeing Diller waving down at her from his perch atop the wrecks. "Ah ... God damn ... guess you know ..."

She moved forward to lean a hand on the fence.

"Don't!" screamed a lot of people in unison, causing Gail to snatch back her hand as if she'd just been electrocuted, which was nothing if not ironic.

"'Tis electrified," explained Bunny.

She nodded and placed her hands on her knees.

Beth stepped forward. "What the hell are you doing here, Gail?" she asked, her tone noticeably icy.

"I ... overheard them telling Gardner. Came to warn you."

"So?" asked Beth. "What do you care? You're one of them." She turned to the rest of the group. "When I went up there a few weeks ago to demand answers about what happened to Leo, it was Gail here who threw me out."

Gail, with a wince, straightened herself up and nodded. "I did. For what it's worth ... I was trying to stop you getting into trouble."

"No, you weren't."

Gail looked at her for a long moment then averted her eyes. "No, I wasn't."

"So, what's made you swap sides now?"

"They shot Pete." She continued to stare at the ground as she spoke. "That Gardner bitch, this morning. She asked – asked, mind you – if anyone didn't want to be involved in hunting these boys down. Pete stood up, said it wasn't his bag, went to leave, and she shot him in the back." She looked up suddenly and glowered down the road to where two bikes sat with their riders on them, watching. "MOTHERFUCKERS!" she screamed.

Bunny glanced up at the bikers. He guessed they were probably calling this in right now. Asking whoever was in charge how they should respond.

"So," snapped Beth, genuine anger in her voice, "they shot a man down in cold blood and because this time it was someone you cared about, you all of a sudden give a shit?"

"I didn't see what happened to Leo," she said.

"I bet you knew about it, though."

Gail paused then nodded. "That bastard Jake made some remarks. My guess is him, Ronnie and possibly Tommy were involved. They all came in late that night. I don't know where they buried him."

Bunny looked across at Beth. There was knowing and there was *knowing*. Despite what she'd been telling herself and everyone else, she'd been keeping that flickering candle of hope going, same as anyone would. Bunny saw the heartbreaking moment play out on her face when that hope died. She looked as if she might sink to the floor there and then, but suddenly a wave of anger surged through her.

"So you knew that and you said nothing to the sheriff when he came asking? Nothing to the state police when they came asking? Nothing, when we had teams of people out combing the hills, trying to find him?" She took a step forward and all but spat out the final word. "Nothing!"

Gail bit her lip and nodded again. "Yeah. I should be ashamed of myself, and I am, for all the good that'll do. I wanted out, though. *We* did – Pete and me. First guy I've ever met in my whole sorry life who treated me right. We were getting out, but you can't just up and leave somewhere like that. We were waiting for the right moment and then ... then they killed him. Maybe I deserve that, but he didn't." She looked at them now, tears streaming down her red face, making her mascara run. "She shot him down and not one of them, not one of those sons of bitches that were supposed to be his friend lifted a finger." She started pacing now. "And you know what they did with him? They just dumped his body out back in an oil drum. Beside the dumpsters. Like trash. Like goddamn trash!" She stumbled and fell messily onto the side of the road, landing on her backside. "He wasn't trash," she said, before dropping her head between her knees.

Beth covered her face with her hands and Cerberus the dog jumped up on her, balancing his one front leg on her thigh, whining with concern. The others simply looked at each other – nobody knew what to say.

It was Smithy who spoke first. "We should probably open the gate and ..."

Beth's head flew up. "No! She's not coming in."

"But—"

"But nothing. This is my place. Mine and Leo's. A woman who was ..." She looked up at Rory. "What's that phrase you use? An accessory after the fact. Yeah, a woman who was an accessory after the fact in his murder doesn't get to come in just because she's suddenly realised she's been hanging out with the scum of the earth. No!"

Sister Joy moved over to stand beside Beth. Then, after a couple of seconds, she spoke in a quiet voice. "I get it. I mean, I've lost people too, and the pain. The pain is something else. Those responsible need to answer for what they've done."

"You're damn right!" said Beth through gritted teeth, running the back of her hand across her cheeks to wipe away the tears.

Joy nodded. "But this isn't the way."

Beth's eyes widened. "Do you think she'd let me in if the situation was reversed?"

Joy shrugged. "I don't know. To be honest, I don't care. An eye for an eye and the whole world is blind. All that pain, all that grief, none of it is going to feel one ounce better because you leave her out there to die. And she will. Everybody deserves a second chance."

"No," said Beth. "Not her."

"Okay, then," said Joy, raising her voice. "Open the gate."

"I said she can't come in."

"She's not. I'm going out. Because I'm not throwing her to the wolves, regardless of who she is or what she did or didn't do. Because I know I've done things as bad as she has. Hell, a whole load worse. And if she doesn't deserve a second chance, then I don't either. If this is how it is, then this is how it is."

Beth looked at Joy for a very long moment before turning on her heel and walking away towards the cabin, all three dogs following in her wake.

"Fine," she shouted without looking back. "The bitch can come in."

THINGS THAT MAKE YOU GO BOOM

Beth lifted the old crate and felt a splinter dig into the soft flesh of the palm of her left hand.

"Argh, goddamn it!" She tossed the crate down. "Eff you, you useless piece of splintery trash." She tried to look at her hand in what fading light was available in the old mill as the sun set outside. A flicker of movement in the corner of her eye caught her attention and she jumped. "Jesus!"

"No," said Sister Joy, "definitely not him." She held out a bowl. "Carlos and Diller made a delicious and nutritious chilli in your kitchen."

"I know. They came and asked permission."

"Such polite boys." Joy proffered the meal again. "Here."

"No, thanks, I'm not hungry."

"Yeah, I don't really care if you are or not. It's been a long day, it's going to be one hell of a long night, and you need to keep your strength up, so eat the chilli."

Beth took the bowl and plonked herself down on one of the crates she'd just moved. She held her face over the chilli and inhaled deeply. It did smell good. Some part of her body that she'd been ignoring suddenly got a word in edgeways and acknowledged she was in fact famished. She picked up the spoon and took a couple of mouthfuls. "Jeez, that is good."

"Yeah," said Joy, looking around at the clutter of broken machinery, random bits of wood and discarded furniture that sat amidst the sea of crates and cardboard boxes. "I've heard nothing but good things."

Beth raised an eyebrow at this.

"I don't eat meat no more," Joy clarified. "Amongst many other things. Diller made a nice vegetarian one for me and him, though. Apparently, he's not eating beef any more. Something about making a deal with a bull that I didn't really understand."

Joy sat there in silence as Beth finished the bowl. As she waited, she produced a green apple from somewhere and started polishing it meticulously on her T-shirt. She must have brought it with her as Beth knew for a fact that she didn't have any in.

"Better?" Joy asked, when the last morsel had been scraped up.

"It turns out I was hungry after all."

"Told you." The subject of food now seemingly closed, Joy inclined her head towards the crates and boxes. "So, why don't you tell me what you think you're doing here?"

Beth noted the phrasing. "What I'm trying to do is find some extra ammunition for my grandpa's rifle or his shotgun. Not having much success."

"Is it likely he'd bury it under all this crap?"

"Hard to say. As you can see, he was quite the hoarder. We were always meaning to clean this place out properly but ..."

"Got away from you," said Joy. "That happens."

Beth turned back to the crates and started poking through the one she'd just uncovered. Joy seemed disinclined to go anywhere else, so she just sat there.

Eventually Beth couldn't take it any more and spoke. "So, I guess I made a fool of myself earlier on."

"No," said Joy, "you didn't. You were angry and you had every right to be."

"For all the good it did me."

Joy clucked her tongue. "Yeah, that's the thing – anger has its place, but most of the time, it's just a spectacular waste of time. Usually, it's just there because we're using it to push other stuff down."

"Is that right?" said Beth. "Why do I feel like I'm being analysed?"

"Oh, no, not by me."

As Joy spoke, Beth took out a promising-looking cardboard box and opened it up to reveal some, but not all, of the pieces of a chess set. She showed it to Joy then tossed it aside wordlessly, before turning back to the box. "That's a relief. I was worried you were going to go digging around in my fractured psyche."

"There's no need to go digging," said Joy simply. "It's right there on the surface. Thank you, by the way."

This got Beth's undivided attention. "For what?"

"That Jake guy had me cold. Second shot and I'd have been dead."

"And now he is," said Beth. She had been trying for flippant but couldn't nail the landing.

"Yeah," said Joy, "and the funny thing, which isn't funny at all, is that you know you had to do it. You know he was going to keep shooting at you, me, anyone in that general direction. You know he was a terrible person and now, thanks to Gail, you one hundred percent locked on, cast in stone, know that he killed the man you love, and you're angry as hell."

"I am."

"But not about that part."

"Excuse me?" asked Beth in a quiet voice.

"That's the worst of it," said Joy. "You're angry at yourself. Because your mind is telling you that you should feel good about it, justified, righteous, and all you want to do is lie down and cry because you killed a man."

Beth stopped rummaging, a trio of old books held limply in her hands, forgotten, as tears filled her eyes. "I thought you said you weren't here to analyse me?"

"Yep. I guess I lied about that. Unfortunately, we don't have the time for you to work through all the stages of whatever by yourself, so I figured I'd supercharge the process."

Beth sniffed then slammed the books back into the crate before turning around. "Is this an area you're qualified in?"

"What? Therapy?"

"No. Killing," said Beth. "Didn't I hear how you're all about the non-lethal approach and all that?" Even as she said the words, Beth hated herself. This woman had done nothing except save her life, so why was she spitting vitriol?

Joy bit into her apple, chewed several times then swallowed before speaking again. "I am now, but that's not what you're asking, and yes, in answer to your real question, I've taken life. Several times."

"And did they all deserve to die?"

Joy regarded her apple carefully. "I don't know if I'm qualified to answer that. What I will say is, some of 'em were real bad people. Real bad. And most of the time, it was self-defence. Or it was defending someone else. Put it this way – the law knows about the majority of these incidents, and I've never served time for any of them, so take from that what you will. I also know that every one, no matter how justified, no matter how awful the other party, weighs on my soul."

Beth bit her top lip. "And how do you deal with that?"

"Oh, it's not easy, but here's the thing – it shouldn't be easy. If you're the kind of person who takes a life and feels fine about it, that's when you're truly broken. You're beating yourself up because your mind is a tornado of conflicting thoughts and you can't get them straight. I'm here to tell you, all that says about you is that you're a good person. Sorry if you thought you were going to get to be one of those stone-cold killers, because that ain't you."

"So if it's us or them, tonight or whenever," said Beth, "the bastard horde of fuckwits currently assembling at our gates—"

"Am I going to start filling body bags?" finished Joy. "Nope. I certainly don't intend to. My path isn't yours, though. A couple of years ago, I was told I was supposed to be dead in months, weeks.

Hell, if those doctors were honest, I think they were surprised I was still perambulating at that point. I had my moment of, call it what you want, and I decided to live whatever life I have left a certain way. By a certain code. I'm not saying it's for everybody, but it seems to be working for me. For a start, I'm alive, for some inexplicable reason. Don't know how long for, but then, hey, none of us do. We could all be dead in the morning."

Beth nodded. "I know that's a phrase people say all the time, but it does feel particularly pertinent to our current predicament."

"Yeah," agreed Joy. "We're outnumbered, outgunned and we've got all kinds of morals going on over on this side of the fence, whereas the other side seems to have absolutely none."

"How are you standing there saying all that and not sounding that worried by it?"

Joy shrugged. "I'm supposed to be dead, remember? It's hard to get that wound up. Besides, I'm a member of the Sisters of the Saint. Impossible odds is kinda our thing, baby."

"Is this the order of nuns you're a part of?"

"Yep."

"You don't sound like any nuns I've ever heard of."

"Ain't that the truth," said Joy, standing up and patting down the back of her trousers. "But I don't think we have the kind of time to get into all of that. Ask me about it some other occasion, though. There are stories."

Beth smiled. "I'll do that."

"And in the meantime," said Joy, "give the treasure hunt another half hour tops then come in and sit down. I'm sure you can take a shift on guard at some point, but before then, I think your dogs are missing you."

"They've got Carlos."

"Yeah, but you're still you." Joy started walking away shouting "Half an hour," over her shoulder as she did so.

Joy left the mill and had almost reached the cabin when Beth's hollers brought her back.

When Joy returned, Beth was standing back and pointing at a

wooden box that had been sitting under the crate she had just moved. Joy edged forward carefully and looked at where she was pointing. "Is that ..."

"I'm pretty sure it is."

"Well, well, well," said Joy. "That's certainly a development."

SIEGE MENTALITY

Sieges, thought Bunny, were in many ways a lost art form. Troy, for example. Now, there was a proper siege. It had it all – heroes, villains, wife-nicking, big horses full of more than just teddy bears. The film didn't do it justice, of course, but that's the way of these things. Brad Pitt had been terribly miscast as Achilles. Him being almost invulnerable was reasonably credible, at least, compared to the idea that a city with any women still alive in it would leave him waiting outside for ten seconds, never mind ten years.

These days, most so-called sieges involved some nutter taking hostages and threatening to do something awful. Bunny had once been involved in one in Dublin, where a bloke took his ex-girlfriend hostage and said he wouldn't release her until Bono stopped wearing those ridiculous sunglasses. It was unique among sieges in that the hostage appeared to be entirely onboard with the demand. Frankly, a great number of the Garda in attendance expressed support too – unofficially, of course. The couple used their time together to discuss the issues that had blighted their relationship and made significant progress in the reconciliation stakes, as was evidenced by the fact that when the Garda armed response unit broke the door in, they found the pair coming to a very amicable resolution on the kitchen table. Bunny got an invitation to the wedding. Bono did not.

This siege was a very different beast. He was sitting up on one of the, what he supposed you could call, towers of wrecked cars that Beth and Leo had constructed. In front of him was a thick sheet of metal with slots in it, making it a tremendously defensible position as far as these things went. It even had a ladder, which meant he could limp up there and take a shift on guard duty, same as everybody else.

They were taking it in turns to keep watch on what the opposition was up to outside the gate. It was an odd situation; Team Gobshite could attempt to storm the place at any moment, but they seemed to be taking their time. That worried Bunny. His philosophy in any conflict was to try to make his opponent act rashly. The Sportsmen had proven themselves to be largely feeble-minded fucknuggets whose ignorance was matched only by their ineptitude; he guessed this more considered approach was thanks to this Colonel Gardner woman. The only advantage he and his allies had was a lead in the smarts department and it looked like that might be lost. Now they were just eight people trying to hold off an army.

Eight sounded like a workable number of people in terms of defending a position, until you started to break those numbers down. One was Carlos, who might weigh in at a fistfight, but he wasn't going to start shooting at people. Neither was Diller. Beth – it was hard to know what was going on there, and Bunny was treading lightly. Gail, the former bartender – she, on the other hand, was wildly keen to get hold of a gun and start firing. They'd almost had to wrestle one off her. The reality was, they only had three working guns anyway, and a pitiful supply of ammunition. Bunny guessed that if left to her own devices, Gail would have long since fired every bullet they had at the men outside the gate, and then attempted to bludgeon them to death with anything else she could get her hands on. The woman was clearly not perfect, but you couldn't fault her fighting spirit.

The unsporting Sportsmen's barricade were lines of vehicles, to which they'd added piles of wood, sheets of metal and some bales of hay they'd somehow liberated from somewhere. They looked a lot like barricades being constructed by people paying undue attention to ensuring their trucks' paintwork went undamaged. They'd gone about setting up these barricades while bobbing and weaving to avoid incoming fire that wasn't coming. Nobody on Team Junkyard was firing because they were holding on to the bullets they had until they really needed them. More surprisingly, nobody on the other side was shooting either, and Bunny highly doubted that stemmed from a desire to conserve ammunition. The only thing less likely was that it stemmed from a desire for a peaceful resolution. The shouted comments directed at Beth from the other side of the fence had made it clear that while an asshole in life, in death Jake was headed for martyrdom, and they intended to avenge him.

Team Gobshite soon came to regret starting the war of words. Team Junkyard had them entirely outgunned in those stakes. Denied the access to firearms she craved, Gail had taken to psychological warfare like a duck to water, or more accurately, like a match to gasoline. She'd come up to sit beside Bunny and it had ended up being quite the show. Rule number one – never, ever piss off a bartender. They know everything. And Gail did not hold back. One lad's problems with erectile dysfunction got an airing. The revelation of who really stole three hundred bucks from someone's wallet last year didn't go down well either. Nor did the detailed explanation of exactly how one of them cheated at poker. One guy at least found out why his marriage was failing, although the bit where it transpired his best mate was dropping around to offer his wife support that went considerably beyond that of the moral variety was Bunny's favourite part. It caused an actual fistfight. Only intervention from a third party who dived in to disarm one of the participants prevented it from turning into a full-on firefight. Still, nothing raised morale like watching your enemy knocking seven bells out of each other.

Eventually, someone in the opposition ranks came up with the idea of playing loud music to drown out Gail entirely. It appeared to be a Kid Rock album. It was true what they said. In war, there truly were no winners.

Gail stood up to scream, "Bunch of pussies," before Bunny

quickly dragged her back down, in the most gentlemanly way possible.

"For feck's sake, Gail. I know they've not been shooting yet but, and take this for the compliment that it is, I think they might be willing to make an exception for you."

"I hate those sons of bitches so much," she hissed with real venom.

"I'm getting that. To be fair, I think they are too. There are three dogs wandering around behind us, and I'd imagine they've picked up on the vibes by now as well."

"Sorry, it's just ... I dunno, just ... They just let Pete die and did nothing."

Bunny didn't really know what to say to that. Gail didn't seem to expect anything. She just looked off into the distance and watched the sunset.

"Actually, not to change the subject," began Bunny, while definitely changing the subject, "but I think you and I need to have a debrief."

She eyed him suspiciously. "I ain't taking mine or anyone else's briefs off."

"No," said Bunny quickly. "Quite right. I meant, I've got some questions. You might have some information that could be of help to us in our current predicament, and we can use all the help we can get."

It turned out Gail was a regular fount of knowledge. The Sportsman's League had come into possession of all these guns about a week ago. Jake and a few of the others had disappeared for a couple of days and came back driving the big eighteen-wheeler they'd seen parked in the Huntsman's Lodge's parking lot. There'd been mention of ripping off an army shipment, which explained a lot.

She also revealed that the vast majority of their membership had been sent out in two-man teams first thing that morning to look for Bunny and the boys. They didn't have enough radios, so they'd been instructed to send up a flare if they located their quarry. This explained why they hadn't come in all guns blazing just yet. They were probably only just getting back from a long day of finding feck all. At least one of them had got overexcited and sent up a flare, which is why Agents Draper and Newton had run off. Bunny had to acknowledge that over the course of a couple of days where their luck had shot past bad into shocking and dangerously close to must-have-driven-a-truck-full-of-mirrors-off-a-cliff, this was a welcome bit of good fortune. If Gardner's two attack dogs had been readily available to her, he doubted their side would have adopted their current wait-and-see approach.

"How come you know everything that goes on in that place, Gail?" asked Bunny.

"Well, aside from the fact that most men are drunken idiots who love to hear the sound of their own voices?" she said. Then added, "Present company excepted."

"Well, I can name a few people who'd take issue with that assessment of me, but go on."

"The Lodge is an old building," Gail began. "The air-con and heating systems are both relics, which was why they finally got a new AC unit a couple of months ago. Until that idiot Jake shot the thing up, fucking fool. Not to speak ill of the dead."

Bunny was fairly sure that definitely qualified as speaking ill but he let it pass.

"But there's all the old pipes," she continued. "They all lead into the kitchen that sits off the bar." She gave an odd smile. "I bake sometimes. Did a whole lot today."

Bunny had only recently met Gail, so he genuinely had no idea why she was grinning at him like she was informing him she'd just won the lottery. "Cookies. Lot of cookies."

"Okay," said Bunny. "Bit of a sweet tooth myself. Did you bring any with you?"

"Noooo."

"Right."

"Anyway," she went on, offering no explanation for her glee. "If you stand in the kitchen and open the right vent when the place isn't too busy, you can hear conversations going on in most parts of the place."

"Really?"

"That's right," confirmed Gail. "That's how I heard Gardner talking to Jake and Ronnie earlier today. She and her two bozos turned up unexpectedly this morning, y'see. Oh, and by the way, that Draper guy is, was – whatever – Jake's cousin."

"Interesting," said Bunny, wondering how Draper would take a death in the family.

"Gardner said they got someone seriously badass coming in tomorrow evening to buy most of the guns, but what really got her mad is that the golden one is gone."

Bunny pulled the weapon in question out of the back of his trousers. "This?"

"I guess."

"How much is it worth?"

"Oh, I don't know. What I do know is, she said it has information or something on it. Like, hidden, and that's what this buyer really wants. She said that without it, they only had half the deal and that was going to get them all killed."

Bunny studied the gun in his hands and turned it over. It looked like an ordinary gun once you got past the ludicrous gold-plated thing. "That explains a lot." Like, for example, why everyone seemed so desperate to get reacquainted with them.

"Yeah," said Gail, pointing at it. "That there is one hell of a bargaining chip."

Just then, the Kid Rock album was turned off.

"Hey," yelled Bunny, "I was listening to that."

He said this because, more than anything, he wanted them to believe that it was true.

Gail's face lit up. "Oh, goodie. I've got loads more stuff ready to rock."

Before she got a chance to let rip, a female voice shouted from the barricades outside. "Good evening, ladies and gentlemen."

Bunny looked across at the other tower, where Rory and Diller were sitting. Not that it was necessary, but Rory pointed excitedly and mouthed something. In the fading light, Bunny couldn't tell what it was, but he'd guess it was something along the lines of "that's her".

"I am Colonel Gardner. I met Ms McPherson earlier, but I'm afraid the rest of you have me at a loss."

"Would now be a good time to tell you that you are under arrest?" shouted Rory.

"Is that our missing sheriff?" asked Gardner.

"No," said Rory. "Glad to hear he got away, though."

There was a slight pause. Bunny wondered if that was because Gardner had inadvertently given away something she hadn't meant to.

"Ah," came her voice again. "The son. How lovely. I am glad to see that your family feud is not a full rift."

"It's not that," said Rory. "I'm just glad to hear your stellar record for catching people is still intact."

Bunny nodded approvingly. Get your shots in where you can.

"I would like to speak to whoever is in charge," said Gardner, sounding slightly more annoyed. "Not the child."

"I'm afraid," shouted Bunny, "we don't have one of them. 'Tis very much a collective effort."

"I see. Spoken like a true leader. Are you the man who led your merry band into this trap?"

"Trap?" repeated Bunny. "Seems more like a fortress from where I'm sitting."

"Does it?" said Gardner, a mocking lilt to her voice. "I wonder if you'll feel the same when we burn you out?"

"Oh dear," responded Bunny, holding up the golden gun quickly. "Are you not worried that'll damage your precious golden gun?"

"You're overestimating the value of gold considerably, sir."

"Am I?" Bunny shifted around, still trying to see if he could see anything through the peephole, but in the fading light, all he could make out were vague shapes. "To be fair, I was talking about the valuable information on it. Y'know, the stuff your buyer paid very good money for."

On this occasion, another, longer silence descended outside the yard.

"I don't know what you're talking about," came Gardner's voice eventually.

"Yeah," said Bunny. "And to use a phrase common to my native people – pull the other one, it's got my sweaty bollocks attached to it. You know exactly what I'm talking about."

"You are well informed."

"I'm afraid your boat has a leak."

Gail looked as if she was about to say something, but Bunny shushed her by putting his finger to his lips. Much better to let Gardner stew on that herself.

"While I'm enjoying our little chat," said Gardner, "any time I like, we can overwhelm you, come in and take it."

"Off you go, then."

"But," said Gardner, "I would rather avoid bloodshed."

"Really?" said Bunny. "Am I definitely speaking to Colonel Gardner, because from all I've heard, she's a fecking psycho?"

"Shut up," came the sharp response.

"Sorry," said Bunny, "did I hit a nerve?"

"I will make it very simple," said Gardner slowly. "If you hand over the gun, I will allow all of you to leave."

"Are you sure about that? Because not that long ago, the lads over there were making quite a lot of threats in the direction of the owner of this here enterprise."

"They will do what I tell them to."

"Right," said Bunny. "How's that working out for you so far?"

Gardner ignored the dig. "Because I am a reasonable woman, I will leave that offer on the table until dawn. Then, if you'd rather not take it, I shall rain down hell upon you."

"Well," said Bunny, "I'll talk to the collective and see how we feel. Does this offer cover the dogs?"

"Yes."

"And if we don't take it, what was it you said you'd do again? Rain down hell?"

"Correct."

"Okay," said Bunny. "Just so we're clear, is that the name of the Kid Rock album?"

"You have until dawn."

Before Bunny could respond, the music was turned back on.

Gail nodded approvingly at Bunny. "You've got a real flair for making friends."

COOKIE MONSTERS

An hour later, Colonel Gardner looked around the bar of the Huntsman's Lodge and the sorry excuses for men who were sitting in it. Despite the complete mess they had made of carrying out simple tasks the entire day, they were happily kicking back, drinking beer and shoving cookies into their imbecilic faces. The image of taking a flamethrower to the lot of them washed across her mind, and it warmed the cockles of her heart.

Draper and Newton stood beside her.

"You seriously want us to go into battle with this bunch of idiots?" asked Newton.

"With? No. This troop of inbred buffoons is literally the very definition of cannon fodder. This is what you end up with when it's been too long since your nation has had a proper war. They're the country's version of an embarrassing vestigial tail. What they are good for is shooting and getting shot at, we will handle the rest. It's not like the opposition should be that challenging. Which two set off a flare and sent everyone on a wild-goose chase?"

Newton nodded towards the corner where the remarkably fat man and his little friend were talking between themselves. "Those two."

"Yeah," said Draper. "Man, what I'd give to put a bullet through that lardass's brain."

"Not just now," said Gardner. Then added, "Although, when this is over, feel free."

"Whatever happens, I want to take out the bitch who killed my cousin."

Gardner gave him an assessing look. "We do not make emotional decisions."

"You can do what the hell you like," said Draper. "I'm getting revenge."

She narrowed her eyes. "I think you've forgotten who is in command here."

"Yeah, yeah. Are you, though? In case you haven't noticed, we aren't in the army any more, and so you don't outrank us. We're not a unit, we're a criminal gang."

Before Gardner could respond, Newton stepped in and placed a hand on Draper's chest. "Okay, let's all stay nice and calm. We're almost there. I'll go check on the barriers, make sure they're doing their jobs. In the meantime, we should probably make sure these idiots don't get too drunk."

"Good point," said Gardner, moving forward to address the room. "Gentlemen."

All heads in the room turned to face her.

"I appreciate you've had a long day. I'd strongly suggest that you cease all alcohol consumption immediately and get some rest."

"Yeah," said Ronnie, standing up from one of the tables at the far end of the bar. "She's right. We all need to be fresh tomorrow so we can kick the asses of these insurgents and seek vengeance for our fallen brother."

Gardner turned her back on the men so that only Draper and Newton could see her exasperated eye roll.

"In fact," continued Ronnie, "I think we should dedicate this valiant battle to a great man and a true patriot ..." He raised his glass. "To Jake."

The rest of the room got to their feet and echoed, "To Jake."

"Christ almighty," said Newton. "Guy's a saint now."

Draper turned to glare at him. "He was family."

"Not mine."

The two men locked eyes fiercely before the tension was broken by Gardner. "Honestly. Look at them, sitting around with their beer and their cookies. Where did they even get the cookies?"

Something scratched at the back of Gardner's mind. She stepped forward again and addressed the table of four sitting nearest to her. "Where did all these cookies come from?"

"There's a massive tray full of them," a gangly man said nervously. "There's probably some of them left."

"Yes, but where did they come from?"

One of the other men chipped in. "Gail makes 'em for special occasions." He lowered his voice. "To be honest, these aren't as nice as they normally are, but hey, can't hit the bullseye every time."

"Gail?" repeated Gardner. "The bartender, Gail?"

All four men nodded.

"The woman who earlier today ran out and joined the opposition, probably just after she took those cookies out of the oven?"

Three of the men at least had the intelligence to look concerned by this unfolding of logic. The fourth guy was still munching away happily on his cookie.

Gardner screamed so loudly that somebody at the far end of the bar dropped their glass and it smashed on the floor. "Jesus Christ, you people are unbelievable!" She rested her hand on her gun and several of the Sportsmen ducked. She turned around to resist the urge to thin the herd, and instead walked back to Draper and Newton. "Stop. Eating. The damned cookies!"

WHEN TOMORROW COMES

Smithy and Diller sat up on the tower, side by side in the darkness save for the occasional beam of moonlight that broke through the clouds. Any other light source was out of the question for obvious reasons – namely that it'd give a bored Sportsman something to take a pop at to liven up his evening. Smithy couldn't tell, with all the comings and goings, how many of them were over there right now. That Gardner woman had given them until the morning, but it wasn't as if they were going to take her at her word that they could all have a lovely night's sleep without incident.

"Do you know what this is like?" asked Diller.

"*The Magnificent Seven*?"

"That's exactly what I was going to say!"

"Would I be Steve McQueen?" asked Smithy.

"I was thinking of the remake."

"The remake?" repeated Smithy, sounding appalled. "Are you out of your mind?"

"I am not," said Diller. "Three reasons – firstly, Denzel."

"Okay, I'll give you that," conceded Smithy. As they had oft discussed, Denzel Washington, Meryl Streep and Tom Hanks were the holy trinity of modern Hollywood. Good in everything and good stuff got made just because they were willing to be in it.

"Secondly," continued Diller, "the villagers in the original are a bit whack. I mean, seriously – an entire village of farmers living in Wild West times, and none of them have seen a gun before? Weak."

"Okay – you might have a point there."

"And thirdly, the new one's got one of them Sarsgaards as the big bad. I know there's, like, fourteen of them, but that family can act."

"Okay," said Smithy, "but you got to see it in context. The original redefined the genre. I mean, Yul Brynner."

"Did you know that he and McQueen hated each other? It was McQueen's big break, but Brynner was paranoid about looking short on film. He kept making piles of dirt to stand on for his marks, and McQueen kept kicking them over."

Smithy chuckled. "In which case, Bunny can be Brynner and I'll be McQueen."

"What about Charles Bronson?"

"That's Joy, obviously."

"To be fair, I don't think Bronson was as kick-ass as her. I mean she took out an SUV with a tree."

"Yeah," agreed Smithy. "As an environmentalist, it's hard to know if that's a win or a loss, but as one of the guys being chased, I was sure happy about it. She's a worthy Bronson."

Diller nodded. "I guess that'd make me Robert Vaughn's character, then – the guy who lost his nerve and was too scared to shoot."

"What?" said Smithy. "Don't talk crazy, D."

"It's true. You're all out here, standing your ground against insane odds, and where do you want me to be? Back hiding in the cabin."

"That's bullshit," said Smithy. "Nobody, and I mean nobody, is questioning your bravery. I've seen you literally ride your bike into a van moving at high speed to force it to stop. That's one of the most courageous things I've ever seen. Violence isn't your thing, and I – no, we all – respect that. You don't have to prove anything to anybody.

Plus, we don't have any more guns. Do you want to be out here throwing rocks at guys packing assault rifles?"

"Couldn't hurt," said Diller.

"It really, really could. This is deadly serious, Dill."

"I know that."

"Also, somebody has to take care of Carlos. Anything happens to him, those two nuns are dead, and more importantly, he's an innocent in all this. If you two need to go hide under the horse, you do it."

"Not to point out the obvious flaw in that plan," said Diller, "but if you're all dead, there won't be anyone to let us out. We might as well stand behind the dragon and see if we can direct its flame at ..."

Diller sat there, staring off into the distance.

"Erm, Dill," said Smithy, "don't know if you've realised, but you just sort of stopped talking mid-sentence?"

Diller hopped up, careful to remain crouched so as not to pop into anyone's line of fire. "I have to go."

"And do what?" asked Smithy, instantly suspicious.

"I've got an idea."

"What is it?"

"Don't worry about it."

"Nothing makes me worry more than you saying don't worry about it."

"I'll see you later."

Before Smithy could utter another word, Diller was down the ladder and away into the night.

"Dill! Goddamn it."

Smithy peered into the night and considered going after him, but was distracted by a pinging noise. Out of his back pocket he pulled the display unit Beth had given him and looked at it.

According to it, they had company.

THE MAN WHO FELL TO EARTH

It was a matter of principle.

Jake may have been a jerk, but he was Draper's cousin and family is family. Draper had never been to Paradise before, but every summer, Jake and his dad would come down to visit their place outside Reno for a week. Jake's dad would dump his son then head to the casinos to go blow whatever money he had saved up on booze, gambling, and Draper guessed a couple of other things, too. He and Jake had been friends as kids, but then, being friends as kids is really pretty easy. "Want to go poke a dead lizard with a stick? Cool. Off we go." Later in life, people develop interests and opinions and, consequently, a higher propensity for being an asshole. It seemed Jake had availed of that opportunity. Draper, on the other hand, had been in actual foxholes. Stupid prejudice didn't last in there very long. Cover fire was cover fire, didn't matter what colour skin the person providing it had.

If he'd been entirely honest with Newton, Draper would have admitted he had no idea Jake was into all that White-power bullshit these days, and when it had come out, it had been embarrassing. Newton had barely spoken to him since this morning, and he'd never seen him this mad. The guy was an iceberg, legendarily so, so for him to have gone off at him, this really must've bothered him.

Still, that aside, some bitch had killed his cousin, and she was going to pay for that. Some mouthy Scottish dude had that stupid golden gun too, which was messing up the deal that was going to give Draper the nest egg he needed, now that he was pensionless and persona non grata to the military that had been his only real family since the age of eighteen. He could kill two people in one trip and settle all of this. Hell, if the opportunity presented itself, Draper could take them all out. He was going to do as much as he could with his knife, too. That was kind of his signature move. The personal touch and the woman who killed his cousin deserved such considerations. Besides, if Draper handled this whole situation, he'd remind Newton what a badass he was and why they'd planned to go into business together when this was all done. That, and they'd be able to get the hell out of this one-horse town ASAP.

Cloudy night, limited vision. Dry. No wind. These were perfect conditions for abseiling. The climb up here had been tricky, but he was trained to deal with exactly that kind of situation. Hell, any situation – that was the point. Admittedly, night-vision goggles would have been handy, but they'd come loaded to deal with a simple handover of weapons, not the invasion of a small country. Besides, they were up against amateurs. The only reason this bullshit wasn't already over was that he and Newton had been off the board, on a wild-goose chase because one of these idiots they'd been forced to work with saw what was probably a deer and set off a flare like a teenager seeing his first titty.

Draper kneeled down at the cliff's edge, staying absolutely still for a couple of minutes. No sounds from below, at least nothing he could make out over that dumbass Kid Rock album they were playing on loop to piss off the opposition. It was annoying, but on the upside it'd also conceal any noise from his descent. Not that there'd be any. Draper was the master at this. Case in point, the trick to limiting exposure was dropping just enough rope so that the line ended a couple of feet from the ground, and he started to feed it down carefully now. The guys in the squad had always been amazed by his uncanny ability to get this right every time.

Satisfied that he'd dropped enough, he tied off the rope on the couple of climbing bolts he'd inserted securely into the top of the cliff. That done, it was Australian rappel time. Facing downwards so you could see what was coming. In one smooth motion he was over the side and gone. Harness tight to his back, right hand feeding the rope, left hand holding his Glock. Nothing was more fun than running down the side of a cliff. This was living.

Fifty feet ...

Forty feet ...

Thirty ...

Twenty ...

He heard it before he felt it. A twang of something being fired and then, a half-second later, electricity coursing through his body. The instantaneous spasm caused him to fall the rest of the way, the Glock flying out of his hand as he tumbled through the air.

He hit the ground hard, but recovered enough sense to go to pull his knife. He stopped at the cold, hard sensation of the muzzle of a gun pressing behind the back of his left ear.

"I really wouldn't, if I was you, fella," said the voice. "'Tis already a long night and none of us wants to draw lots to see who cleans up what little brains you have. Hands behind your back."

Several sets of feet gathered around him suddenly. Reluctantly, Draper did as he was told. He felt a pair of hands slapping cuffs on him, then he was pulled up to his feet. A short Asian woman with a shaved head stood in front of him.

"How the fuck?" said Draper.

"Which part?" asked the voice behind him. "How did we know you were up there? Well now, would you believe a gent called Leo installed motion-detectors up there, as well as everywhere else? Or was it how did you get taken down in mid-air like that? Well, turns out that Joy here has a Taser with a nice bit of range and accuracy."

"Yeah," the Asian woman agreed, wielding the odd weapon that looked more like a plastic laser-tag toy than a real gun. "Those spikes currently attached to your body are part of a design that's still patent pending, so we'd appreciate your discretion."

Draper ignored her, as his eyes fell on the woman standing nervously behind her. "You're the one who killed Jake, aren't you? He was my cousin. Before this is done, I'm going to kill you slow. Real slow."

Draper crumpled to the ground as fifty thousand volts passed through his body.

"Oops," said the Asian woman. "My bad. Still getting used to the buttons."

ONLY THE LONELY

Zoya sat on the couch, laptop on her knees, and tried to resist the urge to bite her nails. The light of a new day was touching the sky outside, which meant that she'd been up all night. Dionne, before she and Tatiana had left, had told her to get some sleep, but there was no chance of that. She was a night owl at the best of times, and that was when everybody she knew wasn't in mortal danger, or worse. She glanced at her cell phone, which lay beside her on the couch, and resisted the urge to call or text Dionne again. She'd get in contact when she had news. No point in pestering her.

Zoya checked the laptop screen again. The Sisters, being the Sisters, had all manner of ways of getting in contact. From here, Zoya could monitor every one of them, bar a couple of physical drop boxes. There were numbers they could call or text. Mailboxes where they could leave messages. Email addresses they could mail. She had a live feed of a video camera in an all-night bakery in Queens where you could just walk in, and facial recognition would send an alert. All kinds of ways. Nevertheless, two days later, Sister Dorothy had not availed herself of any of them. Zoya was trying to think of reasons why that would be. Any reason bar the extremely obvious one. There was all that and the fact that Diller and his crew were also now missing. It was pissing her off immensely, and she was looking forward to telling somebody about it, just as soon as anybody she was willing to talk to had reported in alive.

She almost knocked the laptop to the floor when it pinged. A message ... but not the one she was hoping for. This one was from the address used by the people holding Bernadette and Assumpta. Some weird part of Zoya felt bad for being more focused on Dorothy and Diller and the rest. In a way, Bernadette and Assumpta, while in terrible danger, were also oddly safer than the rest of them. They were hidden away somewhere, and their captors needed to keep them alive if they ever wanted to get hold of Carlos Breida, or rather the secrets that lay locked in his head. Still, given the obsessive hunt that the Ratenda Cartel had launched for all of those involved, she couldn't rule out that something bad might have happened to them too.

The email contained just one video file. She started the process of running it through the suite of programs she'd customised to make sure it contained no nasty surprises then, while they were doing their thing, she walked into the kitchen and rechecked the fridge for something she could drink. Orange juice. All they had was orange juice. She needed something caffeinated, carbonated and, ideally, something health campaigners were currently trying to get banned – that way you knew you were getting the good stuff.

She poured herself a glass of OJ and headed back into the living room. As she sat back down on the couch, the laptop trilled a trumpet sound effect to indicate that the video was certified clean.

She looked at the file on the screen for just a moment. Dionne preferred to handle all this stuff directly, but she wasn't here. Zoya could wait, but what if it was time-sensitive? Some things couldn't wait, especially as they didn't know how long whatever Dionne was heading into was going to take to resolve. Like it or not, Zoya was the one who had to deal with this. She worked her fingers and rolled her head around her neck. Just do it. Don't think about how bad it could be, about what images you might be about to see. Just do it. These people, whoever they were, needed to keep Bernadette and Assumpta alive. That was assuming, of course, that the Cartel hadn't caught up with them already.

Stop thinking about it. Just do it. Do it. Do it.

Zoya stabbed a finger at the keyboard and the video file started to play.

There was a burst of snowstorm static and then the picture changed to show a dirty tiled floor before spinning around to reveal Bernadette. She was sitting on a plastic chair, with a bland brick wall behind her. Tied to a similar chair next to her sat Assumpta, gagged and blindfolded, with a gun held to her left temple. Both of the women looked bruised and haggard. Bernadette still had a little swelling above her right eye, and she looked thin. It was hard to see Assumpta's face, but the knitted sweater she was wearing was ragged and full of holes.

Bernadette looked down the lens, a little groggy, her eyelids slightly hooded. Then her focus moved to someone behind the camera to the left.

"Alright," she said, "I'm doing it." She raised a piece of paper she was holding in her hand and read from it. "Time is running out. If we do not hear from you in the next forty-eight hours with a plan to hand over Carlos Breida, one of your sisters will lose a limb. This will continue every day until you hold up your end of the bargain." Bernadette paused and licked her lips. Her eyes darted in Assumpta's direction for the briefest of moments before returning to the page. "Do not test us on this." Bernadette raised her gaze once more and stared down the lens defiantly. Then she turned her head to look at Assumpta again. "Alright, I did what you—"

The image froze. The video over.

Zoya picked up a cushion and hugged it to herself. This was all too much. Bunny, Diller and the rest better reappear soon because the clock was ticking. She looked around her, at the mansion she bizarrely found herself sitting in.

She'd never felt more alone in her entire life.

BAKE OFF – WAR CRIMES WEEK

Bunny held his hand over his mouth as he yawned. It had been a long old night and, despite the advice he'd been giving to everyone else, he hadn't got any sleep. In his defence, the man-dropping-from-the-sky incident had given him a jolt of adrenalin, and then there was Diller's big idea, which had not only kept Bunny awake, but would also quite possibly give him nightmares for years to come. Besides, Team Gobshite over the road had had the music blaring out all night, only turning it off a few minutes ago.

The aforementioned man who fell from the sky, who was now their prisoner, had been predictably uncooperative. Eventually, it had been easier to gag him, in order to stop the torrent of threats and abuse coming from him. Mr Draper was quite the piece of work. Really, there was limited information they needed from him, anyway. They knew they were trapped, and while the exact logistics of the plan of attack might not be known, they knew Gardner and the Sportsmen were coming for them first thing in the morning.

More importantly, this Draper fella appeared to have been going on a solo run, given that nobody else seemed to be up there on the top of the cliff. The idea that somebody could start lobbing grenades down on top of them had been unnerving. Beth had assured them it was quite the climb to get up there, but Leo had been good enough, thankfully, seeing as he'd installed the motion detectors. If he hadn't ... Well, that also didn't bear thinking about. The only practical reason Bunny had to believe Team Gobshite would not use grenades, or whatever else they had at their disposal, was that they needed the golden gun he held in his hand, and they needed it intact. He'd examined it several times now and still couldn't figure out how it was supposed to hold information, but he was really thankful that it did.

Sure enough, since before first light, there'd been an uptick in the comings and goings outside the gates, as the opposition had manoeuvred itself into position. Admittedly, as they'd done that, there had been some unusual activity. Several members of the Sportsman's League kept running off into the woods. Whatever they were doing in there, Bunny couldn't figure it out.

He was on the tower on the right again, with Diller beside him. In the original plan, Diller had been supposed to stay in the cabin with Carlos, but he'd decided he wasn't going to do that, and Bunny decided that was the lad's decision to make for himself. Besides, he enjoyed the company. On their left, Rory and Beth sat nervously, watching on from the other tower. The one thing Team Junkyard had gained from the attempted overnight incursion was another gun. Draper's Glock, along with his two spare clips, was now in Smithy's possession. Gail had made an impassioned case to be the one to have it, but she'd been overruled. She sure was keen for a fight, though. Just as well, because one was definitely coming.

Speak of the devil, Gail's head appeared at the top of the ladder behind them. "How we looking?"

"They're still moving around," said Bunny. "Aren't you supposed to be in position?"

"I'm getting bored."

Bunny swore under his breath. "Believe me, I could take a whole lot more boredom given what the alternative is."

"Hey," said Diller, "there's nothing over in those woods, is there?"

"I don't know," said Gail. "You think I spend my spare time going out on nature walks? I ain't going near it. The woods are full of wild animals and shit. No, thank you."

"Would you look at that," said Bunny, nudging Diller. "You've found yourself a kindred spirit."

Diller ignored him. "It's just that the guys keep running in and out of it."

"Let me see." Gail pushed in beside them, despite there really not being room up there for three people. She started looking over the barrier eagerly.

"Keep your head down," hissed Bunny.

"Oh my god!" Gail exclaimed with great excitement. "I think it worked. It did, it worked!"

"What worked?"

"Well," she began, turning to them, "I didn't want to say nothing as I thought they wouldn't be that dumb, but I guess they were."

"Will you stop speaking in riddles?" urged Bunny.

"Alright, keep your pants on, Irish. Yesterday, I knew I was getting the hell out of there, but I wanted to show those sons of bitches what I thought of them before I left, so I baked a load of cookies."

"Right," said Bunny. "Feels like you're sending a bit of a mixed message there."

Gail laughed. "Oh, no, I wasn't." She popped her head clear over the parapet and shouted, "Hey, boys, how did you enjoy them cookies?"

A couple of shouts of abuse came back by way of reply.

"If you're wondering what the secret ingredient was," she hollered, "remember when the bull was constipated that time for, like, a week? And then he did that shit that was the size of a truck tyre? Well, we still had half a bottle left of the laxative the vet prescribed. Seemed a shame to waste it."

Bunny pulled her down as a trio of shots zoomed overhead.

"What!" said Bunny.

"Yeah," said Gail, a look of undisguised glee on her face, before she raised her voice again. "These boys were always full of shit, but I'm guessing they aren't any more."

Bunny looked out through the peephole again. "Shitting hell."

"Yeah," said Gail. "I imagine that's what those jerks are in right now."

"Oh my God!" Rory shouted over to them. "They keep running off into the woods and ..."

It was there when you knew what to look for. The visible members of the Sportsman's League didn't appear to be loving life. A couple of the ones in their sightline looked as if they weren't leaning so much as propping themselves up against the barricades.

"Jesus, Gail," said Bunny. "You're a genius. I mean, a monster too, but definitely a genius."

"Thanks, Irish."

"Brings new meaning to the phrase an army marches on its stomach, only this one is running on its arse."

Bunny then burst into laughter and soon found he couldn't stop. Diller eventually patted him on the shoulder. "Are you okay?"

As he wiped tears from his eyes, he tried to get his breathing under control. "Sorry, sorry, sorry. 'Tis just ... The irony is unbelievable."

"I don't get what you mean."

Bunny slapped Diller on the back. "This whole thing started with them not letting us take a shit, and it's going to end with them being unable to stop. Christ on a pedalo, that's damn near poetic."

If Bunny needed something to help him stop laughing, it came his way a couple of seconds later when the distinctive voice of Colonel Gardner shouted across from the barricades opposite. "Good morning."

SHIT JUST GOT REAL

Colonel Gardner lifted the walkie-talkie to her lips. "In position?"

"Confirmed."

Newton was a man of few words normally, but she had always appreciated his focused approach when working. He was an island of professionalism in a sea of ... well ...

It had been quite the night. The bellyaching had started about 2am, around the time she also noticed that Draper had gone AWOL. Grown men whining like children because their tummies hurt. At 3am the first fight broke out in the toilets after certain parties decided that other parties had been hogging the facilities. She'd ended up sending Newton in there to inform them that he would shoot the next man who caused trouble.

Some people started going outside at that point. Eventually, the toilets inevitably broke and then everyone had to go outside. The stench permeating the building was so foul that Gardner, for fear she might just start shooting, had gone across to the warehouse and stayed there. There'd been something soothing about lying on top of a crate full of weapons, surrounded, literally, by tonnes of the stuff. One of the guards they'd put in place was standing outside smoking. Admittedly, modern weaponry was well past the point at which a naked flame was a threat, but there was still a principle to the thing, so that guy had learned a short sharp lesson, which had the added bonus of decreasing his chances of breeding. Gardner had grown to hate this group of men more vehemently than she'd ever hated an enemy, never mind an ally. For a group that appeared to espouse racial superiority, they offered cast-iron proof of what happened when a gene pool remained too shallow.

When she'd gone in to muster the men at 4:30am, she was greeted by the most pathetic of sights – a room filled with groaning, simpering fools. Newton left, as agreed, to get in position, and Gardner, with the assistance of Ronnie, this sad collective's supposed leader, had got their supposed fighting force mobilised and ready to head for battle. Ronnie was one of only a couple of those present who hadn't eaten any of the cookies, seemingly because he was watching his weight. It was nothing if not ironic, given that almost everyone else present had probably lost several pounds of it overnight. The only downside of Ronnie having been spared was that it meant he was able to keep talking. At one point he somehow connected the dots between his sad-sack collective being laid low by cookies and the liberal media. Gardner hadn't really been listening. She kept finding herself fantasising over and over again about killing everyone in the room. Normally, that was just something she did in airport lounges to pass the time.

And now, finally, here they were, on the front line. The men surrounding her were pale and sweaty, but they were here. Their numeric advantage was massive. Most of what these idiots needed to do was just pull a trigger when instructed to do so. Even they couldn't screw that up.

"Top of the morning to ye," the voice from behind the fence shouted back in response to her greeting.

She was fairly sure the Irishman was being ironic, but irony lagged only behind mercy on the list of things in which Gardner had no interest.

"So," she began, "you've had the night, as agreed. Have you made a decision?"

"You say that, but you didn't exactly play fair. Have you lost this?"

Gardner looked around the side of the truck and down the central aisle of the junkyard. Sure enough, as she'd suspected, there was Draper, being pushed forward by a small Asian woman with a shaven head, and that annoying bartender. His hands were cuffed, his feet were manacled, and he sported a gag in his mouth.

"He was acting independently," shouted Gardner.

"Was he?" responded the voice. "Tut tut. First most of your lot lose control of their bowels, and now you've lost control of your men. Sets a bad precedent, doesn't it?"

"You make a good point."

She stepped forward, raised her rifle, aimed through the mesh fencing and, from sixty yards, put a bullet straight through Draper's head.

———

"Jesus!" screamed Bunny.

He looked down to see Draper's body falling to the ground as Joy dived for cover behind the nearest stack of wrecks and Gail sought refuge on the other side of the aisle.

"What in the hell!"

"What the ..." started Joy. This was the first time Bunny had heard her sound in the least bit fazed by anything.

"I told you, this bitch is crazy," screamed Gail. "Goddamn it, I got bits of him all over my shirt."

"You okay, Joy?" shouted Bunny.

"Better than him," she responded. "Why did she do that?"

It was an extremely good question. "Why the feck did you do that?" shouted Bunny over the barrier.

"To demonstrate what happens to those who do not follow orders," came the response.

"You're a fecking psycho!"

"Do. Not. Call me that!"

"'Tis what you are."

"The deal on offer was you hand over the golden gun and we let you leave. Yes or no?"

"Right," said Bunny. "And you seriously expect us to believe you'd keep up your side of the bargain? You've shot two people on your own side that I know of. Have a cookie and then blow it out your arse."

"Fine," said Gardner, "have it your way."

Through the peephole he could see her standing behind the truck, raising a walkie-talkie to her lips. Her eyes. She wasn't looking across at them, she was looking above their heads.

"Down!" screamed Bunny, grabbing hold of Diller and throwing them both off the tower.

RAIN OF FIRE

Bunny heard Beth scream as the shot from behind hit her in the left leg. Rory was standing over her when the second bullet caught him in the left shoulder, spinning him off the tower and down to the ground behind it.

Thankfully, Beth had the presence of mind to roll herself off the platform just before the third shot hit it.

"What the hell?" shouted Joy from her position behind them.

"Sniper," responded Bunny. "Up on the cliff."

Diller stood in a crouched position and shouted over to the others. "Are you okay?"

"No!" screamed Beth. "I've been shot!" She was holding her hands to her left thigh, where a steady flow of blood was already evident.

Rory attempted to stand but collapsed backwards, blood blossoming from the shoulder of his shirt. "I'm ... shoulder."

"Hang on," said Diller. "I'm ..." Before he could move, a hail of bullets rained down from the barricades across the way, pinning them down.

In the area outside the cabin behind him, Bunny heard the front windshield of the VW Beetle shatter under the indiscriminate onslaught from the Sportsmen.

"Christ," he muttered, before shouting, "Joy, you got anything in your bag of tricks that can take out that sniper?"

"Not from down here."

"Fantastic." Bunny looked around him, trying to come up with some kind of plan, now that the one they'd cobbled together had been blown to hell. "Alright," he said. "They've still got to get around the electric fence. We just need to cover the gate. Slow them down. Buy us some time." Time for something, anything, to swing in their favour.

Before Bunny could add anything else, Diller sprinted and dived across the divide between the wrecks.

"Jesus!" screamed Bunny. "Are you suicidal, Dill?"

Diller hauled himself upright. "I'm fine."

Bunny shook his head. Lucky beat smart every time, but luck would one day run out.

Diller helped Rory up but the deputy sheriff pushed him away and pointed to Beth. "Help her. I'm okay."

As he spoke, Gail crawled on her hands and knees from the row behind. Rory walked unsteadily back to the edge of the pile of wrecks and shouted across to Bunny. "I'll cover the gate. You deal with that."

"What?"

Bunny looked to where Rory was pointing. The semi-truck from the eighteen-wheeler that had been in the parking lot of the Huntsman's Lodge was now roaring up the road towards them. Bunny realised that his crutch was still up on the platform but he had no time to worry about that now. He eased himself to his feet.

"Shite," he said. "I think they've got a plan to deal with the fence too."

"What are we going to do?" asked Rory, as he sneaked a peek around the edge of the barrier before swiftly pulling his head back in to avoid the hail of semi-automatic fire.

"Improvise," responded Bunny, because he couldn't think of anything else.

He drew a breath and watched the truck roaring towards them.

They couldn't even try the insane idea of climbing the rope Draper's incursion had left behind and attempt to get to the sniper, because the rope was no longer dangling down from the cliff.

Their only hope was the reason it wasn't.

EWOKS OF OREGON

A couple of miles down the road, Smithy sighed heavily. The reason for this was the barrel of the shotgun that had just been pressed into his back.

Shit. Caught cold. Embarrassing.

"Don't move," warned the voice.

Everything he'd been through was going to be for nothing. The time he'd spent clambering back up the rope Draper had come down, his arms screaming in pain from the effort – nothing. Stumbling down the hill in the darkness, at one point being convinced he was going to break his neck as he lost his footing and tumbled down a slope, then narrowly avoiding busting his head open on a rock – nothing. Worst of all, he was the one chance, the way of somehow saving his friends from having to attempt to fend off a full-on mass assault, and instead, he would be contributing absolutely nothing to the effort – nothing.

You couldn't even call it a plan. The word plan implied there was, well, a plan. This had all been rather spur of the moment. He'd looked up at the rope hanging down the cliff face where Draper had attempted his infiltration and thought, I reckon I could climb that. From there, he'd had to act fast. He'd taken Draper's gun, his knife and his harness and, with a little assistance, he'd begun to climb up the rock. He'd done a bit of climbing previously, and he'd watched that film *127 Hours*, but that wasn't near enough expertise to climb a sheer cliff face in the dark, all the while hoping there was nobody waiting at the top. He'd lost his grip on the rope several times, and if it hadn't been for the harness, he'd have fallen to his death. Thankfully, when he'd somehow reached the top, there hadn't been anyone there waiting. If there had been, he'd have been done for. As it was, he'd laid there panting for a few minutes, wondering if his arms might fall off.

From there, the plan was, essentially, let's have a game of capture the flag. While Gardner and the Sportsmen were up the road, busy getting ready to attack the junkyard, Smithy could mount a one-man counter-offensive and take out the warehouse full of guns. The trick was to say it all quickly, because if you tried to lay out, step by step, how it was supposed to happen, you'd quickly realise there were massive gaping holes where bits of actual plan should be. Smithy had been hard at work trying to figure out how to fill a particularly tricky one of these holes, that when he'd been so engrossed in thought, he'd allowed himself to be caught cold.

He'd managed, against all probability, stumbling, bumbling and fumbling his way through the woods in the dark to find his way back to the Huntsman's Lodge. He was in the trees across the road from it and had watched in the slowly dawning light of morning as the last of the Sportsmen had pulled out, heading for the junkyard a couple of miles down the road. The problem was, the last of hadn't actually been the last of. Gardner wasn't an idiot. She'd left six men guarding the warehouse. Admittedly, they were behaving weirdly. Smithy had watched them for ten minutes and they seemed to be taking turns to head off into the woods. Their body language was odd, too. Lots of belly-holding and tightly wound, mincing walks. It was as if they were all ill, which was probably a help in some regards, except it meant they were never all in the same place at the same time. It was already incredibly hard for one man to catch six cold, but they needed to be in the same location to do that. Irony of ironies, he'd been trying to figure out how to do that, when he himself had been taken by surprise. He was not having a great few days.

"Raise your hands, slowly," instructed the voice.

"Alright," said Smithy, complying because he had no choice.

"And keep your voice down."

That last bit surprised Smithy, enough for him to risk a glance over his shoulder. "Sheriff?"

"Shush."

"What are you doing here?"

"I'm guessing, the same thing you are. Trying to find a way to take out that warehouse and hit these bastards where it hurts, but I just thought you and me should have a word first, seeing as how we left things the last time we spoke."

"When you betrayed us, you mean?"

The wince in the sheriff's voice was almost audible. "Yeah, that. It's no excuse, but I was scared for my son. They offered me a wad of cash to look the other way, and in a moment of weakness I took it. I didn't want Rory to waste his life trying to win unwinnable battles."

"He clearly doesn't feel the same way."

"I know," said the Sheriff, removing the gun from Smithy's back. "He's stronger than me. Gets that from his mother. I ... I ... let him down badly. And everybody else too."

The pain in the man's voice was there for anyone to hear, and whatever anger Smithy had melted away. He turned around. "Well, the good news is, I think we've still got a chance to make it right."

It was only then that Smithy noticed they were not alone. Sheriff Davenport took a step back to allow Smithy to get a good look at his three companions and nodded in their direction.

"This here is Kimberley Reese, Janice Dockery and Cartavious Randall."

They were, respectively, a blonde girl in her twenties with a heart-shaped face, the woman in her early sixties he'd seen on Main Street when she'd run across the road to tend to Jake after he'd been shot, and a man who must be touching eighty, and who was worryingly still aiming a shotgun at Smithy while giving him a mean stare.

"Cart," said Janice Dockery. "You can stop pointing the gun at the man now."

The old man grumbled something under his breath and angled the gun away a few inches.

"How did you all get here?" asked Smithy.

"I've lived here my whole life," snapped the old man. "I know these woods like the back of my hand."

"Are there any more of you?" asked Kimberley.

Smithy shook his head. "Not here. They're all in the junkyard."

"But you have a gun?" asked Janice.

He nodded.

"So," said the sheriff, "with our two shotguns that makes three. Still not enough."

They turned as one at the sound of distant gunfire coming from the direction of the junkyard. It had started.

"It's going to have to be," said Smithy. "Has anyone got any ideas?"

Janice turned to Kimberley. "Sweetie, remember when I had a word with you a couple of months ago, about you washing your car in a bikini top?"

Kimberley scrunched up her face in disbelief. "And you think now's the time to bring that up again, Janice?"

"Desperate times, desperate measures."

MOMENTS OF WEAKNESS

Tommy Drake made his way into the woods, as Maurice trailed behind him.

"Why the hell you following me?" snapped Tommy.

"I need to go too."

"Well, get your fat ass away from me. I don't want to see you taking a dump."

Tommy's mood, not unlike the smell that now seemed to linger everywhere, was foul. Yesterday, some lunatic woman had electrocuted him then broken his nose with a beanbag, and he'd had to stand there and explain it to that crazy Gardner woman, half expecting her to shoot him on the spot. As if all that wasn't enough, and it definitely was, he'd been poisoned by a cookie and given the worst diarrhoea he'd ever experienced.

"If I ever get hold of that bitch, Gail ..." started Maurice.

"Shut your tubby ass up, Maurice."

"What?" he snapped back. "Spiking a cookie. It's so friggin' un-American. It's like burning the flag."

"Just – stop flapping your gums."

Tommy couldn't go any further. He tossed his rifle to the ground, dropped his pants and hunched down in front of a tree. As he relieved himself, he was disgusted to see Maurice doing the same only a few feet from him. "What did I tell you? Get away from me."

"Screw you," barked Maurice. "I told you I need to go too."

"Not in front of me. I don't want to see that."

Both men looked up at the same time as Sheriff Davenport stepped into the clearing, a look of revulsion on his face and a shotgun in his hands. "I don't want to see it either," he said. "I would say put your hands in the air but ... Just stay away from your guns."

"Shit," said Maurice.

"Yes," said Sheriff Davenport, holding his free hand to his nose, "you can say that again."

———

"This is bullshit," said Walter.

Carl looked to the sky and shouted, "Would you shut the hell up, Walter?"

"Well, it is," he responded. "They all get to be down there fighting in a battle against these insurgent bastards and we're sitting here with our thumbs up our asses, guarding a dumbass building."

"Personally," said Stevie, "I'm alright with not getting shot at."

"Yeah," agreed Doug, "and keeping the hell away from that crazy Gardner woman."

Doug was still feeling very sensitive after what she'd done to him last night, just because he'd been having a cigarette. Nobody had said you couldn't smoke. Admittedly, that encounter might finally be the thing he needed to make him quit.

"I'm just saying—" started Walter.

"Nobody wants to hear what you have to say," sniped Carl. "So why don't you ..."

He trailed off because he and the other three had all noticed the exact same thing at the exact same time. To be fair, a hot girl running up the road towards you, wearing just a pink bra and a pair of cut-off shorts, would get any red-blooded man's attention. She was waving her T-shirt above her head. "Boys, boys, can you help me, please?"

Stevie gave a low whistle. He'd seen her around town a couple of times, but she'd been all snooty before, wouldn't even look at you.

She ran up to them, still waving her shirt about. All four of them stood up a little straighter.

"What appears to be the problem, honey?" asked Carl.

"Well, it's just, you see ..."

She really did have a smoking-hot body.

"I saw you boys over here and I just thought, they look like the kind of pathetic dumbasses who would get distracted easily."

"Drop your weapons."

Carl spun around to see two men standing on either side of their group. One was that damned dwarf and the other was an old duffer holding a shotgun.

"What in the"

"Drop 'em, now," said the dwarf.

Carl, Stevie and Doug looked at the two men, looked at each other, then did as they were told.

"Well, that was the grossest thing I've ever had to do," said the girl, turning her back on the men and putting her T-shirt back on.

Walter, meanwhile, still held on to his gun.

"Drop it," ordered the short fella, pointing his weapon at Walter.

Walter, however, kept looking at the old man. "Right. I'm supposed to believe this old-timer has the balls to ..."

Old Man Randall's hand twitched upwards then Walter screamed as Cartavious shot him in the leg. He collapsed to the ground.

The old man calmly took a step closer. "I fought in a war you've only seen in the movies." He racked his shotgun and ran it over the rest of the group. "Never mess with a man's Wordle streak."

THE CHAINS THAT BIND

Bunny leaned against the pile of wrecks, careful to keep himself out of sight from where he presumed the sniper to be, while also protecting himself from the constant stream of gunfire coming over the barricades in front of the main gates. He was watching the truck, which had now turned around and was reversing towards the fence on the right-hand side of the yard. He'd initially thought they were going to ram it, but their solution appeared to be depressingly smarter than that. The concrete columns would have stood up to such a frontal assault. But no, he could see lengths of thick rope piled up on the back. Hooks on the end of them. They were going to try to grab the fence and pull it down.

Behind him, Rory was doing what he could to defend the front gate. The Sportsmen had brought ladders to scale it, but once one of them had been shot in his excitement to be the first over, the rest of them had lost some enthusiasm for the endeavour. Rory was now firing the odd reminder, every time somebody stuck their head over, while trying to avoid getting shot himself as hailstorms of bullets headed his way in response. It was like trying to fight the sea with a water pistol. Before they'd taken Beth away, Diller had left her rifle beside Rory. It wasn't much but every little bit helped.

For his part, Bunny was struggling to come up with an idea to combat the truck. He fired a couple of times, but the four men who were now crouched down behind it were taking good advantage of the cover it offered, so all he ended up with were two fewer bullets.

"Joy," he shouted.

"Yeah," came the response from the row behind him, "I'm watching it."

"Any ideas?"

"Nothing that'll stop the truck, but I can make it unpleasant for them."

"I'll take anything you've got."

"Bunny?" shouted Rory. "They got a second ladder and I'm running low on ammo."

"Go," shouted Joy. "I got this."

———

Gail and Diller had Beth propped up between them. She was barely conscious and had lost a fair amount of blood. The plan, such that it was, was to get her back to the cabin, which they'd placed barricades in front of yesterday, in preparation for a last stand. It was also where the first-aid kit was located. To reach there from where they were, they needed to hug the side of the wrecks to get as close as possible while in cover, but that still left twenty yards of open ground between them and the porch. Suddenly, that felt like an awful lot, but it wasn't as if there were other options.

They had made all of five yards' progress when a sniper's bullet thudded into the ground beside Gail's feet and they all hit the deck. Diller and Gail scrambled back into the cover of the wrecks, leaving Beth lying on the open ground in front of them, semi-conscious, looking around in confusion.

"Shit," shouted Gail. "I thought you had her."

"I thought *you* did," responded Diller.

"Well, ain't we a pair." Gail raised her voice. "Beth, you're going to have to crawl back this way a little and then we'll come get you."

"Don't," shouted Diller, throwing out both his hands in a stopping motion to emphasise the point.

"What?" said Gail.

"She's a sitting duck. If he wanted her dead, she already would be. I think he's waiting for us to try and go get her so he can take us out."

"Bastard! So what are we supposed to do?"

Diller jumped to his feet and took a few deep breaths.

"Okay, I'm going to make a run for the cabin."

"What? That's crazy."

"Yeah," he confirmed. "When I do it, I'll get his undivided attention. You go get Beth."

"But that's suicide."

Diller shrugged. "We all got to die somehow, might as well do it running."

———

The truck stopped reversing three feet in front of the fence and the men crabbing along behind it duly sprang into action. Two of them started firing into the compound, providing cover for the other two as they grabbed the thick ropes with hooks on the end from the back of the truck.

Joy stood in the lee of the wall of cars, her beanbag shotgun in her hands. It felt like she'd brought a tissue to a pillow fight, but the code was the code. It didn't mean she couldn't spread a little non-lethal joy, no pun intended. She counted to three, took a couple of steps forward to clear her angle then hit the secondary trigger to launch the grenade. With a satisfying pop it arced through the air and thunked down on the back of the truck, exactly where she'd been aiming. She enjoyed the briefest moment of pleasure hearing the hiss of the tear gas releasing, and then a jolt of fire coursed through her stomach. The sniper's bullet had ripped through her vest and sent a searing pain across her right side. Joy fell to her knees. Damn it, the bastard had relocated. The Kevlar was designed to stop shots from a handgun. It never stood a chance against a high-powered sniper rifle shot.

She rolled back behind the wrecks as a second bullet hit the ground where she'd just been. She placed a hand inside her vest to check the damage and then lifted her T-shirt, already sticky with blood. She was lucky – the shot had only sliced into the side of her abdomen, avoiding any organs. Using the wrecks for support, she eased herself back to her feet, found one of the emergency bandages she kept in the lower pockets of her trousers and slapped it on the wound. It wouldn't stop much of the bleeding, but it would hopefully slow it down from ripping any further as she moved, and she was going to have to move.

———

Diller took off sprinting, running straight towards the cliff for a few feet before veering right, just before a bullet pinged into the ground in front of him. He spun left, ran back a few steps. Another bullet landed to his right. *Left again. Left.* He didn't see where the third bullet hit. *Reverse. Zig right.* Bullet fired. *Zag left. Stop.* A bullet hit the ground to the right of his foot. *Then sprint left.*

He kept doing this, trying all he could not to fall into any kind of predictable pattern.

Left, no right.

He was getting dizzy now.

Left ... Right ... Left. No, forward, no ... He was so busy second-guessing himself, he tripped over his own feet and fell to the ground. He started rolling as soon as his knees hit the dirt, and he felt, more than saw, a bullet as it landed at most an inch from his side.

He stopped himself and rolled back the other way.

Then he leaped to his feet and ran forward.

Luckily, seeing as he had no clue where he was now, he'd somehow ended up with the cabin in front of him.

He dived onto the porch, his lungs burning, heart pounding and every fibre of his being singing.

That felt pretty brave.

———

Bunny pulled the trigger on the golden gun but was rewarded with nothing but an empty click. "Shite, I'm out."

He looked across at Rory, who was leaning heavily against the stack of wrecks on the far side, his shirt drenched in blood from his wound. Beth's rifle was dangling from his hands. "I'm ... I think I got ..." Rory patted his belt and his pockets. "Nope, I'm out too."

Bunny glanced at the gate again. How long would it take for the opposition to figure out that they were in a gun battle where only one side was shooting? "We need to fall back and—"

Both he and Rory looked up simultaneously when they heard the sound.

THE SHOT HEARD AROUND THE WORLD (WELL, OREGON)

Sheriff Davenport and Old Man Randall moved their six prisoners back across the road, well away from the warehouse. Smithy, meanwhile, set about awkwardly shooting his way through the lock on the warehouse door. Their prisoners had sworn blind that Gardner and Ronnie had the only keys to it and Smithy believed them. It made sense not to leave these jackasses with access to any more weapons than they already had. Besides, any inclination the rest of them had to hold out on them was no doubt removed when the mouthy one got shot in the leg by Cartavious Randall. Janice Dockery had taken a look at the injury, deemed it a flesh wound and bandaged it, while her patient whined and blubbered like a man who hadn't called somebody's bluff and lost.

Smithy's sense of urgency was greatly added to by the sound of a gun battle raging in the distance. He tried not to think about what that could mean. Finally, after putting several shots into the lock, it looked as if the metal was going to give way. He was aware he was shooting at a building full of weapons, but given that his objective was to destroy the things as fast as possible, he had no choice, and besides, the warehouse exploding in a fireball was his aim, so at least he'd have accomplished his goal while killing himself.

After a couple of quick shoulder charges, the door gave way. Inside, Smithy found what he was looking for almost immediately.

A minute later, he was standing back on the other side of the road, Janice Dockery beside him. "Are you sure about this?"

"Sure?" said Smithy. "Hell no, but have you got any better ideas?"

"Not right now."

Smithy raised the rocket launcher and set it on his shoulder. "I'm afraid right now is when we need them."

"Are you insane?" shouted one of the prisoners. "You got any idea how much all that weaponry is worth?"

Smithy looked down the long metal tube in his hands. "I know how much it's about to be worth."

The thing didn't come with a manual so he just started flipping anything he could find. There was a big red button on the right-hand side that looked particularly promising.

"Stand back," he warned Janice.

"Are you sure it's the right way around?" she said while retreating. "I saw that in a movie once."

"I guess we're about to find out."

Smithy took a deep breath and pressed the red button. Nothing happened.

He pressed it again. Another anti-climactic nothing.

"Have you taken the cap off?" asked Old Man Randall.

"Is there a safety?" asked Sheriff Davenport.

"Everybody shut up," snapped Smithy. He'd just noticed a small button on the top that he hadn't flipped. He did that then repeated the process. This time, there was no sense of anti-climax. If anything, there was too much climax.

The rocket took him off his feet as it shot out of the launcher and screamed across the road. A half-second later, the force from the explosion knocked most of them down.

The noise, the sheer pressure of the blast was overwhelming, and then there was the heat. Even from where they were standing you could feel it. Bits of the warehouse were scattered over a wide area. They were thankfully just outside the blast zone, but not by much. A massive plume of smoke rushed towards the sky from the flaming husk of the building, and many of the surrounding trees were now bent back or had been knocked over entirely. Several small secondary fires had started to burn.

Smithy picked himself up and shouted, "Everyone okay?"

Sheriff Davenport recovered quickest, keeping his gun trained on the prisoners. "Nobody get stupider," he warned, before looking around.

"Oh my God," yelled Kimberley, "that explosion must've been visible from space."

"I don't know about that," said Janice, "but they'll have definitely seen it down in New Bridge."

"Yeah," agreed the Sheriff. "We don't need a telephone signal now. Every cop and emergency service within thirty miles will be hauling ass to get here."

Smithy looked around. "Oh, right." He hadn't thought of that.

REASON FOR LEAVING LAST EMPLOYMENT?

Colonel Gardner, still standing behind the barricade on the far side of the road, looked up at the large plume of smoke which confirmed that the massive explosion that had just echoed around the mountains had indeed come from the direction of the Huntsman's Lodge. She screamed. A raw, visceral, wordless shriek of rage at the injustice of it.

"Oh, man," howled Ronnie beside her. "That's got to be all them weapons."

She looked at him. "Oh, really? You figured that out all by yourself, did you?"

"I just ..."

"We left six of your fools guarding it. SIX! How is this possible?"

"I ..."

Gardner could sense the other Sportsmen in the vicinity moving quickly away from them. Her knuckles were white now as she gripped her rifle. "We are soooo screwed. Do you understand that? How badly we are screwed?"

Ronnie looked as if he might cry.

Gardner cast a glance back at the junkyard. This changed things.

The "subtle approach", taken in an effort to make sure the golden gun and its precious content weren't damaged, was now at an end.

She threw open one of the crates she'd brought with them and withdrew the anti-tank missile launcher.

Members of the Sportsman's League dived out of the way as she moved around the barricade and fired it at the gate opposite them. When the smoke had cleared, the gate was left a ripped and mangled mess with a great big hole in the middle of it. Gardner raised her walkie-talkie. "Newton, cover me, I'm going in."

"No."

"What?" she snapped.

"I don't know if you noticed, but our payday just went up in smoke. I'm out."

"Finish the job."

"Screw you, you psycho. In fact ..."

Some part of Gardner's brain that wasn't screaming for vengeance picked up enough in his tone to make her dive for cover just as a bullet whistled over her head.

"This is mutiny," she hollered into the walkie-talkie.

"What this is, is my resignation. I should never have signed up for this. Screw you, and screw every one of these assholes. Actually, maybe it's time to even things up a little."

One of the Sportsmen who'd been keener than his colleagues to carry the fight to the opposition collapsed in the middle of the road as a bullet hit him in the leg. A couple of seconds later, the engine of the truck, the hooks of which were now attached to the fence, stopped revving as the driver slumped over the steering wheel.

"Holy shit!" screamed Ronnie. "He's shooting at us now."

"Now, if you'll excuse me," said Newton. "I've got a long walk out of here." And the radio went dead.

BLOW IT OUT YOUR HOLE

Bunny picked himself up, having been knocked off his feet by the force of the explosion as a rocket hit the gates, ripping them asunder. As he struggled to his feet, he saw that on the other side of the aisle, Joy was bending over Rory, who had collapsed onto the ground.

"Is he alright?"

"Lost a lot of blood," replied Joy.

"Shite," said Bunny, noticing her side. "You're wounded too."

She shrugged. "Borrowed time anyway." She started picking Rory up. "I'll get him back to the cabin. Cover us?"

"I'm out," said Bunny.

"Then you know what you have to do."

He did. Whatever information was somehow on this stupid golden gun couldn't get into Gardner's hands.

The bullets raining in from the other side of the gates had stopped, so when a shot from the sniper rang out, it was distinctive. It was swiftly followed by a second, which Bunny could have sworn went well over his head, and then, inexplicably, he saw one hitting the driver of the truck, taking him out.

"What in the ... I think the sniper has changed sides!"

Joy now had Rory on his feet and the two of them were staggering away, like two drunks destined not to make it home. "Finally," she shouted over her shoulder. "A little luck goes our way. Now fall back!"

———

Gail clambered to her feet and grabbed Beth's arm. "C'mon. We need to get you to the cabin."

Beth pulled away. "No, leave me alone."

"Can't do that. You're in the open and defenceless here."

Beth glared up at her, anger in her hooded eyes. "I didn't ask for your help."

"I know, but you're getting it anyway."

"And I didn't ask you to pull me over here."

"Cool. If you're suicidal, I wish you'd told me that before I had to drag your ass out of the firing line while the Black kid nearly got his head blown off a dozen times by a sniper."

Beth went to say something then stopped, as if she'd run out of energy.

"Okay," said Gail. "To be clear, you hate me. I hate me. How about we both use that energy to get you from here, over to the cabin, before we both get killed by someone we both hate even more?"

Beth's head drooped. This needed the big guns.

"And I'm pretty sure Ronnie or that crazy Gardner woman wouldn't draw the line at killing your dogs either."

Beth's eyes flew open and, with a great deal of effort they collectively managed to get her back on her feet.

"Still hate you," slurred Beth.

"I know, honey. Me too."

———

Colonel Gardner and Ronnie crouched behind the barrier for a good minute before Gardner stepped back and drew herself up to her full height. "He's gone."

"Are you sure?" asked Ronnie.

"Yes."

"How can you know?"

"If he wasn't, I'd be dead by now." She held her rifle in front of her. "Let's go." She raised her voice. "On me."

Ronnie looked around. None of the Sportsmen were there to follow her command. He scanned the treeline and spotted countless figures disappearing into the woods. "Guys. Come back."

"Fuck you, Ronnie," shouted a voice. "And that crazy bitch. Even her own sniper can't stand her."

Ronnie turned back towards the Colonel. She'd presumably heard the remark, but she was staring at the gate.

"We don't need those fools. There are two of us, and if you haven't noticed, the other side aren't shooting back. My guess is they're out." She slammed a fresh clip into her rifle. "Let's finish this."

"Right behind you," said Ronnie, lifting his own gun with a nod.

———

Bunny managed to retrieve his wooden crutch from the top of the tower then, propping himself up with it, started limping down the right-hand side of the compound. On the other side of the wire, the truck lay abandoned, the fence half down but still mostly in place. He'd noticed the Sportsmen running, but that still left Gardner. She didn't strike him as the sort that would ever stop.

They were broken. From where he stood, he could see Diller running out of the cabin, with Carlos and the three dogs in tow, going to help Gail as she supported Beth, and Joy who was all but carrying Rory's limp form in a fireman's lift. As far as Bunny knew, almost everyone on their side was wounded or worse, and they were out of ammo and options. If Gardner was coming, she wasn't going to hit much resistance. He reached the end of the line of wrecks and looked back up the aisle. Sure enough, there she was.

———

"Okay," said Gardner, scanning everything in front of her. "I'll go after the Irishman and you …"

She realised she was talking to thin air. As she turned, she caught sight of the back of Ronnie Pierce as he ran into the woods like his life depended on it. It did. She fired a volley of shots but, dodging his way through the trees, she could see him make good his escape.

"Screw you, Ronnie. I don't need you. I don't need any of you."

She turned back and started advancing down the central path, stepping over the body of her own man who she'd shot a few minutes beforehand.

"Draper," she said in acknowledgment, without looking down. "You look different. Have you changed your hair?"

She giggled to herself.

She could do jokes.

———

Bunny steadied himself then broke into a limping sprint, heading for the bullet-riddled remains of the Volkswagen Beetle.

"UP CORK!" he screamed at the top of his lungs as a burst of gunfire followed in his wake, confirming he did indeed have Gardner's undivided attention. He managed to collapse behind the vehicle as a volley of bullets clunked into it. A stolen glance confirmed that Gardner was now striding down the central aisle towards him.

He stuck out his hand and waved the golden gun around. "Looking for this, by any chance?"

A trio of shots whizzed past as he snatched his hand in.

"Looks to me like you're out of bullets," shouted Gardner, sounding positively cheerful.

"Yeah, looks to me like you're out of friends."

"I don't need any help with this. You and I need to spend some quality time alone."

"I hate to break it to you," said Bunny, "but if you mean that in a sexual way, you're really not my type."

"Don't flatter yourself," said Gardner.

Bunny was carefully trying to judge her location from her voice as it got steadily closer.

"I mean," continued Bunny, "I know some people subscribe to that whole crazy-people-are-the-best-in-bed theory, but I'm of an age where I enjoy the cuddle as much as the fumble."

"You talk too—"

Bunny, carrying his crutch more than using it, ran as fast as one and a half feet could take him, trying to block out the screaming pain in his ankle. He'd judged it well enough, having waited for Gardner to draw level with the Beetle. There, she had to move to get a clean shot as he scrambled for the opening in the wall of wrecks that led back to the cave.

He made it through, collapsing onto the ground as more bullets whizzed over his head. His ankle wasn't going to allow him to walk another inch. He crawled a further couple of feet and then, with every ounce of energy he could muster, he hurled the golden gun up the path.

"I surrender," shouted Bunny, holding up his hands.

He could hear Gardner's laugh from around the corner. "Do you really think that will save you?"

"Nah," said Bunny. "I think your record in the area of shooting unarmed people is pretty clear."

"But you have a gun."

"I don't, actually. I just chucked it away."

He saw Gardner's head pop quickly around the corner before she moved around it in one fluid movement. Her gun was trained on him, her eyes scanning all around them to confirm they were alone.

"Ah, I see you've moved the dragon sculpture."

They had. It now sat in the mouth of the cave, with the golden gun lying on the ground behind it, Bunny having managed to successfully arc his throw.

"We did," confirmed Bunny. "Location, location, location. 'T'was my friend Diller's idea. He's got a real eye for these things."

"Yes," said Gardner, looking up the path. "Am I right in assuming that the gun is that glint of gold on the ground I can see just beyond it?"

"Might be."

"Hmmm. I'm afraid your transparent little plan here is rather pathetic. You see, I've seen the dragon's fire-breathing trick already. Not much of an element of surprise."

"Oh," said Bunny, "that's a shame."

"Yes." She looked down at him.

"I'd ask you to make it quick, but ..."

"Correct," she said. "I won't. You've been a massive inconvenience to me."

Bunny laughed.

"What's so funny?"

"I mean," said Bunny, "we're a long way beyond it now, but for the record, all my friend wanted to do was use the fecking toilet, and your buddies created this massive inconvenience for all of us."

"Couldn't he have just gone in the woods?"

"Ara," said Bunny, "the lad doesn't like going outdoors. 'Tis a quirk."

"Sounds like his cowardice is going to get you all killed."

"He's not a coward," said Bunny, with real feeling behind it. "Bravest lad I know."

To Bunny's surprise, Gardner stepped around him and started moving up the path towards the entrance to the cave. "I'm sure he'll die well, then."

"Christ," said Bunny. "Like there's really such a thing. We all just die."

"Speak for yourself," she said, her eyes darting to take in the details of their surroundings, looking for some form of trap. "Since you destroyed the weapons shipment, you've made my life rather difficult, but still, if I can get out of here with what's on the data card in that gun, I will still have a way forward."

"Can I ask – I'm mad curious – what the hell is on it?"

She laughed again. "I honestly don't know. I just know that it's worth a massive amount of money. It was a former mentor's get-out-of-jail-free card."

"And is he in jail now?"

"Oh no, he's dead."

"Bad luck."

"Trust me," said Gardner, "there was no luck involved." She stopped six feet from the dragon and glanced around again, confirming they were completely alone. The lights were on in the cavern and she could see there appeared to be nobody back there. The golden gun was indeed lying on the ground inside the entrance tunnel, just beyond the scrap-metal sculpture. "A dragon guards the treasure, how amusing. I always did enjoy these little puzzles."

"Well, 'tis nice to have a hobby."

"By the way," said Gardner, "I haven't killed you yet as I want to make sure I have the gun, and then, really as a matter of principle, I will kill everyone who works with you, slowly, and you can watch them die before you do. I don't normally let emotion creep into my work, but recently, I've decided to stop being so cold and logical about these things and, y'know, have a little fun."

"Has anyone ever suggested to you that you might need to, like, talk to someone or something?"

"Oh, don't be tedious. It is the great flaw in our society that we think every mind that breaks from the norm has to be fixed or medicated or sit in a circle talking endlessly about its feelings." Gardner stuck out her tongue and made a retching sound.

"Yeah, I'd agree with that statement in general. It's really just you who, I think, should do all those things."

Gardner ignored him. "It has some kind of motion-activated sensor, the dragon. So, let's assume you're not hoping the little gout of flame is going to burn me alive. I can't see any evidence of accelerants on the ground, so I'm going to guess you've souped it up a little. Yes, that'll be it. Maximum flame."

"By the way, remember how I said my friend Diller was the bravest lad I've ever met? I've got a cracking example of this if you'd like to hear it?"

Gardner took a few steps back and to the side. "I'm assuming you're trying to annoy me so that I'll give you a quick death."

"No, honestly, 'tis a great story."

"Not interested," she said, unclipping the walkie-talkie from her belt. There was nobody on the other end of it to speak to now, anyway.

"Suit yourself," said Bunny.

"I will."

And with that, she tossed the walkie-talkie in front of the dragon.

DRAGON'S BREATH

Nine hours and twenty-seven minutes earlier

When Joy ran back into the Old Mill, Beth was standing back and pointing at a wooden box that had been sitting under the crate she had just moved. Joy edged forward carefully and looked at where she was pointing. "Is that ..."

"I'm pretty sure it is."

"Well, well, well," said Joy, "that's certainly a development. I strongly suggest you slowly back out of the building."

"But—"

"But nothing, Beth," said Joy, as calmly as possible. "That's dynamite. Only, you see all those crystals around it? Yeah, that's dynamite that hasn't been stored properly, which means we breathe on it the wrong way and this building is going to have one hell of a sunroof.

———

Nine hours and nineteen minutes earlier

Bunny, Smithy and Diller were now standing in the yard with Beth and Joy.

"Is there any way we could use it?" asked Bunny.

"Okay," said Joy. "Let me make this real clear. I get the idea that dynamite, given our current predicament, sounds pretty enticing, but this stuff has been sitting there for God knows how long, and those are nitroglycerin crystals around it. Jiggle it, drop it – hell, even touch it – and there's every chance you'll blow yourself to smithereens."

"She's right," said Smithy. "Place I used to live, they found an old box of it in an abandoned mine. They had to evacuate and do a controlled explosion."

"See?" said Joy, nodding in agreement. "Even the guy who dangled out the side of a car thinks this is a bad idea. Everybody stay well away from the dynamite."

"Right."

———

Four hours and thirty-seven minutes earlier

Diller and Smithy had been sitting on the tower, discussing the plan for the morning and Diller's part in it. At least they had been.

"Erm, Dill," said Smithy, "don't know if you've realised, but you just sort of stopped talking mid-sentence."

Diller hopped up, careful to remain crouched so as not to pop into anyone's line of fire. "I have to go."

"And do what?" asked Smithy, instantly suspicious.

"I've got an idea."

"What is it?"

"Don't worry about it."

"Nothing makes me worry more than you saying don't worry about it."

"I'll see you later."

Before Smithy could utter another word, Diller was down the ladder and away into the night. Smithy then got distracted by an alarm going off, a man falling from the sky, and then his own subsequent decision to climb the rope the man had left behind. Not for nothing, as Smithy reached the top of the cliff, he remembered that he'd meant to ask Bunny to check in with Diller to find out exactly what his big idea was.

———

Three hours and four minutes earlier

Even on wheels, the dragon was heavier than Diller expected, but luckily, Carlos was as helpful as he was strong. More importantly, he didn't ask questions, which was very handy, as Diller didn't want to give anyone answers.

———

Two hours and twenty-six minutes earlier

Bunny, having just left the cabin, was heading back over to the tower to relieve Rory from his stint on sentry duty when he stopped and drew his gun. A figure was standing in the middle of the yard, stock-still.

"Jesus, Dill," he hissed, "you scared the life out of me."

"Sorry," came the response.

"I nearly shot you."

Bunny now noticed that Cerberus, the three-legged dog, was standing in front of Diller, looking up at him excitedly.

"What are you doing?"

"Funny you should ask," said Diller. "I'm sort of waiting, hoping Cerberus here will get bored. You see, I've got an object in my hand, and I think he thinks I'm going to throw it. So I've been standing here for about ten minutes."

"Why? You're not scared of ..." Bunny's heart jumped into his mouth. "Is that?"

"Yeah. Dynamite. Three sticks of it."

"Three?"

"Yeah. I only wanted one, but they were stuck together."

"And why the hell have you picked up highly volatile dynamite?" Bunny was trying very hard not to scream.

"I had an idea."

"What idea?"

"Could you maybe call the dog away, and then, once you're both at a safe distance, I'll explain it."

———

Two hours and four minutes earlier

This was insane. Bunny had done some mad things in his time, but this was the craziest thing he'd ever seen anyone do. Ever. He limped along behind Diller, at the requested safe distance. Diller had explained the idea, and while it was indeed lacking all sanity, he was also far enough into executing his plan that stopping was no longer an option. Bunny didn't bother informing anyone else as more people panicking wasn't likely to improve the situation. Besides, he was panicking enough for everybody.

Walking slowly, with, it had to be said, a remarkably steady hand, Diller was making his way in the dark towards the mouth of the cave. The image popped into Bunny's head of people bringing the offering up to the altar at Mass, only instead of the bread and the wine, Diller was bringing three sticks of highly unstable dynamite, and instead of a priest, a large metal dragon lay in wait for him.

"Wait," hissed Bunny from behind him.

"What?"

"Have you turned off the motion-detecting thing on the dragon?"

"Yes," snapped Diller. "I did that when we moved it, and could you please stop urgently whispering things at me."

"Right, sorry. You're doing great."

"If you mean I've not dispersed myself over a wide area yet," said Diller, "then yes, I'm doing great."

Bunny watched on as Diller, like a man bearing his own coffin, solemnly walked up the rest of the path and slowly, so very slowly, slipped the sticks of dynamite between the dragon's teeth.

"Oh dear," said Diller.

"What?"

"The dragon's head – it tilts down."

"Right?"

"So things will tend to, sort of, fall out of it."

"And you're only thinking of this now?"

"Well, that's not very helpful."

"Jesus," said Bunny. "As last words go, those will have to do."

Diller, not even daring to breathe, slowly, oh so slowly, pushed the trio of sticks into the mouth. They were sticky and itchy, not to mention extremely lethal. His fingers had unhelpfully started to shake. He gathered himself and pushed the end of the bundle with his fingers, nudging it slowly forward. The sticks were now off the palm of his hand and inside the mouth. He felt a little resistance and stopped pushing.

"How's it going?" asked Bunny from behind him.

"Still not dead."

"Right. That's good."

"I'm taking my hand away."

Bunny looked on in silence for a minute before he spoke again. "You've actually not—"

"I know I haven't," said Diller. "It's just ... Right, fine, here we go."

Diller took a step back and removed his fingers from the dragon's mouth. He watched as the sticks shifted slightly and then stayed in place.

He turned to walk back down the path, but about halfway down his legs buckled underneath him. Bunny dived forward and grabbed him.

"Are you alright?"

"Erm," said Diller, feeling sort of giddy and numb at the same time, "I guess."

"Right," said Bunny, getting him back onto his feet. "That was the single bravest thing I've ever seen."

"Thanks."

Then Bunny clipped him around the ear. "And if you ever do something like that again, I'll kill you myself! Ye fecking lunatic!"

"Damn it," said Diller.

"What now?"

"I'm going to have to very carefully go back and turn the motion sensor back on."

———

Two seconds earlier

Gardner tossed the walkie-talkie in front of the dragon and Bunny ducked, covering his head with his arms.

Nothing happened.

And then it did.

OUT FROM UNDER

For the second time in his life, Bunny awoke to someone licking his face. He was relieved to see that on this occasion it was a dog.

Cerberus, he with the three legs and the sunny disposition, was standing over him. Smithy shooed him away.

"You're alive!" said Smithy.

"Right back at ye." Bunny blinked a couple of times. He had dull aches, lots of bruises and a splitting headache. Overall, though, he'd woken up in worse states. "What the hell happened?"

"You were kinda under a bit of a mountain when it fell off."

Bunny looked up. Even for a junkyard, the place was a mess. The entrance of the cavern had caved in and the explosion had caused half the cliff face to crumble away. Either side of him, wrecks of cars were, well, still wrecks, only more so, and they were no longer in neat piles.

Smithy started to help Bunny up. "Half an old Ford landed on you and some rocks, but given that you'd just set off a big explosion, you came out of it remarkably well."

"To be fair," said Bunny, "I didn't set it off. Gardner did. I presume she is somewhere under all of that. Or at least some bits of her are."

"Let's let mountain rescue or whoever worry about that, shall we?

We need to get the hell out of here. I stole us a car – successfully this time."

Smithy located Bunny's miraculously still-intact crutch and together they walked back down towards the cabin.

"Is everybody alright?" asked Bunny.

"No," said Smithy. "Almost nobody is alright, but they're all remarkably still alive. Janice has opened her own little triage station and is tending to them now."

"Janice?"

"A nurse. Formidable woman. You'd like her, but no time for intros, I'm afraid. We need to make a break for it and fast. I don't know if you noticed, but a real big explosion went off a while ago and it's sort of put Paradise on the map."

"Which explosion do you mean?"

"Good point," said Smithy. "For the record, mine was bigger."

"Well, 'tis not the size. It's what you do with it."

"Of all people," said Smithy, "you don't need to tell me that. Besides, you get bonus points because yours didn't start a minor forest fire, which I feel terrible about. Although there are already fire trucks over there getting it under control. Tragically, the Huntsman's Lodge is also ablaze."

"Meh," said Bunny. "I've kinda gone off that place."

————

Five minutes later, Bunny, Smithy, Carlos and Diller were all in a car, attempting, once again, to get the hell out of Paradise. Diller was driving, despite not having any form of licence, because Bunny had a bad foot, and Smithy couldn't do so without some alterations that they did not have time for. Besides, while it was technically illegal, they happened to have built up a bit of goodwill with the local sheriff's department.

Joy, back on her bike, was riding point in front of them.

"Is Joy okay?" asked Bunny. "She had a nasty-looking wound on her side."

"Who knows," said Smithy. "She's carved from rock. From what I can gather she's already supposed to be dead but even the Grim Reaper is a little scared of her."

"I feel bad about the dragon," said Diller.

"What?" said Bunny.

"We destroyed some of Beth's work and, come to think of it, we buried the cavern with all the rest of it in it."

"Are you crazy?" said Smithy. "She's got a buried cavern full of art and one hell of a story. If she's half as smart as I think she is, everyone who is anyone in the art world will be here in a few weeks when they dig it out."

"Hmmm," said Diller, "I guess."

"I really liked the dogs," said Carlos.

"Yeah," agreed Bunny, "they were nice."

"And look ..." Carlos pulled something out of his pocket and Bunny turned around in the front seat to look at it and the big fella's grinning face.

"Beth gave me a new yo-yo."

"Ah, excellent. All's well that ends well."

In the distance, the symphony of sirens started to grow.

———

A few minutes later, after passing through Paradise, they came to the landslide blocking the road. Several of the locals had come out in force and were already busy trying to clear it, forming a chain to shift the smaller rocks off the road. On the other side were the flashing sirens of ambulances and a patrol car.

As they pulled up, two patrolmen who had been working on the removal stood up and eyed them suspiciously.

"Ara crap," said Bunny. "Let me do the talking."

He opened the passenger door.

One of the patrolmen put his hand to his holster. "Alright, hands where I can see them."

A couple of the locals stopped what they were doing and

exchanged glances, before one of them stepped forward. "Oh no, officer, these people are fine. They're just some tourists who got caught up in this whole mess."

The patrolman looked back at him. "Well, if you're sure, Mr Clarke?"

The man nodded. "Absolutely." He smiled at Bunny. "I do hope this experience won't put you off coming back to visit Paradise in the future?"

"No," said Bunny, "'tis a lovely town."

"Well, it was, and it soon will be again," said the man before silently mouthing "Thank you".

Then Bunny sat on the hood of the car to rest his ankle, with Sister Joy slurping down a can of Fresca beside him. They watched on as the other three boys, some townsfolk and the emergency services cleared the road and opened Paradise for business once again.

———

Handily, about fifteen minutes after their little convoy had got going, they'd met a minibus driven by two very annoyed nuns coming up the road towards them. This meant they could dump the sort of stolen car they were driving, and the troublesome quartet was able to rest in the rather comfy seats in the rear. Most of the drive back to Los Angeles was taken up with the rather awkward explanation of where they'd been for the last couple of days.

For the record, during the journey, they only stopped once for gas, and nobody got out to use the facilities.

EPILOGUE 1 – NATURE FINDS A WAY

Ronnie Pierce had no idea where he was.

For three days he'd been out here, alone, in the wilderness. He hadn't eaten; he hadn't slept. A stray bullet had caught him on the upper arm, too. Well, not stray. Gardner had definitely been aiming at him. Remarkably, it had only grazed him. That was the good news. The bad news was that the wound had gone all red, and yellow liquid was now seeping out of it. That was bad. Real bad. Ronnie didn't know much about medicine, but he knew that.

He still carried his gun, for all the use it was. He'd used up the last of his ammo yesterday, trying to shoot fish in the river.

Initially, he'd been running, trying to get away, but then at some point, without making a conscious decision, he realised he'd turned around and started walking back uphill. Back towards Paradise – at least in theory. While the idea of getting away appealed, the idea of dying from a septic wound did not.

Besides, what had he actually done? Alright, a lot. But what could they actually prove? Even if they could, if he played it right, he could say he was trying to defend the country from the deep state. Gardner was sort of government or something, after all, and all of this was really her fault. The powers that be would probably want to hush the whole thing up. He might even get a pay-off. A nice little lump sum to keep quiet about what he knew. Yeah.

He could move to Florida. He'd always liked the idea of Florida.

Ronnie could figure it all out once he got home.

God, he was thirsty. Feverish, too. He had to keep moving, though. If he lay down, he might not get back up again.

He came to a clearing, the late-evening sun breaking through the branches and warming his face. He was sure he recognised it.

Yes!

He was less than a mile from town. Nearly home. Everything was going to be okay.

Then he heard the noise behind him.

That distinctive huffing noise.

He turned around slowly to see the bull pawing at the ground in front of him.

Ronnie looked into those large eyes and saw nothing but pure hatred staring back.

"Billy, hey. Okay, I'm sure you're mad, but listen ..."

Billy, being a bull, did not listen.

He charged.

It went as well for Ronnie as you think it did.

———

Almost a week later, Billy got picked up by animal rescue and ended up on a dairy farm where he spent his days assisting in the continuation of the species and generally having the time of his life.

The farmhands did notice something peculiar, though. The otherwise mild-mannered bull did go absolutely crazy if he ever smelled hot sauce.

EPILOGUE 2 – THIS IS A MAN'S WORLD

There were two of them. They referred to each other as Boogie and Whiteboy, although it was a safe bet that neither of those names got repeated at the table over Thanksgiving dinner. Come to think of it, it was quite possible these two young men weren't ever welcomed at anyone's table, either for their strength of character or their conversational artistry.

Whiteboy held his hand to his nose and grimaced. "Man, Boogie, it smells like shit down here."

"No kidding, dumbass. We're in a sewer. What you think it's gonna smell like?"

"I know, I'm just saying."

"Well, shut the hell up. Your gums flapping is shifting the smell around even more."

Whiteboy glanced around behind them. All they had for illumination were the strip lights and one flashlight that Boogie held, a sure sign of his seniority in the relationship. Everything was relative, of course. Given that they had been ordered to go trudging around sewers, it was unlikely they were high-flyers in the grand scheme of things. Whiteboy had to make do with the light from his phone. He was the nervous one. Boogie was the angry one, although the reason for the anger was unclear. He may just have been one of those men whose default emotion was anger.

"Couldn't we just—"

"No," snapped Boogie. "They said find the target and stay where you are until someone comes. That's exactly what we're going to do. Didn't you hear what happened to that Santana dude when he didn't do exactly as he was told?"

Whiteboy looked down at their target, revulsion in his eyes.

She was sitting on a raised block, inches above the flow of what she was telling herself to think of as water, because it was more palatable than the more accurate alternatives. Covered in all manner of filth, dehydrated and exhausted from what felt like an eternity dragging herself through the sewers of Brooklyn, Sister Dorothy was willing to bet she had looked better. When the two men had found her, their first comments conveyed their amazement that she was alive. She echoed the sentiment. She'd gone down the chute with nothing but the clothes on her back – no food, no water, no weapons, and her phone had not survived the landing. She didn't have her medications either, which she had been reliably informed were keeping her alive. She was exhausted, lightheaded, nauseous, but then she defied anyone to spend two days limping, staggering and crawling through the sewers of Brooklyn and come out feeling healthy. She hated that damned wheelchair, but found herself missing it now more than she could have possibly imagined. Sleep had been out of the question as she'd needed to fight off the rats. At least here, the "water" wasn't too deep. There had been points when it had been waist high. As deaths went, the thought of drowning down here felt like one of the less dignified ways to go.

These two men weren't the first to come looking, but finally, this time, she'd been unable to stagger to cover. At no point had she given up but there was only so far bloody-minded determination could drag a body, especially one as weak and broken as hers. Still, she had tried. Nobody could say she hadn't tried.

Whiteboy looked around nervously. "Maybe try calling her again?"

"Call her?" echoed Boogie, incredulous. "Do you ever pay attention? The lady don't speak. I sent her a text. She responded saying she was coming. End of story."

"It's just ... you know there are gators down here?"

"What?"

"Alligators."

"That's bullshit, man. One of those urban legends."

"My uncle Mike's friend says his barber—"

"Shut up, dumbass. Your uncle's friend's momma's gynaecologist's dog don't know shit. Shut the hell up. There ain't no monsters down here." He pointed at Dorothy to emphasise his point. "You think if they were roaming around down here, this mad old woman would still be alive? She's been crawling around down here for two days. She'd have been a snack a long time before now."

Whiteboy turned to look at her. "You seen any monsters down here, lady?"

Dorothy looked through them as if they weren't there. "There are monsters of all kinds down here."

"See!" said Whiteboy.

"Would you shut the hell up, dumbass. She's pulling your chain." Boogie addressed Dorothy directly. "Stop trying to play your mind games. That ain't gonna work on me."

"I wasn't talking to you."

"Well, I'm talking to you. You got any idea of what you got coming?"

"No," said Dorothy, continuing to look behind the two of them. "Why don't you tell me?"

"They going to do whatever it takes to get you to talk. The Cartel, man. They're experts at this. Ice-cold animals. Keep you alive for ever. They break a man like that." Boogie clicked his fingers. "Imagine what they gonna do to some old lady. You best tell 'em what they want to know, right now."

"No," said Dorothy. "I won't be doing that."

Boogie laughed. "You think you got a choice? Torture. Worse. You ain't much, but they'll find some messed-up dudes to come in and they going to do some real nasty stuff to you. *Loco* dudes straight outta prison. A whole line of 'em. Count on it. There ain't gonna be much romance!" Boogie laughed again. He looked over at Whiteboy, who was too busy staring the wrong way down a tunnel to pay attention.

"I'm curious," said Dorothy. "Do you have a mother? Sisters? A daughter?"

"You mind your business," snarled Boogie. "You got yourself into this shit, you'll get what's coming."

"What did I do exactly?"

"That isn't my business. All I know is, you pissed off the man, big time."

"Yes," said Dorothy pointedly. "My actions have often annoyed men."

"Yeah, and you about to find out – it's a man's world, lady. A man's world."

"Is that right?" said Dorothy, still not looking at either of the men, because her question wasn't addressed to them.

Boogie took a step forward, his hand raised. "I'm sick of you not looking at me when I'm talking. Show me some respect or else I—" And then he screamed because, out of seemingly nowhere, at least from his perspective, Lola appeared beside him.

Dorothy had been looking at her, standing back there in the dark, for quite some time. One of, if not the only advantage of spending that amount of time in a sewer system, is that your night vision becomes superb.

Lola looked at Whiteboy, who was pointing his gun at her.

"Oh, shit, sorry," he said, quickly shoving it back into the pocket of his jacket.

"Damn," said Boogie, "you scared me. Like, you came out of nowhere. That was ..." He trailed off, noticing the rather blank and bored expression Lola was giving him.

He turned the flashlight onto Dorothy, who had to shield her eyes from its brightness.

"We found her. The old lady. This is her, right?"

Lola looked down at Dorothy and then, after a long moment, she shook her head.

"What?" said Boogie in disbelief. "C'mon, it definitely is. It's her." Then he saw her face. "I mean, no disrespect, but ... we were told to find an old African lady somewhere down in the sewers. This has got to be her."

Lola raised her eyebrows then gave a pronounced shake of her head.

"But—"

Dorothy cleared her throat. "I am who you are looking for."

"See!" said Boogie.

Lola glanced between the two men, then looked down at Dorothy again and sighed heavily.

She shrugged her shoulders and then, with terrifying economy of movement, shot both men in the head. It happened so fast that both bodies splashed into the water at the exact same time.

"You didn't have to kill them," said Dorothy.

"That is rather ungrateful," said Lola.

"I appreciate the assistance, of course, but I did not feel—"

"Feel what you like," said Lola.

"Are you going to help me up?"

"No. Just because I'm not on their side doesn't mean I'm on yours."

"Would you like to talk about—"

"No, I would not."

"I see. Will you help me to get out of here?"

"No."

"And how do you suggest I do so?"

Lola bent down, patted the jacket of the man formerly known as Boogie and, when she found it, tossed his phone over to Dorothy, who managed to trap it against her body.

Then Lola turned and started walking away down the tunnel.

Dorothy called after her. "I have his phone should you want to—"

"I won't."

"But—"

"I won't."

Dorothy nodded then spoke to herself. "We will see." She glanced up at the ceiling of the sewer then repeated, "We will see."

FREE YUMMY EASTER EGG

Hello,

Caimh here. Ever wondered what's going on in my mind when I write a book? Well, now you can find out. Scan the QR code below and come with me on a journey through my warped imagination!

In this exclusive video – which is only available via this link – I discuss the process behind the writing of *Other Plans,* my favourite scenes and characters plus how the idea for this book came about, and where the story might be heading next.

This video contains lots of spoilers for this book, so if you've skipped ahead but you haven't read the book yet, then turn back now, ye weirdo!

You can also view the video here: https://youtu.be/_6yy-XtoyZ8

Drop me line if you have any questions or let me know what you think and if you'd like more behind the scenes content.

FREE STUFF

Hello again, lovely reader-person,

And that's a wrap! I hope that you enjoyed Bunny being back in the States. His hunt for Bernadette, Assumpta and ultimately, Simone, will resume soon.

If you're new to the Bunny experience make sure you've signed up for my monthly newsletter for free short stories, audio stories, and the latest goings on in the Bunnyverse.

You'll also get a copy of my short fiction collection called *How To Send A Message*, which features several stories featuring characters from my books. To sign up go to my website:

www.WhiteHairedIrishman.com

The paperback costs \$11.99/£9.99/€10.99 in the shops but you can get the e-book for free just by signing up to my newsletter.

Oooh, and you can also listen to the Bunnycast and The Stranger

Times podcasts too for more audio exclusives and short stories. They're available from all the usual places or through my website or **thestrangertimes.co.uk.**

Cheers muchly and thanks for reading,

Caimh

ALSO BY CAIMH MCDONNELL

WRITING AS C.K. MCDONNELL

The Stranger Times (The Stranger Times 1)

This Charming Man (The Stranger Times 2)

Love Will Tear Us Apart (The Stranger Times 3)

Relight My Fire (The Stranger Times 4)

Visit www.WhiteHairedIrishman.com to find out more.

THE STRANGER TIMES: C.K. MCDONNELL

There are dark forces at work in our world so thank God *The Stranger Times* is on hand to report them. A weekly newspaper dedicated to the weird and the wonderful (but mostly the weird), it is the go-to publication for the unexplained and inexplicable . . .

At least that's their pitch. The reality is rather less auspicious. Their editor is a drunken, foul-tempered and foul-mouthed husk of a man who thinks little of the publication he edits. His staff are a ragtag group of misfits. And as for the assistant editor . . . well, that job is a revolving door – and it has just revolved to reveal Hannah Willis, who's got problems of her own.

When tragedy strikes in her first week on the job *The Stranger Times* is forced to do some serious investigating. What they discover leads to a shocking realisation: some of the stories they'd previously dismissed as nonsense are in fact terrifyingly real. Soon they come face-to-face with darker forces than they could ever have imagined.

The Stranger Times is the first book from C.K. McDonnell, the pen name of Caimh McDonnell. It combines his distinctive dark wit with his love of the weird and wonderful to deliver a joyous celebration of how truth really can be stranger than fiction.

Visit thestrangertimes.co.uk for a taste of *The Stranger Times* world.

What people are saying:

'A gag-filled romp ... in the spirit of Terry Pratchett. Ripping entertainment from start to finish.' *The Times*

'I loved this book. Great premise – great story – great characters . . . hugely enjoyable.' **JODI TAYLOR, bestselling author of *The Chronicles of St Mary's* series**

'A filmic romp with great characters, a jet-propelled plot, and a winning premise' **ERIC BROWN, T**he *Guardian*

'Wonderfully dark, extremely funny, and evocative of Terry Pratchett – which I think is the highest compliment I can give.' **ADAM KAY, bestselling author of *This is Going to Hurt***

'I tore through *The Stranger Times*. Like an entertaining collision between the worlds of Mick Herron and Charlie Stross, it's a novel that proves ancient eldritch horror is no match for old-school journalism.' **CHRISTOPHER BROOKMYRE, bestselling author of *Black Widow***

'The one-liners zing, the dialogue is a tennis match of witty banter' *The Financial Times*
    Available now

Made in United States
Orlando, FL
09 November 2023

38763968R00198